Penguin Modern Classics

THE OTHER SIDE

Alfred Kubin was born in 1877 in northern Bohemia. In his autobiography he reveals himself as an unstable, visionary being, who as a boy had a 'burning curiosity' for corpses; who was 'gripped to an incredible degree' by the writings of Schopenhauer and Nietzsche; who had moments of hysterical insight and exaltation; and who spent some time in a mental home. He made his reputation – still considerable in Germany and Austria – as an artist. For a time he belonged to the Blaue Reiter group, founded by Marc and Kandinsky. When Marc proposed that the group should produce an illustrated edition of the Bible, Kubin chose the Book of Daniel, and it was as an illustrator that he chiefly worked for the rest of his life. Kubin wrote *The Other Side* in twelve weeks during a period when he found himself incapable of drawing; it is his only novel.

ALFRED KUBIN

THE OTHER SIDE

Translated from the German by Denver Lindley

Illustrated by
the author

Penguin Books

Penguin Books Ltd, Harmondsworth,
Middlesex, England
Penguin Books Australia Ltd, Ringwood,
Victoria, Australia

First published in Germany as *Die andere Seite* 1909
This translation published in Great Britain by
Victor Gollancz 1969
Published in Penguin Books 1973

English translation copyright © Crown Publishers Inc., 1967

Made and printed in Great Britain by
Richard Clay (The Chaucer Press) Ltd
Bungay, Suffolk
Set in Linotype Pilgrim

ALFRED KUBIN

die andere Seite

Contents

PART ONE

THE SUMMONS

CHAPTER ONE

The Visit

I

Among the acquaintances of my youth there was one remarkable man whose story is well worth rescuing from oblivion. I have done my best to record accurately, as befits an eyewitness, some of the strange events connected with the name Claus Patera.

However, as I was conscientiously setting down my experiences, a peculiar thing happened to me : certain scenes imperceptibly crept into the narrative, scenes that I could not possibly have witnessed and that no one could have described to me. The reader will learn what sort of strange phenomena of the imagination were evoked in a whole community by the nearness of Patera. It is to this influence that I must ascribe my mysterious second sight. Let him who seeks an explanation consult the works of our ingenious psychologists.

I met Patera sixty years ago in Salzburg when we both entered the secondary school there. At that time he was a rather small but broad-shouldered fellow, with nothing remarkable about him except a head of curly hair and a classic cast of countenance. Good Lord, at that time we were wild, boisterous youngsters and paid scant heed to each other's looks. Nevertheless I must add that even now, at an advanced age, I vividly recall his immense, rather prominent light-grey eyes.

After three years I transferred to another school. My contacts with my former classmates grew fewer and fewer until finally I left Salzburg to go to another city, and for many years I completely lost sight of everything I had known there.

Time flowed by and with it my youth. I had had some colourful experiences and was now in my thirties and married. I was making out moderately well in life as a designer and illustrator.

2

And then – we were living at that time in Munich – one foggy November afternoon a visitor was announced.

'Come in!'

The visitor was, so far as I could tell in the twilight, a man of average appearance. He introduced himself briskly. 'Franz Gautsch. May I please have a half-hour's talk with you?'

I agreed, offered him a chair, and had a lamp and tea brought in.

'How can I be of service to you?' My initial indifference changed first to curiosity and then to astonishment as the stranger unfolded his tale.

'I have some proposals to make to you,' he began. 'I am speaking not for myself but in the name of a man whom you perhaps have forgotten but who remembers you very well. This man is the possessor of riches that are, from a European point of view, hard to credit. I am speaking of Claus Patera, your former schoolmate. Please do not interrupt me. Through a strange accident, Patera inherited what is perhaps the largest fortune in the world. Your former friend thereupon set about realizing a plan, one that required, as you will see, almost inexhaustible resources. He had determined to create a Dream Kingdom. The story is complicated, but I shall be brief.

'First of all, a suitable area of three thousand square kilometres was acquired. One third of this territory is mountainous; the rest consists of a plain and hills. Great forests, a lake, and a river lend variety to the small Kingdom. A city was laid out, and villages and farms. The need for these was immediate, for at the very outset the inhabitants numbered twelve thousand. Now the Dream Kingdom has sixty-five thousand residents.'

The stranger paused and took a sip of tea. I remained silent, much puzzled, and was only able to say, 'Go on.'

And then I heard the following:

'Patera cherishes a profound aversion to all forms of progress – I repeat, to all forms of progress – especially in the domain of science. Please take my words absolutely literally, for in them lies the principal purpose of the Dream Kingdom. The Kingdom is cut off from the surrounding world by a wall around its periphery and protected against any attack by its strong fortifications. A single gate provides access and egress and makes possible the strict supervision of persons and goods. In the Dream Kingdom, a place of asylum for those who are disgusted with modern culture, all physical needs are provided for. The lord of this country, however, is far from wishing to found a utopia or any kind of state of the future. Though physical need, as I have said, is impossible there, the noblest aims of this community have nothing to do with maintaining the material wealth of the population or of the individual. No, not at all! But I see you smiling in disbelief, and in fact it is almost impossible for me to describe in prosaic words what Patera actually has in mind for the Dream Kingdom.

'The first thing to note is that every person who is accepted by us has been predestined to this, either at birth or by some later stroke of fate. Highly developed sense organs, as is well known, enable their possessors to perceive relationships in the world of the individual that simply do not exist for the average person except at rare moments. And you see, it is precisely these what you might call non-existent things that constitute the quintessence of our aspirations. In the final and profoundest sense, it is the unfathomable foundation of the universe that the Dream People – as they call themselves – never for an instant lose sight of. Normal life and the Dream World are in many respects opposites, and precisely this difference makes any agreement between them very difficult. Faced with the questions, What actually goes on in the Dream Kingdom? How do people live there? I simply have to remain silent. I can only describe superficial aspects, whereas it is a part of the Dreamer's very being that he strives for the depths. Everything is designed for the most complete spiritualization of life. The

13

sorrows and joys of his contemporaries are alien to the Dreamer; naturally they must be alien because of his wholly different standards of values. Perhaps, as an illustration at least, the concept "mood" comes closest to the heart of the matter. Our people experience only moods or, better still, they live only in moods; all outer being, which they shape at will through the maximum possible cooperative effort, furnishes in a sense simply the raw material. Needless to say, abundant precautions are taken that this does not run out. The Dreamer, however, believes in nothing but the dream – his dream. With us this is cherished and developed; to disturb it would be an unimaginable act of high treason, hence the strict inspection of all persons who are invited to join the community.

'To be brief and get to the point' – Herr Gautsch put down his cigarette and looked me calmly in the face – '*Claus Patera, Absolute Lord of the Dream Kingdom, charges me as his agent to present you with an invitation to come and live in his country.*'

My visitor spoke these words in a somewhat louder voice and with great formality. And now the man fell silent.

At first I too was silent, which my readers will find understandable. In fact, it was impossible to resist the idea that I was in the presence of a madman. It was actually hard to hide my nervousness. Casually, I manoeuvred the lamp out of my visitor's reach; at the same time I adroitly pushed away a pair of dividers and a small scraping knife – dangerous pointed objects.

The whole situation was extremely awkward. At the beginning of the Dream story I had thought it might have been a joke that some friends had taken it upon themselves to play on me. Unfortunately this hopeful possibility grew fainter and fainter, and for the last few minutes I had been nervously calculating my chances. To be sure I knew that the best course with the mentally ill is always to fall in with their delusions. But still! I am by no means a giant; in fact I am a timid man at bottom and rather weak. And here in my room sat this great fellow Gautsch with his judicial countenance, his eyeglasses, and his pointed blond beard.

Such were my thoughts at that moment. And yet I had to

say something; my visitor was obviously expecting me to. In case there was an outbreak of violence I could always blow out the lamp if need be and slip quickly – knowing its layout – out of my room.

'Yes, yes, of course! I'm perfectly delighted! I just want to talk it over with my wife. Tomorrow, Herr Gautsch, you will have my answer.' I spoke reassuringly and got up.

However, my guest remained perfectly still and remarked dryly, 'You misunderstand our situation at the moment, and that does not altogether surprise me. Very likely you do not believe me at all – if indeed your ill-suppressed nervousness does not point to a more serious sort of suspicion. I assure you, I am perfectly sane, as sane as anyone. What I have communicated to you is absolutely serious. That it sounds strange, marvellous – well, yes, I willingly admit it. Perhaps you will feel calmer when you have looked at this.'

Whereupon he drew a small package out of his pocket and placed it on the table in front of me. On it I read my exact address; I broke the seal, and held in my hand a smooth leather case, grey-green in colour. Inside I found a small miniature, a strikingly original head-and-shoulders portrait of a young man. Brown curls encircled a face of unmistakably classic stamp; large, overbright eyes stared straight at me out of the picture. It was Claus Patera beyond question. In the twenty years during which we had not seen each other I had hardly thought once of this schoolmate who had disappeared from my world. At first sight of the remarkable portrait, that considerable period of time vanished from my mind. I saw again the old school porter, with his respectable-looking goitre partially hidden by a carefully tended beard. Again I saw myself surrounded by schoolboys, and one of them was Claus Patera, disfigured by a stiff bowler hat, an article of clothing forced on him by the deplorable taste of his foster aunt.

'Where did you get this picture?' I cried, suddenly feeling in a brighter, more enterprising mood.

'But I have already told you,' my visitor replied. 'And your fear seems to have disappeared, too,' he went on with an inoffensive good-humoured smile.

'Surely this is all nonsense, a joke, a fraud!' I burst out with a laugh. But in fact at that moment Herr Gautsch seemed to me a completely normal, respectable man. He was thoughtfully engaged in stirring his spoon around in his teacup. Surely some sort of joke lay behind all this; later on I would find out about it. Of course, my imagination had simply played me another of its little tricks. How could I have decided so quickly that a decent fellow was crazy simply because of a story like this? In earlier days I would have parried this sort of thing with equal humour. Dear God, so we're getting older! I had completely regained my composure and cheerfulness.

'You really do believe in the picture, don't you?' Gautsch said. 'Your friend, whom it represents, has had the most varied fortunes. He spent only a few years at the Latin school in Salzburg. At fourteen he ran away from his foster aunt and wandered about in Hungary and the Balkans with a troupe of gypsies. Two years later he arrived in Hamburg. He was an animal trainer at that time, but he changed professions, became a seaman, and found employment as a cabin boy on a small merchantman. So at length he arrived in China. The ship lay in Canton, along with many others; they had brought cargoes of millet and rice to forestall a threatened famine. After unloading, the vessel had to remain for several days in the harbour because the goods destined for Europe – human hair and a fine grade of china clay – were not yet ready for shipment.

'Patera made use of this leisure time to take many trips into the country. On one of these occasions he rescued an elderly and distinguished Chinese lady from death by drowning. Having lost her footing in the mud deposited by a recent flood, the aged woman would undoubtedly have met her end in one of the tributaries of the Canton River. The chance onlookers – they can almost never swim – wrung their hands and screamed but did not venture into the swirling brown flood. Your friend, an expert diver, chanced to be passing by. Unhesitatingly he sprang into the water and after a hard struggle with the waves dragged the unconscious woman to shore. The lady was restored to life. She was, it turned out, the wife of one of the richest men on earth. Though feeble and old, he was quickly brought to the scene in a litter and embraced the young man wordlessly. Patera was taken to a great country estate. What deliberations went on there we do not know. The net of it was that Hi-Yong, who was without children of his own, adopted the cabin boy as his son and immediately installed him in his house. Three more years passed, of which we know only that trips were undertaken by Patera into the unknown interior of Asia. And then we see him grieving for his adopted parents: Hi-Yong and his wife had died on the same day. Their heir now found himself in sole possession of fabulous, uncounted riches.'

'And now we come to the Dream Kingdom,' I interjected, still in high good humour. 'The idea is decidedly novel. If you'll allow me, I'll give it to a literary friend of mine who will undoubtedly make a good story out of it. May I offer you one of these?' And I held out cigarettes to the stranger.

He declined, heaved a businesslike sigh, and then remarked in a completely calm, matter-of-fact tone, 'As I have already said, it is clear that you take me for some sort of fraud or teller of tall tales. But after all, I have not come here to convince you of the existence of the Dream Country but rather to invite you there in the name of my superior. For the moment I have fulfilled my mission. If you are absolutely determined not to believe my story, there is nothing at all I can do about it today. In any case, I request a receipt for the safe delivery of the picture. It is quite possible that I shall have other commissions to perform for you in the very near future.'

Gautsch rose and made a slight bow. I must admit that his simplicity of manner did not strike me at all as that of a swindler. Moreover, I still held the case in my hand. Opening it again, I felt a leather flap that I had overlooked the first time. Under it was a white card on which were written in ink the words: 'If you are willing, then come!'

And once more, in a faint and dreamlike way, there arose in my mind a picture of the vanished past. That indeed had been my old schoolmate's handwriting, overlarge, straggling, inchoate and clumsy – 'desperate' is what a teacher had once called it. To be sure, the six words were set down with firmer strokes, but the writer was obviously the same. A peculiar un-ease took possession of me; out of that beautiful face the eyes stared at me, ice-cold. One could be trapped by such eyes; there was something catlike about them. My former merriment was gone, my mood was strange and cloudy. Gautsch continued to stand there waiting; he must have noticed my inner excitement for he was observing me intently.

We both remained silent.

3

In the long run no one can escape from his own temperament; it will always determine the way his life finds expression. In my own markedly melancholic makeup, delight and disgust lie very close together. This unusual nervous constitution, an inheritance from my mother, affords me the greatest joy but also the bitterest pain. I mention my excess sensibility because it will help the reader to understand my behaviour in many later situations.

I had to admit that Gautsch now seemed to me a thoroughly reliable man. I felt sure that he must have some sort of connection with Patera, and obviously there was something true about the Dream Kingdom. Perhaps I had misconceived the whole thing, taken it too literally. The world is big, and many odd things had already happened even to me. In any case, Patera was very rich; very likely all this sprang from some kind of whim, an expensive, elaborately conducted hobby. For me, an artist, something of this sort was always very understandable.

With sudden cordiality I extended my hand to Gautsch. 'Please excuse my strange behaviour, but many things are clearer to me. Your story interests me intensely. Please tell me more about my old school friend.' So saying, I pushed the chair towards him again.

My guest seated himself and said politely, 'Certainly, I will go on with my earlier statement and tell you more about the Dream Kingdom and its mysterious master.'

'I am all attention.'

'Twelve years ago my present Master was staying in the Tien-Shan, the extensive Mountains of Heaven, which lie in Chinese Central Asia. His principal interest there was to hunt certain extremely rare animals, which are now only to be found in those regions. Among others, he wanted to shoot a Persian tiger; to be specific, it had to be a specimen of a small, most unusual long-haired species. After its tracks had at last been located, he set out one night on the hunt. With the help of his native gunbearer he soon succeeded in ferreting out the animal. But before they were able to fire a single shot, the fierce beast flung itself on its two pursuers. The Asian jumped aside in time, Patera was thrown to the ground. Then luckily his com-

panion succeeded in averting the danger. With a single shot in the head from very close range, he killed the animal. Patera emerged with a mangled hand. This wound necessitated a long stay in the region. Indeed, the wound refused to heal until it was treated by an old man, the chief of a remarkable blue-eyed tribe. This small race – it consisted of only about a hundred members – was also conspicuous because of its perceptibly lighter skin colour. Thrust into the midst of a pure Mongolian population, the descendants of the great Kirghiz horde, it lived completely surrounded by them but did not intermarry with the neighbouring peoples. Strange secret practices were said to prevail among them even at that time, but unfortunately I cannot tell you anything about them. In any case, it is certain that Patera was accepted by the tribe and took great interest in them, for when he departed, leaving rich gifts behind, it was with the promise that he would come back again soon, very soon. The leaders accompanied him a long way, and it is said that the farewell was extremely solemn. Patera was deeply moved by it.

'Nine months later he returned to this region for good. In his retinue there was a high mandarin as well as a whole company of engineers and surveyors. A great camp was built in the territory of the Master's blue-eyed friends. The latter expressed the greatest joy at seeing him again. An engineer whom I know, who is still living today in the Dream Kingdom, once described the circumstances to me. Great activity followed, with the result that a large area of land was surveyed and bought. It was on these several thousand square miles that the Dream Kingdom was founded. The rest can be quickly told. A whole army of coolies under expert supervision laboured day and night. The Master constantly urged speed. Two months after he got there, the first houses arrived from Europe, all of considerable age and showing signs of disrepair. They had been cleverly cut up into sections and now they were immediately put together and placed upon foundations that had already been laid. Naturally there was head-shaking at the appearance of the dirty, smoke-stained old walls. However, gold flowed in streams, and everything happened in accordance with the Master's wishes. Everything worked perfectly. A year later, Perle, the capital of the kingdom, must have looked very much as it does today. All the tribes that had formerly lived in that area withdrew along with the workmen; only the blue-eyed people stayed.' Gautsch paused.

'But I don't understand at all,' I said. 'What system does Patera use in buying these houses?'

'Well, that is beyond my comprehension, too,' he replied. 'They are all ancient structures; many, indeed, are in ruins and would be worthless in anyone else's eyes, but others are massive and well preserved. Formerly they were scattered all over Europe. These buildings of stone and wood assembled from all quarters – the Master specifies each one to obtain – must have a quite special value for him, otherwise he would hardly have sunk so many millions in acquiring them for his city.'

'For heaven's sake, how much is this man worth?' I asked in amazement.

'Oh, who can answer that?' came the sombre reply. 'For ten years I have been in his service and I have certainly paid out close to two hundred million for purchases, indemnities, transportation charges, and other expenses. Agents like me live in all parts of the world. One cannot form so much as a reasonable guess at the extent of Patera's riches.'

I groaned. 'Sir, I believe you, but I can't begin to understand it. It all sounds so bewildering. Now tell me, if you will, how the people live there.'

'I will try to explain as much as I can; there is no time to tell it all. Moreover, I am not a regular visitor to the kingdom but am there only occasionally. Just what, if you please, would you like to hear about?'

Naturally I was interested in aesthetic questions. Gautsch explained the attitude towards art in the Dream Kingdom.

'We have no individual museums, picture galleries, or any of that sort of thing. Precious works of art are not put in collections, but here and there you will see many splendid separate pieces. Everything is shared, so to speak, by being put to use. Also, I cannot remember a single instance of a painting, a bronze, or any other work of art of recent date being acquired. The sixties of the last century mark the absolute limit. Incidentally, a few years ago I myself sent out a case of good Dutch paintings; there were two Rembrandts among them, and of course they must still be there.

'Patera is more a collector of antiquities in general than an art collector, but he is that on a grand scale. As you already know, he even buys large buildings. But there is more to it than that. He has a memory that goes beyond my understanding; he holds in his mind almost every object in his kingdom. These have been sought out and purchased by agents like me on his orders. We constantly receive descriptions of desired objects, with the most exact information about details, as well as where and in whose possession they are to be found. The goods, for which we often have to pay very high prices, are then carefully packed and shipped to Perle. That means a great deal of work,' he added.

'It often baffles me where our Master gets his astounding knowledge of all these things. Although I have been in his service for many years now and should be used to it, I am constantly being amazed.

'Valuable objects and what is obviously old trash are demanded with equal insistence. How often I have had to search for worthless rubbish in some middle-class family's attic or wine-cellar or in some remote mountain farmhouse! Often the people themselves did not know they owned the thing in question – a broken-down chair, old fire tools, a pipe-rack, an egg-timer, or something of that sort. Sometimes, when the object was just too shabby-looking, it was presented to me with a laugh. Frequently though, I had trouble convincing the people that they had what I was looking for. In the long run, however, it was always found. Canny peasants for the most part managed to drive shrewd bargains. Yes, I have had a lot to do. Just last week, I sent off a shipment of old pianos. There were some very dilapidated instruments in the lot.'

'Oh, I love old things,' I interrupted at this point.

'Well, of course you would feel perfectly at home. Out there everything one needs is available. The food is excellent, compared with the miserable fare usually set before travellers in the Orient. One lives in comfort, and there is stimulating company everywhere. You will even have a coffeehouse to go to. What more could you ask?'

'You're right,' I cried enthusiastically. 'There is nothing better than a simple, well-ordered life. But what about the people who live there? Whom do you meet out there?'

The agent cleared his throat, his eyeglasses flashed, and he said, 'It's true that I have not yet told you about the people. Well, like every other place, you'll find charming people there.'

'For example?'

'Well, first of all there is a solid, well-educated middle class, including the many members of the civil service. And then there is the military, attractive and well worth knowing – the officers in particular. Also, one must not overlook the large group of private scholars. And finally there is a whole class of less easily defined people – painters, free-lance artists, and so on, just as in every other place.'

'And above all, my friend – the Master himself?' I interrupted.

'You will not encounter him very often. Patera is too much occupied, overloaded with his work. Just think of the responsibility! Naturally all these people fit into the overall plans,' he went on rapidly. 'You were chosen, as far as I know, because some of your drawings made an impression on the Master. You see, you are not altogether unknown there. In order to keep the manner and style of life as pure as possible, it is necessary to have that impregnable barrier around the kingdom that I've already mentioned. The Master's subtle policy finds its fulfilment by that means. In fact, he has hitherto succeeded in excluding from the country all those who do not belong.'

I approved this idea enthusiastically, already determined in my mind to accept the invitation. I promised myself a rich artistic harvest from this adventure.

How feeble and unreliable the heart of man is! Had I had any conception of the fate that awaited me out there, I would never have answered the summons, and would no doubt be a different man today.

4

At this point I must mention that that was the year in which one of my most cherished ambitions lay very close to fulfilment. It was a trip to Egypt and India, which until now had been impossible for lack of funds. My wife had just come into a small inheritance, and this was to supply the money for the journey. However, as always in life, things were to turn out other than we expected.

When I told Gautsch of my plans, he voiced my own idea. 'You will simply alter your itinerary. Instead of India you will go to the Dream Kingdom.'

'But my wife? I don't want to travel without her!'

'My instructions are to invite her too. If I have not mentioned that up to now, I hereby make amends.'

There were few reasons for hesitation left, but my wife's rather poor constitution forbade risking serious hardships.

'Oh, don't worry,' said the agent, reassuring me on that point. 'The general state of health with us is excellent. Perle lies at the same latitude as Munich, but the climate is so mild that even the most serious nervous cases soon find themselves feeling perfectly fit. As a matter of fact, a large number of the Dream people were once regular guests at sanatoriums and health resorts.'

'That makes all the difference. In that case, I accept,' and I shook Gautsch's hand warmly.

'As for travelling expenses' – he glanced quickly around my room and went on considerately – 'a small contribution might perhaps be acceptable.'

I laughed and replied, 'Well, if you would like to contribute a thousand marks, why not?'

At this the agent simply shrugged his shoulders, drew out his chequebook, hastily wrote a few words on it, and handed me the paper.

It was a cheque on the Reichsbank for 100,000 marks.

5

When we hear an account of something marvellous that lies far outside ordinary human experience, an unresolved doubt always remains in our minds. And that is as it should be. Otherwise one would be an easy mark for every teller of tall tales and the first confidence man to come along. For this very reason, however, a fact has a stronger impact than any story.

This was the case now. Gautsch had already won my confidence. But when I held in my hand this large sum – for me a real fortune – I experienced a strange emotion. A slight shiver ran through me, and with tears in my eyes I said, 'Honoured sir, please excuse me, but I have trouble finding words to express my gratitude. Not for this large sum of money – not that! But, you see, when one has striven all his life long towards a dream and then suddenly it comes true, it is a great and beautiful moment. This is what has happened to me today, through your generosity. Accept my thanks!' With these or similar words I expressed my great excitement.

Gautsch, who seemed likewise to have become very serious, replied in a grave voice, 'My dear sir, I am only doing my duty. If in doing so I give you pleasure, that pleases me. You owe me no thanks. I am simply acting for a higher authority. I can only give you this word of caution: be silent about the things you have learned today. Tell no one about them, except, of course, your wife. I do not actually know what the consequences of a breach of our rule would be. But Patera's power is great, and he desires the Dream Kingdom to remain a secret.'

'Then perhaps it was careless of you to tell me so much about it? After all, you could not possibly know what attitude I would adopt,' I remarked.

'That isn't exactly how matters stood, sir. I *knew* that you would come!' Whereupon he pressed my hand and turned towards the door. 'It is already late. I shall come back tomorrow at this time to give you all the details of the trip. Talk this over with your wife and give her my respects. Good night.'

He had gone.

The ten minutes until my wife came home from shopping seemed endless. I had to talk. I had to tell someone about this incredible business. I needed someone.

Now she was here.

The fun of surprising her naturally came to nothing, for my wife read my excitement in my face. At the astounding news she certainly pricked up her ears, but she could not refrain from asking derisively, 'Are you in your right mind?'

'I am indeed, my love. I too considered Gautsch a swindler or a madman before I became convinced of his respectability and nobility of character.'

And now I triumphantly played my trump – the cheque. In this case, too, it had a stronger effect than the story. After she had advised me to find out early next morning whether it was good, we fell to considering the journey and all that it entailed.

'But what about the picture? Show me the picture!'

It made an overwhelming impression. After she had looked at it for a long time she leaned back and whispered in a resigned voice, 'Do you really think you have to go? That man

horrifies me. I don't know what it is, but he looks frightening.'
She was close to tears.

'But my child, what an idea!' I hugged her, laughing. 'This is
my old friend Patera, a fine, likeable fellow! If he makes use of
his money in an artistic way, I think all the better of him for
that.'

'Wouldn't it be wise for you to try to find out more from
some other source?'

'I don't know what you mean. I stand surety for my friend.
That the cheque is good will be proved tomorrow, and the
Dream Kingdom seems to me a marvellous idea. After all, we
were planning to go to India. Don't you ever want what pleases
me?'

My last words sounded almost reproachful. I tried to quiet
her, and she ended by agreeing with me and admitted that her
opposition had been excessive.

'You will certainly have a pleasant time there. And then just think what inspirations there will be for me. And the money, that's splendid, isn't it?'

She became cheerful once more and started to busy herself at once with the practical problems of the move. For my part, I already felt myself completely a Dream man and began to weave fantasies of the future. Again and again I looked at the picture and at the cheque, and I fell in love a little with both of them.

Day was breaking when we finally fell asleep.

6

An hour before it opened I was at the bank. In return for my cheque I received a thick packet of thrice-counted bills. As soon as I held this treasure in my hands I made frantic haste to get into a cab and convey my riches to safety.

At home a letter from Gautsch was waiting for me. To his regret he could not come again; new orders prevented him from doing so. He urgently advised us to make our trip as soon as possible, before the onset of winter storms on the two seas we would have to cross. The letter ended with good wishes for the future. Our itinerary was enclosed: Munich, Constance, Batum, Batu, Krasnovodsk, Samarkand. There we would be met at the railroad station. Our description had been sent on ahead; all I needed for credentials was Patera's picture.

We had already decided upon closing the house. All the preparations for the journey were carried out smoothly and expeditiously with my wife's diligent help. My mood of elation persisted up to the end. On the last day we spent in our old home, however, a feeling of melancholy came over me. I don't know whether it is the same with others, but departure from rooms that have become dear to me always affects me strongly. Once more a piece of life was slipping away from me and would henceforth be only a memory. I walked to the window. Outside it was dark, everything barren with autumn. I actually felt a pain at my heart as I stared into the night sky, sewn with tiny stars.

Then a friendly arm was put around my neck.

We planned to take the evening train on the following day, a Friday, and decided to spend most of the day in a hotel near the station. I already had two tickets to Constance on the Orient Express. To acquaintances whom I chanced to meet, I mentioned casually that we were on our way to India. At nine o'clock that evening we were in our seats on the train.

CHAPTER TWO

The Journey

I

Now I shall hurry on with my account; travel descriptions are to be found everywhere, far better ones than I am able to write.

Railroad journeys, as everyone knows, are for the most part a crowded and uncomfortable experience. From Budapest on, a slight Asiatic atmosphere made itself felt. How did this show? In the interests of this book I do not intend to insult Hungary. Thank God, by the time we were in Belgrade I had got to the point where I no longer clutched at my breast pocket every ten minutes to make sure my treasure was still there. After all, it is not necessary for everyone to know where one carries one's money – not even in Serbia.

Usually I am somewhat irritable in railway compartments. This time things were appreciably better; however, we were travelling with every conceivable comfort. I gave myself over to happy dreams, rejoicing at all the pleasures still before me. If only my wife had been more cheerful. Unfortunately she lay there, brooding, and complained of a headache.

Once Bucharest was behind us, I too had had enough. Two nights on a train, however comfortable, are no trifling matter. We spent the last hours almost like wild animals in a cage. And so when the Black Sea came in sight early next morning we were ready and waiting to descend. With the first rays of the rising sun, we arrived in Constance. There was a great tussle over the baggage.

The steamer that was to take us to Batum belonged to the Austrian Lloyd Line. It was clean and comfortable, which was especially fortunate for my wife. After a bath she had pretty well recovered from the railway journey and was happy at the sight of the fine day and the sea. I stood on the afterdeck and looked at the disappearing mainland of Europe. Soon there was nothing of the coast to be seen but a narrow streak. That too disappeared. I stared back intently, imagining for a long time that I still saw it.

At my wife's suggestion I was very reserved with my fellow travellers. And I had to agree she was right. If one is brimful of an idea, as I was on this trip, it is so easy to betray one's destination. And what might happen then could quite possibly be very unpleasant. When Gautsch had exacted the oath of silence from me, he had not seemed to be joking in the least. Anyone who broke that oath would end up by not being admitted to the Dream Kingdom and would have to pay back the travelling expenses. A fine bargain that would be! And so I was extremely taciturn, which was not especially difficult. There were no Germans on board, and I do not speak any other language. So I devoted myself all the more intently to thoughts of the Dream Kingdom, imagining all sorts of fantastic things.

This mood dominated me completely. Only when we transferred to the railroad train was I, to my irritation, snatched out of it. My wife, on the other hand, was very pleased by the roominess of the Russian railroad carriages. Ah yes, Russia! That was a country to my taste: large, bountiful, uncultivated, yet able to produce comforts the instant the clink of coins was heard; wealthy men like us can get along anywhere these days. Long life to the Tsar, I thought, and rejoiced, too, at the few drops of slav blood coursing in my veins. This whole favourable view of the Russian Empire was due principally to the accident of our having been quickly ushered through Customs.

One week after our departure from Munich we were in Krasnovodsk. The Caspian Sea was already behind us; we had made the crossing in a few hours in a Russian ship. I have never seen such a greasy hulk. My opinion of the Tsar fell rapidly, but I had to grant him one thing: the Caucasus, what we could see of it, was very fine indeed.

I too had become tired of travelling. It was hard to sit cooped up in a pen, even when you could look at half the world with no effort. To the devil with it – I like to be able to move about.

From then on, those who approached the train, with faces more and more completely concealed, seemed to be no better than rabble. We were travelling through a wasteland straight towards Merv. Oases left and right. New kinds of food offered the opportunity of ruining one's digestion. For me this was superfluous; my excessive smoking had already produced the same result. Too bad I had not counted the cigarettes I had smoked between Munich and Merv; but now the problem of tobacco began to haunt me. Yes, what about my tobacco? To pack it between the covers of books was a promising idea but hardly practical. In desperation I begged my travelling companion to put her coiffure at my disposal for smuggling purposes – I had in mind a kind of enormously high chignon – but I was met with refusal. Finally, the best idea occurred to me. With patience and perseverance, I stuffed the tobacco into my air cushion. That worked out all right; I kept patting the cushion, and I never let it out of my sight. I *had* to have my tobacco; the Russian kinds are too strong for me; in this respect I am an individualist. That a couple of roubles might have spared me all this trouble naturally never occurred to me, for I had been used to travelling as a poor man. But soon the cushion would be empty – and what then? Sadly I brooded over possible means of rescue. I decided to put my hopes in the Dream Kingdom; Gautsch looked like such a responsible man. And once more I deliberately wrapped myself in thoughts of the future.

My wife, moreover, was feeling well. The longer this trip lasted, the fresher she became. She was getting used to it, she said. I could not understand this, but secretly I felt envy tinged with admiration.

In Merv we had a short stop. On a side track stood a freight train on which were loaded wagons filled with old iron and lumber. A shipment for Perle? I wondered, staring at them. Dream freight?

My wife began to be worried about me. My happy preoccupation with the future disturbed her. 'You are missing the whole pleasure of the trip. All this strange scenery, the fantastic costumes – none of it seems to exist for you. Before, even on short trips, your sketchbook never left your hand. Now you hardly glance out of the window.'

She sighed – and she was certainly right. But I said nothing; sighing women are one thing I cannot abide. And then she patted my hand. 'Whatever splendid things the future may hold for us, it's not a good idea to leave present reality completely out of account.'

At that I moved to the window of the compartment. There was a colourful crowd in the train shed. All sorts of races were there – tall Georgians, Greeks, Jews, Russians in furs, Tartars, slant-eyed Calmucks, Germans too. A thousand interesting things to look at! Traders were haggling over furs, orating and shouting; Turks were there with their veiled women. An Armenian tried to sell me fruit and kept insisting that I take a packet of saffron as well. To be used for what?

The excitement increased. Departure time had come. Towards the rear of the train great rolls of silks were being loaded. Each time one was lifted in there was satiric comment. I thought I could make out the word 'junk'. A handsome man in a red Circassian uniform, undoubtedly an officer, was saying good-bye to his friends. He got into a neighbouring compartment. All this, and more besides, was plucked out of the darkness by the three lamps on the station platform. Decidedly a picturesque scene.

The train began to move. Just then, at the back of the shed, I caught sight of a pile of barrels. I had been acquainted with them since Baku – they had made the whole ship stink.

'Are you enjoying it, darling?' my wife asked.

'I am just making a note of how accurate the travel books are,' I replied dryly.

2

That night was not a comfortable one for me. In those days I was a man who worshipped adventure, but it had to be a real adventure, something extraordinary, not a cliché. The unbroken ten-day trip had taken its toll of my energies, and I was in a miserable mood. I twisted and turned on the berth and complained to my wife. 'The Dream Kingdom is a fraud – just wait and see. They will drag us off into some inaccessible corner and there we will have to admire Patera and his dung heap, simply because he is rich! As far as I am concerned, a rich man, merely because he is rich, counts for nothing. As for our money, I can foresee that won't last long. They'll get it all away from us by charging outrageous prices.'

I was depressed, full of hopelessness and disillusionment. We kept on travelling eastward, and everything, despite its Oriental look, was exactly the way one could have imagined it at home. And what is there still to come, I asked myself. A few villas and houses, a foreign colony, a park? And for the sake of these heavenly splendours am I to allow myself to be shaken half to death in a railroad train?

My wife tried to comfort me as best she could. 'If we don't like it, then we can just travel home again,' she said. 'Up to now there is really no reason to be so depressed.'

'That agent was a cunning devil; I should have thrown him out. Why didn't you warn me?' I asked reasonably.

'And the money?' she inquired, laughing.

'Please don't keep mentioning the money. When anyone is as rich as Patera, he can easily part with a million or so to have respectable people around him.' Yawning, I turned my back on my wife. Women never understand you.

Already half-asleep, I heard my travelling companion's further comment. 'Aren't you somewhat overestimating the value of our company?'

Wisely I refrained from answering.

The stirring of our neighbours signalled our arrival in Bokhara in the early dawn of a clear day. Turbans and lambskin caps were visible from the berth. From now on it seemed to me the trip went much faster. No doubt coaches had been dropped or a new engine had been attached. That same afternoon we were due to arrive in Samarkand.

I got up cheerful. The scenery outside was splendid. The desert, which I had come to know all too well, had given place to green fields. Though it was November, there was no hint of chill. Herds of camels and horses, watched over by droll-looking youngsters, enlivened the scene. The idea of being close to the cradle of humanity excited my mind. One could actually see representatives of perhaps fifty different races, though not all of them worthy examples. Through this region in ancient times ran the great highways of the world. Even Alexander the Great . . . Enough, I am not going to write a travel book.

Anticipation drove the blood into my cheeks; eagerly I leaned out of the coach windows, first on one side and then on the other. And there – there you could actually see something rising in the distance. A long conglomeration of houses, minarets, churches – Samarkand! Samarkand! The sun was reflected in colourful splendour from the blue and green glazed tiles. The colours increased in intensity as we approached. And now at last an uninvited, happy intoxication overcame me, but along with it the question: Where will disillusionment come in? After all, what lay before us was something wholly unknown.

When the train stopped in Samarkand I was in a soberer mood. As we got out and began to look around, a man approached us. A cross between an Armenian and an East Prussian was the way I classified him.

'You, sir, and your wife, have been announced in advance by Herr Gautsch.' A bow. Fluent German.

'Where shall we go?' I asked, not too cordially.

With another bow, directed towards my wife as well, he presented himself. 'Kuno Eberhard Teretatian, agent. You have something to show me?'

Privately I bestowed a laurel leaf on my instinct for races as I handed the Eurasian the etui with the picture, which for the last half-hour I had been clutching in my hand.

'Thank you, that is quite sufficient. You and your wife have three hours. It is now two o'clock: at five the caravan will start. I propose that you rest in my rooms and refresh yourselves.'

In the meantime, at a signal from the agent, two huge porters had loaded our luggage on a cart and gone off with it. We strolled along beside Teretatian, having refused the carriage that had been put at our disposal.

'We'd rather go on foot. How far is it to your house?'

'A good half-hour, sir.'

'Well then, forward, sir, in God's name!'

3

What an Oriental city looks like is, I assume, known to everyone. It is exactly the same as one of our cities, only Oriental.
This way and that we wandered through streets and across
squares, moving constantly through scenes from the *Thousand
and One Nights*. At the end of half an hour we came to a
quieter section, apparently on the edge of the city. Our guide
stopped in front of a house and said, 'Here we are.'

We were shown into a room on the ground floor. Our
luggage had already arrived; I saw it in the courtyard. A
splendid meal was served on the carpeted floor in pleasant surroundings, which disposed me somewhat more favourably towards our host. This second agent of Patera's was far more
courteous than the first, almost obsequious.

'Well, what's new in the Dream Kingdom, Herr Teretatian?'
I exclaimed in high spirits, busy the while with figs and
bunches of grapes.

'Nothing new, not much that's new. Simply the theatre. No
doubt you have heard about that, sir.'

'But I don't know the slightest thing,' I cried, alert for anything that had to do with the Dream Kingdom.

'A new inspiration of the Master's! The building has been up
for a month. Just last week several freight cars of scenery,
backdrops, and old wigs caused me some headaches in transfer
and shipment. You will have to leave that here, dear madam,'
he went on, pointing to a gleaming alcohol cooker that my
wife was just bringing in from the courtyard. She missed his
words because she was looking with enchantment at a small
child playing outside.

'What do you mean?' I exclaimed, nudging my wife.

'Alas, yes, there's no help for it,' he said regretfully. 'Just a
short time ago an opera singer was here – she became quite
frantic when I had to reject her wardrobe. You would do well
to follow my advice; it will save you a lot of trouble.'

I listened to the man speechless, my eyes staring.

'But I have to have my things,' I cried angrily.

'Sir, you know perfectly well that your worry is groundless.

You will not be robbed of anything, you will not lose anything. You can be reassured, sir.'

'Perhaps we can leave our things in safekeeping here?' my wife said, turning to me. 'For a few days we can manage well enough with the bare necessities. Then your friend will have our trunks sent after us.'

The agent was quick to make use of his new ally and continued to persuade me. 'Even the opera singer is contented now. After all, sir, you are not travelling into the wilderness, and in two days you will find everything you need in Perle.'

'What's that? Did you say two days? From the map I thought it would take at least a week!' I was astounded.

'Then you are not altogether clear about the route, sir,' our host said, smiling politely. 'Even with frequent stops for rest it could not take more than three days.'

'Well now, what in fact *can* we take along?' my wife broke in.

'Our agent for Bavaria must have explained that to you already, madam. The rule is that only objects that have been used can pass the gate.'

'I haven't brought old junk with me!' My patience was exhausted.

'Oh, do as he says,' my wife said. 'This gentleman will be kind enough to inspect our things.'

We went outside and submitted our trunks to his scrutiny. To be on the safe side, I immediately put my tobacco-filled cushion under my arm. One after another our pieces of luggage were opened. A remarkable appraisal. A camera together with its accessories was immediately rejected, followed by my binoculars, glasses of excellent quality. At the sight of my shaving equipment, the fellow exclaimed, 'For God's sake!' My wife's travelling case was thoroughly investigated. He seemed to hesitate over our clothes. When my fine overcoat in the latest fashion – a garment I was very proud of – came up, he said, 'You will certainly want to have this altered, sir. After all, you will not want to be conspicuous.' However, when he came to my wife's underclothes and started to inspect that too, I intervened. 'That stays with us. None of it is to be touched.'

My books were closely examined, but they were old, and he let me keep them.

'You and your wife will not lose a single thing. Nothing will be taken away,' Teretatian kept repeating in a very businesslike voice. But during the operation not the slightest detail escaped his notice.

'Now everything is in order.' He made a deep bow.

It was four o'clock. In the remaining hour I bought various things for myself in Samarkand to take the place of the articles that had been so to speak confiscated. I acquired a splendid old samovar – not as practical as our cooker but handsomer. When I returned, two roomy carts with immense wheels were standing ready. A camel was hitched to each. I looked dubiously at this depressing equipage.

'You and your wife, sir, will ride in comfort; we have spread blankets inside. The guide is a reliable man and has been instructed to follow your wishes.'

Catching sight, as I was getting in, of two generous baskets of provisions, I became compliant once more. I thanked our host and shook his hand. At the head of the column rode our guide, a small Kirghiz, mounted on a horse with a long mane. Beside each cart rode a man, and at the end of the column two servants in yellow caps and dark kaftans. Thus we departed.

Now I was embarked on my adventure.

4

When the rest of the city had long since disappeared from sight, the towering mausoleum of the great Timor was still visible. It stood out in violent hues against the vivid colours of the sunset.

Beside me my wife looked like nothing so much as a large bundle from one side of which a head protruded. She was fighting against sleep and could speak only indistinctly; I soon gave up trying to talk to her. Inside our wagon, which was fitted with a cover, it was dark. The landscape became more and more barren and stony; everything around us was tinged with a cold green. My rapidly growing weariness prevented further misgivings on the subject of our risky venture. We were both very exhausted.

Now and then, leafless bushes, cacti, and salt trees swam by in the uniform green twilight outside. The wagon jolted in a uniform rhythm. From the head of the column a long-drawn-out, plaintive melody drifted back to us. That sound can only be produced by a small instrument, I thought, and at once fell asleep.

We are all wanderers, without exception, all of us. As long as there have been human beings it has been so, and so it will be for ever. From the oldest nomadic folk to the present-day tourists, from predatory expeditions to the latest voyages of discovery, however different the motives, wandering has persisted. Foot, hoof, wheel, steam, electricity, gasoline, and whatever else may come – the means are unimportant – wandering persists. Whether I stroll to the coffeehouse or travel around the globe, I am wandering. And with me all the animals wander, sometimes here, sometimes there. Our ancient earth leads the way as the first great exemplar. An instinct, a law of nature! However weary you may be, you have to join in, always farther. Real rest is possible only when one is through with wandering. And all men secretly rejoice in wandering – only they do not admit it to themselves. Many do not even know it. There are those who have already been around and about a great deal and do not want to wander any more, or are sick in bed, or cannot wander for some other reason; these are the ones who travel in their minds, in their imaginations, and they, too, often go a long way, a very long way. But to stand still – no, that is not possible.

Once I woke up for a moment. Outside was bright moonlight. We had just halted at a cistern, and I heard the animals being watered. My wife's eyes were shut tight and she had a serious expression on her face. It's good that you're asleep, I thought; you will be refreshed in the morning.

It seemed to me that we were in the mountains. As the wagon jolted on again towards the Dream Kingdom, I myself fell asleep once more. It had been a long time since I had slept myself out.

Suddenly I realized that something was happening. The wheels had stopped turning.

'We have arrived. You have been asleep a long time.' Someone was tapping me on the leg.

Still drugged with sleep, I was not one bit interested, and I stayed where I was.

My wife, already very brisk, brought her wiles into play. 'Get up, we're here, in the Dream Kingdom!' she cried in her siren's voice.

I said helplessly, 'Yes, yes, I'm coming, I'm coming.' But I remained lying there. That's just the way I happen to be.

A semi-official voice spoke beside the wagon. Now I looked ridiculous even in my own eyes. I shook off sleep and clambered out.

First one's eyes had to adjust themselves; all one could see was a grey mist, pierced here and there by a few hazy lights. At my first step I almost collided with the wagon towering there beside me. In front of it, a monstrous, ill-defined form – the camel! Now I could see better.

'Please come this way,' a firm voice called. 'Your luggage is in order. Have you your credentials?'

The speaker was a tall, bearded man in a dark uniform and peaked cap. We were standing beside a low blockhouse dimly illuminated by a few lanterns. The official returned my picture and directed us to pass through the entrance quickly so as to reach the train in time.

What entrance, what train? I thought, feeling my way forward.

'Look – look at that,' I heard my wife say.

And now for the first time I discovered in the veil of mist an immense, high wall. Suddenly, unexpectedly, it loomed up before me. Someone carrying a light was walking in front of us towards an enormous black hole: *that was the gate to the Dream Kingdom.* As we approached I noticed its huge dimensions. We entered a tunnel, keeping as close as we could to our guide. Then something strange happened. I had already penetrated some distance into the vaulted passage when I was overcome, as though at a blow, by a wholly unfamiliar and dreadful sensation. It began at the back of my head and ran down my spine; my breath stopped and my heart beat wildly. Helplessly I looked towards my wife, but she herself was white as a corpse, deathly fear mirrored in her face. In a quivering voice, she whispered:

'I shall never come out of here again.'

But now a fresh wave of strength came to reinvigorate me; without a word I held out my arm to her.

PART TWO

PERLE

CHAPTER ONE

The Arrival

Beyond the gate it was very dark. The fog no longer weighed on my chest, and a mild breeze was blowing. Close by, we heard whistling and intermittent rattling. Now we could see red and green signal lights, and we hurried towards a low building that loomed ahead. The man with the lantern said, 'That's the railway station – you are just in time!' At the window we were given tickets, second class, to Perle; the first trip was free, we were told. When we walked out onto a lonely platform, the engineer was already signalling for departure, and we were summoned into the train. 'We will travel third class!' I shouted, hoping to see more people there, for the second class seemed entirely empty.

As we got in, I felt something heavy being pressed into my hand. 'Here is the money. Every newcomer receives it.' The voice was receding into the distance before the words were finished. I put the money into my pocket.

After a number of fruitless efforts, the engine finally got the train into motion. Its speed was moderate; more moderate still was the light from the smoking oil lamps in the coach. Looking back, I was just in time to see the high wall towering up into the night sky. Like a prison wall, I thought, inspecting it with interest as it grew dimmer and dimmer in the darkness.

Of the country through which we rode I could see little. Our engine threw a faint light on trees, bushes, watchmen, shacks. Generally speaking, it was just like any other night train-trip.

The conductor entered our compartment, and I said to him, 'Your lamps smell awful. It's enough to make one sick.'

'There have never been any complaints before.'

'How much longer to Perle?'

'We will be there in two hours – at midnight.'

'Can you recommend a hotel?'

'The Blue Goose is the only one for you. The smaller inns would not be to your taste.' He spoke very pleasantly, and disappeared into the outer corridor.

At some of the stations I noticed long sheds and mountains of chests and bales. At one stop I bought a basket of cold supper for my wife and a bottle of wine. I paid for it mechanically with the money that had been handed to me. Then we noticed with astonishment that I had kreutzers and florins in my pocket; there was also a small roll of gold coins.

My wife was sunk in thought. Probably she was still suffering from her shock at the gate. Yes indeed, overstrained nerves! It was high time for us to be in a place where we could rest.

Two workmen got in and carried on a desultory conversation. As they were getting ready to leave at the next stop, one of them said good-bye and looked at me as though he knew me. He seemed familiar to me, too. One keeps meeting the same faces again and again all over the world. Actually I envied him. He could get out of the train now, and I had to go on tolerating the smell of oil. Fortunately it would not last much longer. What a miserable trip!

A short time before we reached Perle, the train crossed a swampy wilderness. Then it began to slow down, and finally it stopped. I looked out – yes, we were there.

There were few people about; behind the station a single droshky was standing. We roused the driver and told him to take us to the Blue Goose. I peered out eagerly at the streets through which the miserable vehicle went clattering.

'So this is Perle, the capital of the Dream Kingdom! Why, this is the way it looks in our worst slums!' I said, indignant and disillusioned, pointing at a tumbledown building.

There was little life on the streets. A pedestrian passed by only occasionally. The lighting was of the most miserly kind – an occasional gas lamp at a street corner. Often I could have taken an oath that I had seen one of the houses before. To my wife, too, many things seemed familiar. 'But at home we are not so parsimonious with light,' I muttered grimly.

The hotel, though not first rate, was at least fairly clean and comfortable. I had tea brought to our room, which was large and pleasantly arranged. The furniture, to be sure, seemed rather a mixture. Over the leather sofa hung a large picture of Maximilian, Emperor of Mexico; above the bed, the unhappy Benedek of Königgrätz. 'What is he doing here?' I could not help asking the chambermaid.

Anyone who has gone without seeing a proper bed for ten days will understand that this sight was dearer to us than all the dream riches in the world. As my wife examined and approved the beds, she said, 'I'm very happy about the mild air we have here.' I was already stretched out on the delightful feathers, and I replied, yawning, 'That's the one cheery thing so far.'

The new day must have been far advanced when I realized that I had been lying there for a long time open-eyed. A room with red wallpaper? ... Now I have it ... Right ... I am So-and-So, an illustrator ... I am lying in a hotel bed in the capital city of the Dream Kingdom, and my wife is sleeping beside me.

Completely rested and fresh, we got up and dressed. I was filled with intense curiosity about the things I was going to see. After eating breakfast we went out. The weather was cloudy.

CHAPTER TWO

Patera's Creation

Here I will interrupt the narrative of my personal experiences to give the reader certain facts about the country in which I was to live for almost three years. The conditions I observed day by day were most remarkable, and I never gained a full understanding of the connections that existed between them. All I can do is set down everything as I myself saw it or learned of it from other Dream people. My conjectures about these conditions are scattered throughout the book. Perhaps some of my readers will think of better explanations.

In the most general terms, the country seemed like Central Europe – and then again how different! Yes, we had a city, towns, large estates, a river, and a lake, but the sky above was always cloudy; the sun *never* shone, *never* were the moon or the stars visible at night. The clouds hung low over the earth in unvarying uniformity. To be sure, sometimes they piled up during a storm, but the blue sky was perpetually hidden from us all. A learned professor, whom I shall have occasion to mention again, believed there was a causal relationship between this persistent cloudiness and the extensive swamps and forests. The fact is that during those years I did not once see the sun. This depressed me greatly at first, as it did all newcomers. Occasionally the process of cloud-building would reveal conspicuous bright areas, and once or twice towards the end of my stay, oblique rays shot from the horizon over our city, but as for a triumphant break-through, nothing of the sort happened, not ever.

How the earth, with its fields and forests, looked under such a sky is easy to picture. Natural green was nowhere to be seen; all the grass, plants, bushes, and trees were dyed a dull olive, a greenish-grey. The flowers and shrubs that at home have bright colours were dim and subdued. Whereas in normal landscapes the blue of the air and the yellowish-red of the earth form the basic colour scheme and the other hues appear to be interpolated between them, here grey and brown predominated. Variety and vividness were absent. The Dream Country was harmonious in appearance – that much had to be admitted.

The barometer always pointed to 'Continued cloudiness and rain,' but the soft, damp air that had met us on arrival usually prevailed. The seasons showed a similar lack of contrast. Spring lasted five months; there were five months of fall; twilight all night long marked the short, hot summer; perpetual dusk and a few snowflakes characterized the winter.

To the north the kingdom was bordered by a lofty range of mountains, the summits constantly veiled in cloud. This highland descended abruptly into a plain, accompanied by a mighty stream, the Negro, that fell in wild cascades down a rocky cliff. Spreading out from the narrow valley at the cliff's base, its waters flowed on, broad and sluggish and strikingly dark, almost inky in colour. Then the river described a wide curve, and it was here that Perle, capital city of the kingdom, had been built. Dim and melancholy, it stood in colourless uniformity on the barren soil. One would have said it must have been there for many centuries; actually it had existed barely a dozen years. The founder of the city had not wished to mar the solemnity of the scene. No strident new buildings had been erected; as we had been told by Gautsch, Patera had had old houses shipped from all parts of Europe. They were structures appropriate to this place; selected with sure instinct in accord with a single idea, they harmonized completely. When I arrived, the city numbered about twenty-two thousand inhabitants.

To make precise orientation possible – something I consider necessary for the understanding of later events – I have included a small map for the reader.

As this sketch shows, Perle was divided into four principal sections. In the smoke-blackened station district next to the swamp were located the bleak administration buildings, the

Archives, and the post office. It was a cheerless, commonplace neighbourhood. The so-called Garden City, residence of the rich, lay next to it. Then came Long Lane, which was the business district. Here lived the middle class. Towards the river, this quarter became village-like in character. Between Long Lane and the foot of the mountain lay the French Quarter. This minor section of the city with its 4,000 inhabitants, Rumanians, Slavs, and Jews, was considered disreputable. The mixed and colourful population was crowded into ancient wooden houses, the streets were narrow alleys dotted with evil-smelling dives; the place was not exactly the pride of Perle. Hanging over the whole city and dominating it was a monstrous structure, vast and ungainly. The high windows looked out threateningly far over the countryside and down upon the people beneath. With its back against the porous, weather-beaten cliff, the huge building projected into the centre of the city to the Great Square. This was the Palace, Patera's residence.

With the mountain range to the north, the river to the east, and the swamp to the west, the city could only expand towards the south. There, to be sure, next to the cemetery, were large, still unoccupied areas: the Tomassevic fields, named for a deceased former owner. But all attempts to build there had proved unlucky. Before the roofs were in place, the structures fell into ruins. Conspicuous among them was an abandoned brick kiln, which looked like the grave of some pharaoh or one of the great kings of Assyria. No Europeans were allowed to settle on the other side of the river. That was the Suburb, a small community with special privileges, to which I shall return in a later chapter.

As for the population, it was recruited from sharply different types. Outstanding among them were people of exaggeratedly fine sensibilities. *Idées fixes* not yet obsessive, such as love of collecting or of reading, a mania for gambling, hyper-religiosity and the thousand other forms assumed by refined neurasthenia – these were as though made to order for the Dream Kingdom. In women, hysteria was the most frequent phenomenon. The masses also had been selected with an eye to the abnormal or to one-sided development: splendid specimens of drunkards, wretches dissatisfied with themselves and the world,

hypochondriacs, spiritualists, daredevil ruffians, blasé characters seeking adventure and old adventurers seeking peace, legerdemain artists, acrobats, political fugitives, murderers wanted abroad, counterfeiters, thieves, and others of that ilk found indulgence in the eyes of the Master. In the proper circumstances even a striking physical peculiarity resulted in a call to Dream Land; hence the many pendulous goitres, enlarged noses, and mountainous hunchbacks. Finally, there was a considerable number of people who through some dark destiny had acquired strangely bizarre natures. It was only after prolonged effort that I achieved a good eye for these carefully concealed differentiations of character, often hidden under improbable exteriors.

The average population varied between 20,000 and 24,000 souls and was being constantly replenished by the newly invited. Additions through birth hardly counted. Children were not especially liked. The general attitude was that they by no means compensated for the nuisance they caused. The prevailing view was that they simply cost money, often until they were fully grown, that they seldom and unwillingly repaid any of it and almost never showed gratitude to their parents for the gift of life. On the contrary, they often seemed to think that this gift had been forced upon them. The blessing of children was synonymous with the curse of parenthood. That children could be droll and diverting, good God, you could appreciate in the examples already extant. These provided small incentive to get offspring for oneself. People lived not in an uncertain future but in an animated present, from which no one got any advantage. Who wanted to put further strain on his nerves, or make a woman look older? *One* child was usually all a couple produced; families with several had brought their infants with them from outside. An instance of nine children will be mentioned later because of its uniqueness. Besides this, most Dream people were not especially well suited to be fathers and mothers.

There are a few more particulars to add about those institutions that make a country function. A small army was maintained, which followed its profession with enthusiasm, and a really admirable police force, whose principal areas of activity were the French Quarter and the supervision of Customs. All services were managed from the Archives, a low, sprawling structure – the one, in fact, that had caught my attention on arrival. Yellowish-grey, dusty and bleak, it aroused at first glance a desire to yawn. It stood on the Great Square and was the official seat of government. A car-track connected all these quarters, and a usable though grass-grown road ran out to the distant mountain valleys.

By far the majority of the Dreamers were German by birth. One could get along with that language in the city and with the country people as well. Other nationalities hardly counted. And now I believe I have set down all that is needed to serve as a sketchy background to the real story.

CHAPTER THREE

Daily Life

I

The first thing that struck us was the way the Dream people dressed – what a joke! Their clothes were completely out of fashion. This was especially evident among the so-called fine folk.

'Why, these people wear the clothes of their parents and grandparents,' I remarked with amusement to my wife. Hopelessly outmoded high hats with flaring crowns, frock coats of figured material, overcoats with high collars – that was the way the gentlemen dressed. The women got themselves up in crinolines and oddly old-fashioned coiffures, with little hoods and fichus. The effect was exactly like a masquerade.

But my wife and I, too, caused a sensation, and after a few days we felt compelled to conform. My wife became accustomed to a little semi-crinoline, and I wore with distinction a morning coat, a deep-cut waistcoat of flowered material, and a stock of the 1860s period. I could not bring myself to further concessions. I indignantly rejected the narrow, pointed shoes that were urged upon me. But we became used to these external changes more quickly than one would have thought. It was only a short time before I looked with astonishment at new arrivals in their strange gear.

On our first day, my whole concern was to settle at once in a suitable home. Falling in with my wife's desire to be as far away as possible from the uncanny Palace, we began our search on the outskirts of the city. To find a place in the attractive Garden Villas was out of the question. We were wandering at random down Long Lane for the third time when a middle-sized, two-story house with bow windows on the second floor attracted my attention. It seemed familiar to me, as though I had known it from childhood. 'Why, here's what we're looking for,' I exclaimed, pointing. 'We'll find a place on the second floor!' My wife was amazed at my certainty. 'How can you possibly know for sure?' she asked with a teasing smile. I had no answer, of course; it simply seemed inevitable. And, thank God, I was right; there was an apartment of three rooms and a kitchen to be had. A hairdresser, whose shop was on the ground floor and who was also the superintendent of the building, took us up and showed us the place. The rooms looked attractive and inviting, the furnishings were pretty, and the price moderate. We moved in that same afternoon.

The house belonged to a physician by the name of Lampenbogen.

2

So then we became full-fledged citizens of the Dream City. A dozen times a day I had to take back my early suspicion that everything here was the same as at home – that is, during the first few months. Later I forgot my home entirely. In Dreamland one became so accustomed to the improbable that presently nothing seemed out of the ordinary.

Although I had not really intended it, I soon found a job. I was taken completely by surprise. On the third day, a very lively little man came to see me.

'I'm publisher and editor of the *Dream Mirror*, the popular illustrated newspaper, and have my own printing presses,' he said gushingly. 'It's fine that you're here; we've been waiting a long time for a man like you. Castringius, my first assistant, is unfortunately somewhat played out, and now we fill our need for pictures by buying up any old woodcuts we can find in Perle and printing them. Just look at our last number!' He drew out the sheet. 'Kochem-on-the-Mosel; Minister Count Beust and a circle of his relatives; Indians in war regalia. Is that nice? Is that dreamlike? Is it even interesting?' He

was shouting indignantly and waving the paper. 'No, no, my friend!'

He paused thoughtfully for a moment and wiped the sweat from his forehead. Suddenly he drew out a neatly written contract. All I had to do was sign: four hundred florins a month for an entire year, whether I supplied much or nothing at all. It was a real joke. I had never seen an agreement like it before, and naturally I immediately scribbled my name. In the Dream Kingdom people made up their minds very quickly; no one reflected for long; all businesses were uncertain. However, now I had a permanent position; I was an illustrator for a respectable newspaper and I represented, in a word, *something.*

That's what was most important in this country: to represent something, anything at all – a loafer or vagabond if necessary.

My editor gleefully unscrewed the handle of his walking stick. It contained a little glass; out of the cane itself he poured a large schnapps for me. 'To seal our bargain!' he said significantly.

'As soon as you can, bring me something sensational, something horrifying. The fact is, I want to improve the quality of the paper,' he added genially. Then he pocketed the contract with obvious satisfaction, bade me good-bye, and went tripping out in his black-and-white checked suit.

3

Anyone coming to the Dream Kingdom would not notice at first the constant fraudulence of business life. Casually observed, buying and selling went on just the same as elsewhere. But that was simply the surface, and laughably superficial at that. The whole economic life was 'symbolic'. No one ever knew how much he owned. Money was brought to you and then taken away again, you handed out and you took in. We were all to some extent pickpockets, and I too soon learned many of the dodges. Most things depended on glibness. To impose an illusion on one's opponent, that was the trick. In the beginning, I was alarmed at the extent to which Dream people were subject to suggestion, but for good or ill I had to come to terms with this fact, and I myself became steadily more enmeshed in my own fantasies and those of others. The alternation of good fortune and bad, of poverty and riches, was much more rapid than in the rest of the world. Events constantly tumbled over one another. But no matter how confused things were, one felt a *strong hand*. Behind even the most incomprehensible circumstances one detected its secret mastery. It was the mysterious force by virtue of which everything was held together and did not topple into the abyss. It was the great Fate that watched over us all. An immense Justice, reaching even into hidden places, it brought all events back into balance. If a man were in despair, saw no escape from disaster, then he sent his innermost prayer to that address. That limitless power, full of a dreadful curiosity, an eye that penetrated into every nook and cranny, was omnipresent; nothing escaped it. The Dream people were deadly serious in this belief; all else was transitory.

4

I shall now give a few examples of our business practices. On one of our first days in Perle I decided to buy a map of the city. I went into one of the big second-hand stores in our street, I believe it was the one next to Max Blumenstich's.

'A map of the city? The new ones haven't come in yet. No doubt an older edition will do.' There ensued a rummaging and searching among stags' horns, chandeliers, and old strongboxes, but there were no maps to be found. Finally, the clerk brought me a dreadful cast bronze inkwell. 'Take this, it is certainly something you can use. You have to have it, it's a necessity! Only seventy-two florins.' In melting tones, he employed all his powers of persuasion. I gave him one florin and received a pair of nail-scissors into the bargain.

Newcomers tried to make a killing out of these circumstances, but soon were forced to see that they had been reckoning without their Host. The Dream Fate was relentless; riches painfully scraped together disappeared in an instant. The smartest operators had to pay impossible prices for the absolute necessities of life, or there came a succession of deliveries C.O.D. If these were refused, far more unpleasant things were likely to happen. Sickness, for example, and the doctors' charges were exorbitant. Creditors whom one had never seen before turned up and demanded their money. There was no protection against them, for they brought witnesses. So everything evened out in the long run, and one had neither profit nor loss. No bargain could be struck with the invisible reckoner. As soon as I had grasped this strange procedure, all went well.

At the end of the first fortnight, a servant in livery came to our apartment. His master – he mentioned a distinguished name – was waiting impatiently for the five drawings he had bought. The servant had orders to fetch them. What could I do? I packed up five of my best pictures and wrote a letter of apology to go with them. What became of the drawings I have no idea at all.

Every day I visited the coffeehouse on the other side of our street. Once, when I was coming home, I met my wife carrying a huge basketful of splendid vegetables – asparagus, cauliflower, fine fruits – plus a couple of partridges.

'All this came from the grocer's. Guess what it cost,' she said happily.

'Well?'

'Twenty kreutzers for the lot.'

Then I showed what I had bought in the café – a box of wax matches – and admitted I had been forced to pay five florins for them.

At times one's pockets were full of money, and then they were empty again. Actually, you could get along quite well without money. You had only to act as though you were giving something. On occasion, you could even take the risk of accepting something for nothing. But it all amounted to the same thing.

Here illusions simply were reality. The remarkable thing about it was how such fantasies arose simultaneously in a number of different minds. The people talked themselves by sheer will power into their imaginary worlds.

For example, the prosperous head of a household wakes up one morning with the conviction that he has been completely ruined. His wife weeps, his acquaintances condole with him. The bailiff is already there to seize the property, the chattels are auctioned off, a new owner moves in, perhaps on the same day, servants carry out only the most essential household objects and transport them to some miserable narrow dwelling. In a month, all is well again, for there has been a new and happy turn of fortune.

The people of real wealth led a life of great luxury. Their misfortunes lay in another direction but were equally easy to see. For this reason, class envy played no great role. One was tied to one's job and had one's own satisfactions and irritations. If things went moderately well, one could be content; in general, the Dream people loved their country and their city. I worked quietly at my job as illustrator for the *Dream Mirror* and made various, at first fruitless, attempts to pay a call on my friend Patera.

Unfortunately, every sort of thing interfered, exactly as though some devil of mischance had taken a hand. First I was told that the Master was so overloaded with business that he could see no one. Another time he had gone on a trip. Then I heard that tickets for audiences could be obtained at the Archives. I went there. I walked through the gate, decorated with coats of arms, feeling as guilty as an anarchist. The door-man was asleep. I tried to find my way alone and entered a spacious antechamber. About a dozen officials were there.

For probably a quarter of an hour, no one noticed me at all, as though I were invisible. Finally, one of the functionaries asked me gruffly what I wanted. However, he did not wait for my answer but went on conversing with his neighbour. A somewhat pleasanter character bowed to me and inquired about my business. His wrinkled yellow face fell into severe furrows, he took a few puffs at his long pipe, and then motioned with it towards the next room. 'In there!'

On the door was a notice: Do not knock. Inside, a man was asleep. I had to clear my throat three times before any sign of life came into his completely rigid, deeply reflective pose. Then I was favoured with a glance of majestic disdain.

'What do you want?' he growled. 'Have you a summons? What papers have you brought with you?'

Here there was not the same curtness as outside; on the contrary, information came bubbling out.

'To receive your ticket for an audience you need in addition to your birth certificate, baptismal certificate, and marriage certificate, your father's graduation diploma and your mother's inoculation certificate. Turn left in the corridor. Administration Room 16, and make your declaration of means, education, and honorary orders. A character witness for your father-in-law is desirable but not absolutely essential.' Whereupon he nodded condescendingly, bent once more over the desk, and began to write with, as I could see, a dry pen. I stood there completely bewildered. Lucky that I was not asked to show all my receipted bills.

In embarrassment I stammered, 'Perhaps it will not be possible to produce everything that is required. I have only a passport. I came here as Patera's guest. My name is So-and-So.'

As I said this I received a shock. The austere official suddenly sprang to his feet. 'A thousand pardons! You have been expected for a long time. I will take you immediately to His Excellency.' Now he was courtesy itself. Was one to believe that there could be two hearts in a single breast? I did not understand it at all.

Then began an interminable wandering through empty corridors, offices where people jumped at our arrival as though caught red-handed, empty chambers, and chancelleries filled to the ceiling with deeds and portfolios. Finally we arrived in a large waiting room where a conglomerate crowd was sitting about. My guide and I were at once admitted to a sort of sanctuary. His Excellency was seated there entirely alone, waiting. The poor functionary, despite his pretty bows, was fiercely reprimanded, and dismissed.

His Excellency was a very distinguished man. You could tell that even from the furnishings of his room. But it was clearly discernible in his person as well. He had, for example, an immense amount of gold lace sewn to his clothing, and a long line of honorary ribbons to boot. A broad red band ran diagonally across his chest. Whether there were further marks of distinction underneath I cannot say. Presumably so.

We were alone. In contrast to the others in the Archives, he was very cordial. I was enchanted at this distinguished consideration. After listening to me, he said cordially, 'But that is a matter of course, most honoured sir. The invitation will be sent to you immediately.'

Then he got to his feet and began to speak in a mechanical fashion, as though addressing an audience. 'Gentlemen, gentlemen, in the interests of the public welfare and our prestige, the government accepts full responsibility. I stand ready to present your respective requests before the highest authority. In the matter of care for the poor, you will find my ear is always sympathetically inclined. Our next goal must be the completion of our theatrical enterprise. I count upon your energetic support. The experience we have acquired in giving free rein to certain institutions in the French Quarter vouches for our ... gentlemen ... I am convinced, I speak to you from the bottom of my heart, if ... if ... if...' The orator lost the thread of his discourse; he stared at me with bemused glassy eyes. I helped him out of his embarrassment by bowing, expressing my thanks, and taking my leave. In my heart I felt no great regard for the Archives, and I did not disturb their tranquillity again.

This experience, of course, was something that happened only to newcomers. If you followed this course, nothing positive was ever achieved. The most urgent requests were sent back because of minor errors in filling out the forms. With inescapable certainty, you could count on all plans being thwarted. For example, I actually received the invitation to the audience quite promptly; on the following day, however, came a notice that it was invalid.

In the Dream State, the Archives served as a pure parody of government. If it had been removed, things would have gone just as well and just as badly as before. The enormous piles of deeds – collected from all quarters of the world – had nothing whatever to do with the Dream Kingdom. To put the matter bluntly, this atmosphere of officialdom, heavy with the dust of old papers, was used simply to produce a special breed of *Homo sapiens*, which contributed its note to the variety of the whole.

The true government lay elsewhere. For the time being, I gave up my attempted visit, in part because other matters occupied my attention.

5

The house we lived in stands before my eyes today as clearly as though I had seen it only a few weeks ago.

On the ground floor was the hairdresser's shop. He was usually on the premises himself. He was a blond bachelor with a pince-nez and was very well read, his passion being philosophy. On this subject he let his thoughts run riot. His information was vast and confused, and he was by no means niggardly in sharing it. 'There are many things I could tell,' he would remark, giving me a piercing glance.

God knows what he took me for, but from the start I enjoyed his confidence. 'Kant – there was the great mistake. Ha ha ha! You can't sail around the Thing-in-Itself as simply as that! First of all, the world is an *ethical* problem – I shall never be persuaded to the contrary. You see, Space woos Time; their point of union, the present, is death; or, what amounts to the same thing, the godhead, if you wish. Thrust into the middle is the great miracle of becoming flesh: the object. This in turn is nothing except the external aspect of the subject. Those are the fundamental principles, my dear sir. There you have my whole theory.'

'Yes, I can see you are a thinker,' I used to reply.

He lived day in and day out in lofty regions, and his barbershop would have gone to ruin if it had not been for Giovanni Battista. He, in point of fact, was only a monkey; but what a monkey! A quite uncannily gifted and energetic animal. With him for helper, one could safely pursue the problem of ethics. Giovanni had risen from the ranks in his profession. He had betrayed his talent one day by making lather of his own accord; the barber recognized in him, too, 'the subject' and turned the monkey's skilful hands to account. His quick, sure razor strokes were famous in the whole neighbourhood. On Wednesdays and Saturdays he even went to the homes of their private customers. One would often catch sight of him, earnest and workmanlike, hurrying down Long Lane with his bag. More honest and more reliable than a man, he was the true soul of the hairdressing business. There was only one thing that distressed his master: he had little understanding for philosophy.

'You are a Stoic!' the barber would shout at him after lecturing him at length. He never gave up the secret hope of converting Battista to higher aims.

*

I have to confess that whenever I look back on my first year in the Dream Kingdom I am overcome by a feeling of yearning. At that time things were mostly good; yes, those days I count as among my best. Stimulated by all the new experiences, my work was going easily and well. In the afternoons around five o'clock I would meet my friends in the coffeehouse. From its windows I could watch all the comings and goings in the streets. The traffic, to be sure, was not great; in Perle most people preferred to stay at home. In the inner city, for instance, the streets were conspicuously empty. But for this very reason, despite the lack of animation on the sidewalks, what one actually did see became through familiarity a cherished sight.

Bit by bit I felt my way deeper into all this. I found hand-holds, firm positions amid the confusion, and in this respect the houses played a leading role. It often seemed to me that the people were there only on the houses' account, not the other way about.

It was the houses that had true, strong individuality. There they stood, silent but full of significance. Each one had a definite history of its own; one simply had to wait and bully it out of the old structures little by little. The buildings differed greatly in their moods. Many of them hated themselves and were jealously competitive with one another. There were ugly grumblers among them, like the dairy across the street; others seemed impudent and abusive – my café is a good example. Our house was an acidulous maiden aunt, the windows squinting out, malicious and eager for gossip. Evil, definitely evil, was M. Blumenstich's big store. The blacksmith's shop next to the dairy was solid and jovial; next to it, the river inspector's little cottage was irresponsible and frivolous. But my particular favourite was the corner house on the river; that was the mill. It had a merry, white-washed face, and wore its mossy, shingled roof like a cap. On the street side, high up, a rough-hewn balcony protruded from the wall like a good cigar, though its expression towards the top, around the garret windows, was a bit sly and ambiguous. The mill belonged to two brothers. Or did the two belong to it, like two sons possessed by a mother?

There is a great deal I could relate if I were sure my readers would understand these complicated relationships in the way I would wish. For instance, after a while I seemed to notice that the houses in one street represented something like a family. Even if they quarrelled among themselves, they seemed to present a united front to the outside. In desolate Perle ideas came to me that would never have reached my consciousness in the busy cities of the outer world.

But it was when my sense of smell became miraculously

sharpened that I penetrated more deeply into these relationships. This happened after I had been there about six months. From then on, my nose was arbiter of my sympathies and dislikes. For hours at a time I wandered about in all the old byways, sniffing and snuffling at everything, and as I did, a whole new, limitless domain was opened to me. Each worn object shared its small secret with me. My wife often smiled; she found it funny when I snuffled knowledgeably at some book or music box. Indeed, I was almost like a dog. Nor can I explain all this precisely; it was a matter of sensibilities so refined that they baffle the understanding.

First of all, there was a certain indescribable odour that pervaded the whole Dream Kingdom and clung to everything. Sometimes it was quite strong, sometimes it was barely perceptible. Where it was concentrated, this peculiar smell could be described as a mixture of flour and dried codfish. I could never find an explanation of its origin. Far more definite were the odours of individual objects. I analysed them carefully and in the process I was often seized by a strong revulsion. I was liable to become insulting in the company of people who seemed to smell wrong. But in all these living beings and apparently lifeless objects, assembled though they had been through a bizarre whim, an ultimate inexplicable unity could be detected, despite their diversity.

6

Everything one saw in the Dream Kingdom was dull and dim. How far this went was brought home to me one day while I was being shaved. Giovanni was serving me with his accustomed elegance, but the condition of the razor and the copper basin was disturbing; they were tarnished.

'What's the meaning of this?' I said to the barber, who was just then reading to me a difficult passage from Leibniz's *Monadology*. 'Your assistant could certainly keep these things in a little better condition.'

'What's that?' the great philosopher inquired in astonishment, looking like a man who has fallen from the clouds.

'I mean this basin and this razor need polishing.'

'Yes, what is one to do? That's just the way things happen to be. I am careful to avoid innovations.'

To pin him down, I pointed at the mirrors. 'Just look at them, a fine job of cleaning you've done there!'

At that his philosophy deserted him; he was in a dilemma. 'Yes, the mirrors!' Then, reflectively and hesitantly, he said, as though the words were being forced out of his mouth, 'But mirrors are absolutely nothing at all!'

It was obviously painful for him to speak of the subject.

'I did not mean to insult you,' I said in a conciliatory tone, and left the shop.

No matter! It was pleasant to live among those tarnished, ancient objects. I have no hesitation in including the following letter, which was written entirely in the mood that possessed me at that time. Besides, it contains a description of a strange practice relating to the Cult, about which I intend to tell later on. I mean the Great Clock Spell. This letter was in a notebook found among my odds and ends when the Dream Kingdom had been destroyed. There was also the list of sacred objects that is given later on, written on pages that were otherwise covered with wholly illegible writing. On the inside cover of the notebook there was a rough sketch map of the city of Perle, together with some hasty notations that I had set down in the early days for my own orientation.

The letter, written in the third month of my residence, was my first attempt to establish contact with the outside world. Two years later I got it back marked, 'Addressee unknown'. The envelope was a mass of postmarks and scrawls. The letter and the notebook are the only tangible evidence of the Dream Kingdom that I can show to visitors.

Dear Fritz:

You will find it hard to believe, but here I am in the Dream Kingdom. And I can give you only one piece of advice: pack up your belongings at once on receipt of this letter and join me here. Perle is a real Eldorado for the collector. The city is a museum in itself. Naturally there's a lot of rubbish, but there are splendid pieces as well. Today I saw a carved Gothic table, a pair of silver sconces (16th century), and one of those fabulous Renaissance bronzes (a boy riding a bull by our Cellini) which you have always doted on so. Last week we ran riot in porcelains; I must be silent about the low prices, otherwise I should have to fear for your health. And such gems are to be found every day and everywhere by anyone who has the nose for them. There is nothing but old things here. We live like our grandfathers before the revolution of 1848 and thumb our noses at progress. Yes, my friend, we are conservatives! Every fifth house contains an antique store, and the people here live from bric-a-brac. There are architectural extravaganzas to be seen as well. In the Palace at least twenty different styles have been effortlessly combined. And besides that, the

amusing discoveries! You would not believe it unless you saw!
Just so you will understand my high spirits, I will tell you about the
last joke I observed. It is what they call 'the Great Clock Spell'.
Just listen to this. In our main square there is a heavy, massive grey
tower, a sort of squat campanile. It houses an old clock, whose face
occupies the upper third. At night we read the official time from its
illuminated dial, and all the other clocks in the city and in the
country are regulated by it. Now there would be nothing remarkable about this if it were not that the tower has in addition a quite

uncanny quality. It is this: it exercises a mysterious and incredible attraction over all the inhabitants. At certain hours this ancient pile is surrounded by crowds of men and women. A stranger stops in bewilderment to observe the odd behaviour of this gathering. The people tap their feet nervously on the ground and glance up again and again at the long, rusty hands above them. If you ask them what is happening, you receive distraught, evasive answers. Looking more closely, you notice two small entrance doors at the foot of the tower. Everyone is pushing toward them. When the crowd is large, lines are formed and the women watch anxiously, the men angrily, to see that everyone stays in his proper place. The farther the hand advances, the greater the tension becomes. One after another they disappear into the tower; each one remains a minute or two inside. When they come out they all wear a deeply satisfied, almost happy, expression. Small wonder that my curiosity was aroused. When I had an opportunity, I questioned one of my new coffeehouse acquaintances as to what this was all about. I got short shrift for my pains. It was, he said, very improper to speak of this sort of thing, besides it was a proof of stupidity. 'So that you may know once and for all, it is the Great Clock Spell! Just make a note of that!' His indignation only increased my curiosity.

My original supposition that this was some sort of device, perhaps a camera obscura, or a panopticon, collapsed. Quickly making up my mind, I went to see for myself one day, but was sadly disillusioned. Do you know what was inside the tower? But you could never guess. You come into a small, angular, empty cell, decorated in part with mysterious drawings, probably symbolic. Behind the wall you hear the mighty pendulum swinging back and forth. Ticktock, tick-tock. Over the stone wall water streams uninterruptedly. I behaved like the man who came in after me, I stared hard at the wall and said, loud and clear, 'Here I stand before you!' Then you go out again. My expression must have been one of bewilderment.

Women have their own side with a separate entrance, which is indicated by a small sign as is customary everywhere in the world. But the most remarkable thing is this: since the day I had that experience I can feel myself succumbing to the spell. At first it was only a little tug as I was passing the tower. The next day my uneasiness grew greater and greater—the spell simply dragged me there. And so I gave in to this foolishness; resisting it did no good. And now all is well. There are smaller towers situated throughout the city, all copied from the original. Every farmhouse in the country is said to have its own clock niche. Day after day I go to mine at the appointed hour. All right, go ahead and laugh at me. 'Master, here I stand before you!'

Painting here does not amount to much. Works of art are prized for their usefulness. I understand there are a few aged painters living here and there, and what I have seen of their work, dark, thinly painted canvases, are belated imitations of the old Dutch school. Really splendid things. Ruysdaels, Breughels, Altdorfers, and the primitives are to be found now and then in the houses of the rich. The banker Alfred Blumenstich, our Croesus and director of the Dream Kingdom Bank, has a precious gallery containing even a Rembrandt and a genuine Grünewald, of whose existence no one in your part of the world has any idea. 'The Seven Deadly Sins Eating the Lamb of God' is the title. No one uses lively colours here – you do better with simple drawings.

I have a very good situation with the illustrated *Dream Mirror* – four hundred florins and easy working conditions. I have not met my single colleague, the illustrator Nikolaus Castringius. If you come I can almost certainly find you a place on the paper.

Don't be annoyed at me for stopping now. I look forward to our reunion!

Your old Friend,
Dreamer and Illustrator

N.B. You can stay with us in a romantic house on the outskirts of the city, quite undisturbed, just like being in the country.

As can be seen from my letter, at that time I was still in a cheerful frame of mind. The shadow aspects, which were then just making themselves felt, will be described at the end of this chapter insofar as they had already come to my attention. Before that, I want to make some comments about the Cult – or what I took to be a cult.

7

This was a subject as fascinating as it was complex. I never got to the bottom of it, not even later on. In it, I suspected, lay the solution to many riddles. If my researches produced negative results, that is not my fault, for in this matter hostile fate interfered with my serious efforts, and my discoveries remained all too meagre.

All the great religions of the old world were represented here to a greater or lesser degree. However, this was simple make-believe, a hollow sham. Educated people admitted this without question. They were intelligent freethinkers and would not readily submit to any rigid hierarchical scheme. Besides, there were many lucid minds among them. And yet there was a residue there: the fatalistic belief in a subtly equitable fate, and all sorts of incomprehensible and mysterious notions. These were not something to be smiled at. I made that mistake once myself, to my regret.

In the first three months of my stay, I became acquainted with a sympathetic young gentleman in the coffeehouse, Baron Hektor von Brendel. He was thoroughly distinguished in mind and manner, a man of the world, slightly neurasthenic and languid, but by no means stupid. His mild, unobtrusive melancholy was what first attracted me to him. Later on, we saw each other daily.

'You have been here for three years, Brendel,' I said to him once when we happened to be alone, sitting at our usual table. 'I see every reason to believe that there is some sort of secret band of believers here in the Dream State, a kind of Masonic Order. Do you know anything more about them? Can you perhaps enlighten me a bit? Their rites? Their customs?'

He looked at me sidewise, coughed, and asked drily, 'What is it that makes you think so?'

'Oh, nothing definite; ideas about fate are certainly nothing new. But in a general way it's this stubborn clinging to the same old-fashioned way of life, this lack of any interest in progress – and one thing more.' I told him about the business with the barber and his copper basin.

He listened to me seriously, slowly rolling a cigarette, and remarked with a mournful smile, 'To be quite candid with you, my friend, yes, there is certainly something there. But despite my best efforts I know very little more than you do.'

'Oh, come!' I was disappointed. 'Don't you know anything at all about the matter? I can be silent if necessary – that goes without saying.'

Brendel reflected for a moment and then spoke in a half-whisper. 'There are certain things that people stand in awe of. I

don't know, however, whether it will be of much help to you
if I name a few of the sacred objects.'

'Oh, please do me that favour!' I begged him, aglow with
eagerness.

'Well then, eggs, nuts, bread, cheese, honey, milk, wine, and
vinegar are especially holy.'

'Aha!' I cried cheerfully. 'A health cult based on the digestion. Splendid!' I could not suppress a slight note of ridicule.
'Why not tea, coffee, and sugar at the same time?'

At that, Brendel turned his back on me and paid his bill. A
gust of wind blew the door open, and warm, damp, earthy air
rushed in, strongly mixed with the exciting Dream Kingdom
smell. With a curt farewell Brendel walked out; I looked after
him through the high, cracked windowpane. It was dark outside. No, that was not the way I should have gone about it; I
had frivolously forfeited an opportunity. Next time I would be
more circumspect.

Soon after this, I discovered that food and drink were not the
only religious objects; hair, horn, mushrooms, and hay were
equally holy. Even cow dung and horse dung had a special
significance. Among the internal organs, the liver and the heart
were especially important, as were, in the animal world, fish.
Tanned hides took on some mysterious meaning. In the opposite category, and seeming to symbolize specific dangers, were
steel and iron and certain alloys. I learned all these particulars
from farmers and hunters, taking long walks into the open

country for this very purpose. Everything I could extract from these taciturn people, bit by bit, I made a note of; I shall not, however, set down the whole list because it is unnecessarily long. But one more point may be of interest: there were certain lonesome spots in the woods and swamps where no wanderer dared go at twilight; all Dreamers avoided them if they could because of their sinister reputation.

I might have been clearer about this whole matter, not groped around so much in the dark, if I had just once seen with my own eyes the Temple on the lake. According to all reports, this sacred edifice must have been a fabulous marvel. It was situated on Dream Lake and lay a good day's journey from Perle. Artificial lagoons and a quiet park surrounded it, and within the Temple the most precious treasures of the Dream Kingdom were said to be stored. It was built of the noblest material – which I suppose was rare marble – and so cunningly constructed that it appeared to hover between heaven and earth. The great hall was decorated in brown, grey, and green – Patera's colours. In the secret underground chambers symbolic statues had been placed. Alas, the Temple was open to visitors only once a year, and even then special influence was necessary. At the beginning, I hoped that my personal friendship with Patera would serve to gain me admittance. But my visit to him kept being postponed – and then later on came *the events*.

Tireless though my investigations of the Dream religion were, I achieved little real knowledge of it; there was a sort of fatality in the way I kept being rebuffed. Once I was invited to the house of Blumenstich the banker. There was a crowd of people there, and the atmosphere was cheerful. The master of the house had just received a decoration for the bathhouse he had built, and the occasion was being celebrated in customary fashion.

Dinner was over. The men were smoking comfortably over coffee and liqueurs. I thought to myself, Here are the cleverest people in all Perle gathered in one place. If I can't find out something tonight, I never shall. Thus encouraged, I broke boldly into speech and told about my disappointments, my fruitless endeavours to find out about the real Cult of the Dream people. My words ran on smoothly, eloquently; they flowed from my tongue as though of themselves. Finally, I believed I had convinced everyone of my burning thirst for knowledge, and I requested those present to enlighten me. Then I stopped; I could not have gone on, for my throat was parched. Everyone was silent, disconcerted, and embarrassed.

Two dignified elderly gentlemen with intelligent faces, dressed in elegant Biedermeier style, had already moved into the next room. I had put my chief hope in them.

At last the master of the house spoke, scratching his black muttonchops. 'Young man, have you ever been in the settlement across the river? Take a look at that ancient community sometime.' His voice sounded sharp and rather disparaging. I felt as though a heavy weight had been removed from my back – at least one of them had spoken!

The conversation then ran on about indifferent matters. No one paid attention to me any longer. Only my editor, who was there too, commented in an explanatory way, 'Oh you know, these illustrators!'

No help for me there. Sunk in thought, I soon left the house. 'I shall never get to the bottom of it,' I shouted into the night.

As I passed the clock tower I felt its pull. Was there perhaps a connection between this other matter and the Clock Spell? One dared not talk about that either. That, too, was bad form. What was the source of this embarrassment? It seemed that I had been an *enfant terrible* again. But what was there about the Suburb, that tiny, ancient village across the bridge that no one paid any attention to? Lame excuses! I was determined to get to the bottom of this fraud! Clenching my fists, I swore I would do it.

8

Now it is time for me to go on and describe some of the shadow side of our life, otherwise one might come to believe that things there were simply amusing. The entertaining aspects of our life brought a great deal of unpleasantness with them. To begin with, the house we lived in. Under our rooms lived an old maiden lady, Princess von X. She was as ugly as a sick rat, and quarrelsome into the bargain. This creature caused my wife in particular much vexation. She was miserly and rich, but her life was such a closely guarded secret that no one really knew anything more than that about her. The old woman obviously found her satisfaction in constant bickering. If I was still moving around in my room at nine o'clock in the evening, she would knock on the ceiling, a sign that she wanted quiet. When she saw us coming down the stairs, she would begin complaining. A row of pots and dishes for milk and similar deliveries stood constantly outside her apartment. Once I broke an earthenware jug in the darkness. Well, that was the end! Open warfare! She even tried to blacken my reputation with the barber. He, despite his philosophy, still retained respect for 'royalty'. However, once when she carried it too far and insulted my wife in the hallway, I really attacked her: 'You're the Princess of Filth. That's what you look like standing there!' (The old sow had not done her hair.) That had some effect. From then on, the great lady withdrew into her apartment, very much on her dignity, whenever she heard me coming. On one occasion she did this so precipitately that one of her patched bedroom slippers was left lying in front of me. I kicked it out of my way, and to my amazement gold coins tumbled clinking down the stairs.

'Housebreaker, murderer!' she screeched, and roused the whole house against us.

Incidents like this made our lives bitterly uncomfortable. But 'the student' caused us even worse annoyance.

He had two rooms on our floor, and he was a drunkard. His face was expressionless and puffy; scars on both cheeks made him look as though he had a mouth three times the normal size. To even things up, he seemed to have only one third of the average human intelligence.

This neighbour of ours led an unabashed nocturnal existence, and whenever he tried to find his way to bed, he mistook our door for his. Almost every night we awoke in alarm at his curses and hammerings. I remonstrated with him countless times, but what good to us were his apologies? The nuisance continued. Finally there was nothing for it but to make peace and reconcile ourselves.

But there was still more to come. Certain days seemed bewitched. I select a few items from among many.

At five in the morning, a mason rang at the front door, carrying a pail of mortar and the tools of his trade. He asserted loudly and positively that he had received orders to wall up the windows in our apartment. Another time, late at night, we were treated to a serenade. A gypsy orchestra performed in front of our door – of course it was due to some mistake. Visitors came with the most varied requests; strange articles were delivered and never picked up again. A package of old cheese rinds was once left in our apartment for two weeks. When I had finally thrown it out, three army officers appeared and rudely demanded their property. House-to-house beggars

were in full cry in Perle. But often much more unpleasant incidents occurred. For example, one evening just at twilight a number of men dressed in black dragged a coffin to our door. This was where it was to be delivered, was it not? My poor wife was very disturbed about it.

I do not want to make too much of these misunderstandings and the continual knocking at our door. However, there were other happenings that were uncanny, hardly credible. We had as our maid of all work an elderly woman who came to us by the day. She suffered perpetually from toothache, and I never saw her without a cloth wrapped around her head. She cooked well and produced savoury dishes, something that required no great art, given the excellent, fresh foods available in the Dream Kingdom. After a couple of weeks, I could have sworn that under the old skirts there was a different person; it was no longer the elderly housekeeper. Naturally I said nothing about this to my wife, but unfortunately various things had caught her attention too.

'Have you noticed,' she said one day, 'I believe Anna is dyeing her hair. Since yesterday she has become blonde. Wasn't she always a brunette?'

'Now, now, just a bit of vanity!' I remarked with disingenuous innocence. However, I had been disturbed about Anna for quite a while. A time came when the matter could not be ignored. On the preceding day, a vigorous middle-aged woman had served us; today, an old woman with the face of a crone was busily setting the table. My wife clutched my arm; we were both as though turned to stone.

'But it's the same scarf around her head, isn't it?' I stammered, glancing at my wife's eyes, which were wide with fear. We exchanged our observations in whispers; she, too, had had suspicions for a month.

'No, even if she did the work of ten, I won't have her! I'd rather do it all myself.'

I had to dismiss Anna, and for a few days I stayed at home. Then I made an arrangement with the barber, for a consideration, to have Giovanni Battista help my wife in the mornings with the housework. This turned out splendidly. My wife became very fond of the intelligent creature. The only thing he was not allowed to do was to disturb my drawing table. We had to be careful about this, for he felt he was something of an artist himself and kept trying to help me and improve my work. As far as I could, I made myself useful too, by doing the marketing, for instance. But you had to keep a sharp eye on the tradespeople, otherwise you brought home the strangest things. One day I bought a couple of mutton chops at the butcher's very cheap; when I proudly unwrapped them at home, there were small mousetraps in the paper instead of the chops; there was a piece of a mouse's tail still hanging from one of them. 'So, hoodwinked again – the devil!' I thought.

9

And then those noises! There were disturbances all night long, and they were insidious.

Disreputable crowds, including prostitutes from the bordellos in the French Quarter, penetrated into our neighbourhood. Sounds of roaring, whistling, brawling, would draw close to our window and then recede. Drunkards leaving the café gave long monologues; crazed with drink, they shouted insane curses. That was something one could not get used to. The houses were built at various angles to the streets, and the corners and projections thus formed threw back every sound as a redoubled echo. Strident cries rang out from the inner city; now shriller, now lower, they were picked up by building after building and handed on. There was no known reason for this. And then all would become quiet until a coughing and tittering began. To wander at night through the alleys of Perle was a torment. Dreadful abysses opened up to one's aroused sensibilities. From barred windows and reeking cellars resounded moans and groans in every register. Behind half-open doors one heard suppressed outcries so that one thought involuntarily of stranglings and murders. When I turned my anxious steps towards home, there were a thousand – no, ten thousand – taunting voices behind me. Gateways yawned as though eager to swallow me. Invisible voices enticed you towards the river bank. Blumenstich's store grinned maliciously; the dairy was like a treacherous, hidden trap; even the mill was not quiet, its chattering never ceasing all night long. Many a time, haunted by fear, I took refuge in the coffeehouse on my way home. Meanwhile, alone at home, my poor wife was filled with dread. A cupboard would creak, or a glass fly into splinters. She imagined she heard horrid words coming from every corner of the room; often on my return I would find her sweating with fear from her morbid imaginings. These sleepless nights had a ruinous effect on her nerves; soon she believed she was seeing living shadows and ghosts everywhere.

And always there was that indefinable substance that one smelled and finally felt with one's whole body. In the daylight, no one admitted to having seen anything; the city was the same as usual, dead, empty, inert.

CHAPTER FOUR

The Spell

I

One night I returned from the coffeehouse and climbed the stairs to my apartment. At the prearranged signal, my wife opened the door. She had been crying and seemed badly shaken. On the table lay the little case with Patera's picture.

'Why is that out here? Has something happened?'

'I have seen him – yes, that man there!' Her words were disconnected and confused. 'I can't understand it at all, but there's no chance of my being mistaken – those eyes belong to only one person.'

'But please, tell me about it.'

And now in broken sentences, her breathing laboured, she related the encounter.

'I was coming home from the market and I was just turning into Long Lane – it was already getting dark, and so I was hurrying to get home – when I heard quick footsteps behind me – it was a lamplighter – he almost touched me as he passed. At that moment he turned towards me for an instant – and said in a low voice, "Excuse me." But it was horrifying – just think ... your friend Patera ... that's who it was.'

She actually screamed the last words; tears were running down her cheeks. Sobbing, she buried her head on my shoulder. Much dismayed myself, I tried hard to calm her. 'You are mistaken,' I said as quietly as I possibly could. 'You must certainly be mistaken! The twilight – at that time of day it's so easy to make a mistake. What can you be thinking of? Patera, the owner of everything here – is it likely that he would be running around as a common lamplighter?' My voice was unsteady; I, too, was very frightened.

'Oh, don't talk that way, you only make it worse! His face was completely expressionless, like a wax mask, only those eyes ... there was a blind stare in them ... I still shudder when I think of them!' Her hand was hot and feverish. I insisted on her going to bed. I tried to cheer her up with trivial coffeehouse gossip, but I could not distract her thoughts from her experience. I was terrified myself.

Life now became more bedevilled, more exasperating, than ever. Despite the steady monotony of the days, there was no repose; one could never be sure of what the next hour would bring.

Gradually I became sick of the Dream Kingdom. Of course, my wife's encounter with the lamplighter had been a hallucination. My friend Patera certainly had other things to do besides playing carnival jokes. And yet a hallucination is always a warning. The tortured nerves were beginning to rebel.

2

I finally met Nik Castringius. I am really uncertain whether he found me sympathetic. He had had to give up his position on the *Dream Mirror* and was now doing free-lance work. I found him genuinely original, much nicer than the two friends with whom he used to come to the coffeehouse, De Nemi and the photographer. Castringius was no good at all at pretence;

anyone could read envy and jealousy in his face. For this very reason he was completely harmless and you could take pleasure in what good qualities he possessed. A really wicked man seldom becomes an artist – a small meanness now and then, perhaps, that's all. Our sensations leave no time for planning large-scale frauds. We lay ourselves bare in our work so that all the world can see at a glance what a villain the artist could have become in other circumstances. Art is a safety valve!

Before my arrival Castringius was in his simplest period. Three or four lines, and the picture was finished. He called this 'grandeur'. His most significant works were called 'The Head',

'He', 'She', 'We', 'It'. It must be admitted that this put no limitations on the imagination. For example, a head in a flower vase – one could interpret that any way one liked. Then after I had achieved a reputation, Castringius had to aspire to something more. 'The deepening of the subject, that's the secret!' was his dictum. And now came drawings such as 'The Mad Pope Innocent Participating in the Cardinal's Quadrille'.

The illustrator lived in a small attic studio in the French Quarter. In this section of the city he could conduct his life in accordance with his own tastes. It was there that he had found De Nemi. The latter was a swine, a lieutenant in the infantry, and a regular guest at Madame Adrienne's. His ideas were concerned exclusively with what went on there. His talk never strayed far from that subject. His uniform was always dirty, and his eyes always inflamed.

There is not much I can say about the photographer. He was an Englishman with a long face, straw-blond hair, a satin coat, and a billowing tie. He still used the old wet-plate process and ten-minute exposures. In Perle they had not got beyond that. He was a taciturn man and liked mixed liqueurs.

We talked about the theatre. I had visited the place only once. *Orpheus in the Underworld* was being given; the audience consisted of exactly three people. Although the acting was good, it was a disagreeable evening. The three onlookers made the great theatre seem even more desolate. The music sounded uncanny in the empty hall. The actors seemed to be playing for their own entertainment. I was sitting in the gallery. Suddenly I was overcome with the feeling that this great dingy hall was the Stadttheater in Salzburg, long since demolished. When I was eleven, it had represented for me the quintessence of magnificence. What I saw now was well-worn benches, torn dark-red upholstered seats, and cracked stucco. Opposite the stage was a large dark loge; over it in gold letters, 'Patera'. I sometimes fancied I caught sight of two gleaming points of light within its shadow, points that lay very close together.

De Nemi, who seemed to be well acquainted with happenings backstage, argued convincingly that the theatre could not succeed. 'What use is a theatre in Perle? We act out our own dramas!' people said, and stayed away.

The theatre did indeed go bankrupt. The troupe was dissolved. The minor actresses gradually found their way into the brothel, while still maintaining their standing as chorus singers, ballet dancers, and so forth. The rest formed a variety troupe; Blumenstich put up the money. De Nemi was delighted, as he was an enthusiast for music halls. I had little interest in the subject.

The host of the coffeehouse wandered from table to table, greeting the guests with a sly, mindless smile. He cast anchor beside the chess players, his expression growing serious. But the fellow knew nothing of chess; he was too much of a simpleton. I yawned and looked out of the window.

Sacks of grain were being unloaded beside the mill. I could distinguish the two owners clearly: the one always cheerful and laughing, the other taciturn and glowering. In the matter of dress, these were the two most conservative men in the city. They still wore the bag-wigs and buckled shoes of former times.

A carriage was driving by, an elegant lady reclining in it. 'Do you know her?' De Nemi asked, nudging me. 'She is your land-

lord's wife, Frau Doktor Lampenbogen.' He laughed cynically, and the other guests grinned. The carriage was on its way to the bathhouse.

I called for the check. Anton, a cheat of the first rank, tried to give me bad money – assignats of the First Republic. But for once the trick did not work and he had to beat a retreat, grinning impudently.

3

My poor wife could no longer free herself from her state of anxiety. She became visibly paler, her cheeks grew more sunken, and every time I spoke to her unexpectedly she gave a nervous start. This could not go on, and only the fact that I still had not succeeded in paying a call on Patera postponed our departure. Without his specific permission, leaving was out of the question. Ten formal applications signed by me lay in the Archives, but only a few ambiguous words of comfort came from on high: 'During the present season the Department of

Audiences is on vacation,' or, 'The attention of the petitioner has been repeatedly directed to the requirement that only persons engaged in respectable bourgeois professions have any prospect of being granted an audience. He should therefore adhere to these time-honoured traditions and look about for such employment at once,' etc., etc., etc. I was filled with indignation and determined to have a straight talk with my friend about this official caste, so damaging to the public interest. 'They'll be sorry for this!'

Something else weighed heavily in the balance against our departure: *our money was gone!* Yes, simply gone! Not one pfennig of the hundred thousand was left.

'So that's where we stand, just as I prophesied in the beginning!' I said bitterly to my wife when I realized the situation. The poor woman could not really do anything about it, and so I spared her further lamentations. Whatever had happened, thievery or not, the money had disappeared for good, and we were now entirely dependent on my earnings.

Thus our second year in the Dream Kingdom was coming to its end. My wife was constantly tormented by her terrifying hallucinations, even in broad daylight. The kitchen lay at the back of our apartment; through its window one could look down into the courtyard of the dairy. In the middle of the courtyard was a well; farther back, a pair of stable doors.

'There are ghosts in that well,' she declared. She had often heard strange hissings and knockings there, she maintained. I had not noticed anything. However, to please her, I undertook to go over and inspect the place, and I went. Under the pretext of wanting to see the dairy. I knocked at the door and summoned out a Swiss, who was hard of hearing. A large tip put an end to his hesitations. I could look at anything I wanted to, he shouted in my ear, and then retreated once more into his room. Left to my own devices, I set to work at once on my exploration.

Quickly I passed through a whole series of ill-lighted rooms. The building was set fairly deep in the earth, and only a dim light penetrated from high up through the small barred windows.

A large number of round flat vessels stood on long wooden

trestles, and in the corners there were vats, also of wood. All were full to the brim with milk. A vaulted side chamber served as a repository for a variety of implements. The walls were hung with metal pans, wooden plates, and trays. I looked hastily for the courtyard; but instead of finding a way out in that direction, I encountered only darker rooms in which huge cauldrons hung over dead fires. A sharp smell of cheese assailed my nose. There, in fact, they lay, of all sizes, stinking and dripping, in even rows; a repellent place, dim, long and narrow, the mouldy walls covered with spiderwebs.

This could not be the right way – I hurried back. In that uniform maze of cheese, butter, and milk, I could not find my way. I blundered into an obviously unused part of the cellars. The arched ceiling was low, and rusty iron chains hung down from heavy hooks. It was hardly possible to see; the slippery floor seemed to slope downward. Suddenly I stumbled on greasy steps and found myself in complete darkness. Deep night and the icy air of the cellar – somewhere above me I heard a door slam. Thank God, I had a few wax matches in my pocket. Then all at once a sound reached me from far away, very far away. It was like distant hammering but grew louder and louder with uncanny speed. By the light of a match I saw I was in a passageway. Suddenly panic seized me. To get away, just to get away, was my single thought. I ran, striking my

head repeatedly against the oozing walls. But behind me the up-roar grew – a dreadful regular beat, like a gallop. My matches were growing fewer, and the bad air kept the flame from rising. The reverberant noise came nearer; clearly I was being pursued.

Now I could easily distinguish a groaning and heaving. This sound struck to the marrow of my bones and I thought I was losing my mind. I dashed on, as though under a whip, but soon my strength was exhausted and I fell to my knees close to unconsciousness. Helplessly I stretched my hands out in front of me against the oncoming menace; on the floor, the last of my matches flickered.

Then it came, rushing onwards – a cold wind pulled at me – I beheld a white, emaciated horse. Although I could only see indistinctly, I noticed its horrible condition. The great mare was almost dead from hunger and flung out its huge hoofs with the strength of desperation. The bony skull was stretched far forward, the ears lay back; the creature dashed past me. Its dull, lifeless eyes encountered mine – it was blind. I heard its teeth grinding, and as I looked, shuddering, after it, I saw its flayed croup gleaming with blood. The mad gallop of this living skeleton went on unchecked. As the pounding died away, I felt my way forward, tormented by the sight of that terrifying bag of bones. Soon, in the distance, I saw a gas flame, a way of escape. It swam indistinctly before my eyes, for I was over-come by nervous shock. My tongue was paralysed and my body like stone. When the attack was over, I dragged myself towards the light. A stairway appeared – another light. Then I heard people's voices and entered a familiar room. I found myself in the coffeehouse.

4

My entrance had not been noticed. Outside it was twilight, and the lights had been lit. Sitting down in a quiet corner at the rear of the room, I tried to collect my thoughts, understand my monstrous experience, and get rid of my distressing dizziness. I was not long alone. A dignified elderly gentleman in a white neckerchief came over to the corner and sat down at my table.

'It is a little quieter here,' he remarked.

I made no answer; my head was still whirling with confusion. Presently he said in a gentle, sympathetic tone, 'This must be the first time it has happened to you. You have been badly upset.'

At this I looked up. There was something kind and friendly about the man. 'What do you mean?' I asked wearily.

'Why, the blow! Just look around!' And he made a sweeping gesture.

Now for the first time I realized that something must have happened here too. Considering the number of customers, the place was remarkably quiet. Exhaustion and confusion could be read in every face. 'Why, what has happened?' I was beginning to be afraid again.

'Just look at the people! Of course it's all over now.'

I began to trust the speaker; he was candid and engaging.

'I noticed at once that this was the first time for you; it is a curse!' He sighed. All the guests seemed plunged in thought; a few were whispering. Then occasional words were audible again here and there. In the middle of the room broken glass was being swept up. The two chess players were staring at each other as though hypnotized. I begged my companion to explain the strange atmosphere that surrounded us. From his fine curly white hair, which went well with his rather oddly sentimental eyes, I judged he was in his late sixties.

'You have not been very long in the Dream Kingdom, at least not many years?' he began.

'It will soon be two years.'

At a signal from me, Anton, who had regained his briskness, brought cognac. Gradually, things in the coffeehouse returned to normal.

The old man went on: 'Of course, it is hard to adjust yourself if you have known a different life. Here we all stand under *the spell*. Whether we like it or not, a necessary fate is working itself out. We should be glad about it, too; it could be much worse. This way you can at least laugh occasionally at the immense nonsense. Many, very many, are at times unwilling to cooperate. The newcomers, especially, tend to rebel. If the inner rebellion against what is unalterable becomes too strong, however, then comes the blow; everyone feels it; this was a day of that sort.'

He fell silent; a smile, troubled and resigned, flitted across his face. I was speechless. I was on the track of an enigma. Perhaps it was the great enigma that had disquieted me for so long? I told the old man the strange and disagreeable things that had happened to me, also the recent frightful mystery, which still lay heavy on my heart. I left nothing out.

Sympathetic and pensive, my companion listened to my tale. He shook his head slightly and bent towards me:

'My dear young friend, don't brood unnecessarily, never rebel against your inner voice. Of course you are right. There are mysteries everywhere here, but they are inexplicable. Those who are full of curiosity are sure to get their fingers burned. Console yourself with your work; one can work perfectly well in Perle. I, too, had the same experience as you at first. You see before you an old friend of nature, and so you will certainly believe me when I tell you that I suffered a great deal from what was unnatural in this country. But in time one makes an adjustment; I have been living here for almost thirteen years, I have fitted myself in, and I find much that is of interest. You simply have to be undemanding; then even the smallest things can afford you joy. For example, I am a collector of lice, dust lice.' His eyes brightened, and with a secret smile he went on in an animated voice:

'I'm on the track of a new species. Yes, the Archives contain marvels, of which very few people indeed have any suspicion. Office sixty-nine is now my hunting ground. His Excellency has graciously put it at my disposal. That's where my hopes lie! – But now I have to go.'

At these words, he drew an old green case from his pocket, took out a pair of horn-rimmed glasses, and put them on his nose. Before going, he made an old-fashioned bow and introduced himself: 'Professor Korntheur, zoologist.'

I looked after him, full of sympathy. The originality of his attitude, his abundant, snow-white hair, his engaging face which still betrayed a youthful idealism, the meticulous cleanliness of his clothing, extending even to his grey gaiters and galoshes – in a word, everything about him pleased me.

But I was worn out with the day's excitement. With a dull oppressive feeling I mounted the stairs to my apartment.

My wife lay on the divan completely exhausted, which was just what I had expected. She said nothing, and for my sake tried to pull herself together; I, too, was silent, for I did not feel like lying.

In bed, I tossed and turned, constantly imagining I heard that frightful, hammering noise and saw a sightless, haggard eye. My mind was occupied almost exclusively with the information the professor had given me. A *spell* – and the *blow* –?

I brooded over the meaning of these words. Ah yes, plenty of remarkable things had happened to me here; just a short time ago, I had seen a crowd of boys behind the house making a great din with rattles and drums. When I asked what they were up to, they replied: 'We are playing the accompaniment!' This nonsense enraged me; I found madness everywhere. At first it had been a novelty; we had sat at the window and watched intently the burlesque happenings on the street below. In the last month, however, there had been no laughter in our home. My wife was slowly declining in health. At the same time, the uncanny occurrences increased in number. I no longer dared tell everything to my helpmeet for fear of placing her in immediate danger. So I locked up my cares in my breast and felt lonely and constantly out of sorts. Where would this end? I myself was going to pieces!

5

A few days later, I was walking along the street. It was just before the New Year, but this meant little in that winterless land. I was stealing past the familiar rows of houses; one acquires a special gait in Perle – slow, hesitant, uncertain, prepared at every instant for an accident. A few isolated street lamps showed me the way. The proper lighting for Dreamland! Out of the general fog that veiled and magnified everything, details sprang at me with an unnatural aspect: the posts of a doorway, a store sign, an iron fence.

I was coming out of the nuns' old Gothic cloister, which housed a children's hospital in one of its wings. There I had bought two bottles of strengthening medicinal wine for my sick wife. As I was passing the chapel that formed a part of this complex, I noticed in the shadow of the portal a black bundle. I heard a few mumbled words, and the naked stump of an arm was thrust out entreatingly. Indifferently I threw a few coins into the dark corner, but at the next instant I stopped short as though rooted to the spot. What sort of strange old woman's face was that among the dirty rags? I had to look closer, a mysterious compulsion forced me to. Against my will and filled with disgust, I bent over the beggar woman. It was not her stinking breath or toothless mouth that held me captive, but a frightful pair of bright eyes, which drilled into my forehead like the teeth of a viper. Completely shaken and feeling half-dead, I reached home. Was this reality, or the terrifying product of an overwrought imagination? It seemed to me as though I had looked into the abyss.

Incidents like this were overtaxing my nerves. I determined to go and see Patera the next day; if necessary, I would force admittance; I would scream and shout. He was my friend, he had invited me, it was his responsibility whether we should be destroyed or not. The mindless residents of the Dream City must certainly have a false conception of him. Why were they so timid and oppressed, and why did they answer evasively when I talked about the Master? My friend had not deserved this.

A malignant star stood over this day. My wife had migraine and was groaning; I made cold compresses for her and then threw myself exhausted on my bed. At this moment – perhaps about one o'clock in the morning – came shouts and knocking at the door of our apartment. Angrily I thought, 'It's that sot from next door!' Presently I heard him muttering my name rapidly again and again. I was furious at this lack of consideration and, springing up, slipped into my dressing gown and took a walking stick from the corner of the room. This time I was going to teach the scoundrel a proper lesson! I opened the door into the corridor. There he was, blowing his beery breath into my face. Could I possibly spare a few cigars – just as a loan – and wouldn't I do him the honour of calling on him – my wife too was invited – he was going to make a punch.

I could not contain myself for anger. 'Damn your impudence, can't you spare others your crazy tricks? Get out of here at once or I'll throw you down the stairs, you good-for-nothing!' I was shouting at the top of my voice, everything inside me seething.

With a wild, drunken laugh, he stammered, 'Well, well, just come on over!' He seized me by the arm, trying to drag me with him. I lost all self-control, A quick kick in the stomach sent him sprawling on the floor. What made the wretch think he could behave this way? Furious thoughts crowded my mind.

'This time I'm going to make a complaint, no more delay, I'll have justice. This accursed house is intolerable!' Consider my position: exposed to hideous experiences week after week, my wife ill and causing me grave concern, the money gone – only enemies and derision on every hand. Wild hatred against the whole of Dreamland robbed me of my senses. Shaking with rage, I sprang up just as I was, ran down the stairs, and made straight for the Palace. Compensation was what I meant to demand, compensation for the indignities I constantly had to endure, and if Patera had to be dragged out of bed, then I would do it. I ran up Long Lane towards the Square. A heavy fog hung over the pavement; the gas lamps were like glowing yellow stains; I saw not a single passer-by, only the dirty, wet pavement. I rushed along half-delirious, busied only with the words I would use to describe all these humiliations to Patera. I spouted my accusations out loud; splendid turns of phrase occurred to me spontaneously, and I found gripping sentences to tell of my misery. But now I suddenly froze. As I looked down, I had to realize that I was not in proper attire to visit a distinguished man. An old dressing gown of a flowered material, under it my nightgown, and below that one bedroom slipper – the other had been lost as I ran – that was all. At the Square, the fog had lifted somewhat; there stood the Palace. It towered into the night like a gigantic die. The illuminated dial on the clock tower was like an artificial moon. The cold and damp brought me to my senses; I recognized that my plan was silly. No, this was not the right moment or the fitting costume for making a complaint. In my nightgown, carrying a cane, at past one o'clock in the morning, bareheaded – how would I look?

Sobered, I turned around and started on my way home. I wanted to take a shortcut through a small side alley; the chill was very uncomfortable. My wife would be painfully anxious about me. But tomorrow – tomorrow would be the day of revenge! To warm myself, I broke into a slow trot. A lighted window appeared; I ran towards it. Music, the tinkling of a piano, raucous voices, song! A bright light fell across the street. Damnation, I must not be seen like this! But I had already been noticed.

'You there, just step this way!' Two sinister-looking figures approached me. Now I knew I had gone astray. I was in the French Quarter.

Here things were still very lively. Soon I was the object of great curiosity. I was ashamed and angry; they were laughing at my ridiculous dress. I cursed and walked on quickly, with more and more people following me; coarse jokes were cracked, and I began to be worried about how all this would turn out. I could not find my way in those disreputable alleys and culs-de-sac; it was all very distressing; Castringius would have been completely at home.

If only I had known where the police station was! But, looking right and left, I could see only filthy dives and dens of vice. All the drains steamed and stank. I walked as fast as I could. A young man with make-up on his face seized a corner of my dressing gown and tore it off. I caught him with a hard blow to the ear. But it would have been better if I had not done it. Now the excitement really began. With hoots and yells they began to chase me. A gigantic, puffy woman came towards me and tried to trip me up. I sprang away from her easily but lost my cane as I did so. She rolled in the filth of the street, my nightgown in her hand as a trophy. This gave me a short head start. Like a frightened greyhound, I sprinted on. Never had I been so sure of my strength. But behind me the wild tumult increased; half of the French Quarter was on my heels; shrill whistles pursued me; the footing grew more slippery; I had to watch out not to fall. 'Soon I'll be exhausted; there's no chance of getting away,' I said to myself, and fear pounded at my temples. Bottles and knives were being thrown at me; I began to zigzag through the alleys, and at every corner I shouted as loud as I could: 'Help! Police!' But no help came, and behind me I could hear the crazy crowd laughing in derision. Naked and desperate, my mouth wide open, I literally flew along; no rescue, no hope in sight. Finally – I was desperately out of breath by then – I saw a tall, narrow house blocking the alley. All the windows were bright; over the doorway hung a red Chinese lantern. The door was open; I dashed up the brilliantly lighted staircase. The walls were painted in bright colours and ornamented with palm trees. On the second floor a woman came towards me, a graceful vision resplendent in a long silver-lamé gown, her hair down, her arms magnificent. She was not especially surprised to see me in that state but said smiling, 'Not here, sir. You must certainly have made a mistake. Number Five is over there!'

Comforted but shamed by her kindliness, I stammered breathless apologies, covering my nakedness with my hands. Then I opened the door she had pointed to. Damnation, there were two people already there, stark naked also. I slammed the door. The crowd was now beginning to surge up the stairs, at their head a policeman – now one had come – who roared: 'Where is the fellow? I will bring charges! But first the exits must be closed!' Then the mob.

My rescuer had disappeared; my bleeding feet seemed to weigh a ton. Breathing hard, I climbed up more flights and saw written in big letters on a door, like an order, the saving word, 'Here!' Help from heaven once more! With the remnant of my strength I opened the door and then bolted it behind me – safety for the moment – but the mob was already pounding on the outside. A thousand voices were shouting, 'Open up, open up!'

I glanced around like a hunted animal, and a sudden desperate decision flashed into my mind. At the risk of a fatal fall, I forced my way through a narrow window and reached out for some sort of handhold. Sure enough, a rod, a lightning rod! And with a marvellous sureness that I cannot understand, I clambered down it. Around me stillness and night. Then I collapsed; my legs would no longer carry me.

I was lying on a pile of dung. A collector of night soil on his nocturnal rounds lifted me up and took me home in his evil-smelling cart. My wife was watching from the window as I arrived. She had had a terrifying quarter of an hour; that was the length of time I had been away.

Several days later, I caught sight of a pack of dogs on the street playing with a brightly coloured object to which a cord and tassel were attached. I recognized my old dressing gown; ownerless property, it had simply been lying about the streets of the Dream City. My enthusiasm for Patera's creation was decidedly a thing of the past.

6

My plans for protest had to be postponed once more for the next few days. Our home was a sorry sight. My torn and swollen feet were swathed in bandages, and my wife did not leave her bed.

Lampenbogen's house had a cellar apartment at the rear. Here a family with nine children lived in destitution. Nine children! A unique situation in Perle. The husband was a dissolute brawler and good-for-nothing, supported by his emaciated and perpetually pregnant wife. The latter now looked after us, for the monkey came only occasionally in the evenings for a visit. At those times, at least, we had a few agreeable hours. He used to sit down beside my wife's bed, pick up her knitting with his rear hands, and knit rapidly. At the same time, he liked to scan old copies of the *Dream Mirror*, which he held in his front hands.

Our current maid sometimes brought her two eldest daughters with her, and this gave me an opportunity of confirming a discovery of my wife's, that children born in the Dream Kingdom have no thumbnails on their left hands. My editor's little girl, as well as the two sons of His Excellency the administrative president, all had this defect. And so in honest Frau Goldschlager's family there must have been nine missing thumbnails.

As soon as I could walk again I went straight to the doctor. My wife's rapid pulse disturbed me. I had often thought earlier of calling on Dr Lampenbogen, who as owner of the house often came there. But I have always distrusted doctors, and

caution was perhaps more than ever indicated in this land of uncertainty. 'A doctor is a businessman like any other,' I told myself. 'If you order a pair of boots from a shoemaker and he demands payment without having delivered them, you simply laugh in his face. But with a doctor, you have to pay even if he has not helped, even if he has actually done harm.' Lampenbogen was a rich man, the owner of a fine villa, a pretty wife, and a carriage. His rent from the apartments brought in a handsome sum, and so it was no wonder he had grown so fat. Everything turned out right for him! (There was, to be sure, a rumour that his wife was flirtatious.) I, by contrast, was no more than a bag of skin and bones.

And so the doctor arrived. He came into the apartment in his fur coat like a walking cube. While he made the examination I admired the back of his neck. A fine roast! I thought with relish. He advised a change of air; we had best go to the mountains for a few weeks. My state of health did not please him at all. At my protest that I wanted to look up Patera first, he said: 'That is an idea you had better forget!' and left.

Our small group was ready for the trip. Frau Goldschlager pushed my wife in a wheelchair. We waited for the coach at the post office in the Square, and then were duly loaded aboard. The whip cracked. Turning around, I caught sight of Frau Goldschlager's pendulous belly and the farewell smile on her unlovely face.

Just beyond Perle, the street crossed the railway tracks. We were bound for a small village in the mountains where we had been promised comfortable lodgings in a forester's house. The somewhat neglected road ran in serpentine curves through the infamous swamp. We passed a ruined city, fragmented remnants of the very ancient past. A few pelicans were the only living things we saw. Beyond this wilderness the country was more inhabited. We went by large pastures, potato fields, even vineyards. And then came elaborate farms, their straw roofs blackened with age. Everywhere the inhabitants stared after us, often they waved. These rough-looking peasants in leather clothes sat on benches in front of the houses; some were carving wooden figures just as square-cut as themselves. Despite the fact that many of them resembled toil-twisted animals, they pleased me more than the city dwellers. They seemed less distraught and tormented. Here strange mystic practices had evolved and here they were still held in strict observance. The road divided; at this point a thin tower rose like a pointing finger over a chapel completely covered with frescoes. The coachman motioned with his whip. 'The road to the right goes to the Great Temple.'

Now we entered a narrow valley. High up on the steep rocks there clung grey, barely distinguishable huts, the dwellings, I was told, of ascetic anchorites. Gradually it grew dark; the clouds hung lower and massed themselves into yellowish-brown piles as though for a thunderstorm. The landscape was now solemn and splendid in its uniformity; we were at the foot of Iron Mountain, a dangerous region at certain seasons of the year because of the violent magnetic discharges. Today, too,

the tension was oppressive; we saw ball lightning rolling along the metallic summit. 'The mountain is made almost entirely of iron,' our coachman informed us. It was strange; not even dry brush or wilted grass was to be seen anywhere on it. There it stood, dark rust-coloured, blocking the valley.

Suddenly my wife refused to go on. The air up there, she said, oppressed her even more than in the city, and she foresaw no improvement from a stay in such country. I felt the same way; my hair was standing on end from the electricity in the atmosphere. So it was better to turn around at once. I only regretted that I had brought the sick woman so far.

We got out at a wayside inn and waited for the stage coach that went back to the city. The people at the inn looked after my feverish wife and helped her very kindly as we got into the coach. And so we rode back again. Darkness fell as we reached the swamp. A foul, stupefying smell rose from it. In the light of the coach lantern I caught sight of several Mohammedan graves, half-sunk in the seething, slimy water, their headstones marked with turbans. The ground mist choked us. There was a rustling and slithering; the demons of the swamp were on the move. My wife was suffering from chills and pressed herself close against me. It was two o'clock when we rode into the city. Now I knew that I was bringing home a mortally sick woman.

7

Next day I went to see the doctor and report on our ill-fated expedition. He was not in his villa. On the way home my attention was attracted by two men. They were following a lady, who turned into Long Lane in front of me. Now I recognized the men; the first was my neighbour the student, and the second, De Nemi. At this moment they seemed to notice for the first time that they were pursuing the same objective. A clash ensued before my eyes. What happened between them I cannot exactly say. All I saw was that they went together into a dark entryway, from which at the next moment the student's hat flew out into the filth of the street. To keep from being recognized and involved, I went diagonally across the way as fast as I could. There stood the hunted lady in front of the window of a lending library. I believed I had seen her somewhere before. She was tall, very elegantly dressed, and had a thick knot of reddish-brown hair at the back of her head. Her face was turned away from me. She could not have been aware of the pursuit, for she made an abrupt turnabout and came back in my direction. It was Frau Melitta Lampenbogen; I admired the perfection of her undulating walk. Then her glance struck me – like a blow – I grew faint. *The eyes of the old beggar woman!*

There was no peace that night. Comings and goings on the stairway, knockings and rattlings. No possibility of sleep. At six in the morning there was renewed disturbance in the corridor. I went out. Three men were carrying a black coffin down the stairs; the door to the student's apartment stood open.

In the coffeehouse it was said that the student had been killed in a duel. Still another rumour was abroad. One of the two owners of the mill had disappeared – the young, constantly cheerful one. Suspicion of fratricide rested on his brother. Nothing was known for sure.

'Two inspectors from the Criminal Bureau have searched the mill,' Castringius whispered to me confidentially. He was eager for sensational material because he wanted to get back on the *Dream Mirror*. A colourful illustration, 'The Student's Wounds', was immediately rejected.

I was in a difficult position. Frau Goldschlager had not appeared that day, and I decided to go and look for her in her rabbit hutch. The place was really a horror, filled with a quite uncommonly repellent odour. A midwife stopped me at the door; Frau Goldschlager had had a miscarriage the night before. And so I accepted the generous offer of Hektor von Brendel to put his servant, an old grey machine of a woman, at my disposal for running errands. During the three days since I had recognized my wife's dangerous condition, I had been as though out of my mind. Anger and resentment had disappeared; I could no longer shut my eyes to my own situation and I dragged myself around listlessly. Dull and despondent, like a beaten dog, inwardly gnawed by unrest, I did not know what to do with myself. I could not stay at home; to sit and look on wrung my heart. A walk in the open air was the only thing. I gave the coffeehouse a wide berth and made my way to the river bank. Formerly I had found much pleasure here beside the silently gliding stream. Unintentionally I fixed my eyes on the mill. It was quivering as though alive. Vague and pallid in the glimmering mist, as though made of some gelatinous substance, it seemed to be exuding a nameless fluid that made me vibrate to the tips of my toes. Behind the dusty window stood the miller, dark and full of hatred, staring down at me.

Now, past the tanner's, the stockyard, the brick works, I came into more open country. The heavy, damp air and the dismal croaking of the frogs suited my mood. Before I realized it I was at the cemetery and I stopped to light a cigarette. Then through the cast-iron gate I caught sight of the gravestones, and I shuddered. Gritting my teeth, I began to run through unfamiliar streets. I repressed the melancholy that was overcoming me. Inside I felt cold contempt for everything, especially Patera.

'Where are you hiding, you torturer?' I shouted at the empty gardens as I hurried by, but the leafless bushes and bare trees gave no answer. Onward I ran, splashing heedlessly through puddles. A slight fever heated me and drove me across squares and through alleys I could not remember ever having seen before. A decrepit horsecar – more a decoration than a useful vehicle, it seemed to me – caught my attention. I had not known that this form of transportation existed in Perle. But I was too upset to pause for long over such thoughts, and before I realized where my feet were carrying me, I was standing in front of the Palace. The lamps were just being lighted.

Set into a corner pillar of the Residence was a marble plaque that riveted my eyes:

AUDIENCES WITH PATERA FOR EVERYONE DAILY FROM FOUR TO EIGHT O'CLOCK.

Shaking my head, I read this several times, mumbling it half-aloud to myself. Then a wholly preposterous thought flashed through my mind: 'This is all a huge joke – we are just too stupid to understand it.' Convulsive laughter shook me; I could have murdered Patera. Leaning against a pillar, I fought for composure. Then I simply strode through the open portal as though it were a matter of course. I mounted a broad staircase; under the enormous arches I must have looked very minute. Higher and higher I climbed. Through the bow windows I could look down into the city. Around me everything was still as death – only my footsteps resounded. I was so completely absorbed in my own thoughts that I paid no heed to the strange situation I was in. I had an unaccustomed feeling of lightness, that much I still remember. I opened gigantic white double doors and made my way through suites of huge chambers. Each time a cold draught of air met me. 'Surely no one can live here,' I murmured repeatedly, as though trapped in a dream. Large, carved armoires and upholstered chairs draped in dust cloths stood in each room. Once I saw a slim, upright figure hurrying straight towards me. But that was an illusion: a mirror in the wall had reflected my own image.

When I had gone through many halls and chambers, I finally came to an immense gallery that seemed to curve backwards. On the walls hung darkened, life-size portraits in ebony frames; to my right was a row of bow windows. At the far end was a small, low door, which I cautiously opened. I found myself in an empty, medium-sized room, its walls hung with a heavy, leaden-grey material. The twilight made everything indistinct. However, I noticed this much: there was no other door – this was the end. And then I paused for an instant and considered what to do. There was nothing here – it was as silent as a tomb.

I was on the point of turning back when from all sides arose that peculiar smell that I kept encountering over and over again in that country. It filled the whole room with its stupefying intensity; I heard what sounded like a low, dry laugh. And sure enough, by the wall opposite I saw the face of a sleeping man. Accustomed now to the half darkness, I distinguished a figure dressed all in grey lying on an elevated couch. I moved a step forward. A head of extraordinary grandeur: I recognized my friend Patera. No mistake was possible; I had looked too often at that picture. The pale countenance was encircled by dark locks, the eyelids were closed, but the mouth quivered and moved unceasingly as though about to speak. Fascinated, I stared at the wonderful symmetry and beauty of that head. With its broad, low forehead and the wide base of the nose, it was more like a Greek god than a living man.

An expression of deep pain lay on Patera's features. Then I could hear words, whispered hastily in a low voice. 'You complain that you can never see me, and yet I have been with you all the time. Often I observed how you scolded and doubted me. What shall I do for you? Tell me your wishes!' He fell silent.

Stillness reigned in the room. My throat was dry, and only with the greatest effort was I able to say, 'Help my wife!'

The head rose a little. Slowly Patera opened his eyes. Instantly I was overcome with a dreadful weakness. Numb and motionless, I had to meet that awful glance. Those were not eyes at all, they were like two brightly polished metal discs, two small, gleaming moons. Expressionless and lifeless, they were directed at me.

The voice whispered, '*I will help.*'

The figure rose to its full height; his head hung over me like a Medusa mask. I was spellbound, incapable of movement; my mind kept repeating, 'This is the Master, this is the Master!' The eyes closed again.

Then I witnessed an incredible drama. A horrifying animation took possession of the face, the expressions, like the colours of a chameleon, changing unceasingly a thousand, no, a hundred thousand, times. Like lightning that countenance became successively a young man, a woman, a child, an old man. It grew fat and then emaciated, developed wattles like a turkey, shrank together to diminutive proportions. In the next instant it was inflated with pride, it stretched, extended itself, expressed contempt, kindness, malice, hatred, developed furrows, then became smooth as stone – a terrifying mystery of nature. I was unable to turn away; a magic power held me as though rooted, and I shook with dread.

Then animal faces appeared: the head of a lion, which grew pointed and sly like a jackal; it changed into a wild stallion with flaring nostrils; became birdlike; then reptilian. It was ghastly; I wanted to cry out and could not. I had to watch these terrible grimaces, hate-filled, yet tinged with a base buffoonery.

And finally – peace returned. Like retreating heat lightning, occasional spasms crossed his face, the fading masks disappeared, and once more the man Patera was sleeping there before me. Only his curbed lips trembled feverishly.

Once more I heard the uncanny voice. 'You see, I am the Master! I, too, was in despair. Then from the ruins of my fortune I built a kingdom. I am the Master!'

I was overcome with a deep sympathy for him. With an effort I asked, 'And are you happy?'

But the beam had reached and paralysed me. Close in front of me I saw those dreadful eyes. Patera had come down and was holding my hands. Inside and out I was as though coated with ice. He cried, 'Give me a star, give me a star!'

His voice took on a beguiling tone, it flattered and seduced. I saw his white teeth gleam, his movements were heavy and awkward. I understood almost nothing of what he said in his hoarse, urgent voice. His breast heaved, the veins in his pale throat seemed at bursting point. Suddenly his face grew as grey as the wall; only the wide, dilated eyes continued to blaze, holding me in their inexplicable spell. He must have been torn by a truly monstrous, more than human, anguish.

Patera rose to his full height, his hands clawed into emptiness. Then a curtain fell between us. I heard an inarticulate groan and the dull sound of a fall.

I turned around, but I had to support myself against the window frame, for I felt complete paralysis coming on. Starting at my tongue, it took hold of my whole body. Beneath me in the Square, men and animals for a moment became stiff as wood, only for a moment, then everything went on again.

As soon as I could move I rushed down the stairs, completely convinced that I had lost my mind.

8

I was unhinged, quite incapable of collecting my thoughts, when I reached home. Lampenbogen was there but on the point of leaving. He had brought with him a sister of mercy from the convent. Catching sight of me, the doctor immediately drew me into the window embrasure. He spoke very solemnly, and though I was in no condition to understand his words, his monumental calm made me feel better. 'Just don't give up hope,' I heard him say. 'This is a serious nervous depression, perhaps the crisis. It's quite possible, however, that your wife will survive the attack. One must never abandon hope completely. Call me, of course, if anything unexpected happens tonight. In any case, I shall look in tomorrow.'

He left. As I have said, what had just happened and why he spoke as he did were not clear to me.

The nurse went in and out of the room with towels and basins in a quiet, businesslike way. I felt half-dead, quite unable to rouse myself to any sensible action. I wandered around the apartment in a daze, yet aware of my uselessness. Surely my wife could not be so very sick; when I approached her bed timidly, on tiptoe, she lay there sleeping; she even looked a little better, less emaciated than during the last week, and her face had a rosy hue. Then I talked to the nurse. Well yes, an attack, a sort of stroke – that was what the invalid had had during my absence. The nun was chary of words; late in the evening she prayed half-aloud. Slowly, intimations of the dreadful seriousness of the situation came to me. In the midst of my confused thoughts, which dwelt on the Master of the Dream Kingdom, came flashes of memory of the chills and fever my wife had suffered from that night in the coach. But I *could* not believe the worst, I *would* not believe it.

That night I bedded down on the divan in the living room, which was also my workroom. No chance of sleep. Towards morning I got up and looked at Patera's picture. The invalid seemed to be quiet; only once during the night did I hear her utter a few sounds. Towards nine o'clock I went into her room, where everything had been aired and tidied. My wife looked at me in bewilderment; it was obvious that she had trouble recognizing me. Despite her improved appearance, she was very weak, and I could barely understand her words. The nurse was satisfied with the night's developments; the fever had gone down, and the patient really seemed fresher.

The nurse left us for a while to fetch supplies. I sat down on the edge of the bed and took my wife's feverish hands in mine. Full of hope and intent on sparing her the effort of speaking, I talked about everything I could think of that might cheer her. I spoke of the Temple that stood by the lake and of its wonders, the jewels and riches that were stored there, for I knew that jewellery was a minor passion with her. I described the mirror lakes and the deep, leafy parks as though I had wandered through them for days at a time. She looked at me steadily, almost cheerfully, and even ran her hand over my head once or twice. I was happy that my tales pleased her and I went on eagerly. I talked about the gilded boats and the snow-white swans on the lake; my pictures became colourful – there in drab, colourless Dreamland. In glowing words, I described the abundant flowers, the variegated orchids, the dark-red roses, the lilies on graceful stalks. I believed firmly in the magic power of my words. I talked of blue forests, of forget-me-nots, of millions of glittering dewdrops under the early sun. I spoke of the twittering of birds and of the joyous, triumphant notes of silver bugles. That is where we would go, into that light and splendour – flee, if necessary. There she would get well. While I was choosing the most seductive words and luxuriating in dreams of the future, my wife – had fallen asleep.

I sat there in deep discouragement, crushed. Inconsolable hopelessness had laid hold of me again. There lay the invalid with half-closed eyes; the deep flush on her face no longer seemed natural. I forced back the tears that were rising to my eyes; the nurse was entering the room.

And then unexpectedly Herr von Brendel arrived and inquired most sympathetically about my wife's condition. He had brought flowers, too, pale yellow tulips. I drew him into the living room; at last, a healthy person! I literally clasped him in my arms.

The doctor came as he promised. He stayed a long while, and before leaving he led Brendel into the kitchen, where they had a short conversation. After that, he quickly took leave of me and went down the stairs. His last words were, 'Chin up, and keep on hoping!'

Brendel proposed that I go out with him. 'We can spend the day together. Here you are just in the way and you won't get anything proper to eat.' He purposely avoided mentioning my sick wife.

And so we went to the coffeehouse for breakfast. To be sure, I had no appetite at all, but I had to go somewhere. I was really fond of Brendel. He was a charming, uncommonly obliging man who had only a single weakness: he was one of those sentimental Don Juans – and there are worse things than that. Far from being a skirt-chaser like De Nemi, who was only interested in mechanical, mindless sensuality, Hektor von Brendel was truly in love – he was always in love and always with a different lady. Anyone who took him for a confused, immature youngster because of this excessive weakness for women would have been mistaken. With complete devotion he pursued his imaginary ideal, an ideal that alas, he never realized – that is, of course, lastingly realized. His current love, 'the raw material', as he called her, always had to be re-moulded. He begrudged neither effort nor money to this; he advanced patiently and methodically step by step, following a very complicated system of his own based on experience. After settling the question of how she should dress – this always went very easily because of his large income – came the many intellectual categories: behaviour, expressions of affection, etc., etc. Most of the contenders stumbled over these require-ments and found themselves out of the running. Undiscour-aged, Brendel selected new 'raw material'. The next stages ('whole-hearted trust', 'refined intimacy') were too much for almost all the candidates. He often raved to me half the night about some new idol. He was severe on himself, criticized his procedures, made improvements, changed his methods, but he never succeeded in producing the state he described as 'maturity'. The fault lay in a false psychology, but then he really did have bad luck too. One lady betrayed him, another turned out to be a bore. He was perpetually condemned to sampling tidbits.

Today, out of consideration for me, he was silent, although I should have preferred him to talk. The stories of his adventures were not without comic charm and often amused me con-siderably. At each 'parting' he gave a tastefully arranged fare-well dinner, in the course of which sorrow was already being transformed into new hope. Chivalrous and decent, he bore no one a grudge for a 'mistake'. And he knew how to console himself; the material, after all, was inexhaustible and perpetu-ally interesting.

A choking anguish rose from my stomach, compressed my heart, and pressed upon my entrails. I smoked and drank, but found no relief. The deep impression that the living statue in the Palace had made on me and the recognition of my wife's critical condition ran together. I was caught in a disaster from which I could not shake myself free.

The miller from across the street came in, rushed to the bar, and gulped down several glasses of rum, standing; without speaking to anyone, he went out again. The two chess players sat there as always, like Chinese gods carved in wood.

Brendel took me with him to the Blue Goose, where he usually ate, and after the meal we went to his apartment. He gave me coffee, and showed me a pretty collection of water colours, scenes of the Dream Country. About five o'clock in the afternoon I could stand it no longer. I made my apologies for the bad day I had given him, thanked him, and went home. I had stayed away much too long as it was, and I could not understand how I could have been so lacking in love.

My anxiety became a torment, driving me on like an engine. I dashed up the stairs – and then dared not enter – I listened at the door – nothing! – she was lying in the second room. Once more I took a deep breath – and then opened the door.

The first thing I saw was Lampenbogen's fur coat. Trembling, I entered the sickroom. The doctor silently acknowledged my greeting; he had turned back his cuffs. My wife, lying on the bed, looked old and withered. A nameless dread filled me at the sight of her, and I fell on my knees. I entreated the doctor, 'Help her! Help her!'

The huge man patted me on the shoulder and said, 'Control yourself – you are young!' I groaned.

The nurse tried to give me a glass of water; at that, I leaped up as though struck by a whip and pushed her aside.

Bending over the tumbled bed, I stared in desperation at my dying wife. She was completely still except for the dreadful chattering of her teeth, like a little machine – an incessant clicking, dry, harsh, distinct. I felt the deepest sorrow of my life; in my horror I could not grasp what was happening. Her wrinkled skin was greenish; sweat streamed from all her pores – I tried to wipe it away with a cloth – then the clicking stopped. Her mouth and eyes opened wide. Her face became white as chalk – she was dead.

As though at a great distance I heard the nun praying and the doctor leave. I knelt down beside the bed and softly, tenderly, spoke with the dead. The years we had spent together rose before me. I murmured to her not about the Dream Kingdom but about the times when we had first known each other. I thanked her for all our joy. I brought my mouth close to her ear, for no one else need hear. I whispered that I had interceded for her with Patera, that the Master would help. There was a childish faith in me that he would. As I said this, I touched her head, and it fell heavily to one side into the yellow lamplight. Now for the first time I saw the change: an alien thing with bloodless lips and pointed nose lay before me. I did not know my wife in this guise. Huge, lustreless pupils looked through me – a spasm shook me – babbling senseless words, I ran out – out into the foreign streets. I paid no heed to anyone, I was seeking some dark hiding place. But I could find nowhere to stay. All night long I ran about, a babbling ghost; all fear had left me. I stammered out every childhood prayer that lingered in my mind. I was lonely – there was nothing lonelier than I.

The next day, too, I spent in hiding; I hoped death would seek me out. That night, there were whistling and crackling sounds around me, constantly I thought I saw the image of Patera, a misty grey simulacrum that hovered in front of me. In the first light of morning I staggered wearily up the stairs to our apartment. My head was empty; I was mocked by the vague hope that perhaps all this was imaginary.

In the room where she had died everything was in disorder; a stale, sweetish odour struck me. The bed was empty, the bedclothes tossed aside. On the night table there were overturned medicine bottles and three lumps of sugar. It was all incomprehensible – hopeless. I went down to the street again. There stood Lampenbogen beside his carriage.

He took me by the arm. I recoiled. A new calamity?

'Just a few words – I've been looking for you. You must not let yourself go this way. I will take you with me; in half an hour your wife is to be buried. What you need is a home, a family. I hope you will not refuse an invitation to move into my house for the time being – my wife, too, would be pleased. One survives this sort of thing. You will grow calmer.'

Without saying a word, I got into Lampenbogen's carriage. Beside that large, corpulent figure, I felt very thin. People looked at us from the coffeehouse; out of the window Anton made a deep bow; the chess players were oblivious.

In a few minutes we came to the cemetery. From a distance I saw a group of people in the porch of the little chapel, and bit by bit I distinguished familiar faces: Hektor von Brendel; the owner of the coffeehouse; a priest; a few people I did not know. They were all standing; there was just one thing that was not standing – a simple coffin covered with a black cloth. Rain began to fall; the wetness penetrated my clothing and gave a kind of comfort to my taut, dry skin.

The priest murmured a prayer, and the coffin was carried to the grave. I walked first in line behind it. 'In there lies my wife,' I thought. I pictured her as though she were still alive. 'Surely she knows everything that is happening here, that I am walking behind and simply letting things happen.' Meanwhile I was treading unsteadily on the wet brown grass, and then I made an effort to think only of my own behaviour. 'They must not see my sorrow. That can wait until later on when I am alone.' I kept constantly in my mind's eye a large, printed word, 'courage, courage, courage', repeating itself in an endless line, and I bit the inside of my cheeks. At the same time I looked with curiosity to see where the grave had been dug. There it was, among many, many other graves. When we arrived, the black cloth was removed from the coffin. I found I was in a sort of half-dream. Adroitly the men lowered the coffin into the earth. I glanced down very briefly; the picture engraved itself with dreadful sharpness on my mind. 'This is your last look, your final farewell to your life's companion.'

I withdrew with unsteady steps; Lampenbogen held me by the arm. Everyone bowed.

At this moment a man came hurrying up from the cemetery gate smoothing his high hat with his sleeve. It was the hairdresser. He took my hand and said solemnly, 'In death the Subject becomes the diagonal between Space and Time – let that be a comfort to you!'

By the cemetery wall to the left I saw the big vault of the

Alfred Blumenstich family, an iron sphinx with a knight's helmet and closed visor on a white marble base.

I was glad it was all over and had gone so smoothly. Then I got into Lampenbogen's carriage again and we drove to his villa.

9

It was certainly kind of the Lampenbogens to take in one so bereft as I. To be sure, I would have driven off with anybody; from now on I did not care where I went.

'The Lampenbogens aren't sacrificing a thing. They don't care that my wife is dead,' I thought as the maid opened the door to the dining room. It was six in the evening. The doctor's wife had already greeted me when we arrived, saying she hoped I would be at home in her house and would soon forget the 'dreadful event'. 'Yes, yes, the dreadful event,' I had answered mechanically. 'There is much sorrow in life,' Lampenbogen had remarked as he placed a box of cigars on the table in my room. After I had got over my astonishment at having to live in a different room from now on, I made myself presentable and went down. Outside it had been cold and raw; here it was warm and luxurious.

The lady of the house seemed concerned about me, and this was comforting; the impression I had just had must have been an illusion. Now I looked calmly into her eyes; they were almond-shaped and grey-green; they were thoughtful and seemed constantly to be searching for something in you. 'So this is the woman they gossip about so much,' I thought to myself. 'Why, that's ridiculous.'

We sat down at the table. Lampenbogen's elephantine body occupied a whole side. He was a gourmand. As he ate, his face became distended; you could see and hear how much he liked his food. I had no interest at all in eating, although my stomach was empty. But at table Lampenbogen became a totally differ-ent man, a sort of 'ordained field marshal', if one may use such an expression. Reverently, yet with a commanding atten-tion, he surveyed the dishes, and if they were not immediately served to him he snapped his fingers sharply. He would categorically demand that dishes just carried out to the kitchen be brought back again. 'How often do I have to tell her, the dumb ox?' he snapped, growing red in the face. At these moments he resembled Fukuroku, the Japanese god of good fortune.

He prepared the salad himself at a small side-table, adroitly managing two forks, and I noticed how skilfully he moved his fat little hands. He must be excellent in the operating room, I thought. In the end, however, he seemed dissatisfied with his work. 'You can't get anything decent here any more,' he growled, glancing with contempt at a whole battery of coloured bottles and cans. 'A Cross-section of Lampenbogen' would be a good subject for Castringius.

'Why, you're not eating anything at all!' he cried, as the cheese was being served. His wife called him to order. 'Now Odoaker, you understand...' Incidentally, I noticed that he had a finely shaped nose like mine. That, however, was the only point of similarity between us.

After dinner I got out my cigarettes. Sighing regretfully, the mountain of fat rose to its feet. 'Unfortunately, most unfortunately, I have to go to the club tonight, just when it would be so nice to sit here with you.'

I expressed my regret. 'Where is the club?' I inquired.

Of course he immediately invited me to go with him; there was a bowling alley in a back room of the Blue Goose, he said. I declined, saying that for today that would be a bit too much.

'Well then, God bless you,' he said, shaking my hand.

His wife received a pat on the cheek. In contrast with his weight, there was a certain subtle grace in Lampenbogen's movements.

We were alone.

'Your husband is in robust good health,' I remarked, just to say something.

'Yes indeed,' she replied.

The atmosphere became a little strained. I was worried about the night to come and wanted to stay where I was as long as possible. I observed this beautiful woman closely. She was wearing a bouffant blue-and-white striped dress, and her luxuriant hair was confined in a net, as was the fashion at that time in the Dream Kingdom. Her face seemed strikingly small, the forehead narrow, the eyebrows sharply curved and rising at the outer ends. Her nose was rather short – a snub nose; her mouth very full and broad with slightly negroid lips. Her finest features were her alabaster skin and her hair. She was tall for a woman.

I was amazed that in my situation I could observe her so closely. Melitta got her sewing out of a basket and then seated herself beside the fireplace in which long birch logs were crackling. The luxurious dining room, panelled in dark-brown wood, was slightly overheated. Outside, the trees creaked in the storm, and occasionally a gust of rain rattled against the windows.

I waited for my hostess to speak; that night I was bad company. But she was silent. And so I had to rise to the occasion. 'Dear lady, you have very beautiful hair,' I said casually.

'It is really nothing special. Once I had more. It's prettier when it's down.'

A sudden feeling of panic seized me. I felt myself growing pale.

What happened then is something I shall never fully understand. During the last few days I had gone through the most dreadful emotional torments a human being can endure. I was broken, crushed, and desperate.

Can there be some law that gives a pendulum-swing to our natures? Why else at that precise moment should a little thought have arisen suddenly and quietly, forcing me to be coldly and calculatingly observant? Almost simultaneously I felt immense, dim powers begin to stir within me. All this went on somewhere in the depths; at the surface of my consciousness I was indignant at myself. But now, like lightning, everything changed and coalesced into a single, unwavering intent; this had been somehow ordained by fate. I was as self-possessed and calculating as a serpent. Seen from the outside, I was just a man sitting there smoking.

Melitta put her sewing aside and said quietly, 'As a painter, you must, of course, know about beauty.'

I was completely master of my thoughts, and these were crystal-clear. Now I wanted to act. But first I must test the

situation. 'When your hair is down it must be a truly marvellous sight,' I said, taking refuge behind the smoke.

'You would be disappointed, I'm afraid.' At this she quickly bent over her work again with a little laugh.

Oh well ... I was definitely not interested in this sort of flirtatious game; it had never really been to my taste. Impassively I got up and remarked with impersonal gallantry, 'Too bad your husband is not an artist.' (A diversion to make my opponent advance and reveal herself.)

And as expected: 'My God, he doesn't notice anything at all!' It was said with a slight, contemptuous shrug of the shoulders – just what I had hoped. Now she was mine. Despite the fact that nothing had happened, the situation was completely clear.

The chambermaid came in. 'Is there anything else?'

'No, you may leave.'

'What would you say if I dared ask you to take down your hair?' (I could risk this question before springing the trap, for a refusal would have been ridiculous.)

'On the day of your wife's funeral?' (A pretended thrust.)

'Besides death, there is life as well.' I kept up the play-acting. Nevertheless I felt some revulsion, but what could that do against the force that had taken possession of me?

'Well then, if you like and if it would console you.' (Ah, a hidden sting for the widower, her last parry.)

How stupid this woman is ... just like all the others – the thought came of itself. Melitta stood up and began to undo her hair.

'Won't the maid come back?' I asked calmly in a low voice. (This was both a compact between us and a precaution to keep the skirmishing from going on indefinitely. Besides, I felt a growing confusion in my thoughts.)

Softly she replied, 'We are safe.' (What more could one ask?) Two splendid auburn braids tumbled down her back. She went behind the high screen at the hearth and freed her hair completely.

I was surprised; nevertheless I felt called upon to exaggerate. I regaled her with my detailed knowledge of the subject, bit by bit introducing words of passion. After all, I was not exclusively interested in her hair. A feeling of oppression began to choke me. I foresaw that if I went on talking my words would become disjointed.

'Your hair is unique, surely you will not forbid an artist to see more? Please, please,' I said coaxingly, and saw that Melitta was blushing.

'God knows you ask a great deal,' she replied with coquettish indignation. Her blush proved that her resistance was melting. My trembling fingers were allowed to substitute for those of her lady's maid.

In the adjoining boudoir two small sconces provided a dim light. I wanted to rouse Melitta from her state of impassivity and at the same time I rejoiced in that impassivity. I smelled the intoxicating scent all too familiar in Dream Land – so far as I was concerned my wife had never existed.

.　　　.　　　.

On the street it was quiet. The night storm had subsided, though it was still very damp and cold. A sabre rattled, and two pedestrians went by.

'A tip for the devil . . .' It was Castringius' well-known bleat. I ran, and kept on running to get as far as possible from the Lampenbogen villa. No one and nothing could take me back there.

At the coffeehouse, I drank a strong punch and said with a sort of gallows humour, 'Alone at last!' After the third glass, I struck a balance of what I had tried for and what I had accomplished in my life: a look into the void. I was just like Brendel and his love affairs. I pursued an image of happiness, and it made a fool of me. I wanted nothing more to do with this apes' comedy. At the fourth glass I was sunk deep in plans for suicide. Better not exist at all than be a fool among fools.

Meanwhile I was tormented with remorse at what had just happened. I pleaded with the dead for forgiveness. For several hours she had been buried in the damp earth, hemmed in and abandoned in her wooden prison, while I still had to bear the burden of the living flesh. Even then I was mocked occasionally by lascivious thoughts, which rose in me and burst like bubbles.

At the fifth glass I came to a decision: 'Here I shall drink my fill, then into the river.' My tongue burned from constant smoking and my skull buzzed.

At the next table they were talking about the mill. Jacob, the missing miller, had been seen the week before crossing the river farther down on a ferry boat. A road led from the landing place through boundless, primeval forest, a wild, unexplored region of the Dream Country. At night, real symphonies of hell came from that side of the river. 'Perhaps the miller lost his way and was killed by some wild animal' – this was the general conjecture, though some continued to talk about his brother with the darkest suspicion.

I drank black coffee and came to the realization that I was not capable either of suicide or of continuing to live. 'I will lead the half-life of a vegetable between these two possibilities and await the stroke of death like an ox led to the slaughter –

it cannot be long delayed.' A glance in the mirror showed me a sick and puffy face.

It was now three o'clock in the morning. I ate three servings of ham and a raisin cake besides; a wolfish hunger had seized me. The last guests to appear were Castringius and De Nemi. The illustrator saw me at once, but I picked up *The Voice* and pretended to be reading it. Both of them understood what I meant. My name stared up at me printed in spaced type – a short obituary of my wife. I could not refrain from looking over the newspaper at Castringius' hands. One of them, the right, was hanging across the back of his chair. A shocking implement, it must have been the product of regressive evolution, possibly some intermediate form. But Castringius gave people to understand he wished to be counted as a member of the human race. A ship's screw, that's what I called the short, fleshy fingers with their broad, hornlike, yellow, cracked nails. Because I knew that at bottom my colleague did not like me, I was elaborately polite to him.

The owner came to my table, half asleep, and inquired whether I intended to keep my present apartment. 'Good God, no!' I exclaimed, and told him that at the moment I was without a lodging place – did he know of one?

'Certainly, in my house.'

He had a small room, as long and narrow as a corridor. There I spent the rest of the night and there I remained. The bed stood in a dark alcove screened by a curtain. The room was as familiar to me as though I had never lived in any other; it reminded me of my home because of its worn, yellowed leather hangings, the old-fashioned grandfather's clock, and the pot-bellied tile stove.

Tired to death, I fell asleep at once and did not wake up until a day and a half later, when my drawing desk was delivered.

I was seized with a feverish desire to work; in the half year that followed, I produced, under pressure of my sorrow, my best things. I drugged myself with work. My drawings, done in the dim and mournful spirit of the Dream Kingdom, gave secret expression to my anguish. Diligently I studied the poetry of mossy courtyards, hidden attics, shadowy back rooms, dusty spiral staircases; gardens gone to seed and overgrown with nettles; the wan colours of tile and parquet floors; blackened chimney-pots and the world of bizarre fireplaces. I played constant improvisations on a single, melancholy, underlying theme – the misery of bereavement and the struggle against the incomprehensible. In addition to these numerous drawings, which I disposed of to individuals or submitted to the *Dream Mirror*, I did several small series of works intended only for the few. In these I attempted to direct creation of new forms according to mysterious rhythms that I had begun to feel: they writhed, coiled, and burst against one another. Then I went even further by giving up everything but line, and developed a peculiar linear system, a fragmentary style that was closer to writing than to drawing. Like a sensitive meteorological instrument, it expressed the tiniest variation in my moods. 'Psycho-graphics' is what I called this style, and I intended some day to write a commentary on it. I found the relief I so much needed in this new area of creativity, but far from being reconciled to fate, I continued to live an essentially hybrid existence.

Night after night I thought about my wife's death, searching for an explanation. I was in part to blame; hers was a healthy, realistic nature that could never strike roots in this phantom kingdom. I should have recognized this fact in time and given up the whole adventure.

When I began to go out among people again, I discovered all sorts of changes; things in the Dream Kingdom were going from bad to worse, if that were possible, and all was in confusion.

One day Frau Goldschlager, who had formerly been our servant, was carried out of the house dead, the third corpse in six months. Her nine poor children were now in sorry case.

Hektor von Brendel was said to be involved in an affair with Frau Lampenbogen; would *she* achieve the state of 'maturity'? De Nemi was visiting Lampenbogen, less on Melitta's account than because of a bad sickness, the result of his gallantries. The news I heard of Giovanni Battista was all cheerful; he had become a master of his trade, and the hairdresser had bought him an annuity.

No large increase in the population was noticeable, and little attention was paid to the occasional newcomers. To be sure, these talked a great deal about the world outside, with its progress and its wonderful inventions. But we Dreamers were not at all interested; we would say casually, 'Yes, yes, quite so,' and then change the subject. To us, the Dream Kingdom seemed limitless and grandiose; the rest of the world was not worth consideration; we forgot it. No one accustomed to living there ever wanted to leave; the 'outside' – that was a fraud; it simply did not exist.

Late one night I went down to the river. I intended to set out night lines to catch eels; fishing had been a passion with me in my youth.

The strange gaseous vapour still drifted and crackled around the mill; greenish bands of phosphorescence swept across the walls. Near by, I saw unpleasant and disturbing phenomena. Over the mill door were fastened as good-luck talismans an owl's head, a crucified bat still alive, and a deer's foot. In the doorway stood the miller; his pipe glowed. I had always had a horror of this secretive fellow, but tonight I walked past him deliberately and boldly; I had thought out in advance the best place to set my lines – just behind the big grating. As I was about to place them, I heard a low but distinct voice speaking very close to me: 'Psst, psst, take care! Please step a little farther to the left.' I saw no one. Then with a start I became aware of a fat brown face in the sand at my feet. I thought I was suffering another diabolical illusion, but a natural explanation soon presented itself: a criminal had covered himself in the sand and was eavesdropping on the miller. I was relieved.

When I had set my lines I started home again. On the bridge I stopped; the sound of singing, a long-drawn-out strain on a single note, was drifting from the farther shore. In that direction lay the Suburb with its low-roofed houses. I had never been there, having already found distraction enough in the Dream Country. The solemn singing in monotone laid hold of my heart in odd fashion; I listened in silence; an unusual quiet lay on the water. I decided once more that I would go over to the Suburb soon and, as so often, I reflected on Patera's monstrous secrets and what little I knew about them. These things will be the subject of my next chapter.

Then I went for a short visit to the coffeehouse.

I was unable to catch Anton's attention; he was talking animatedly to a tableful of guests, gesticulating with the latest copy of *The Voice*, which was open at the section on new arrivals. I heard him say, 'Now he's here; he arrived yesterday.'

Finally he bestowed his attention on me, all zeal. 'The *American* arrived today,' he announced portentously.

'Who?'

'Why, the American, a man of vast wealth.'

CHAPTER FIVE

The Suburb

I

Elaborately carved, denticulated gables and roofs of straw! It was a tiny village I was entering. Small, low, whimsically shaped houses; tiny structures with cupolas; conical tents. A well-tended garden plot around each dwelling. Seen from a distance, the colony had the look of a model ethnographical exhibit. Here and there in moss-grown confusion stood signal poles with pennants and glass discs and innumerable grotesque figures of all sizes made of earthenware, wood, and metal. The low-hanging branches of venerable trees veiled much of the scene.

This was the home of the original inhabitants of the Dream Country. A strange peace lay over everything. The weather-worn statues on their heterogeneous wooden altars blended harmoniously into the peaceful surroundings, despite their often dreadful and exotic combinations of forms. I wandered about for some time before I met the first inhabitants. Then three tall sinewy figures came towards me down a hill.

At my greeting they bowed their shaven heads and continued silently on their way. They were old men of unmistakably Mongolian type, dressed in pale orange-yellow robes. Soon I saw others. Each was sitting in front of his hut, motionless as a statue, with no visible occupation. One had a vessel containing flowers in front of him; another was gazing at a sleeping dog; a third was sunk in contemplation of a few stones. In Perle they shake their heads over these people, I thought. No one ever came here from Perle, where the inhabitants of the Suburb were almost despised. Nevertheless, this was a proud tribe that traced its descent in direct line from the great Genghis Khan. Of course, there were no reminders left of that Asiatic despot, and those who still lived here were without exception very old. The few women among them were hard to distinguish from the men; in bearing, clothing, and facial expression, all were alike. The most beautiful thing about them was their slightly slanting, piercing blue eyes. What an antithesis all this was to the conditions that prevailed elsewhere in the Dream Kingdom! Out there was haste; here, peace. But these old people must have had their battles too; deep furrows in their faces testified to that.

After this first visit, I often strolled across the bridge to see the blue-eyed people. No one invited me, but no one sent me away either. I was impressed each time by the striking contrast to Perle. I found rest, and I observed quietly and silently. The serene wisdom of these men made a deep impression on me. I thought about it and tried to connect the results of my thinking with my other experiences.

After all, for the past six months I had not been altogether blind to the immensity of the riddle of Patera. The old professor had been right in many respects. All Dream Land was subject to a spell; the dreadful and the undeniably ridiculous aspects of our lives were tied together. The Master really was behind everything, and he mysteriously manifested himself more often than was comfortable. The thought that he was the manipulator of almost 65,000 Dreamers could not be dismissed out of hand, monstrous though it appeared. Where the limits of his power lay I could not possibly discern, for I kept finding evidence that he imparted his impulses to all animal and vegetable life. Collectively we suspected this and accepted it quietly as the seal of fate. The whole thing was so confused that even the subtlest mind could make nothing of it. Patera's nature was unfathomable; so was the power that made all of us in Dream Land into marionettes. It was perceptible in every little detail. The Lord was master of our will; he clouded our understanding. He made us his subjects, his puppets; but for what purpose? We paid him no tribute, after all, created nothing for him. The more one thought about it, the more mystifying it became. Unquestionably this mysterious person suffered; he had epilepsy, and we all shared in his attacks – this was the 'blow'. He would grow old, he would die, and what would happen then? Would every spark of our own strength flicker out with him? In truth, we needed him for everything, simply not to founder. Whence came his immense sources of energy? And here, now, lived a remnant of an old and distinguished tribe, its customs the antithesis of ours. In what relationship did they stand to the Master?

The old men would stare into the distance for hours at a time, expressionless; they would sit bowed for days over some trivial object – a stone, a bone, a feather. Never laughing, rarely speaking to one another, these blue-eyed people were the incarnation of equilibrium. Their measured gestures, and their furrowed faces stamped with the marks of intellectual power, were testimony to this. Their almost superhuman impassivity made them seem burned out. Disinterested interest – these contradictory words keep recurring to me whenever I think of them, and I shall feel their magic to my last hour.

About their age I ventured to draw no conclusion. Their faces were those of ancients, seemingly inaccessible to any emotion. Nor could I read anything definite in their eyes, which seemed in some way illuminated from within. Their teeth were flawless, but the rest of their bodies was emaciated, almost as dry as skeletons.

Three times I saw how they buried their dead, and from this I realized how widely they differed from Christian and Buddhist anchorites. The bodies were clothed in their customary robes and bedded in the earth in moss and leaves, and then the graves were filled up. Each one was buried beside his own hut, and no marker was erected over the levelled earth. There was no excitement, no praying. I derived immense profit simply from observing these points of behaviour.

Here I will interrupt the course of my narrative and description to tell the reader the philosophy of the blue-eyed people insofar as I was able to grasp it.

2

A Clarification of Ideas

What I learned, above all else, was how to appreciate the value of indolence. For an energetic man to achieve this demands a lifetime's effort. Once one has savoured its sweetness, one holds on to it firmly and for ever, even at the cost of constant struggle. Now I, too, tried collectedly to contemplate stones, flowers, animals, and human beings for hours at a time. In the process my sight grew sharper, just as my sense of smell and hearing had already done. Now came the great days – I discovered a new side of the Dream World. Little by little my perfected senses influenced the working of my mind and transformed it. I became capable of an astounding, new kind of wonder. Each object, singled out from its context of other things, gained a fresh significance. That a thing should thus extend from eternity all the way to me made me shiver. The mere fact of existence, to be thus and not otherwise, was a marvel to me. Examining a mussel one day, I saw with blinding clarity that it did not simply exist materially as I had thought till then. It went with everything, with the whole world. At first, my strongest sensations came just before falling asleep or immediately after waking up, that is, when my body was tired and the life in me was in a twilight phase. By degrees I had to fashion a world not yet alive – and I had to do this again and again.

More and more, I felt the common bond between everything. Colours, smells, sounds, and tastes became interchangeable. And then I understood: the world is the power of imagination, *imagination is power*. Wherever I went and whatever I did, I was intent on increasing my joys and my sorrows, and secretly I laughed at both. Now I knew for certain that the swing of the pendulum stood for equilibrium; this could be seen most clearly in the farthest and most violent swings.

At one moment I saw the world as a marvellous coloured tapestry, the vivid contrasts all melting into harmony. At another I surveyed a limitless filigree of forms. In the darkness there surged around me an organ concert in which the tender, touching sounds of nature evolved into recognizable chords. In a somnambulistic way I became capable of wholly new kinds of sensation. I well remember the morning when it seemed to me that I was the centre of an elementary system of numbers. I had the feeling of being an abstraction, the precarious point of balance in a system of forces – a process of thought that I have never experienced since. At that moment I understood Patera, the Lord, the prodigious Master. Now, in the midst of the great absurdities I was one of those who laughed most, without forgetting to tremble with the tortured. Inside me was a tribunal that surveyed everything, and hence I knew that in reality nothing whatever happened. Patera was everywhere; I saw him in the eye of my friend as well as in that of my enemy, in animals, plants, and stones. The power of his imagination pulsated in all that existed – the heartbeat of Dream Land. At the same time I found something alien within me. I discovered to my horror that my 'I' was composed of innumerable 'I's', the one lurking behind the other and spying. Each successive 'I' seemed larger and less accessible; the farthest of them eluded my consciousness in the shadows. Each of these 'I's' had its own view. For example, from the standpoint of organic life, the conception of death as the end was correct; from another, higher level of understanding, human beings did not exist at all and so nothing could come to an end. Patera's rhythmic heartbeat was omnipresent; insatiable in his imaginative power, he constantly demanded everything at once – the thing and its opposite, the world and the void. This was the reason why his creatures oscillated so, back and forth. They had to wrest their imagined world out of the void, and from this imagined world they had to make a conquest of the void. The void was inflexible, and it resisted. Then the power of imagination began to hum and whirr; forms, sounds, smells, and colours began to take shape in every way – and there was the world. But the void devoured everything that had been created, and the world became flat, pallid; life rusted, grew silent, fell apart, and was dead again, was nothing. Then it began all over again from the beginning.

This explained how everything fitted together, how a cosmos was possible. And it was all dreadfully interwoven with pain. The higher one grew, the deeper one must send one's roots. If I demanded joy, then I simultaneously demanded pain. Nothing – or everything. The primal cause had to lie in the power of the imagination and in the void; perhaps they were the same. Whoever has discovered his rhythm can tell approximately how long the misery or the torment will last for him. The madness, the contradiction, must be experienced together. The burning of my house is at once misfortune and flame. Let the victim console himself with the thought that both are imaginary. Patera, who won both, must surely have done that too.

Through our related heartbeats I understood the lower animals. I knew with certainty when a tomcat had slept badly, when a goldfinch was thinking something coarse. These things reflected inside me now governed my conduct. The uproar of the world outside had so exacerbated my nerves, had rendered them so sensitive, that they were now ready to experience the Dream World.

At the end of these evolutionary developments, man as an

individual ceases to exist; and there is no longer any need for him. This road leads to the stars.

3
A Confused Dream

That night I fell asleep with grand ideas. Less grand was the dream I had, but even so I want to include it because it was so bizarre. I saw myself standing beside the great river, looking yearningly towards the Suburb, which appeared more extensive and picturesque than in reality. As far as the eye could see there was a confusion of bridges, towers, windmills, jagged mountains, all pushed together and interconnected as though in a mirage. Figures large and small, fat and thin, were moving about in this chaos. As I started across the river, I sensed that the miller was standing behind me. 'I murdered him,' he growled, and tried to push me into the water. Then, to my astonishment, my left leg grew to enormous length so that I could step effortlessly across into the motley crowd on the opposite bank. And then I heard all about me a multifarious ticking, and became aware of a great number of flat clocks of every size, from church clocks and kitchen clocks down to the smallest pocket-watches. They had short stubby legs and were creeping about in the meadow like turtles to the accompaniment of an excited ticking. A man dressed in soft green leather with a cap that looked like a white sausage was sitting on a leafless tree and catching fishes out of the air. He then hung them on the branches of the tree, and instantly they turned into dried fish. An elderly fellow with an abnormally big torso and short legs approached me; he was naked except for a pair of greasy duck workman's trousers. He had two long vertical rows of nipples – I counted eighteen. With a snort, he inflated his lungs, filling first the right and then the left side of his chest, and then with his fingers on the eighteen nipples played the most beautiful harmonica pieces. As he expelled his breath he moved to the rhythm of the melody like a dancing bear. Finally he stopped, blew into his hands, and hurled them away from himself. Then he grew an immense beard and disappeared

into this undergrowth. Out of a nearby thicket I stirred up a herd of fat pigs; they goosestepped past me, growing smaller and smaller, until they vanished, squeaking loudly, into a mousehole beside the road.

Back by the river sat the miller – I was beginning to feel uneasy – studying a huge newspaper. After he had read it and eaten it, smoke poured out of his ears; he became copper-coloured, stood up and, holding his pendulous belly with both hands, stormed up and down the bank, all the while staring about wildly and emitting shrill whistles. Finally he fell to the ground as though stricken and grew pale. His body became light and transparent; you could see quite clearly two little railroad trains dashing about in his entrails, whirling like lightning around the loops of the intestines. Shaking my head and somewhat disconcerted, I was about to offer the miller help, but my words were cut short by a chimpanzee who, quick as a flash, planted a circular garden around me in which thick, apple-green stalks like giant asparagus sprang up close together out of the damp ground. I was afraid of being imprisoned within this living hedge, but before I could think what to do I was freed. The dead miller, no longer transparent, had had convulsions in which he laid a necklace of many hundred thousand tiny milky-white eggs out of which legions of snails hatched, and these immediately and greedily devoured their sire. A penetrating smell of smoked fish filled the air and caused the fleshy stalks to collapse and decay. In the distance, the Suburb disappeared in a web of shimmering violet threads.

I caught sight of a colossal mussel, lying like a reef at the water's edge. I sprang upon the hard shell. A new disaster! The mussel was opening ponderously, I was losing my foothold, inside quivered a gelatinous mass. I woke up.

PART THREE

DOWNFALL OF THE DREAM KINGDOM

CHAPTER ONE

The Adversary

I

Hercules Bell of Philadelphia made himself the subject of much conversation. He was a multimillionaire, and by no means stingy with his wealth; Dream Land was literally flooded with his gold. He entered into an agreement with Alfred Blumenstich, and soon we realized that the country's finances had been overhauled. No one would accept paper money any longer; no one was allowed to make payments with the small greenish coins that were being withdrawn from circulation. For a time this stewardship produced a recrudescence of luxury in Perle. The city was seized by a mindless vertigo. Day after day the rich gave sumptuous parties; the masses crowded into the taverns and drank and stank. Everywhere toasts were proposed to 'the American', as he was commonly called, in honour of his magnanimity and munificence.

Now autumn was approaching. Happy at having clarified my ideas, I allowed myself a rest. The American had opened headquarters in the Blue Goose, where he had rented the second floor for a huge sum. One evening, formally dressed, I went to the hotel restaurant for the purpose of seeing him.

There I found Castringius and Herr von Brendel, and had a chance to see still another side of my colleague. I had not encountered Castringius for some time, and in this period he had made the acquaintance of Von Brendel. The artist, whose roving eye lighted on me immediately, behaved, to my astonishment, very coolly and condescendingly. He replied to my greeting briefly and absently, as though he barely knew me, and at once turned away. What's the matter with him, I wondered. After all, I had never insulted him, and he always used to be almost importunate. Besides, we hadn't seen each other for almost four months. How odd. I was genuinely pleased at Brendel's presence. He was absorbed in the menu and did not notice me immediately; however, he sprang up as soon as he saw me and cordially invited me to take a place at his table. At first the illustrator raised his eyebrows in displeasure, but he soon recognized the situation, and his arrogance melted away. He extended his ship's screw to me.

The situation was this. Castringius had no idea that I had long been an intimate friend of Brendel's; he wanted to keep Brendel for himself. Since this was not possible, he adjusted himself to the new circumstances; he had a genius for adjustment. At one point, when he had left the table for a moment, Brendel complained about this new friend who jealously dogged his footsteps. He accompanied him to every rendezvous and would then remark that he could easily wait close by. Now and again Brendel made use of the illustrator as a *postillon d'amour*, but even then he had a strange way of fulfilling his commissions. 'I'll never be rid of him,' Brendel commented resignedly. 'Besides, he's so unbelievably cordial. Alas, that's how one has to learn one's lessons.'

'Yes, the true artistic temperament,' I comforted him, laughing.

The evening turned out to be a lively one. Brendel ordered champagne, and Castringius, patting me on the thigh patronizingly, said, 'Now you see how it is, eh?' He did not know that I was indifferent to all forms of alcohol.

There was uproar in the big hall next to us. You could hear speeches and applause. The American had called the meeting; he was said to have sworn to bring order into the Dream Kingdom at last. Later I saw the man himself coming out of the hall. I have never forgotten how he looked. There he stood in the doorway, a man in his early forties, a thickset figure with the shoulders of a colossus. He was wearing tails. His face looked like a combination of hawk and bull. All the features were twisted slightly out of symmetry. The hooked nose was

bent to one side; a prominent chin, a high, narrow, deeply inclined forehead, gave his face an air of reckless daring. His black hair was growing thin at the crown.

The American attracted the attention of everyone in the restaurant. He passed our table with short springy steps. Castringius greeted him eagerly and received a quick nod in return.

'There's a real man. If you could get close to him, there'd be money like hay,' Castringius remarked, staring after him thoughtfully. 'The sworn enemy of Patera, our editor tells me,' he added, filling his glass to the brim.

Smiling sceptically, Brendel clinked glasses with him and said, 'Well, good luck to him and to you.' Nik was getting more benevolent with each glass. In fact, when the gypsy orchestra came in accompanied by a cymbal player, he was cracking nuts with his teeth and patting himself on his short kinky hair. He cried out to the leader, 'Here you see the man with the teeth of a lion.' At Brendel's astonished glance, he explained, 'He's a good friend of mine. Shall I invite him to join us?'

Brendel said that I should decide, since I too was present. But I thought the gypsy leader repulsive. And then the hubbub of the crowd was drowned out by the stentorian voice of the American.

Glancing around, I caught sight of an old acquaintance, Professor Korntheur. In evening dress, with a bright silk waistcoat and a cravat that rose to his chin, the old gentleman was sitting at a side table with a bottle of burgundy in front of him. I got up and went over to greet him. He had a happy, festive air and at once invited me to join him. 'Just for a minute,' I said, sitting down. 'What's the good news with you?'

'Oh, you will never guess, my dear sir. I have her, she belongs to me, this is a great day!' And his kind eyes lighted up ecstatically. 'For ten long years I have searched for her, and finally I have found her. You have no idea what that means to an old man. It rejuvenates you! New life floods through the fragile limbs! Never more shall Acarina Felicitas leave my side.'

I congratulated him. (June and December? I thought. Dear me, I would never have imagined it of this proper gentleman. Very likely a singer from the music hall. Well, no doubt there were some very nice ones.)

'Why didn't you bring her with you?' I asked, privately pitying the old man. (She will do him in, I thought.)

'But I have her right here,' he exclaimed excitedly, drawing out of his coat pocket a little cardboard box covered with silver paper.

'A photograph? A medallion? Please let me see it,' I begged.

'No, my adored Acarina Felicitas herself. There she is, sitting in the corner!'

And sure enough, there in the box sat a dirty little grey insect, a damned dust louse. Now I understood.

In my father's house there are many mansions.

As we were leaving, I asked the maître d'hôtel what had caused all the shouting in the next room.

'Certainly, that's something I can tell you,' he said mysteriously. 'Today the Lucifer Club was founded.'

Castringius, four-fifths drunk, wanted at all costs to take us to Madame Adrienne's. We declined. 'Then the artist goes solo,' he said. And, reversing his coffee-brown coat so that the lining was outside, he marched gravely off. His last words were, 'Good night, babies!'

2

The rich American continued to cause more and more talk. Every afternoon he galloped down Long Lane on a black stallion; from the café we could distinctly see his contemptuous smile as the trembling citizens scurried into corners and doorways to escape his ruthless career. Arriving at the bathhouse, he would tie up his horse, change, and then ride the animal into the river! It took an athlete to control the rearing steed with such ease.

Once he came into our coffeehouse after a bath of this kind; because the various drinks he ordered were not to be had there, he burst into abuse. Finally he calmed down over a glass of grog. Now I could observe him at close quarters; his sharp, diabolical profile was directly in front of me. (Certainly a thoroughly dangerous individual, I had to admit.) His short-stemmed pipe was like part of his face, yet he also carried two huge cases of thick cigars – 'propaganda cigars', he called them. He offered them to everyone; if you accepted, you were already half his. Presently he began on his theories and his societies; even in the coffeehouse he was looking for followers. (The Lucifer Club, the social and political organization he had founded, had been fittingly welcomed by *The Voice*; the official paper had made no mention of it.) He talked a great deal about the outside world, glancing around among us as he did so, as though to see what impression his words were making. I still remember many of the things he said. 'You have lost the sun, you fools! It will serve you right if you lose your whole lives. Why don't you defend yourselves? Look at me – I spit on your Patera!' And, laughing contemptuously, he struck the table with his fist. His shocked listeners flinched, some of them no doubt feeling that lightning was sure to strike an instant punishment for such blasphemy. Timidly they lowered their eyes. The innkeeper crossed himself rapidly a number of times, tapped himself on the breast, and desperately began to pray.

Anton crouched beside the tile stove, whispering, 'Damnation, help! Damnation, help!' The chess players alone were imperturbable.

To drive home the impact of his words, the American spat on the floor, tossed a gold coin on the bar, and strode out disdainfully.

If he did not get everyone on his side, at least he awakened the residents of the Dream City to political activity; in doing this he spawned more mischief than he had intended. Associations and groups shot up like mushrooms. Each of them wanted something different: free elections, communism, the introduction of slavery, free love, direct commerce with the outside, stronger barriers to commerce, removal of the border guard – completely opposing aims came to light. Religious clubs were formed: Catholics, Jews, Mohammedans, free-thinkers, banded themselves together. The inhabitants of Perle formed groups representing the most varied points of view – political, commercial, spiritual – groups that often numbered no more than three people.

The American had not expected this; he had no wish to raise such ghosts. 'Brainless shadows, you are no longer good for anything. The devil owns you to the marrow of your bones. What small intelligence you may have had has been duped!' He expressed these opinions everywhere.

At this time a large influx from the outside world resulted in some strange occurrences – and misunderstandings. The fact is, the newcomers found their doubles were already there; all kinds of irritations and inconveniences followed, for the newly arrived Dreamers not only resembled in body and manner those long in residence, but even seemed intent on copying the clothes of the originals. Laughable though it was, two Alfred Blumenstichs, so to speak, were going about; two Brendels, several Lampenbogens. You rushed into the café to greet a good friend you had not seen in some time – complete astonishment – it was a different man! Lampenbogen would be coming along the street; I would raise my hat; only to encounter Lampenbogen at the next corner again. One day I saw the proprietor of our café four times in a row, and I could have sworn that he was still in his place of business as well. Moreover, I too must have had another 'I', for I would often get a friendly slap on the shoulder and turn to find a stranger, who would then apologize irritably.

One day I became very excited. In Hucksters' Alley, a dark passage leading from the French Quarter to the vegetable market, I encountered a lady who resembled my dead wife as one eye resembles the other. The sight of her awakened painful memories. I followed her until she disappeared into a house with a high Gothic gable. On the doorstep she turned towards me; the similarity in even her slightest movement filled me with consternation. From then on I saw her frequently, and I admit I spied on her a little. Secretly, hardly admitting it to myself, I wondered whether a second happiness might perhaps be possible for me – until one day I saw her on the arm of a thickset man with long artist's hair and a wide-brimmed hat. I discovered by inquiring at her house that she was the wife of a court organ-builder. I felt I had been tricked. In the light fall rain, which dissolved everything in its shimmer, one could not be too careful in order to avoid mistakes. Under his borrowed name, a Castringius II ran up debts in all the bars to the point where credit was denied to the real Castringius.

The League of Joy was founded by the wealthy classes at a great celebration in what was once the theatre. Melitta played a prominent role in this and rejoiced in a sorry notoriety. One day she decamped and for a whole week appeared daily at the music hall in a strip scene entitled 'The Modern Eve'. Although her face was concealed by a mask, everyone recognized her. This scandal brought Lampenbogen and Brendel closer together. Both considered their honour had been wounded, and sorrow is easier to bear when it is shared. Brendel was completely infatuated with her and could change mistresses no longer. Hollow-eyed and miserable, he went around avoiding everyone, even me; he was filled with shame. Melitta, on the other hand, was insatiable in her lusts and not afraid of disgrace. She even yearned for the American. Her strong shoulders and healthy complexion, so rare in the Dream Kingdom, were tantalizing attractions. She pursued him openly, her skirts lifted above the knee, letting fall one after another her handkerchief, lorgnette, and purse. Unschooled in gallantry, the man from

143

the West failed to react to these moves, and as the beautiful lady bent down, turning her derrière invitingly towards the man-tamer, the latter said coldly, 'Just get out of my way, baby,' and pushed her aside. Filled with hatred, she roused Brendel against the cold fish, but without success. The American sent word that he was accustomed to fight exclusively with the horsewhip. That put an end to the scandal.

The Lucifer Club recruited most of its members from the newly arrived Dreamers. These were generally unwilling to have comic old clothes forced on them. Besides that, the usual old-fashioned hucksters' wares, the dilapidated, antique furniture, etc., suited them not at all. People of this kind joined the American's party.

I was often amazed that the real Master should be so passive an onlooker at activities that openly violated the established usages of the Dream State. The proprietor of our café, who did not take sides himself, remarked knowingly, 'Don't worry, he's a deep one.'

The border guard functioned well, as it always had, but inside the walls everything was charged with a sense of impending disaster. The air was more sultry and oppressive than ever; a pale radiance lay over our city; on a few occasions oblique sunbeams penetrated the usually unmoving cloud-cover. The disagreeable blinding light was unsettling; we were no longer used to the sun and would have much preferred a refreshing shower.

Time seemed to move at a different rate. Anxious and excited groups stood on the streets everywhere, and this gave our normally quiet city an artificial appearance of commercial activity. Passwords were hastily exchanged between party members. By and large, despite disagreements about particulars, the whole city was divided into two main groups: those who still believed in the Master, and the others who lent ear to the American. To be sure, the partisans of the latter were not altogether reliable, a fact well known to him. For this reason he continued to press his propaganda.

My readers will remember that there were two daily newspapers in Perle in addition to the illustrated weekly. The official paper was unavailable to the magnate; it remained faithful to the government in its every line. And so he exerted all his powers on *The Voice*, the publisher of which ran a complete disclaimer of responsibility at the end of each revolutionary article. Our editor had to acquiesce in this double game, and probably this was not too hard for him. As a matter of fact, he had been from the beginning the secret director of all three papers, which followed three different editorial policies.

We two illustrators had to go on working in the usual *Dream Mirror* manner; Castringius, to be sure, kept trying to pay covert homage to the American. He represented him as a giant clad in golden armour stuffing his pipe with state papers and debentures; till one day he received a card from Hercules Bell with the one word: Ass.

Suddenly a rumour spread that the American was going to buy *The Voice* and the *Dream Mirror* for a huge sum and publish them himself. First, though, he carried out his master stroke – the Proclamation. To accomplish this, he had to do violence to our unfortunate editor and owner of the press. 'I will not print that!' he declared in panic. But the monster only laughed and blew tobacco smoke in the face of the terrified slave of duty.

'You will print it at once on crimson paper,' he roared.

The unhappy wretch threw himself on his knees and whined, 'Mercy! Mercy I simply *cannot* print that. It would cost me my life!'

At that, the inexorable American drew a revolver from his pocket, held it to the miserable man's ear, and shouted, 'If you don't obey immediately, I'll fire!'

Trembling, white as chalk, the editor took the paper. 'I'm the father of a family,' he sobbed, tears running down his cheeks.

The American supervised the printing himself; when it seemed to him to be going too slowly, the monster fired his gun into the air. By evening, six thousand proclamations were ready; there was not enough red paper for more.

'Well, numbskull, so what's happened to you?' he asked the still panic-stricken publisher. However, to every member of the press crew he gave a hundred gulden in gold.

3

The copy of the proclamation reprinted here was given me by a Russian officer who was present when the Dream Kingdom was occupied. He has generously given me permission to reprint it.

PROCLAMATION!
Citizens of Perle!

When I came here I expected to see a country of fairyland splendour. No doubt that was your expectation as well. For seven long years I applied to Patera for admission to the Dream State. Finally he granted my wish; but it would have been better for me if he had persisted in his refusal. I found a kingdom in which unreason reigns! Only my great pity for you prompts me to open your eyes. Are your lives already forfeit? No! And once again, No! But you are anxious, unhappy. That you must admit, all of you. You have fallen into the trap of a charlatan, a confidence man, a hypnotist! He has cost you your health, your goods and chattels, and your *reason!* Unhappy people! You are the victims of a mass hypnosis! No one listens to his own reason any longer. No, you believe the thoughts implanted in your minds by another are your own ideas! So you let yourselves be badgered to death, and that villain enjoys the game.

But there is still time for rescue. Let everyone who still possesses a spark of strength support me in my plan.

Pay heed now to what I have to say to you. The spell must be shaken off! You only have to *will* it seriously and you are free! Gather around me, form battalions, and storm that thrice-accursed Palace! I put a price of

One Million Gulden

on that devil's head. Do you know the sort of houses you are forced to live in? I can tell you: there is hardly one of them that was not sullied by blood, crime, and shame before it was brought to its present place. The Palace is patched together out of ruins of buildings that were the theatres of bloody conspiracies and revolutions. In collecting them Patera went back to the most ancient times. Fragments from the Escorial, from the Bastille, from ancient Roman arenas, were used in its construction; blocks of stone from the Tower and from the Hradcany, from the Vatican and from the Kremlin were stolen at his instigation – broken off and carted to this place.

Fifty years ago the coffeehouse in Long Lane was a notorious café in the suburbs of Vienna. The dairy was a robbers' den in upper Bavaria. The mill, which was bought in Swabia, has borne for two hundred years the bloody stains of fratricide! These are only examples; I will not tell you all the results of my investigations. My assurance must suffice that Patera bought most of his houses secretly in the most squalid quarters of the big cities. Paris, Istanbul, and others gave of their worst horrors!

Fellow citizens! Now that I have opened your eyes, do not shut them again! Once more I summon you to hasten the fall of this beast. I have a piece of advice to give you: *Let everyone beware of sleep!* That is when the Master enslaves you. In the unconsciousness of sleep you are helpless against him; it is then that he insinuates his deadly ideas; thus he daily renews and strengthens his infernal spell and destroys your will. I am convinced that one day I shall behold in each of you a happy and contented person.

The great world outside has made gigantic strides towards the light of the future. You have been left behind, cowering in a swamp. You have no part in the splendid discoveries of our modern age; the countless inventions that are spreading order and happiness are wholly unknown to the Dreamer! Citizens, you will be amazed when you leave here. The blue of the heavens, the green of the meadows, will smile on you once more; the sun will again conjure up roses on your pale cheeks. Again you will feel immense joy in your children, and will look back with horror on the sterile filth of the Dream State. Be on your guard against every trick of this play-acting criminal!

Down with Patera! Let that be your battle cry!
Join the Sons of Lucifer!

Dixit
                                    HERCULES BELL

Castringius had made a drawing to head this proclamation, a goddess of liberty wearing a diadem and holding a tablet on which were written the words LIBERTY, FRATERNITY, EQUALITY, SOCIETY, SCIENCE, LAW. In her headdress he had arranged an American flag, which wound as a streamer around the margins of the text.

Jaques and his gang were employed to distribute and post these crimson sheets. This adolescent, father unknown, was the son of Madame Adrienne, a notorious procuress and the owner of the better of the two establishments in the French Quarter, from which she never emerged. Jaques, who had the face of a gallows bird, could be found wherever anything depraved was going on; he had the rank of an *apache* general, and his exploits, often of amazing daring, were famous among his crowd. The American met this character in a thieves' kitchen and immediately hired him, paying a generous advance. For Jaques, who earned his living in unmentionable ways, this politician's wealth was irresistible. At the very first meeting he sold himself body and soul and offered to form a bodyguard for his Croesus from the sinister characters in the French Quarter.

To be sure, not everyone was to be bought. For example, the Negro Gotthelf Flattich, a native of the Cameroons and once a stevedore, whom chance had tossed into the Dream Kingdom, withstood the temptation. Bell knew him from an earlier time, for the coloured man had married one of Bell's serving women, also a Negro. Bell had won the man's affection on that occasion by an expensive wedding gift; when he found him again in the Dream Kingdom, both were delighted. Flattich was strong as an ox, and good-humoured as well. One simply had to be careful not to rouse him from his customary phlegm; at such times he was dangerous. Now a widower, he employed his time in training birds. Bell immediately wanted to enlist his services, but his plans fell on a deaf ear. Flattich was a fervent admirer of Patera and for nothing in the world would he turn against him.

He took no part in the revolution, but quietly devoted himself to his beloved pets. He lived in the French Quarter, where he was universally loved. He will appear again in our story.

As a consequence of orgies and debauches, the nerves of the inhabitants of Dreamland had been reduced to a dreadful state. Mental and nervous disorders already present – Saint Vitus' dance, epilepsy, and hysteria – now took the form of collective phenomena. Almost everyone suffered from a nervous tic or an obsession. Agoraphobia, hallucinations, melancholy, spastic seizures, increased in a disturbing fashion, but the people continued their mad pursuits, and the more numerous the grisly suicides, the wilder became the behaviour of the survivors. The bloodiest sort of knife fights began to occur in the inns. I could no longer ever sleep peacefully at night; the uproar from the coffeehouse kept me awake. Recklessness increased until finally there were no limits.

One evening a singer made an appearance in the café; at the beginning things were fairly quiet except for the out-of-tune piano and the applause, but at about three o'clock shrieking and laughing began. I got up and looked out of the window just as the soubrette, completely naked except for a necklace of champagne bottles, was being trundled along the street in a wheel-barrow by the drunken crowd. Lieutenant De Nemi was leading this amazing procession with drawn sword.

The nine motherless children continued to live in my former house, now frequently visited by Alfred Blumenstich, the well-known philanthropist. It was said that his visits had to do principally with the two elder daughters. He would drive up with great boxes of confectionery and disappear inside the house. The father himself kept watch at the door so that Herr Blumenstich should not be disturbed.

Ether and opium began occasionally to take the place of alcohol; people now gave themselves injections openly, to whip up or to relax their exhausted nerves.

That such conditions must lead to a catastrophe was clear even to the least perceptive people. One could not but observe with horror the growing restlessness in the behaviour of the half-maddened crowds. What I found especially unnerving was the shrill, mysterious screams that rose at night from the houses; the accelerated rhythm of events gave life a shadowy quality, literally dreamlike.

If you add to this the oppressive air, the spectral, stormy light – for now and then a blinding glare swept fleetingly across the sulphurous sky – then you may gain some notion of my terror in those days.

And then came the proclamation; it was posted at all the street corners and distributed to every house. The antagonism that had developed between the American's party and the older citizens faithful to Patera could only be sharpened by this. These were evil times.

CHAPTER TWO

The Outside World

For twelve years the civilized world had remained unaware of the existence of the Dream Kingdom. To be sure, there had been sudden and inexplicable disappearances. Sometimes those in question had been glimpsed on trains or ships, but subsequent investigations had proved fruitless. So long as the missing were in trouble of some sort and therefore had reasons for wanting to hide, little attention was paid to the matter. The world has small sympathy with bankrupts.

Society was far more concerned when respectable members of the learned professions, artists, and financiers began to swell the list of mysterious fugitives. In most cases, two or three weeks after they disappeared, relatives received some sign of life – at least a brief note. But what could be made of such statements as, 'Do not search for me, I am comfortably settled'; or, 'Because of unforeseen circumstances, I must entreat you to relinquish all thought of marriage'; or, 'Forgive me for everything, I cannot act otherwise'?

Everyone would have laughed in disbelief if told that these disappearances had a common cause. The police gave up.

The most notorious case was the disappearance of Princess von X. At that time, of course, people were used to the disappearance of prominent ladies, but these were almost always quite young. In this instance it was an old woman who had seemed perfectly content at home. Her trail led as far as the Black Sea, where she had attracted the attention of certain Turkish porters by her extraordinary stinginess in the matter of tips; that was how she had been identified. The only ones to be seriously disturbed by her disappearance were her nephews and nieces, who had been counting on their inheritance. Unfortunately this elderly maiden lady had taken all her money with her. No further trace was found of the Princess von X.

Soon thereafter came the case of the American multimillionaire Hercules Bell, and it was this that made the outside world aware of the Dream State and finally led to action. How this prominent meat-packer heard about the strange country is unknown to me, but he took it into his head to become a citizen of the Kingdom. Instantly there was a rumour that Bell was suffering from mental illness, which he countered by engaging a famous neurologist to keep him under constant observation, and this specialist was able to testify that the American was in full possession of his faculties. For years this eccentric, accompanied by his doctor and two servants, voyaged the seven seas to far countries, seeking the Dream Kingdom. At one time he was seen poking about in the islands of New Zealand; later he erupted into the Indian archipelago. It was in Hong Kong that his doctor deserted him, explaining that he could no longer stand the company of his patient, and that he had been compelled to change his original favourable diagnosis and now considered the American to be ill and suffering from a morbid obsession. The doctor travelled home again, and the magnate continued to follow his chimera.

And then sensational news: the American had dispatched a messenger who turned up one day, carrying a thick letter and a proclamation, in the office of the British Prime Minister. His lordship was asked to believe in the existence, in open violation of all laws, of a society in which an immensely rich and equally unscrupulous potentate exercised malign power. Many thousands of honest Europeans were being held there in illegal restraint. The American appealed to the British as the declared enemies of every form of degrading slavery, and expected from them the promptest and most energetic help.

Although letter and proclamation were written in a crude, strident style, in view of the mysterious disappearance of so many people it was impossible to disregard the appeal for speedy assistance. Even the Princess von X was said to be languishing there in prison. Also, the strange purchases of houses, which had aroused such a stir in the European press and had been thought of as the whim of some Asiatic princeling, now had an explanation. The result was a feverish exchange of dispatches between the governments of the great European powers; swift action without much noise seemed indicated. Russia, as a neighbouring nation, was accorded the mandate to intervene; the customary jealous rivalries found no voice, for the parliaments were not immediately informed.

Within a month a Russian division was mobilized and put under the command of the able General Rudinoff. On their banners they inscribed the words 'For Christian morality and love of one's neighbour'. And in their minds they carried a vision of gold ingots. The Tsar was hoping, incidentally, to acquire a rich province; the legendary country, after all, lay quite close to his frontier.

A covey of newspaper reporters and photographers, speculators and experienced businessmen, were invited in great secrecy and taken along. Naturally, the Chinese ambassadors to all the powers involved protested against this open violation of the boundary of the Celestial Empire, but by that time it was too late, and the gentlemen had to withdraw, shaking their pigtails.

The position of the Dream Kingdom could be fairly accurately determined from the map, but the American's messenger was to go along to guide the troops. However, one day this man was found dead in his hotel room. A dagger was sticking in his belly; on the blade were etched three words:

Silence is golden

General Rudinoff had to make the search alone.

CHAPTER THREE

Hell

I

It is a gloomy morning. Hercules Bell, the American, is still in bed, his arms crossed in a posture of deep reflection. 'I shall win!' he murmurs, a look of pride brightening his unlovely, over-vigorous face. 'I shall win!' he repeats loudly, and gets up.

'I am healthy,' he says triumphantly, stepping naked in front of a big mirror. With a look of defiance he examines his body and goes through exercises to make the muscles swell. 'All solid as a rock!' He strikes himself on his hairy chest. Taking a boxing pose, he shouts triumphantly, 'First prize to Hercules Bell!'

He thinks about the Dream people and automatically spits in the corner. It won't take him long to deal with that spineless rabble.

Then his forehead becomes furrowed. The Suburb has come into his mind. He has only been over there once to take a look at the inhabitants. Humbug – that word sums up his judgement of the ancient tribe; he has never gone back to the village, which he found 'unsympathetic.' Having experienced the formidable coldness of those blue-eyed Asiatics, he has come to the conclusion that the Suburb is unpromising ground for his political activity. Nevertheless, some obscure presentiment makes him continue to fear those strange old men. They are completely unmoved by the beginnings of the revolution and continue to live from day to day in total passivity. Devil take them! The American prefers even the most degraded of the Dream citizens.

He shaves and dresses with care, then skilfully massages his face. His momentary low spirits improve: his major stroke is still to come – a triumph no one suspects. He thinks of the night on which he parted from his devoted servant. At the risk of his life this man, Hercules Bell's personal servant for twenty years, escaped from the Dream Kingdom in order to carry news to the outside world. Connor was now actually beyond the border wall. A genius both in technical and practical matters, he had recognized at a glance that the river provided the one possibility of flight. At the point where it disappeared under the rampart of the wall, Connor dived down and encountered an iron grating. Under the cover of dark, he managed to file through one of the iron bars, thus making an opening through which he was able to force his agile body. Once outside, he signalled to the American, by firing a rocket, that his attempt had been successful. He carried the all-important letter in a rubber bag around his neck; his hardened body would have taken no harm from his nocturnal swim. Now nothing could go wrong! Connor's intelligence and tenacity had been proved in every sort of adventure. In four to six weeks at the most, help would arrive.

'In two months I shall be commander of the Dream Kingdom,' Bell says, filling his two cases with cigars. 'King Patera will lie at my feet!' His eyes shine with malice. But why must he pay the Master, whom he hates so much, the tribute of a secret but ardent admiration? In this lies the whole tragedy of the man.

When, after repeated pleas, he had been allowed to enter the country and had seen with his own eyes the operation of the incalculable powers possessed by Patera, Bell had thought, in his practical way, that the use to which they were put was childish nonsense. With his spirit of enterprise, he would have achieved something very different. At first, he had thought of some kind of joint company with the 'Master,' and would have poured his millions unstintingly into such a project. The whole world could be conquered – truly something greater than this madhouse of a country.

This influential man, bootlicked in America and Europe because of his wealth, found himself treated by the Master like an importunate suppliant. His requests for an audience were tauntingly denied. Not once had he managed to penetrate as far as the Highest and lay before him his profitable proposals. The most unlikely accidents had always intervened. At this, a dreadful hatred for Patera sprang up in his breast. Now he wanted to make his power felt – he was not one to beg! He would compel recognition for himself. And so he threw himself into politics – with what success we have seen.

For whole nights he has tossed on his bed, brooding over the means of taking vengeance on his invisible opponent. Thanks to his wealth and his sustained activity, today his name is feared in the Dream State. His goal, humiliation of Patera, now seems close at hand.

'But this is the time for action, not thought.' He takes out his watch – it has stopped. 'Strange – how long have I been asleep?' He rings for his servant. No one appears. Then he opens the door to the anteroom. There lies his man John fast asleep with his mouth open. Bell seizes the sleeper and shakes him vigorously. Finally John just manages to open his eyes, stares dazedly at his master, and goes back to sleep. This time he cannot be roused.

Furiously but fruitlessly the American rings all the bells, and then goes down to the restaurant. The first thing he sees is the hotel keeper snoring behind the bar. There are a few guests sprawled over the table, their napkins serving as pillows, in front of them half-empty glasses and plates with remnants of food. Leaning against the coat rack stands the bus-boy, sound asleep, holding the *Dream Mirror* clamped between his legs. Bell gives him a push; the little chap collapses, the peaceful look on his face undisturbed.

The American dashes up to his room again, almost falling over the laundress, who is half buried under a pile of clothes. A dreadful thought comes to him. He looks out of the window. Something red is fluttering at the street corner opposite – a strip of paper – a half-torn copy of his proclamation. He sees two men lying on the ground in a filthy corner; from the depths of an entrance protrude the skirt and legs of a woman. Otherwise all is deserted; no life is visible except for two animals with pointed muzzles prowling about in the distance. They are foxes.

Bell steps back. He turns white, and an expression of unspeakable disgust comes into his face. He lets his head sink; three sharp perpendicular furrows appear on his forehead, his nostrils quiver; in an attitude of collapse, he says painfully, 'I'm a bungler. I have lost.' His eyes are almost closed, but it does not quite come to that. Trembling, his body fights against the lassitude. He drags himself to the tub and immerses his head in cold water – that refreshes him. He takes a swallow of brandy; with what remains in the bottle he massages his head. His weakness is conquered. He fills his pipe, puts on his hat, and goes out.

Hercules Bell does not surrender.

2

An irresistible sleepiness had descended on Perle. It broke out in the Archives and spread thence through city and country. No one could withstand the epidemic. The very people who boasted of their alertness had already unknowingly caught the germ.

It was recognized as contagious very soon, but the doctors could find no antidote. The proclamation failed of its purpose, for in the very act of reading it people started to yawn. Everyone who could, stayed at home so as not to be overcome on the street. If one had a safe place to stay, one submitted willingly enough to this new turn of fate. After all, it did not hurt. A great feeling of weakness was usually the first symptom. Then the sick person was seized by a yawning fit; he felt as though he had sand in his eyes, his lids grew heavy, all thoughts dispersed, and he would let himself sink down wearily wherever he happened to be. He could, to be sure, be aroused briefly by means of sharp scents, spirits of ammonia, etc., but he would only mutter a few unintelligible words, and then was off again. With people of strong constitution, the condition could be postponed for a few hours by massage; after that, however, it was the same story. Many cases developed rapidly. One orator was discoursing passionately about political events when he suddenly fell forward over the table, let his head drop, and began to snore rhythmically.

In the coffeehouse Anton could hardly keep his eyes open; however, he went on working. But what people had to do to keep him moving! My God! He was bombarded with lumps of sugar and teaspoons; his forgetfulness was prodigious, and if finally he laboriously produced what had been ordered, the impatient guest had usually fallen asleep himself. Special care had to be taken to extinguish the burning cigars of those who had dropped off.

On the parade ground the soldiers drilled diligently to be ready for the threatened revolt. But the noncommissioned officers could roar to their hearts' content – one man after another simply fell to the ground. There were curious and comic incidents. Thieves collapsed, happily asleep, with their hands still in other peoples' tills. Melitta lay for four days in Brendel's apartment. Her husband was dreaming, sprawled over his dining-room table, his nose in the mayonnaise.

Castringius was stricken while playing cards. He was in a low dive, comfortably ensconced in an armchair and holding the jack of diamonds in his paw. I myself was caught at home, where I had promptly taken refuge. I had just opened the bed and was about to draw the curtains. I only had time to see that bank notes were fluttering one after the other out of the window of the Princess's apartment across the street; a light fall breeze drove them like dry leaves along the alley in the direction of the river. Then it was high time for me to get to bed.

In the first few days after the outbreak of the epidemic, trains ran extremely late since new crews had to be put aboard at every station. Later they did not run at all.

The last number of *The Voice* was printed on only one side, and even that teemed with incomplete sentences and a myriad misprints. The last page, where comic incidents were usually recorded, was missing altogether. Effort was of no avail; Perle was asleep. This condition of complete unconsciousness may have lasted for six days; at any rate, that was the hairdresser's estimate; he based his calculation on the length of the stubble on his clients' chins.

It is believed that during this time only one man in the

whole city did not sleep, or slept only briefly – the American. At least, this is what he himself maintained. One day, as he was wandering down Long Lane like the prince in a modern *The Sleeping Beauty*, he is said to have glanced through the coffee-house windows and seen one of the chess players making a move. From this he concluded that these two, like himself, had been spared by the sickness. Otherwise, however, one simply stumbled over sleepers. Well-dressed ladies and gentlemen, wearing contented expressions despite the oddity of their situation, slept, together with the vagrants, not only on all the benches in the public parks but on stairways and under arches.

As people gradually awoke, many of them were able to go right on with their activities. That was fine, not only for Brendel but also for the wretched nag at the horse butcher's, which during all that time had been bound tight awaiting the final blow. Now the blow fell. For the strange fact was that animals remained immune to the sleeping sickness.

For most people, nothing seemed to have changed, at least in the first few minutes. Cheerful but famished, I went into the coffeehouse and found the hairdresser already there, ravenous too, and in a very bad temper. He had found that a four-kreutzer piece was missing, and this discovery led to permanent discord between master and assistant, who of course, like all animals, had remained awake.

The Dream City awoke and found itself in a sort of animal paradise. During our long slumber another world had taken possession to such an extent that we were in serious danger of being driven out. To be sure, it had been noticed earlier that rats and mice were especially numerous that year. There had also been complaints about the attacks of birds of prey and four-footed chicken thieves. The gardener had even seen wolf tracks in Alfred Blumenstich's park. He was laughed at, but when the next day all that was left of a snow-white Angora goat – the particular pet of the commercial counsellor's wife – was a pair of horns, the laughter stopped.

Who could describe the consternation of the many people who had fallen asleep alone and undisturbed but now found themselves with uninvited company? A big green parrot would be sitting on the windowsill; or weasels and squirrels would peer out inquisitively from under beds. The extent of this invasion was discovered only bit by bit. When the butchers woke up they had to drive a great pack of jackals out of the slaughterhouse. Attacks by wolves, wildcats, and lynxes increased in an alarming fashion. It was disturbing that even our domestic pets suddenly became intractable and unreliable; almost all the dogs and cats abandoned their masters and ran wild of their own accord. The newspapers, which had begun to appear again, reported a case that excited a great deal of attention: a bear broke into the ground-floor apartment of Apollonia Six, widow of the master butcher, and completely devoured the unfortunate woman while she slept. A couple of

gunshots disposed of the beast. Hunters and fishermen coming into the city told improbable stories of monstrously heavy animals they claimed to have seen, but these men are liars by profession, and no one believed them. Then suddenly crowds of farmers and other Dream people from the open country came galloping in on their draught horses. They brought with them their wives and children in heavily loaded wagons, together with their more valuable household possessions. They were extremely angry, and held demonstrations in front of the Palace and the Archives, protesting at the absence of military protection. Herds of buffalo had devastated their fields, and the farmers had barely been able to defend themselves against the bands of great apes that had suddenly appeared and attacked them.

These devils spared no one. Soon afterwards, the tracks of huge cloven-hoofed animals were discovered in the clay soil of the Tomassevic fields on the edge of the city. The situation was critical.

Insects became a dreadful affliction. Voracious grasshoppers descended from the mountains in great swarms, and where they alighted no blade of grass remained. The castle garden was wiped out in a single night. Fleas, earwigs, and lice made life miserable. Every species of these creatures, from the biggest to the tiniest, was subject to the elementary instinct of propagation. Despite the fact that they devoured one another, these four- and six-footed pests increased in an uncanny fashion. What help was it that the authorities handed out weapons and poison and issued the strictest orders that windows should be closed and doors kept shut? The multitude was too great. Volunteer groups of hunters were organized and lent their support to the army and police. The owners of many houses cut loopholes in the walls.

The wife of the coffeehouse proprietor woke up one morning with fourteen rabbits in her bed. Since only a thin partition divided her room from mine, I heard the screeching of the young.

Most terrifying were the snakes. No house was safe from their visits; the reptiles lurked in drawers, clothes closets, coat pockets, water pitchers – everywhere. Moreover, the treacherous creatures were of a terrifying fecundity. If you moved about your room in the dark you would step on their eggs, which burst with a plop. Castringius became noted for his excellence in the Egg Dance, invented by him.

In the French Quarter the vermin soon became unbearable. But even during this animal invasion most people kept their heads. They would shoot a deer from the window and immediately invite their friends in for a hunters' feast. From the garret windows of my former residence, there was a wide prospect over meadows and fields. This terrain was now transformed into a zoological garden of monsters. The river, too, got its share: crocodiles, hunted for years and driven upstream, reappeared. The bathhouse had to be closed because electric eels, whose bite is fatal, had made their nests there.

One of the few rays of light in those dark and trying days was the repeated opportunity to enjoy delicious roasts and rare delicacies.

My old friend the professor enjoyed great prestige at this time. He gave public lectures, instructing the Dream people how to distinguish between dangerous and harmless animals. Armed with an ancient three-barrelled gun, he would be out at daybreak, strolling among herds of gazelles, wild pigs, and marmots, zealously devoting himself to the hunt. The animals soon grew accustomed to this odd, bespectacled huntsman and came to love the old gentleman. His weapon did so much damage to windowpanes that it had to be taken away from him.

At night the greatest precautions were necessary when going out; arms and a lantern were imperative. Our city had been made even more unsafe by deadfalls, wolfpits, traps, and automatic rifles. However, it never occurred to any of the Dream people to deny themselves their pleasures.

3

The level of morality, which had sunk far below normal, was especially advantageous to my colleague Castringius. His pornographic works were much in demand; he was now the artist of the hour. Drawings like 'The Lustful Orchid Impregnating an Embryo' had many admirers. Hektor von Brendel once bought a whole series of these works because his Melitta found them 'a scream'. In fact, she enjoyed the drawings so much that she hung them, nicely framed, on the walls of her boudoir. But this was only a momentary whim; after a few days they were carried off by her devoted Céladon, a dragoon officer. By way of return the officer presented her with a pair of antique emerald earrings. That same night he took the pictures to the coffeehouse, where an auction had been organized. The proceeds were destined for those whose dissolute lives had brought them to the sickbed. Our hospital had no ward for these unfortunates. A good deal of money was collected. Blumenstich – not the secondhand dealer – made up the rest, and the ward was founded soon thereafter in the cloister next to the children's hospital.

The spirit of comedy decreed that I should win the drawings. One day I met Castringius on the street. He was looking for a new place to live. His studio windows had been broken, and there was a hole in the roof. Numerous bats were hanging like bits of dried meat from the curtain rods. As he was telling me this he had to defend himself constantly against the importunate advances of an ibex. I invited him to come up; there hung the pictures. Chilly amazement! 'How do you come to have those?' I explained. He said, 'They are very good work. "The White-Striped Whip" is my most successful picture. It is a synthesis of the morality of the future. There is not a woman alive today who can draw the proper conclusion from it. It is the last word.'

I agreed with him completely, being, after all, the only person in the Dream Kingdom who appreciated his works for their artistic merit. In general, I was quite fond of this eccentric fellow, and why not? Let him who is without sin cast the first stone.

Then suddenly there was an uproar in the street; we went to the window. A crowd of people stood there laughing – and with cause. Just imagine: the monkey had gone on strike! On the previous day Giovanni had left a gentleman sitting half-shaved in the chair because he had noticed a troop of macaques hurrying by. One of the beautiful long-haired females had signalled to him, and our apprentice barber could not resist the temptation. However, the philosopher had succeeded in restraining him by the use of a malacca cane and the argument that time is divisible into small eternities. But now reasoning was no longer of avail. Giovanni scrambled gracefully up the drainpipe, seized with his prehensile tail a bottle that contained the Princess's supply of coffee, seated himself comfortably on the windowsill of my former apartment – now empty because of its dilapidation – and began to play a mouth organ that he had been carrying in his cheek pouch. The old woman screamed, terrified, and tried to belabour the thief with a broom. Giovanni immediately threw away the bottle and seized the broom. You should have seen the old lady then! She disappeared in a rage, only to reappear on the second floor. Giovanni Battista was convulsed with merriment. From my window we could watch every detail of the battle. First he

wrested from the old woman her principal weapon, a pair of
ancient fire-tongs, willingly relinquishing the broom. He seemed
almost to have wings. Using as missiles old bottles of India ink
that I had left behind, he scored a hit every time. The public
shouted encouragement from below. The Princess was swear-
ing like a drayman.

Then he bobbed up again at the front of the house wearing a
woman's old bonnet that was stiff with dirt, and swung himself
out of the window. With comic grimaces he slid down the
drainpipe again. Above him the Princess was shouting for the
police; below waited the hairdresser with his cane. 'You should
be ashamed of yourself,' he shouted at the monkey.

Commercial Counsellor Blumenstich was just emerging with
a satisfied smile from the apartment of his nine darlings. Once
more he had been playing the benefactor in his particular way;
his carriage was ready and waiting. With a mighty *salto mor-
tale* the monkey sprang onto the horse's head, and off they

went! The crowd was delighted and continued its applause until the equipage and its grotesque rider disappeared from sight.

That was just one scene; similar spectacles were the order of the day.

It was a mystery where the overwhelming abundance of animals came from. They were the real lords of the city and obviously knew it. Lying in bed, I would hear the sound of galloping hoofs, as though I were in a great city. Camels and wild asses were running through the streets; it was dangerous to irritate them.

In contrast to this eruption of the animal kingdom, vegetation progressively disappeared; everything green was gone, eaten up or trodden into the ground. The avenue of linden trees leading out of the city in the direction of the cemetery was now marked only with barren stumps. The earth steamed, as though about to spew forth even more creatures. A warm, acrid vapour rose out of small fissures in the ground. The nights were wrapped in a crepuscular light that obliterated everything.

4

Most uncanny of all was a mysterious phenomenon that began with the animal invasion, increased rapidly, and led to the Dream Kingdom's complete collapse – *the crumbling process*. It attacked everything. Buildings made of all sorts of materials, objects collected through the years, everything that the Master had spent his gold for, all this was doomed to destruction. Cracks appeared simultaneously in all the walls, wood rotted, iron everywhere turned to rust, glassware grew muddy, cloth disintegrated. Valuable works of art fell irremediably victim to an *inner* decay, for which no adequate cause could be found.

A sickness of lifeless matter. Mould and mildew invaded the best-kept houses. There must have been an unknown, destructive substance in the air, for fresh food, milk, meat, and later on eggs became sour and rotten in a few hours. Many houses began to collapse and had to be quickly abandoned by their tenants.

On top of that came the ants! They were found in every

crevice and fold, in clothes, in wallets, and in people's beds. The biggest, the black, were in every crack in the walls and, in the open country, wherever one set one's foot. The white, by far the most dangerous, transformed woodwork into powder. The most irritating, beyond question, were the red, for they elected to make their homes on the human body. At first, scratching was considered bad form and was carried on only in private. But what can one do when one itches? In the French Quarter everyone had been scratching for a long time. We had laughed at them – and soon were doing the same thing. The wife of His Excellency the President of the Government, on the occasion of a soirée, boldly set the example.

Animal excrement in the streets and dust in the houses could no longer be coped with; it increased, however desperately people fought against it. Clothes fell to pieces while they were being shaken and brushed. My only surprise was at the continued good humour of the Dream people.

The Lampenbogens, for instance, remained unperturbed. The whole officers' corps down to the youngest lieutenant frequented their house. No doubt he still murmured, 'dear lady,' but she no longer stood on ceremony. In the end she sought out the lower classes. I often observed her on the street performing her customary manoeuvre, the lifted skirt. Curious people stopped and looked at her. Dogs ran after her; but this was no time to trifle with them. Once I saw a dog tear her dress; she ran off in alarm, dropping a tattered letter. I picked it up and later read it.

My Queen of the Ants:

Still completely drunk with happiness, I mentally kiss all your splendours. In my dreams you are my Queen, afterwards as well as before. How did you sleep? Very little, as usual? But just think, now I've found a way of getting at least a little rest. You put your wardrobe on the floor on its back and spread insect powder an inch deep on the bottom, a blanket, more powder, then another blanket. (The nightshirts now in fashion are of no use even when they button at the bottom.) As soon as you get in, you close the wardrobe; a little hole (in the form of a heart?) covered with netting provides for air.

Please don't send me any more letters at the hotel. I hate the

American's crowd, particularly Jaques, who is an out-and-out rascal. Besides, the cooking there has become miserable recently. From now on I'll make the café in Long Lane my midday haunt. Letters to H. v. B. should go there, but no longer entrust them to N. C. He is unreliable and, since his association with the damned American, impudent besides. Is that fatty of yours groaning over the departure of his last tenant? The hairdresser will soon shut up shop too, and the Princess really doesn't pay much. I saw your husband today in his carriage, but at that moment he was busy with his vermin and so didn't take any notice of me at all.

Tonight at nine I shall be waiting for you behind the rosebush, leafless though it now is!

Thine, thine
HEKTOR

N.B. I am still receiving anonymous letters about you – how little the world knows my Melitta!

Soon everyone was carrying a bag of insect powder about. If the Dream people had formerly succumbed to sleep, now they hardly slept at all. Excited, a hectic flush on their cheeks, they wandered around the city until long after midnight. It was safer on the streets than in the collapsing houses. In the last few days the mating instinct of the animals had reached its peak. In every dark corner, in the water and in the air, all sorts of creatures were copulating. Bleating, whinnying, and grunting resounded from their stalls. A bull, maddened by the sight of cows destined for the slaughterhouse, crushed the butcher to a jelly against the wall.

The American was busy stirring up hatred and dissension and making fun of everything. Hardly anyone continued to believe in the Master. The Clock Spell was forgotten; only occasionally did anyone go into the cell, and then he did not remain for the prescribed half-minute; he came out at once. *Now I knew that the downfall of the Dream Kingdom was inevitably approaching.*

One night I heard snuffling and growling on the roof. I looked on with horror while a huge leopard dismembered a rabbit; I heard the crunching of bones, and an icy chill ran through me. My little room was no longer livable; it had two gaping holes in the wall out of which in the evenings there appeared the rear ends of cockroaches arranged at regular intervals like a frieze. For several days a pair of robins nested in my coal bucket. These creatures were harmless and rewarded me for my tolerance by their singing. Unfortunately this pleasure did not last long; the lightning swoop of a predatory falcon put an end to the male.

On one of the last evenings, as I was going to bed, I discovered two scorpions under the blanket. I was about to undertake a search for other pests when my weapon, the boot jack, fell apart. I took up my scissors; they were eaten through with rust. They I noticed that my paper was mouldy and that my ruler, what was left of my drawing table, and my three-legged commode – in a word, all the wooden objects – were worm-eaten and worthless.

What of my own appearance? It was certainly strange. Well, others too, usually cleanly and properly dressed, now

went about in rags. All had mildew on their clothes and shoes. No amount of washing or brushing helped – the mildew came back immediately. The cloth of our suits rotted, turned to rags, fell from us in tatters. We men endured this with dignity, but the poor ladies – let us not speak of them.

5

A great change took place when the houses became no longer really habitable. On the ground floor one could still make do, but to climb the stairs required reckless daring.

One day when the waiter put in front of me a rotten egg, a muddy liquid in a broken beer bottle, and a filthy greasy rag intended, no doubt, as a napkin, my patience snapped and I summoned the owner. He was engaged at that moment in propping up the ceiling with the remnants of a billiard table.

'What's the meaning of this?' I shouted at him. 'There's a pound of verdigris on this silverware. Kindly take all this repulsive stuff away – and the dishrag as well!'

He whimpered, bowing, 'Oh sir, it's the help.'

'Very well,' I said, dismissing him. I got up, took my shabby high hat, and left the café. Where I had been sitting, a small colony of ants had established itself.

Now I only went to the coffeehouse out of habit. It was too unappetizing to linger there for more than a black coffee. Anton was greatly changed for the worse. His hands were always dirty, and you could smell him at a great distance. It was not really necessary to go about looking as Anton did. The layer of filth that adhered to him was called 'matter' by the hairdresser. It was simply revolting! And so I was all the more astounded when one evening, returning home, I heard a low tittering in the corridor, and upon exploring all the corners – for I suspected the presence of some animal – I came upon Herr Anton behind the storeroom door in an amorous embrace with Melitta. She met her death shortly thereafter. Her torn body was found in her bedroom. The locked door had to be broken down. A huge bitch was locked up with her. This crazed beast, its hackles standing, leaped upon the intruders and wounded two policemen before it could be shot. The men died shortly afterwards of rabies. Only faint remnants of Melitta's former beauty were to be seen in the last days of her life. She had tried in vain through extravagant use of makeup to mask the deterioration that had taken place in her.

The two chess players also suffered grievously. These old gentlemen, who were slaves to their passion, finally found every bodily movement so complicated that they had to spend hours in calculation before lifting a hand. Obviously, with the infestation of vermin, such deliberateness placed them in a critical situation. And so a young lady who took action in their behalf received universal praise. She was just having tea when she noticed their distress. Going over to them, she picked the ants and fleas off their clothes. None of us wanted to be outdone. Until then we had just laughed at the chess players' grotesquely distorted faces, but afterwards each of the regular guests made a habit, on entering and leaving, of going over and giving the two gentlemen a short scratching. As can be seen, even in those evil times, not all sympathy for suffering had died.

The American was causing a lot of talk again. He prophesied that the flood of animals would very soon recede, and was proved right to the extent that the larger species gradually withdrew. All the small mammals and reptiles, however, remained for a time, while the birds disappeared entirely except for an enormous number of ravens and white-necked vultures. The vultures, massive, heavy birds, perched like bronze statues on the tree stumps in the avenue and stared imperturbably towards the city as though in expectation. Although the American's prophecies were only partly fulfilled, they brought him a large number of new adherents. From now on, he intrigued even more arrogantly, if that were possible, against his enemy Patera.

I resumed my evening walks along the river bank. The waves had brought ashore innumerable shells, coral, snails, and the skeletons of fish. I often noted with amazement the remains of sea creatures. It was as though the shore was strewn with mystic signs. I was convinced that the blue-eyed people would understand this symbolic language. Without any doubt there were secrets here; the wings of many splendid insects, noc-

turnal moths and beetles, bore marks that must certainly have
been a lost alphabet. I lacked the key to them.

How great you must be, Patera, I thought. Why does the
Lord hide himself so mysteriously even from those who love
him? I walked on in melancholy reflection. On the far shore
the barren trees bent far over the river and trailed their
branches in the black water. Between them gigantic shadows
moved. The crash of breaking boughs reached me distinctly,
and sometimes I saw long necks or trunks, and could not free
my mind from thoughts of monstrous prehistoric creatures.
The darker it became, the more dangerous it was for a solitary
walker. One evening, which was to be of great significance to
me, I turned around in alarm as a board that had emerged from
the water began to snort: it was an alligator baring its teeth.
On my way back, I thought about a misadventure that had
happened the day before, which had had a happy outcome. For
a long time rumours had been circulating about a gigantic
tiger, a pregnant female, which was said to be lurking in the
Palace. Various people maintained they had seen its long back
and short snout through the windows of the gallery. And in
actual fact, on the day before, a beast of this species had leaped
into Alfred Blumenstich's dining room. At the sight of this wild
beast, the plump lady of the house had silently fainted. They
were at table at the time, and Professor Korntheur was a guest.
That worthy gentleman showed remarkable heroism at this

dreadful moment. 'Remain calm,' he said to the horrified guests as he arose. 'Even the most dangerous predators are subject to man because of his superiority; they feel reverence for his upright carriage and fear his noble and masterful glance.' He then advanced upon the animal, taking off his spectacles. Whether it was because of the strangeness of this stiff-legged, scholarly apparition or for some other reason, the tiger whirled and sprang away, to the accompaniment of breaking windowpanes – alas, with the wife of the commercial counsellor in its jaws. Blumenstich wrung his hands. 'Good God, spare my Julie!' he whimpered.

Pursued by servants armed with muskets, the tiger dragged the unconscious woman to the Palace. Everyone in the street politely drew aside. The fire brigade, hastily requisitioned, attempted to drive the tiger away from its booty. It could be heard in the great hall on the second floor snarling ferociously at its pursuers. It was impossible to shoot for fear of wounding Frau Blumenstich. And so they hit on the happy idea of driving the animal off with fire hoses; this proved effective. The streams of water forced the tiger out of its corner in the hall, but it did not relinquish its victim. With an enormous leap, it flew out through the high bow window. The people screamed in horror, but God had mercy on the lady. Frau Blumenstich was left hanging on a window hook, visible to the whole Square, her skirts over her head, but saved. In the general excitement, the tiger slipped away.

Since the dangerous animal had not been captured, there was great consternation. The American proposed a search of the Palace, but despite the recent emancipation from the Master, no one dared follow his suggestion. The army and the police curtly refused their help.

The Master was behaving strangely. If he no longer had any wish to extend protection to Perle, he might at least have made an exception for the faithful. However, he did not seem to be concerned about making this distinction. The city now had quieter hours once again, although most of the population of Dreamland was assembled there.

'Turn over the villas to us!' the mob screamed and howled. The rich surrendered them willingly enough, since they literally had to be wrested from the animals who had nested there. The Lampenbogens' country house had become a sty for wild boars; a huge, surfeited boa constrictor slept on the divan in her ladyship's boudoir. In other ways, too, things were far less fine than the poor men had expected; the most valuable objects had clearly lost the will to live. A fine pattern of cracks appeared in the precious vases and porcelains. The splendid paintings developed black spots, which rapidly spread over the entire surface. Engravings became porous and fell to pieces. The speed with which so many well-preserved and carefully repaired household furnishings turned into piles of rubbish was hardly credible.

And so most of the peasants who had fled to the city finally settled in the public squares and in the fields close to the city.

Now, Lord, you show your might only through terror, I thought as I turned into Long Lane. It had grown dark, and on every hand there was the sound of cracking and rending. Here a tile whistled through the air, there mortar trickled from a wall; a fine rain of sand poured uninterruptedly from holes in the buildings, which grew larger as one watched. One had to clamber over piles of rubble and make one's way around protruding beams and rafters. Death was weaving its mysterious web.

On the roof of the coffeehouse quite close to my mansard, I clearly distinguished a black silhouette moving – the leopard. It must certainly have its lair in some near-by storehouse. No doubt a rifle-shot would have killed it, but we were all too cowardly for that. Arrived in my narrow room, I was overcome by deep despair; for a long time I paced up and down; I had aches in my back and all my joints.

Why do we all still go on living? We are certainly condemned men. If I were to fall ill, not a soul would be concerned for me. Insidious dread crept through me. I do not want to die; I won't! And in desperation I seized my head in my hands. 'There is nothing higher,' said the voice of despair. 'Two legs – bony tubes – support my entire world, a world of pain and error. The most horrible thing is the body.' Dread of death shook me to the marrow. What further miseries will my body suffer – and its thousand organs? To what refined instruments of torture will they be forced to submit? Oh, if I could only stop thinking, but that goes on of itself! There is no certainty that is not opposed by uncertainty! Confusion is unending – I am lost! In my belly I carry filth and loathing, and if ever I rise to a higher passion, cowardice follows close behind. I am sure of only one thing: struggle as I may, I must let the inevitable occur – the approach of death, minute by minute. I do not even possess the strength for suicide; I am predestined to enduring misery. I groaned.

Now I entertained doubts of Patera. I do not understand him; he juggles with enigmas! Very likely he is less powerful than anyone, otherwise he would have crushed the American long since. But he cannot do it! The American is the one who knows how to live. Oh, if I were not so pusillanimous I would appear before him, fall on my knees, and he would bring me aid.

As though undone by fear of death, I knew not where to turn. There was uproar in the street below. Rowdies were being ejected from the coffeehouse – a daily occurrence. Across the street in his lighted room, the hairdresser was bowed over his books.

6

Then I felt a series of tuggings inside me in rapid succession. I had to stand up – there it was again – what did it mean? Gradually, I was filled with an obscure feeling of compulsion. Now the tugging and knocking began again, more urgently – 'Yes, yes, what is it?' – I concentrated, surrendering myself completely to those vague sensations. 'Patera!' The word rose from inside me. 'Patera – the Palace – come!' It grew constantly more persuasive, more urgent, frightfully distinct and clear. In the dark, I descended the stairs with perfect sureness, without a thought in my mind. I was being pulled and pushed at once, and I resigned myself wholly to this guiding power. No one paid attention to me. When I was able to think again, I was halfway to the Palace. In God's name, what am I doing, I thought, what must I do? I wanted to turn around. 'At the next corner I'm definitely going to turn back!' It was no good! I had to go on. I tried to cry out to passers-by, 'Help me, help!

Hold me!' My jaws were clamped shut. And then I saw the imposing Palace, with its huge gate and gaping windows, like a death's head.

I stepped into its darkness. In every direction stretched a labyrinth of colonnades. Mechanically, like a wooden doll, I marched on – one, two, one, two. The long galleries were dimly lighted by hanging lamps; I entered the great halls. All the doors were ajar – I heard a sound – the melodious striking of a clock – in the draught, the doors opened of themselves – a crash! Christ have mercy, the tiger! From then on I was tormented by this image, and under its fierce compulsion I almost ran, careful to make as little noise as possible. Frequently I thought I heard my name called, quite loud and then softly, close beside me; but for nothing in the world would I have looked around. In the bare, untenanted rooms lay broken furniture; the stale air, reeking of mould stifled me. I passed through spacious chambers, each dimly lighted by a single candle. Tumbled beds, draperies torn down, windows walled up, magnificent tile stoves, their fires dead, Gobelins hanging awry. Up little dusty staircases and through long, silent corridors I hurried like a sleepwalker. Then I saw the familiar low oak door. 'Patera, Patera,' I thought uninterruptedly. 'Patera, Patera.' This door, too, was ajar. A silver lamp hung from the ceiling of the chamber; its small, flickering flame illuminated the torn rags of a canopy – except for the faintly visible pattern of the mosaic floor, I saw almost nothing – I stopped. *Now it was possible for me to stop!* There, there! – that face! – already my temples were bathed in cold sweat.

Patera stood there wrapped in a silver-grey garment like a veil – asleep on his feet. Unsurmountable dread overcame me at the sight of him. In the deep, greenish shadows of his eyes lay superhuman suffering. And then I noticed that the nail was missing from the thumb of one of his large, beautifully shaped hands. I suddenly remembered the children born in the Dream Kingdom. Once more I heard whispering like that on my first visit.

'I have summoned you –' It sounded as though from a great distance. This time, no distinct play of features followed. The muscles swelled, rolled, and contracted, but no recognizable expression resulted. The features grew slack; only the lips quivered and played horribly in the otherwise blank countenance. And then the sound began again, very low, as though muffled by a veil. At first I heard only a meaningless and disconnected whisper. Then all at once I began to understand and could follow the words.

'Do you hear the dead singing, the light-green dead? They decay in their graves, painlessly, softly. If you thrust your hand through their bodies, you touch only fragments – and the teeth, the teeth do not fall apart easily. Where is the life that moved them, where is the power? Do you hear the dead singing, the light-green dead?' Patera's acrid breath assailed my nostrils, I felt myself growing faint. Then the Master sat down on his elevated couch and threw off his gown – this time he was seated upright, his torso bared, his long locks falling over his shoulders; I had to marvel at the broad, noble limbs. The shimmering white body was like a statue. I concentrated the last of my strength in a single question: 'Patera, why do you permit all this to happen?'

For a long time there was no answer.

Suddenly he cried in a resonant, metallic bass, 'I am weary!'

I recoiled in terror. At the next moment I was staring into those lustreless eyes – *I was under the spell* – his eyes were two empty mirrors reflecting infinity. The thought came to me that Patera was simply not alive – if the dead could see, that would be their look. Inside me there was a command to speak. But I could only stammer; I babbled, and was myself astonished at the way I sounded. A question rose up, as though from some primeval age; these words must have been spoken billions of years ago, and now for the first time I uttered them. They were heard again here and now.

'Patera, why have you not helped?' Slowly, lifelessly, his eyelids closed; at this I felt relief.

In his countenance appeared an ineffable gentleness; I was charmed by his infinitely soft, sad look. And once more the clear whispering began.

'I *have* helped, I will help *you*, too!' It was like music; a wholly delightful weariness overcame me – I bowed my head, my eyes closed.

A laugh made me spring to my feet – laughter that shook me to the marrow of my bones, a hellish laugh. In a harsh glare of light, where Patera had stood, the *American* was standing in front of me . . .

How I succeeded in escaping from the Palace I no longer know. I ran and screamed. Men tried to check me in my flight, but I must have evaded them, for when I regained control of my body, I was cowering in a coach house. In the upholstery of a capsized carriage I noticed a litter of dead ant-eaters.

The derisive laughter still echoed intermittently and stridently in my ears, but it no longer moved me. My nerves had been stretched past the breaking point. *Fate, in whatever guise it might appear, could no longer tear me from my enduring calm.* Still incapable of sustained thought, I nevertheless felt myself strong in the awareness of my own impotence. Even though I could not understand or solve these paradoxes – why, after all, should that trouble me? All terrors had disappeared; the horrible vision, which had enabled me to grasp Patera's double nature, closed the abysses of my doubts and dreads.

7

This encounter explains why I was able to survive the final terrors that descended upon the Dream Kingdom. My lack of feeling was my nature's shield. The final agony of the Dream State was acted out before my eyes like a series of phantom scenes.

I no longer visited my room and I shunned the coffeehouse. Anton was now repulsive to me for reasons other than filth; he would slap the guests familiarly on the back and say, for example, 'What about that friend of yours, eh? He's a scamp!'

'Who?'

'You know the one, sir. It's Castringius I mean.'

Little by little, the residents of the Dream City settled in the open areas. The upper classes camped on the Tomassevic fields, the large building site next to the cemetery. Here a tent city sprang up, extending to the bank of the river. The nights, to be sure, were uncomfortable there because of the oily fog and the damp clay soil. But people did not immediately lose their good humour, and the atmosphere was merry around the fires in the evening. There was dancing and chatter; some people caught fish. These were usually devoured half raw because as soon as they were dead they acquired the taste of decay. Only the mob stayed in the city at night, searching for booty. During the day, if great care was exercised, commerce was possible in the streets. However, many people were injured by falling walls.

Dr Lampenbogen had installed a first-aid station in an abandoned park. I found him at work there, dressed in a grey tunic. He told me that two storeys of the Blue Goose had collapsed; eighty-six dead, seventeen hurt. A meeting had been going on at the time. Miraculously, the American had remained uninjured, but his servant – Lampenbogen pointed to a bandaged and bloody figure on the ground – was hardly expected to survive. He had no luck these days, he complained; most of his patients croaked.

Conditions were bad inside the hut: lack of sanitation, shortage of bandages, rusted instruments. In an old icebox, which he kept carefully locked, the doctor stored cold food and his cupping glasses. I thought it appropriate to offer some words of condolence. He smiled absently and said, 'Well, you know, I'm not the same sort of man you are!' He did not seem especially grieved by the loss of his Melitta.

The government paper and the *Dream Mirror* had suspended publication; *The Voice* now belonged to the American. It appeared exclusively as extras, and printed the day's sensations in telegraphic style. The paper was hawked about the streets in the evening by Jaques and his gang. It had a big circulation, since it published increasingly exciting news. Pathological phenomena were now the principal subject of conversation. When Dream people met they would often be seized by a sudden automatic compulsion: they all started to make the same involuntary movements, stretching out their hands stiffly and meaninglessly. This stopped abruptly after a few minutes and everything went on as before.

On the occasion of a long speech delivered in an open field, some chance auditor fell to repeating the whole oration rapidly, over and over again, beginning now at the end and now at the beginning, like a runaway phonograph. Speech disorders increased everywhere. Words were misspoken, concepts confused, letters transposed; many people became temporarily dumb.

Many became misanthropes and withdrew into the wilderness.

One had to be extremely cautious about drink; alcohol worked like a poison, although there were exceptions, and sickly people, women, and children could sometimes tolerate it by the litre.

I had one more sight of little Giovanni in Long Lane. He was with a band of chattering monkeys that had settled in the store of Blumenstich the secondhand dealer. Here a moth-eaten kingdom of upholstered furniture lay open to the sky, for the framework of the roof had gradually lost all its shingles. I recognized him among the other long-tailed monkeys by his red belt. I shouted up, but he was not to be disturbed; he was engaged in love-play and had completely reverted to type.

The tensions were unbearable; at night, coils of pale silver light writhed in the sky – long, delicate, pointed hands like Northern Lights. Hermits, dervishes, and fakirs came out of the sandy wilderness and from the mountains to prophesy in the marketplace that the end of the world was near. They exhorted the crowds to repent, but were laughed at for their pains.

Before the finale, one more farce took place: the 'black fish'. This was the name the extras gave to a huge shape that could be seen in the bed of the River Negro a good hour downstream. The big motionless body lay there like a battleship at anchor. People girded themselves for an attack by this new unknown creature. The most exposed portion of the camp on the Tomassevic fields was abandoned. Fear spread, and an observation post was installed in the brick works. Everyone crowded together and stared towards the place where the colossus lay. Oh, they were determined to sell their lives dearly! I too was in the excited crowd, squinting through an old cardboard telescope; unfortunately, because of the dim lenses and the uncertain light, I could see very little.

'It's a Greenland whale,' the old professor, standing beside me, remarked helpfully. 'Hitherto observed only in the Arctic.'

The remarkable creature did not move. The helpless city lay open to the impending danger. Some proposed to bombard it from a distance, but how would it react to such an attack? If irritated, it might spew out poison and destroy the little that we still had left. Better to wait – just possibly it would go away.

In the general confusion, a few daredevils suddenly showed heroic courage. This was the last evidence of healthy human instinct that I observed; later on, everything went downhill. Two farm lads, a soldier, and a hunter, all of them young people, determined to sacrifice themselves for the common good. Their plan was to float downstream in a rowboat, get as close as possible to the animal, and drive it away with hand grenades. Perhaps they could even kill it. It was a brave and reckless venture.

The noble offer was accepted, and everyone ran to see the youthful saviours. A priest in full canonicals prayed over each of the four and administered the last sacrament. Full of enthusiasm and emotion, the crowd jammed the space between the mill and the cemetery.

The young men went off to the sluice. Floating the last half-rotted boat, they drifted slowly downstream. Two of them had to keep bailing constantly. The tiny vessel grew smaller and smaller; now it was already at the bend in the river. They would soon reach the monster. All necks were craned, all breath was held. The crowd kept silent, except for the low sound of scratching. The little expedition came to a stop un-harmed in the immediate neighbourhood of the danger. To everyone's amazement, for a time nothing happened. Then suddenly there was a flash in the distance, and slowly the gigantic animal sank.

A shout of joy from a thousand throats rewarded the heroes.

Amazement was great when the prodigy turned out to have been a hot-air balloon that had come to grief, sunk over the Dream Kingdom, and become ensnared in the willows at the river's edge.

8

Nowhere was the decline of the Dream Kingdom mirrored more clearly than in the practices carried on in Madame Adrienne's beloved establishment in the French Quarter. Hitherto it had prospered in discreet obscurity, supported by the occasional counsel of experienced older men. Now high society in full dress appeared at the interesting and very searching entrance examinations. Castringius conceived the happy idea of distributing illuminated Ph.D. degrees, but this was rejected. It was indicated to him that this was not so much a scientific faculty as a cult.

The disintegration of cloth afforded the occasion for the invention of the famous slit dresses. Even respectable women – indeed these especially – went to the utmost extremes in this; it was they who were said to have originated the idea of the so-called menus; I shall only hint at what these were, and trust to my reader's discreet imagination. If I were to put it briefly and say that they were full of double meanings about love, that would not quite give the whole picture. The menus were printed invitations to intimate festivities. The apparently unobjectionable bill of fare – as, for example, Sandwiches, Roast Venison, Charlotte Russe – denoted technical details of amorous practices that none of my readers will want to explore further.

Even my old café was the scene of orgies; on at least one occasion I noticed piles of obscene pictures being carried in together with mirrors, bathtubs, and mattresses. I asked the host what the meaning of this might be.

'Oh, it's nothing! A little *arrangement*,' he replied with a smirk. When I passed there again that evening, the shutters were closed – something that had never happened before.

Diagonally across the door was a notice: 'Private party'. Uproar, epithets, and frightening laughter poured out.

A few priests who had sought refuge in the city divulged the mysteries of the Temple. How the mob interpreted these can be imagined. To them, the organs of fertility were not symbols of secret delights and powers; instead they were grossly reverenced as gods, in whom alone all hope was now placed. The greatest of all mysteries, the secret of the blood, was likewise disclosed, and therein lies madness. This may well have been the cause of the destructive release of the instincts. Confronted with the numerous dangerous animals, it was natural that people should band together for common protection. With this as pretext, they slept in the tents in groups under a single blanket. This fancy name for this safety measure was 'community sleeping arrangement'.

The air was oven-hot. Pale-blue flames were to be seen in the pools and bays along the river bank. Perpetual twilight reigned in the Dream Kingdom.

One day as I was walking through the encampment there was unusual silence. The Dream people lay about staring at each other from under sunken eyelids. Everyone seemed uneasy and oppressed, as if waiting for something. Suddenly a swelling hum and the sound of stifled laughter began to rise all over the field. Horror laid hold of me. It resembled a sudden outbreak of mental illness. And, like the onset of a storm, the sexes fell upon each other.

Nothing was exempt, neither family bonds nor sickness nor youth. No human creature could extricate himself from the elemental drive; with bulging, greedy eyes, all sought a body to embrace.

I rushed to the brick works and hid myself. I watched the horrifying spectacle through a small hole in the wall.

From all sides rose cries and groans intermixed with shrieks and occasional sighs; a sea of naked flesh rolled and quivered. Cool and uninvolved, I recognized the mindless, mechanical nature of the crass scene. There was something insect-like and grotesque in the convulsive performance. A reddish haze hung over everything; the light from the campfires flickered over the heap of writhing flesh, here and there picking out individual groups. I vividly remember an elderly bearded man cowering on the ground and staring between the legs of a pregnant woman. He was muttering aloud slowly and senselessly – a madman's prayer.

Suddenly, close to me, I heard a loud screeching as though from someone in an ecstasy of pain. I saw that a yellow-haired prostitute had castrated a drunken man with her teeth. I noticed his glazed eyes as he writhed in his blood. A moment later an axe descended; the mutilated man had found an avenger. Those self-defiled were edging backwards into the shadows of the tents; farther off, cries of 'bravo!' rang out where our domestic animals, seized by the frenzy, were copulating.

But the half-sleeping, half-imbecile expressions on those pale or heated faces convinced me that the wretches were not acting of their own free will. They were automatons, machines, that had been set in motion and left to their own devices – their spirits must have been elsewhere.

De Nemi appeared in uniform with some members of Jaques's gang; this had the effect of oil on flames. A piano was dragged up, and De Nemi hammered out a series of popular jingles, repeating them over and over again. The drunken crowd, obeying a bestial voice of command, attempted to copulate by columns. Children were forced on one another. I could see this ghostly inferno extending far into the red mist that hung over the river.

The thirst for blood awoke. A gigantic, filthy fellow sprang up, roaring like a bull, and leaped at a neighbour with a long knife. A murder! Then another! The man had gone berserk. All play stopped. A number of women were writhing on the ground, white as chalk, in hysterical seizures.

Now from all sides rose the howling of those mad for blood. *Only animals could roar that way.* Grim battles followed, and the gibbering maniacs were shot down. The gates to the near-by wine cellars were broken open, and great casks were rolled into the camp. Everyone became drunk. An uproarious crowd withdrew into the bathhouse; some prankster locked the door behind them. Their terrifying cries for help rang out for hours, but the drunken camp paid no attention. Then the cries subsided, and a herd of overfed crocodiles slid into the water.

Some people were violating new graves in the cemetery. A mangy dog, attracted by the smell of blood, threw himself on the carcass of a crushed cat.

Then I became aware of a twisted figure beside me. It was Brendel, who was grinning at me idiotically. 'Brendel, what's the matter with you?' I tried to rouse him.

'Melitta,' he said slowly, quietly laughing to himself. I had heard enough; the poor fellow had lost his reason over the death of his beloved.

When most of the fires went out it became quieter. Then nothing was to be heard but drunken snoring. I was deciding whether I could safely leave my hiding place when a bright fire sprang up, fed by the piano. In its light I saw a broad figure – the American.

He was wearing a tailcoat, as though at a celebration, and was smoking the inevitable short pipe. He made his way among the sleeping figures. A naked woman, half rising, tried to detain him, but instantly got a blow from his whip; a vivid red weal rose on her back. Then he disappeared among the shadows, heading in the direction of the city, from which a rumbling sound was rising.

The American's hour had come.

9

In the city, extras were being sold with headlines about a fresh disaster. The great Temple had sunk into the lake; monks had brought the news. It was thought that the foundations had long since been eroded and that the structure had plunged into the soft sandy bottom. Some of the priests had been drowned while singing hymns. They must have been taken completely unawares, for their trumpets were still ringing out when the building was half-submerged. Everything had happened very fast, the heavy marble walls sinking without disintegrating. Those monks who had escaped with their lives had first learned of their peril when they heard the splash of water pouring through the stained-glass windows. Buoyant because fat, they had easily escaped by swimming. The lights continued to burn deep under the water, illuminating the Temple windows so that they glowed like the eyes of some legendary sea monster. Then one by one they slowly went out; only the silver and gold dome shimmered and gleamed, until finally it too was engulfed by the greedy waves. The body of the Reverend High Priest was washed ashore; the others found their graves in Dream Lake.

There was general mourning for the fabled treasures that had disappeared, shared by me in particular since I had never had the chance to see these wonders with my own eyes.

The large animals all vanished. This brought an unanticipated disadvantage with it. What could one use to still one's hunger? The herds and the swarms of insects had laid waste the fields and gardens. All provisions went bad; eggs, salted and smoked meat, turned rotten. There was threat of famine. Two sisters from North Germany thereupon produced a practical proposal. One of them had studied chemistry and had made certain ingenious experiments, which in her opinion had been successful. The pair offered to detoxify by a secret process the little fish thrown up in piles along the river and transform them into edible food. Despite their good intentions, the two ladies encountered black ingratitude; they were lynched by the enraged mob.

10

It was no longer possible to distinguish night from day; one could barely find one's way in the uniform grey twilight. Since all the clocks had rusted and stopped, there was no method of measuring time, and so it is impossible for me to say how long the period of dissolution lasted. Now and then emaciated beasts of prey were to be seen, but at anyone's approach they took to flight with their tails tucked between their withered flanks. Dried serpents were extracted from dusty corners.

To prevent an outbreak of plague, the residents of Dream City were ordered to throw all corpses into the river. The decree could be obeyed only in very small measure, for now no one would venture into the dangerously dilapidated houses. Broods of rabbits and snakes infested the city. The stench of bodies hung in the doorways. The upper half of Lampenbogen's apartment house had collapsed; a long fireplace and the rear wall towered in the air. A cross section of our former apartment was visible, a few pictures still hanging on the flowered wallpaper of the bedroom. Through a big triangular hole one could see the dirty ceiling of the Princess's state chamber.

The dairy had been invaded by a fungus growth, which bulged out of windows and doors and deformed the whole structure; it hung in great, white tatters from the attic windows. The wooden shack belonging to the river superintendent fell in under the weight of its moss-covered roof.

The coffeehouse died like a coquette, striving to preserve appearances to the end and beyond. Outwardly it seemed intact, but the inside was filled with the wreckage of the upper stories and the attic floor. Strangely enough, one windowpane remained unbroken, and through this one could see two tall antheaps. Within them a few small white bones were visible, and between the two stood a chess table, exhibiting a very neat checkmate.

I made my way through the devastated streets towards my favourite path along the river bank. Here, too, the scene was dreary. As I passed the butcher's an incredible stench assailed me, so that I had to hold the tatters that served me as a handkerchief in front of my mouth and nose. The wall surrounding the courtyard had collapsed on the side facing the river; behind the rubble lay mountainous heaps of animal carcasses. Buzzing came from every direction, and at each step millions of blowflies rose up. I went down to the river to get my breath, for the air was still somewhat more bearable there. Almost nothing remained of the bathhouse. A few planks and piles, thickly covered with green slime and snails, still stood in the water. All at once there was a bright glare. Turning around in a panic, I saw that the mill was on fire. The windows were filled with blazing light. The dry woodwork snapped and crackled. Smoke poured from the pointed shingle roof, and a great flame darted towards the heavens. The front wall fell in with a crash. In the fiery light the machinery of the mill could be seen in motion, like the open body of a man. The wheels still whirred, the millstones turned, the funnels shook. Powder from the meal spread in a fine mist through the glare. The flames seized

eagerly on the decaying stairs and ladders, and slowly, as though reluctantly, one part after another ceased to move – like the organs of one dying.

Last of all, the great meal bin pitched into the flames. Where it had stood I saw a pair of old-fashioned high boots with half-decayed legs still in them – burning rafters concealed the rest. Behind me I heard a hollow voice: *'I have done it! For the fourth time I have done it, and I will always do it again!'* It was the miller. He took a pinch of snuff, drew a razor out of his pocket, tried the edge, and slashed his throat. He pitched to the ground, blood streaming over his breast as though from a fountain. His face was twisted in a satanic grimace.

Thieves invaded the church in the cloister, insolently broke open the tabernacle, and stole the relics encrusted with precious stones. The nuns could do nothing to prevent this outrage, for they themselves were in a desperate situation. A crowd of cripples and invalids, acquainted with every corner of the cloister because of the soup kitchens, stormed the hospital. Their threatening demands for food had to be refused by the nuns, who had nothing themselves. Laughing boisterously, the ruffians demanded recompense of another kind. As in a witches' sabbath the repulsive crew humped and crawled ever closer to their trapped victims. Trying to defend herself, a quite young and beautiful girl knocked out the eye of a man with

double goitre. As punishment she was bound to an iron bed-stead. Mange-covered creatures, crawling with vermin, noses eaten away, purulent eyes, ulcers as big as fists, bent over the helpless woman. In the course of the rape she lost her reason and then expired. The other nuns submitted with resignation to the inscrutable ways of destiny; only the eighty-year-old Mother Superior was spared this test, no doubt as a result of her ardent prayers.

I I

The American kept turning up everywhere, master of the city – yet he almost met with disaster. He appeared with his cohorts in front of the bank. Now they were to be rewarded, these faithful ones, as he had promised them. Everyone was surprised that the massive gate of the great, now rather dilapi-dated, building was standing open. On investigation, it was found that the vault contained eighty-three kreutzers; there was not a single deposit in the bank. Jaques, De Nemi, and the other leaders of the gang looked at the American in dismay. 'Just as I thought!' De Nemi cried angrily. 'Forward to Blumenstich's!' Banker Blumenstich was discovered in his gar-den pavilion in a welter of decayed flowers. He received the gentlemen calmly, his face plum-coloured; he was dead. He had taken refuge there from a swarm of hornets; while he had been shouting for help, the insects had stung him on the tongue, and he had choked to death. Once more everyone looked at the American, who merely said, 'Damnation!'

'You promised us money. Give us some of your gold!' shouted his enraged followers.

'Look for it yourselves under the ruins of the hotel!' the American cried indignantly.

Jaques exchanged conspiratorial glances with the others and, hiding a knife in his hand, advanced on Bell, who was observ-ing his every movement. With a blow of his loaded cane Bell felled the would-be assassin. Imperturbably he put his back to the wall of the pavilion, an automatic in either hand. In a resounding voice he yelled, 'Which sixteen of you want to be the first?'

The gang had thought it would be easy; as they cowered and struggled to get back, the vociferous fellows behind kept pushing them forward. The shots rang out sharp and clear one after another. Around the American rose a wall of bodies, far more than sixteen, for each bullet had penetrated several people. The American stood there bareheaded, proud and erect in his cutaway, his short pipe clenched between his teeth. His forehead, contracted into two lumps, gave his face a devilish expression, and his blank stare had a dominating and restraining effect on the raging crowd. No one in front dared touch him or shoot at him, but the pressure from behind continued. Yielding to it, the lines in the front were forced over the pile of slain, and the confused mass of bodies robbed Bell of all freedom of action. Breast-high and two spans from his own face, those empty masks, parodies of the human countenance, confronted him. His lungs worked mightily, his breath came in gasps as though from a steam engine. 'Down, down with him!' The murderous cries rang in his ears. Then unforeseen help arrived. The sound of lusty cursing drew nearer and grew louder.

'Where is he?' came a voice. 'Where?'

'Gotthelf Flattich – the mighty Gotthelf! Look out! Take cover!'

A colossal, half-naked figure was forcing its way through the mob. Growling, they made way for the approaching Negro, who towered over them by a good head and a half. He had been attracted by the uproar and had recognized at a glance the American's dangerous situation.

'Don't touch him!' he roared in his bull's voice, swinging an iron bar menacingly. His eyes rolled angrily in his black face. Hurling to the ground those in his way, he pressed forward and saved the life of his former benefactor.

12

A crowd had assembled in front of the Archives. Both wings of the great gate swung open, and out stepped His Excellency, followed by several functionaries, a commanding figure in court dress wearing all his medals and a helmet adorned with plumes. From a distance he looked like a bird of paradise. In his

magnificent uniform, he mounted a small, newly erected rostrum. The Dream people all around fell silent.

'Gentlemen, perhaps it has occurred to you that we are living in unusual times. This must come to an end. Order will be
restored. The wish has been expressed in the highest quarters
that all subjects be happy. Our gracious Master has determined
to pronounce an amnesty for all crimes and offences. I have
issued an order that our state prison, the Wasserburg, be
thrown open this very day!'

Derisive laughter greeted this announcement. 'Done long

ago. We have freed them ourselves!' the mob roared with delight. The prison was located on a rocky island in the middle of the River Negro, a short day's trip downstream, not far from the village of Bellamonte.

From then on not a word of the speech could be heard over the tumult. The orator opened and closed his mouth on his lofty perch. Finally, convinced of the futility of his attempts to calm the crowd, he made a little bow and started to descend from the rostrum. As he turned around a storm of laughter erupted; His Excellency's gold-striped trousers had lost their seat. 'Strange – what the people find amusing,' he reflected.

Suddenly there was an explosion – dust – smoke. Many people fainted or were crushed to death. A bomb had been thrown – by whom, no one knew.

The dead and seriously wounded were carried off on stretchers. Shuddering, the Dream people looked at the bloody burdens borne past them in long lines.

Both His Excellency's feet had been torn off. A steel splinter in his body was the cause of death.

13

I heard nothing of this at the time, for I had gone to visit the cemetery. Disquieted by the violation of the graves, I wanted to inspect my wife's tomb. The mound was undisturbed. The small iron cross had been completely eaten away by rust.

From where I stood I could see freshly dug mass graves. In these days the dead were buried hastily; four feet of earth had to suffice. Naturally, the miasmic exhalations attracted wolves, dogs, and jackals, which burrowed in the fresh earth and could often be shot while they were feasting. I saw a dark, humpbacked creature behind the marble slabs of the plundered family vault of the Blumenstichs; it gave a whinnying laugh – a hyena unless I was much mistaken. A leaden sky hung over the burying ground. Trampled immortelles, twigs, and decayed wreaths heightened the oppressive melancholy of the place.

I shivered. I had not slept in a bed for a long time. Then I remembered that I had read an announcement about blankets being distributed at police stations to the homeless. There was a

police station adjoining the mortuary. I went in search of it, hanging my head sadly. A great languor filled me. I had the sensation of walking on springy moss, on hay, on cotton. The cypresses seemed to make way at my approach. Amid the bright shimmer of the gravestones I saw a low building with rough brick walls. Over the open glass door I automatically read the words 'Police Station'.

The room I entered was very scantily furnished. Large rectangular windows set high in the walls admitted a pale light through their milky panes. Statutes in narrow black frames hung on the shabby walls. Facing me, over a closed door, I saw a picture of King Ludwig II of Bavaria. Primitive square gas-brackets extended from the whitewashed ceiling. There was nothing else in the room except a long, dirty table on which lay a horrifying object – a short, swollen body in a uniform bedecked with gold braid and smeared with blood. It was perfectly rigid, with legs slightly bent. The feet were missing. The trousers had been tied below the knees.

'That is the King of Bavaria.' The thought shot through my mind, and I was almost convinced. His sparse, black goatee stuck straight up, but I dared not examine the face closely, for I knew that the treacherous eyes were alive and were following me – I had had enough of such glances to last me for ever.

A diagonal band of light fell through the glass door to my right. 'Perhaps that is where the employees are,' I thought, and glanced through the pane. I started back in horror. I had looked into a long narrow chamber in which hundreds of corpses were stacked. They had been stuffed into grey potato sacks, and these were tied around their necks so that only the heads protruded, the faces greenish, the lips drawn back revealing the teeth. Many were dry as dust, the eyeballs shrunken. Several had been completely packed in the sacks, and their addresses were pasted on the outside. The degree of dislocation of the bodies could be guessed from the position of knees and elbows and the discernible angle of the heads. On the rear wall of this storehouse of corpses hung a tablet, which said in large letters :

HALL FOR THOSE SUDDENLY DECEASED

Making a wide circuit around Ludwig II, I headed for the open air, and then it became clear to me that the short, gold-braided figure on the table was not the King of Bavaria but the President of our government.

'I have a secret,' I said to myself. 'A secret that I am not going to tell. Perhaps he is the King of Bavaria after all.'

14

The melancholy cawing of crows drew my attention. The big black birds were sitting close-packed in long rows on the brick works. Occasionally the whole flock would rise and perform the most precise manoeuvres in the air. In the direction of the river, the sky was still reddened by the burning mill.

Just then I was almost knocked down by a naked man who came rushing across the field pursued by a pack of dogs. He raced towards me straight as an arrow, but at the last moment he made a sharp turn and clambered up a bare tree. The man wore nothing but a pair of patent-leather shoes and a turban made of newspapers. With marvellous strength and agility, which one would not have credited in that emaciated frame, he swung himself into the boughs of the linden and made his way up and up, dexterous as a monkey, in spite of an object that he persisted in dragging along with him. The thing he was carrying kept getting caught in the small branches, and he would struggle laboriously to free it with comically solemn grimaces. The dogs that had been chasing him crowded around the tree, barking up at him as though he were a cat.

Then a detachment of helmeted constabulary hurried up from the direction of the cemetery.

The man in the tree lost his grip on his treasure. With a loud cry the outlandish figure leaped down, snatched up his posses-sion, and dashed away, with the dogs in hot pursuit, a big black Newfoundland close on his heels.

One of the policemen fired at the nearest pursuer. The dog fell, but the man too was hit and collapsed on the ground. Now I saw that it was Brendel. We gathered around him and tried to raise him to his feet. Foam dripped from his mouth; he whim-pered idiotically. The wound beneath his right shoulder bled hardly at all. Little by little he became still and cold. Then a final spasm shook him, and he was dead.

The policemen lifted the dead man, curious to see what he had been so carefully shielding with his body: a decayed head, from which hung long thick chestnut-brown hair. It seemed to be alive. There was motion in the hollows of the eyes and around the tightly clamped lips – a busy throng of maggots.

15

Revolt had broken out in the city. Several squadrons of cuirassiers came from the castle garden to take up positions in front of the Palace, all picked men, showing few signs of the misery of the past weeks. Their breastplates and helmets, to be sure, bore traces of rust, but otherwise they were in good condition.

The rebels were in a strong defensive position behind hastily erected barricades. Under the leadership of De Nemi, the single renegade among Patera's officers, they had broken into an arsenal some hours before and now possessed all the weapons they needed. They had a tenfold superiority in numbers, and this was the source of their courage.

Opposite them, the horses stamped the ground impatiently. The fact that the mob had guns filled aged Colonel Duschnitzky with grave misgivings. He was also disturbed about his horses, which were nervous, ill-fed, and neglected. He had planned to postpone his attack until promised reinforcements arrived, but delay was now dangerous. The rebels might take the Archives before help came, and then the cavalry could not be used. Moreover, the barricades grew in height from minute to minute.

Some of the lieutenants laughed and lighted cigarettes, rejoicing at the prospect of sweeping the streets clean of those rats. An operation of this sort is always a lark to young officers. The men waited, straight as ramrods, semi-moronic expressions on their faces.

Then a shot rang out; a horseman pitched to the ground. The Colonel signalled and rode down the line. At this moment his hard-bitten, soldierly face with its bronzed, leathery skin seemed truly beautiful. He saluted the silent Palace – it was like an *Ave Caesar* – then a trumpet blew the charge, and with a loud hurrah the mass of horsemen threw themselves determinedly against the barricades. Sabres stretched before them, their ghostly horsehair plumes waving in the wind, the riders bent forward over the necks of their charging steeds. The sharp chatter of a salvo met them. Perhaps five cuirassiers slid from their saddles. But – what was far worse – the horses rebelled. They reared, standing straight up in the air, and threw their riders. With piercing whinnies, they stampeded in a wide circle around the Great Square, hurled themselves over the barricades against the rebellious soldiers with tremendous force, knocking down whatever stood in their way. The horses, seemingly endowed with supernatural strength, had gone berserk.

At this point, the expected reinforcements arrived, which only magnified the disaster. The approaching horses sensed the

fierce tumult and were at once caught up in it. Rotten bridles and girths parted, and the riders, without purchase, were thrown headlong to the ground before they knew where the enemy was. Freed of their burdens, the wild herd dashed against the barracks in a shower of sparks.

I was standing in Long Lane when I heard the advancing thunder. Instinctively I climbed onto a little wall beside the coffeehouse – the hooves were already pounding on the pavement. I looked into maddened, protruding eyes, saw the distended nostrils and twisted faces, for an instant smelled the sharp odour of sweat. Then they all disappeared in a cloud of dust in the direction of the fields.

The great vultures sat on the stumps of the trees along the avenue as though on pedestals, fat and indolent, watching indifferently as the herd thundered by. The only thing that excited their attention was a brown nag that kept limping in circles.

The frenzied cavalcade dashed through the whole city. Strays galloped wildly down winding alleys before dashing their brains out against protruding house corners. Several times the main herd piled up in confusion in narrow passages and culs-de-sac, and then it came to the large garbage dump on the city outskirts. There was no way out. The weak were trodden under foot by the strong. Frantic hooves struck, intestines split and splattered. An evil stench arose.

The old colonel would surely have been pleased if he could have seen the splendid results of his charge: uncounted rebels trampled to a pulp. But a white-gauntleted hand was all that remained identifiable of him – the rest was hopelessly intermixed with the mass of limbs, cuirasses, splintered bones, helmets, saddles, and bridles.

16

Before the coffeehouse collapsed completely it had become so rickety that no guest would enter it. The owner blamed his headwaiter for this.

'You look like a pig!' he said mildly. Given the benign tone of this speech, it could only have been its content that inspired the despicable plan in that false-hearted waiter. One night he pushed his unsuspecting employer into the opening to the cellar and slammed the trapdoor shut. The innkeeper's arm was broken in the fall, but otherwise he bounced like a rubber ball because of his fat. Though enraged at Anton, he did not guess the magnitude of the danger that confronted him. The waiter had calculated on accomplices in his crime and, as an adept adder-up of cheques, he had made no mistake. His frightful allies were the millions of rats that infested the subterranean passages and catacombs of Perle.

Feeling his way in the wrong direction because of the darkness, the innkeeper entered the passageway in which at one time I had suffered so much. In vain he seeks an exit. His broken arm swells and begins to ache intolerably. He grows weak, he hears a soft squeaking, a scrabbling and scampering. First singly, then in larger and larger numbers, hundreds, thousands – now he realizes what sort of trap he has fallen into. He tries to run, he strikes out with his good arm, again and again he feels the little grasping hands. Heavy lumps hang onto him. His arm is covered with small sharp bites. He tries to shake the enemy off. Four, five, six times he succeeds. Then he throws himself to the floor to thrash himself free of his hungry tormentors. A hundred rats, perhaps, lie crushed and trodden to death. Thousands take their places and praise the Creator for the good fortune He has bestowed upon them.

Several people told me of the unusual screams they heard, the terrifying curses, pitiable prayers, dull roars, that seemed to come from certain gutters and sewers. The places mentioned were, to be sure, rather far apart, but acoustics in the Dream Kingdom were remarkable.

After the disappearance of his employer Anton kept the café open for a few hours, then he locked up and abandoned the place. He could expect no more income. The two chess players stayed.

By chance, Anton came into association with Castringius and formed a partnership with him. Nik had changed his trade. Now he obtained his living from the savings of others – that is, he stole whatever he could lay hands on. His last work, 'The Leprous Albino Destroying the Original Brain,' was dedicated to the American, whom he gave to understand that the picture was an 'allegorical symbol' and worth a hundred thousand marks; the American could have it for the ridiculously low price of five thousand. Bell laughed and had the artist thrown out. This had happened to Castringius more than once recently.

Raging for revenge, he went over to Patera's side and attacked the adherents of that 'damned Yankee' whenever he could. Once, after a good stroke of business, when he was just about to be up and away, he felt a strange hand in the back pocket of his coat. Seizing it, he became aware that the hand was attached to the waiter Anton! Apologies, explanations – in the end, these two great souls joined forces. Their speciality was breaking into abandoned country houses. They had a hiding place in the Palace garden where they assembled their riches and buried them. One day they had an especially promising project. The villa of the former publisher of the *Dream Mirror*, who had died from the bite of a poisonous snake, was standing empty. Cautiously the pair made their way through the Garden Quarter, keeping as much in the dark as possible. They walked in silence, each busy with his own thoughts. Anton was hoping for an opportunity of getting rid of his friend. Then he and he alone would be the heir. Castringius, on the other hand, was mentally counting over the treasure already won. He was satisfied. A few more happy strikes and he would have enough to lead the honourable and carefree life of an artist somewhere in Europe.

It was hard to see.

'Will it take much longer?' growled the waiter.

'Don't be silly. You've been running all your life! There, that's the last house. Now we're home.'

Now a roof was visible among surrounding trees. At the garden wall Castringius looked cautiously about.

'All's clear so far. Well then, over you go!' he ordered his companion.

The latter did not take kindly to the suggestion; he feared a trick on the part of the illustrator. After prolonged argument, Castringius climbed over, followed by the other. The waiter's stiff shirtfront remained, hanging on the barbed wire. 'A professional hazard,' his friend remarked sarcastically.

They carried out a businesslike search of the house. Neither in the workroom nor anywhere else did they find a thing worth taking. Castringius gave vent to his feelings about the publisher. 'I can't understand it at all. How could I ever have felt respect for that fellow? I hereby dedicate to you this collection of thirteen years of the *Dream Mirror*,' he added maliciously, pointing at a row of books.

Anton, who was staring with disapproval at the broken furniture, retorted, 'Spare me your stupid jokes, you can keep that muck for yourself.'

'Silence, lackey! What do you know of higher things? These volumes contain almost the entire output of an artist who must always remain a stranger to you. Your mental horizon is just barely adequate to embrace the works of my esteemed colleague!' He gave Anton a look of contemptuous pity.

They were rummaging through a wardrobe in the bedroom for anything usable when they heard a suppressed moan. 'What was that?' cried the superstitious waiter, shivering and almost dropping his lantern. A figure half wrapped in a blanket was cowering on the bed, a barely adolescent girl who stared large-eyed at the intruders, frightened half to death.

'Louisy, my publisher's little girl!' Castringius shouted happily. 'She belongs to me, of course!' He went over to the terrified child and bowed.

'If you please, fifty-fifty, as agreed!' The waiter's courage had returned; jealousy flared.

Castringius turned around, his head lowered like a bull – no, he was more like a drunken bullfrog; he glared at the waiter, who was weak from malnutrition. Standing firmly on his short muscular legs and swinging his long arms with his frightful paws, he growled, 'Sir, I have prior rights. I am not going to

share anything with a lout like you. Try me and see.' He bared his teeth, confident of his own strength.

The wily Anton had been prepared for just such a scene since the beginning of the partnership, and he carried his means of defence with him in a bag. Suddenly a handful of ground pepper flew into the face of the mainstay of the *Dream Mirror*.

Blinded, the latter struck out wildly, seized his opponent and dragged him close. The ship's screws locked behind Anton's back, and he collapsed. The tall man and the short rolled crazily on the floor, first through the room, then through the open door onto the balcony. In their furious embrace, neither one noticed that the railing had been broken off. They flew from the balcony onto the roof of the washhouse, slid downwards, and pitched into the open cesspool.

There was a muffled splash.... Then a few bubbles rose to the surface.

17

'Love of the flesh is simply the will of the Thing-in-Itself to force its way into the temporal world. How can you be so presumptuous as to compel the Thing-in-Itself? You make no distinction between the Thing-in-Itself and other things. From a philosophical point of view, I am compelled to condemn your actions.'

This was the hairdresser's view of the saturnalia taking place in the Tomassevic fields. Since he refused to put an end to his tirades, which were so inappropriate to the day's festivities, the crowd slipped a noose around his neck and hanged him from the sign over his shop. He dangled there under a brass basin. Seeing him thus, a wit tore down a cardboard sign from the wall of a house and tied it to the legs of this authority on Time and Space. It read: 'For rent.'

Lampenbogen lived high to his last day, while reducing his patients' rations first to a half and then to a quarter. Since Dream people took this sort of thing in bad part, a small hospital revolution broke out, vigorously supported by the orderly, who would rather have been free to take part in the great events going on outside than carry on with his disagreeable tasks in the ward. The icebox still contained three roast chickens, a packet of chocolate, and a slab of cheese. The patients demanded a share of these private stores, although the condition of the food was far from appetizing. Lampenbogen refused. Then he must die, they said. He didn't want to do that either. The enraged patients quickly reached an understanding among themselves, and fell on their doctor. The bedridden looked on while the orderly, assisted by the others, subdued him. A miserable woman with a broken jaw painstakingly poured chloroform drop by drop over the doctor as he lay groaning in his fat. Sick people are rarely compassionate, they have suffered too much themselves.

When they had reduced their victim to unconsciousness, they broke open the icebox and helped themselves to the dainties inside. Lampenbogen they skewered on a gas pipe – a long and tedious operation for the weakened patients. The orderly made a fire so as to obliterate the traces of the outrage. So Lampenbogen ended his existence as a roast *en brochette*,

and, what's more, badly done; his back was almost raw, barely warmed through; the belly, on the other hand, was completely charred. Only his sides were nicely crisped.

18

A hatless old man is hurrying anxiously down Long Lane in the direction of the river. The tails of his housecoat flutter behind him like wings, his waistcoat is half undone. He nods his head vigorously, entirely absorbed in talking to himself. Arriving at the water, he stops indecisively for a few moments. Lecturing to himself, he moves up and down the sandy shore with the solemnity of a heron. The River Negro murmurs – now hungrily, its waves licking up the sand from the shore by spoonfuls, now breaking into mystic, polyphonic song. A dim lantern attached to the pillars of the bridge throws dancing spots of light on the surface of the stream. Finally, with decision, the old man wades into the water. First the waves come only to his knees; methodically he gets out a glasses case and puts his spectacles on his nose. He returns the case to his pocket. A few steps more – the water now reaches to his lean hips. He has to fight to retain his footing against the current. Pressing his hands to his heart, he utters odd and fervent declarations of love. Now he gets out a small unidentifiable object, which he holds near-sightedly in front of his eyes. Then he bends his face to the water as though to examine it; it is already up to his neck, now up to his nose – and then all there is to be seen is a little island of white hair. A gleaming oblong spins and circles, rocking on the waves like a tiny ship on the stream – it is a small box covered with silver paper – Acarina Felicitas!

19

The swamp was devouring the station. The building itself had tipped over, the platform was covered with slime and bulrushes; through the rotting doors the morass crept into the waiting room, the melancholy song of toads resounded from the benches and cushions. Over the buffets crawled salamanders and grubs. All the countless creatures that had infested

Perle, laid waste its gardens, and terrified its inhabitants had originated in the swamp, which extended for many miles into the grey darkness.

But it not only bestowed life, it took it away. Countless Dreamers – peasants and fishermen – slept in its wet earth. And yet how harmless this treacherous swamp could appear, while the serpents coiled under its mossy surface! Without a sound it could launch ghostly flames as high as a house, to the consternation of the nesting waterfowl. It could nourish itself abundantly on its own life – its tigers ate its wild pigs, its foxes hunted down its deer.

This wilderness was considered holy in Dream Land. At certain places stood age-old moss-covered stones, on which characters had been cut, now weathered and indecipherable. Hunters used to bring the vital organs of their wild game there, fishermen sacrificed the livers of catfish and pike, farmers brought bundles of vegetables and would heap up apples and bunches of grapes in little pyramids. The swamp accepted these gifts graciously at all times and devoured them. In earlier years Patera went there often and even ventured to approach these holy places alone at night. I was told that he made offerings in the name of the Dream people to 'the swamp Mother' – and renewed his union with her through mysteries in which blood and sex played pre-eminent roles. Now he had not been there for a long time, but people knew all about these secret rites and used to swear 'by Patera's blood'. The results were visible everywhere. An old Temple saying, 'Spilt blood breeds madness', had been fulfilled. I must not fail to mention that the blue-eyed race on the other side of the river kept aloof from all these customs. At a considerable distance from those locations, between the sickly bushes and the stunted pine trees, brightly painted posts had been planted in the ground. These, too, were consecrated places, but of another kind. Here the 'happy nights' were celebrated. On certain evenings at harvest time, the Dream farmers brought their rack carts filled with hay and flowers. These fragrant loads were strewn on the ground a yard deep. A fire was lighted, new wine flowed foaming from the bungholes, the devotees were gaily dressed, and joy was unconfined.

After merry tales, games, dancing, and a sumptuous meal, the warm wind, redolent of fruit, would usually blow out the fire. The couples stayed, each in a separate nest, until morning.

The big rickety train-shed beside the station still smelled like a menagerie. The acrid filth of the animals that had made their lairs there mingled with the slimy black water, forming big lakes. Now a figure wrapped in a hooded cloak was busy in the damp, sand-choked hall; this lonely fireman banged and tinkered energetically at an old rusty locomotive. He examined all the parts carefully, dousing them lavishly with oil. Then he pulled open the door to stoke the fire again, and his determined, sweaty face was revealed in the red glare – it was Hercules Bell.

Weeks before, he had examined the tracks and set all the switches. Puffing reluctantly at first, the engine finally began to snort, and Bell drove it out of the dilapidated structure. A pair of owls, startled from their sleep, accompanied him. With the aid of a turntable, which he had tested in advance, he managed at length to reach the main line. The supply of coal was sufficient – if worse came to worst, he could replenish it at an intermediate station.

Heated by his exertions, he took off his robe. Raking the fire again, he glanced at the steam pressure and pulled a lever. The ancient vehicle set itself in motion. It was a dangerous journey, for the low railway embankment was half destroyed. In some places swamp water covered the tracks for long stretches. Spray rose in front; the wheels mowed down masses of reeds; a long wake stretched behind.

The engineer inhaled the sulphurous vapours rising from the troubled waters of the stagnant morass. In the distance he could dimly distinguish the whitish ruins of an old Persian settlement long abandoned.

He fed the fire until the boiler threatened to burst; the furnace and adjoining steelwork glowed red, the locomotive rocked on the bent and rusted rails. Belching smoke, it sped past vacated farms, pillaged estates, barren woods. Once Bell had to stop in order to drag the carcass of a half-eaten nag from the rails. Then on rushed the engine, panting and rattling. After two hours Bell stopped again in an open field. He banked the fire, spat hissingly on the boiler, and leaped down. For a time he followed the rails, then turned off into a small valley filled with gigantic trees. Dried vines and hanging moss tried to impede his hurried progress. After a half-hour's walk, he came in sight of a dimly lighted window, behind which a black wall seemed to rise into the infinity of the sky. With steady hand the American opened a little garden gate, crept to the window of the house, and looked in.

An oil lamp with a green shade stood on an ink-stained table. Papers, schedules, sealing wax, and lead seals lay scattered about; there were some tools, nails, and twine on a low balustrade. The showpiece in this narrow room was a very bad life-sized portrait of Patera, distributed by an institute in Perle.

This was the office of the border overseer of the Dream Kingdom. The old man himself was asleep in an easy chair covered in oilcloth. With his bearded chin propped on his hand, he gave an impression of weakness. In obedience to the regulations, he had the key to the so-called little gate, a small door cut in the great wall and designed for single passage, attached to his belt by a snap hook. The yard-long principal key was kept in an iron safe. The old man performed his onerous duties with the assistance of his two sons. Next door was his own house; this in turn adjoined the barracks for the border guard and the customs officials. Both structures were built against the colossal boundary wall.

All these details were well known to the spy. Now it was growing dark with a speed that amazed Bell, accustomed as he was to uniform twilight. He looked around him in astonishment; under the low clouds he was barely able to distinguish the tin roofs of the storage sheds attached to the railroad terminus. Noiseless as a cat, he entered the overheated room and pushed back his cowl. In his right hand he held a heavy iron lever from the locomotive. 'It's too late to worry about one life more or less,' he reflected, looking imperturbably at the sleeping man. The latter stirred without awakening, and his head rolled over on the back of the chair. Then, a well-aimed stroke with the iron bar! It sounded like the palm of a hand striking water. The vigorous blow hit the skull exactly in the centre, splitting it; the eyeballs were driven out of their sockets, imparting a horrifyingly grotesque expression to the bearded countenance of the murdered man. A deep, silent tremor ran through the body, but it remained upright in the chair.

With comic affection, the American bowed to the portrait of Patera. 'Outwitted you at last!' Then he removed the key from the dead man's belt with quick skilful fingers. A dark lantern stood on the floor beside the easy chair. As he was bending down for it, he felt something close hard on his wrist. *It was the dead man*, or rather, just his yellow fingers, against which Bell must have brushed. The corpse lay there helpless and still. But its terrible fingers had such incredible strength that they could have crushed steel like dough. Bell screamed, 'This is Patera's work!' It was clear that the increasing mechanical pressure must shortly crush his wrist; he had already lost sensation in the imprisoned limb. He gnawed at the wrist of his grisly opponent with his teeth – but that was much too slow – his own hand was lost.

At this horrible instant he caught sight of an open knife lying to the balustrade. A leap, and he was there, the corpse flying with him like some monstrous appendage. With expert strokes he severed the dead man's hand from the body; at once the hand grew limp and fell to the floor. Bell's sigh of relief held a note of wonder. From the portrait on the wall Patera, his locks oiled and parted, looked down on him with the same friendly smile. Picking up the dark lantern, Bell ran out.

Arriving at the wall, the American plunged into the mighty tunnel. He was in a state of great excitement; now he would find out whether his plan had succeeded; according to his calculation, help from Europe must be very close. *He needed it, had to have it*; by himself, he could not subdue the Dream rabble, which was growing hourly more dangerous.

He opened the 'small door' and stepped out into the fresh, cold night air. Then he set off the rocket he had brought with him; a fountain of melted gold shot into the dark sky; high above it described a splendid curve and ended in a spray of stars. Feverishly the American waited to see whether the signal would produce any result . . . nothing! In all directions lay darkness and silence – he had calculated wrong! In rage and disappointment, he turned the light of his dark lantern on the monumental bronze door with its ponderous hinges. Should he go back? For a long time he glanced into the distance. There, all at once, a ghostly beam swept across the firmament – for seconds only – then it disappeared as suddenly as it had come. But once again the bluish gleam appeared, like a comet. *It was a Russian searchlight.*

The wildest joy and pride surged through Hercules Bell. He raced back as fast as he could, leaving the gate open for the troops. Breathless, he reached his locomotive. The border guards, true sons of the Archives, had noticed none of his activities.

The American put his ancient machine into reverse, stoking the fire constantly; a long streamer of flame swept backward from the smokestack as the locomotive rumbled through the stark darkness of the barrens. The American's enterprising recklessness had triumphed. Bell blew the whistle in exuberant delight; piercingly shrill and plaintive, its cry resounded in the night. 'And now we will put this country in order!' he promised himself. The ache in his badly swollen hand had become insistent. Vainly he tried to sooth it with machine oil, but the joy of his victory was barely marred.

The sky began to redden in the direction of Perle; a harsh

glare, growing rapidly stronger, was reflected from the cloud cover and soon embraced the whole horizon. The American looked at this new conflagration in concern. Without reducing its speed, the rusty monster was now plunging through the sea of slime. The high black bow wave drenched the engineer in filthy water. The halves of an adder, cut in two by the wheels,

were hurled into the cab and writhed at his feet. Half-submerged, the ashbox hissed in the greasy water; the steam gauge stood at 99 – at any moment the boiler might explode. With a pair of heavy pliers the American held the safety valve shut to keep in the excess steam.

When the station came in sight he halted the locomotive and, leaving it to its fate, rushed into the city. There everything was bathed in a blazing red, the Archives were in flames. Small dust explosions occurred constantly; the conflagration carried burning papers high into the air, where they flew over the city like firebirds. A mob surged through the hot streets howling and laughing.

A shudder shook the American, and he collapsed on a pile of stones. Faint and weak, he spat out the words, 'Patera leaves his successor nothing but excrement.'

20

When the Archives and their treasures went up in flames I was sitting in my favourite place by the river, on whose surface the fiery sky was reflected. The unparalleled events to which I had been a witness in the last few days had shaken me out of my apathy. I felt my numbed heart thawing – the inhuman sufferings of the Dream people threatened to crush me. I wished for death, in whatever form it might come. That this night of horror must bring all to an end seemed only too clear. But why did Fate linger so long and outdo herself, repeating the most hideous tortures?

Now disturbances of vision afflicted the Dream people. At first objects seemed to be encircled by a rainbow. Later, all natural proportions seemed to be distorted; they mistook small houses for lofty towers; false perspectives misled and frightened them; they thought they were hemmed in when they were not. It seemed that the buildings were leaning over the streets or were balanced precariously on too narrow foundations. People approaching were multiplied in number, became crowds! They stepped high to surmount imaginary obstacles, crawled along the ground on all fours, constantly picturing abysses in front of them.

Many succumbed to mass suicide. Persecuted and tormented beyond endurance, they fell helpless victims to dreams in which they were given the command to destroy themselves. Those who remained were so disturbed in mind that they probably were not conscious of their final bitter hours.

Suddenly the rumour spread that Patera himself had appeared. Borne on a litter by four servants, he had come into the marketplace, a pointed tiara on his head, dressed in a green satin robe magnificently embroidered with pearls; he was like a cardinal bestowing his blessing on the crowd. The American was said to have picked up a paving stone on catching sight of him and hurled it at the Master as though demented. The tiara was shattered and fell in the dust, the head – that of a wax doll – split like an eggshell; the eyes were glass balls filled with quicksilver; the magnificent clothes had been stuffed with straw – another mystification, that was all!

The military had long since used up their ammunition. Clad in grease-stained red trousers, they charged at the ragged madmen at the double with fixed bayonets. Inflamed with drink, they were incapable of mercy. The American sided with the soldiers; the latter, once they had heard about the wax doll, greeted Bell's dominating presence with jubilation. The Archives, the Post Office, the bank, were aflame and lighted the streets as bright as day.

Down the slopes from the French Quarter, like a river of lava, slowly poured a mass of dirt, filth, blood, entrails, and carcasses of beasts and men. In this mixture, iridescent with all the colours of decay, the surviving Dreamers waded helplessly. They could only babble now and could not understand one another; they had lost the power of speech. Almost all were naked; the more robust among the men pushed the weaker women into the flood of offal, where they perished, rendered unconscious by the stench. The Great Square was like a gigantic sewer in which, with their last strength, men choked and bit one another and finally expired.

Stiff corpses of dead onlookers protruded from the windows, their lifeless eyes mirroring this kingdom of death.

Dislocated arms and legs, spraddled fingers and clenched fists, distended bellies of animals, horses' skulls with swollen blue tongues thrust far out between the yellow teeth – that was how the phalanx of destruction irrevocably advanced. Stark shafts of light gave flickering animation to this, Patera's apotheosis.

21

The blue-eyed people remained unmoved by all that was going on. They stared across the river calmly. It is true that something must have been happening among them, too, for they had set up great cauldrons in front of their strange dwellings. Day and night they busied themselves around the fires. Obviously some decoction was being made. The wind carried acrid, evil-smelling fumes across, which made people cough. Soon the reek changed to a pleasant odour. The blue-eyed ones, who had formerly been so solemn and decorous, were now dancing around the cauldrons and singing slow, monotonous choruses. The gangs in the city wanted to go across. It had long been know that the Suburb was by no means so tormented by vermin and dirt. However, the bridge had fallen and been swept away. There were no more boats, and an attempt to swim through the reptiles in the river would have been suicidal.

I waited on the bank, sitting on one of the pillars of the bridge. No longer capable of bearing these scenes, which exceeded my powers of comprehension, I planned to put an end to my life. I stared in fascination into the muddy waves that I had chosen for my grave. In the next moment they would receive me. I had a distinct feeling that something of unimaginable magnitude must lie before me. Very slowly and gently, I let myself slide down – *it was like a dream!*

With a gurgling roar, a yawning funnel formed in the water, and a black hole sucked the river into itself. The still glowing remnants of the mill sank in a cloud of steam.

Long Lane collapsed upon itself, and as a consequence I could see the Palace, ordinarily not visible from there. Its shuttered mass towered over the ruins, rising nobly in the bright red glow. I thought the Day of Judgement had come, that now trumpets would ring out. The River Negro poured in raging cataracts into the greedy open mouth of the black whirlpool that had formed in its bottom. Fishes and crabs wriggled in the slime and were left clinging to the water weeds.

Then on the far shore I observed a small band of men beginning to advance across the river – the blue-eyed ones. They strode past me with bowed heads. First came a bent figure with face so furrowed that it seemed splintered, as though a thousand years old. From his remarkably lofty skull hung long smooth silver strands. For a moment it occurred to me that this might be a woman. Then the others! All were tall, emaciated figures. The last, somewhat taller and more erect, turned to look at me. I stared into the most beautiful face I have ever seen, with the one exception of Patera's. The clean contours of the egg-shaped head were as though made of porcelain. With his transparently thin nostrils, his narrow, somewhat flattened

chin, the man seemed to me like a hyper-refined Manchu prince, or an angel from some Buddhist legend. His long slender thighs testified to the utmost evolution of the race. All the hair had been shaved from his skull, over which the skin was stretched perfectly smooth. He looked at me with an indescribable expression in his blue eyes, an expression that could not mean rejection. I followed him.

Then the earth began to stretch and expand like rubber; a deafening roar, as though from hundreds of cannon, shattered the air. Slowly the façade of the Palace leaned forward, curved like a flag in the wind, and buried the Great Square under it.

From all the towers in Perle the bells chimed melodiously, ringing out a majestic swan song for the dying city. I was moved to tears, it was as though I were participating in the funeral procession of the Dream Kingdom.

I followed the blue-eyed men into a narrow passage cut in the rock wall. In the dim light of scattered torches, a long stairway with irregular steps led upwards. My guides disappeared into a rocky chamber cut into the wall at one side. I, however, climbed higher and higher in search of a place of security, and came into the open again to find the sky growing red above me. I found myself in the old mountain fortress. A few cannon were still intact, aimed at the city, but for the most part the gun carriages were broken and the bronze barrels lay askew against the walls. The mountain fell sheer away for several hundred metres. I sat down. Beneath me I saw a labyrinth of passageways. I could hardly believe my eyes; the city had all along been undermined as though by mole tunnels. A wide passageway connected the Palace with the Suburb, others extended far into the country. These tunnels now lay open and were filled with the dark waters of the Negro; everything that still stood was slowly sinking into them. From the other direction the swamp crept nearer and nearer.

The ringing of the bells had ceased, the towers had crumbled; only the Great Clock Tower still stood, its mighty bell humming a deep bass. I saw hardly any remaining life. Only a small band of people seemed to have escaped. They had dispersed in different directions and then come together again at one point, like marionettes controlled by a single string; that is how they looked from high up.

The people down below seemed to be herding about aimlessly. Finally, at the command of an invisible leader, they rushed across the ruins towards the river in one last amazing effort, traversed its empty bed, and hurled themselves against the Suburb.

Out of a huge hole in the earth rushed an ice-cold wind that reached to where I was standing; the fleeing men were thrown in heaps. The mysterious hole inhaled the air it had blown out; boards, beams, and men disappeared into it. It was like watching a whirlwind. Only a few escaped and tried to hide themselves in the little houses of the Suburb. Then the blast of wind stopped, and a camel's head cautiously reared itself from the dark hole. It was poised on an unending neck; gazing about with intelligent eyes, it rose to the height of the place where I was, then it laughed silently and withdrew again.

The huts began to move, then the windmills struck out at the intruders with their arms. The straw roofs raised their ragged

hair, the tents became inflated as though they housed the wind, the trees seized men with their branches, the signal poles bent like pipes. Finally the little temples and houses clambered on top of one another and uttered strange words in a horribly loud, rasping tone, distinctly audible – a dark, incomprehensible language of houses.

Corpses still floated in the canals, which were now slowly draining into the bosom of the earth. Then everything in front of me disappeared, but at the last moment I thought I saw the pyramids of houses in the Suburb come crashing down.

It was as though a sheet of water were falling between me and everything down there below. Fog was descending, through it the conflagration gleamed indistinctly, a few more times I heard a mass outcry, a long sustained *ohooo*, *ohooo*, then I saw and heard nothing more, all was wrapped in fog, I could barely distinguish my hand in front of my face. Soon it grew brighter, a great gleaming disc hung in the sky, innumerable points of light covered the dark blue firmament ... the moon and the stars. For three years I had been deprived of this sight, I had almost forgotten that great world above us, and for a while I had to surrender myself completely to the impression made by the infinite height of the heavens. A piercing cold penetrated me and I looked down shivering. The great cloudbank that had been the Dream Kingdom's sky had fallen.

Then a dull rumbling began in the tumultuous cloud mass beneath me, a thundering as though the Riders of the Apocalypse were invisibly galloping by; it swelled infinitely, broke against the steep mountain wall, was thrown back doubled and redoubled, waned and swelled again frightfully, divided, rang out from the high mountain valleys and over all the passes, and would not come to an end, lasted and lasted, and slowly ebbed.

This was the destruction of the Dream Kingdom.

A grey blanket lay over the land; on the horizon, clear in the moonlight, gleamed the glaciers of the Tien-Shan Mountains.

CHAPTER FOUR

Visions – Patera's Death

I

I was filled with a lightness such as I have never felt before. A vague, sweet perfume rose from within me, my feelings were utterly transformed, my life was nothing but a small, lively flame. Was I asleep perhaps? Was I awake? Was I dead? From the distance I heard a few sonorous cries, like the distinct tones of broken chords. A rooster crowed, and I was aware of soft organ music, a simple chorale. I looked out and saw far below me a German winter landscape, the nostalgic view of a mountain village; the time seemed to be late afternoon, the organ strains came from the open portal of a small church. The village boys were dragging their sleds through the tumbled snow on the streets; women wrapped in great gaily coloured shawls were coming out of the house of God; bent figures stood under the broad eaves of the wooden roofs weighted with stones. Suddenly I recognized all this; it was the place where I had spent my childhood. Every person was well known to me; with a shock of joy I recognized my parents – my father was wearing his customary brown fur cap. I felt no surprise that most of the people down there were long since dead; on the contrary, I wanted to take part in this reanimated past, but I could not move a limb. I saw ravens flying towards the lake, on whose frozen surface costumed figures moved – then everything grew paler and paler and disappeared.

I saw nothing more in the darkness. The organ music filled me so miraculously that I believed my own existence lay in its strains; new, even richer chords kept entering into this concert – and then without warning the harmony broke off.

The city of Perle stood in its old place. Out of the Palace door stepped Patera, he drew in his breath so deeply and loudly that I could hear him. He stretched himself, and in the process grew taller and taller. Now his head had risen to my level, he could have used the whole Palace as a footstool. His face was covered by his long, falling locks. He shoved the streets apart with monstrous feet; bending over the railroad station, he seized a locomotive. Playing on this as though on a harmonica, he expanded in all directions so that his toy soon became too small. Thereupon he broke off the great tower and on it blew hideous trumpet blasts at the sky. His naked body was terrifying to behold. Now he grew boundlessly, he dug up a volcano from which still hung, snail-shaped and twisted, a granite intestine torn from the entrails of the earth. He put this gigantic instrument to his lips – it roared so that the universe shook. The city had long since disappeared beneath his feet. He stood there upright, his torso reaching to the clouds; his flesh was as if made of hills. He seemed filled with rage! I saw him kneel down in the distance, flocks of birds were caught in his long hair. He waded into an ocean, which barely came to his hips, but it overflowed and covered the whole earth. He paddled in the waters with his fearful arms and caught ships and writhing sea monsters. These he crushed and tossed away. He annihilated the mountains with his feet and they squirted up like mud, great rivers poured into his footprints. He was bent on destroying everything. He spurted boiling urine at far-off mountain huts, and their unsuspecting inhabitants were scalded to death in the steam. He splashed about in the yellow-grey deluge, his glowing body wrapped in clouds of smoke. He threw handfuls of people in my direction. He was a mile away, and they descended in a downpour of corpses. Now a mighty mountain range that extended from west to east began to move. I saw that it was the sleeping American. Patera threw himself at full length on his sleeping enemy. While they struggled, the ocean began to boil up in waves as high as houses. I, however, knew that I was in the hand of Fate and remained calm.

An ocean of blood stretched below me as far as my eyes could reach. The hot purple floods rose higher and higher; my feet were wetted by the rose-coloured foam of the surf. A revolting smell came to my nostrils. The red sea withdrew and decayed before my eyes; ever thicker and darker and blacker grew the blood, while occasionally it shone with all the colours of the rainbow. The viscous fluid parted again and again, and the bottom of the sea was visible, covered with soft filth, exuding abominable vapours.

Patera and the American became interlocked in an amorphous mass; the American had grown completely into Patera. This ungainly body, too large to be encompassed by sight, rolled every which way. The formless creature possessed a protean nature; millions of small, changing faces appeared on its outer surfaces; these talked, sang, and screamed confusedly, and then were reabsorbed. But suddenly peace descended on the monster, and it twisted itself into a gigantic ball – Patera's head. The eyes, big as continents, looked like those of a clairvoyant eagle. Now he had the face of one of the Fates and grew older before my eyes by millions of years. The primeval forest of his hair fell from his head, and the bare skull appeared. Suddenly his head turned to dust; I was looking into a glaring, undifferentiated void ...

Far off I saw the American, who was now of the same terrifying stature as Patera. The eyes in his Caesarean head shot forth diamond lightning as he grappled with himself in a demonic paroxysm; his distended veins writhed in a bluish network round his monstrously swollen neck as he tried to choke himself – in vain! With all his strength he struck himself on the breast, which rang like a steel cymbal; the roar almost stupefied me. Then the monster quickly melted down; only his private parts refused to shrink, and finally he clung like an improbable parasite to his incredibly huge phallus. Then the parasite fell off like a dried wart, and the frightful member crawled over the earth like an immense serpent, writhed like a worm, and growing smaller, disappeared into one of the subterranean passages of the Dream Kingdom.

I could see into the earth; in all these passages there lived a thousand-armed polyp; elastic as rubber, it thrust its tentacles

under all the houses, crept into all the apartments, extended under every bed, disturbed every sleeper with its tiny fine hairs and suckers, went on for miles and miles, coiled up in lumps that shone, now black, now olive, now pale flesh-coloured.

Brightness blinded me once more. Two brilliant violet-coloured meteors rose from opposite directions, approached each other, and collided. The air became a white inferno. Multi-coloured lightning flickered and criss-crossed. Then it seemed as though in a few seconds there emerged a series of magnificently coloured sunny worlds with flowers and creatures such as I have never seen on earth. I felt a sparkling, boisterous life stirring confusedly in my soul. For I no longer saw this with my eyes – no, no, I had forgotten myself. I was completely dissolved in these worlds, I participated in the pain and joy of countless beings. Strange and indescribable enigmas were revealed to me.

Somewhere there was a splintering sound. I heard lumps falling. Soft, boneless masses came into being, female in appearance. An intense formative power invaded them; pinpoints of light sprang up, a thousand harmonies filled the empty spaces. The latter in turn flowed together into an indivisible, luminous, aqueous magma. Where only now a sea had roared, an ice crust formed, and this, cracking, threw out geometric figures in all directions.

I was a part of all this and, with the aid of nameless powers, I comprehended it all. After events that were timeless, eternal, after the tensions of an ever more eruptive transformation, all things changed into their opposites. After parturition came an urge towards a central point – and this was achieved in an instant. A soft and blessed frailty permeated the world. Out of faint understanding grew a power, a yearning. It was an immense, self-assertive strength – it grew dark. In distinct, regular oscillations, the universe shrank to a point.

I knew nothing more.

2

A piercing pain awoke me – fortunately – for the cold had increased to such a degree that I had very nearly frozen to death.

225

There opened before me a broad valley partially filled with the violent mists of the night; a far-flung, jagged mountain range; steep alpine meadows. Above this scene arched a soft green morning sky, and the highest snow-covered mountain peaks already gleamed with rosy light. The mists were parting, and separate cloudlets settled on the dark forests. I rubbed my eyes. What country was I in? Fragrant scents heartened me; suddenly the sky turned red; from behind the eternal snows emerged a glorious fanfare of light – I sprang up with a shout. *That was the sun, the great sun!* But my eyes were too weak for this brilliance. I could not endure the brightness and tried to make my way into the shadow of the mountain. From the distant plain came the sound of horns. A dark column was advancing from the horizon! Beneath me I beheld a large field of ruins covered with innumerable trenches heaped up with stones. Shuddering, I descended into the ravine.

I entered a rock hall; its two rows of mighty columns carved with figures reminded me of a cave temple. In a wide bronze basin burned a naphtha flame, a moving orange-yellow tongue. This was the only light, and it barely penetrated into the far corners, where the blue-eyed ones sat. In my fear I was tempted to withdraw, but I wanted to thank them for rescuing me; I had not yet given an instant's thought to the future.

I could not bring myself to step before this solemn, silent gathering in my tattered clothes. I decided to stay hidden in the shadow of a column. Then I was startled by a hoarse sigh. Something dark was moving in the entrance, a heap of black cloth – this was all I could make out in the uncertain light. Groaning, with lagging steps, this creature laboriously approached. A human being? He kept his veiled head deeply bowed, his gown trailed far behind him. He stopped beside the brazier and threw back the veil. Patera? Yes and no! But it was Patera after all! What transformation had befallen him? As though groaning under a burden beyond his strength, he drew nearer; his striking ability to change his appearance at will seemed to have deserted him; now his face expressed only weariness – a nameless weariness. His eyes were half closed. There was something human about him, and I no longer felt the slightest dread. The dead, waxen hue had disappeared, and

once more he resembled the person I had known at school. As though crushed by some ineluctable suffering, he dragged himself hesitantly past me towards the blue-eyed ones. The latter had risen and were awaiting him like statues in a half-circle in front of the brazier. One of the oldest approached and handed him a small vessel, a vase, so far as I could identify it; then the old man fell to the earth in front of the Master; the others had already prostrated themselves and hidden their faces. A deep religious emotion overcame me so that I involuntarily fell to my knees and folded my hands.

With heavy feet Patera described a circle around the burning fountain, and descended several steps to a small semicircular opening behind it. Out of this streamed a light of such unimaginable intensity that I had to hold both hands in front of my eyes. By contrast, the naphtha flame burned with a troubled, smoky light. The Master turned towards us, who lay there motionless on the floor, hardly daring to look at him because of the blazing light. Patera's eyes had now lost all trace of their uncanniness; a large, dark, moist, gleaming blue, they embraced us all with a look of infinite kindness. Then I saw once again that inconceivably pure profile brilliantly lighted against the dark background. With an abrupt motion of his head, he threw his long, thick locks over his shoulders, and disappeared. Slowly the black train of the robe was drawn after him. The bronze door clanged shut.

All rose and walked to the door; I too came out of my hiding place. In the next room, something singular must have been going on. There was a noise as though columns of men were in motion. Suddenly the flame in the brazier flared up wildly, turned green, and expired. We were plunged into utter darkness.

From within came ghastly, long-sustained screams that so wrung my heart that, quivering, I had to hold my hands to my ears in order to retain my senses.

They were piercing tones, as though from a giant saw eating into rock. Finally they turned into the deep, hoarse groaning of a wounded carnivore – this too, little by little, became weaker, and ended in a horrible rattle.

When we opened the door, we found the chamber dimly

illuminated in a bluish light and everything inside it in ruins – melted metal, eroded stones, split boulders. And there – the Master ...!

Twisted into a bundle and thrust against the wall, he lay face down in one corner as though hurled there by some alien power.

The crumpled figure seemed astonishingly small and feeble. The Master and this diminished object must be two entirely different things. I could not grasp it. Could this piteous example of decrepitude conceivably be he who had but now entered this room?

An unimaginable death struggle had deformed the body of the most powerful of earth's creatures. But the mightily arched head, though soot-covered and filthy, was the same that we all knew so well.

The old men lifted him up. When they had washed the body its rigidity slowly relaxed. The distortion disappeared from the face. The eyelids could now be closed, and the rictus gave place to the most exalted expression of peace. *Patera's dark brown locks had turned white in death.*

Laid out on the floor, the corpse appeared markedly longer than before, but to my horror it continued to grow – by jerks, clicking, as though from a secret superfluity of strength. It was some time before this growth ceased. In relation to the length of the body, the mighty head now seemed almost delicate, encircled by its pale mane – marmorial, cold, like the statue of some god of the ancient world.

The body was indescribably beautiful. I beheld a charm and purity of form so great that I could not conceive how anything of the kind could exist upon our earth. I stood before him, the Master, in my rags, and for the first and last time saw true majesty. None of the blue-eyed ones ventured by any action to disturb his silent unapproachability. One after another they went out. Once more I was the last; holding my breath and walking on tiptoe, I stole away. The blue-eyed ones left the mountain; I have never seen one of them since.

I sat down on the lowest step of the stairway, and a spasm of weeping shook me.

CHAPTER FIVE

Conclusion

A wide, wide field of ruins; piles of rubble, a morass, broken bricks – the gigantic refuse heap of a city. It is still wrapped in the bluish mist of early morning. The rocky mountains in the background are beginning to turn gold in the light of the rising sun. The sky, though still darkened, is cloudless. A bareheaded man with a heavy piece of luggage on his shoulder is making his way with firm, elastic strides through the rubble. He is wearing a narrow-tailed morning coat with wide satin lapels, and on his muscular legs are tight pantaloons in the Viennese fashion of the sixties. But these clothes are marred by burns and bloodstains and are torn in many places. He is like a housebreaker trying to escape with his booty. Now he places his burden on a large stone, which seems to offer itself as a table. He pulls off the dirty cover – a brand-new leather steamer trunk with polished brass fittings stands there. From this, Hercules Bell removes a modish outfit together with modern underwear and begins to change. Then he shaves himself carefully, examines his face in a hand-mirror, gets out a new, broad-brimmed panama, and lights his short pipe; a thin bamboo cane with a gold crook puts the final touch to his toilet.

No one could have guessed from his energetic manner and tanned skin the hardships and adventures he had been through; only his hair, formerly pitch-black, has turned a little grey at the temples. Thus the American goes to meet the approaching Europeans.

Lieutenant General Rudinoff had sent a detachment of riflemen ahead as advance guard. The soldiers, making use of all possible cover, crept up to the still smoking ruins of the wall, but with the best will in the world they could not discover a single enemy. On hearing their report, the general determined to advance. Through a field glass a small fort had been discovered, built on a rocky spur projecting from the mountain wall. He ordered several batteries to unlimber and train their guns on the elevated fortification. Then he sent an officer accompanied by a trumpeter and two Cossacks bearing a white flag, to present the enemy with an ultimatum, by the terms of which they were to surrender at once as prisoners of war. All weapons and all possessions were to be delivered to the Russians; any European citizens held in subjection were to be set free immediately. But all the intermediary found was an abandoned area covered with stones, most of which had been ground down to sand. Here and there, to be sure, a few charred timbers still glowed amid the rubble; a lengthy examination of the place did not seem indicated, for the ground was sinking and growing muddy. The ruins were slowly subsiding into the depths.

There was no one there to whom the ultimatum could be delivered.

The general was greatly displeased at this report. There had been all too much confident rejoicing at the prospect of rich treasuries.

And so it was decided to advance to the mountain, exercising the greatest precaution of course, for some of the staff officers held stubbornly to their belief in a pre-arranged ambush, massed batteries, and that sort of thing.

Thus it was that they found the little door in the mountain wall, and on the bottom step of the stairway they found me lying completely unconscious. It is to this happy circumstance that I owe my life.

They treated me most cordially. The journalists, who knew of me from earlier times, demanded constant interviews. Various newspapers insisted on publishing my photograph together with views of the place where the Dream City had stood. I was too weak to meet all the requests that poured in on me, and I referred them to Mr Bell, who had now managed to join the Europeans.

No trace of the temple inside the mountain was found; the rock strata had shifted and blocked all the entrances. The geologist attached to the expedition shook his head in very droll fashion at my suggestion that this sort of change had occurred. I could see that no one believed me – and this incredulity was strengthened by the American, who swaggered about boasting that he had put an end to the whole Patera humbug by destroying the wax doll.

By the way, we two were not the only ones to survive the catastrophe. In the nearby virgin forest some wandering soldiers ran down a crowd of half-naked creatures sitting in the trees and talking and gesticulating violently. They turned out to be citizens of the Dream City, owners of grocery stores. Later on, I learned that they had recovered with amazing speed and had achieved great riches in the big cities of northern and western Europe.

And then as the soldiers were poking about in the ruins, they found a dissected body in a pile of hot ashes; it was dusted off and assumed to be a mummy. The regimental doctor, however, discovered there was still a trace of life in it; he exerted himself and fanned the tiny spark into a flame. Everyone rushed to see the rescued person who, it quickly appeared, was female. A high-ranking Russian officer, bearer of an ancient name, recognized her as his aunt, the Princess von X. He had her properly attired and adorned and took her back to Europe with him.

I myself made the journey home in the company of a doctor by way of Tashkent and, arriving in Germany, I found it necessary first of all to visit a sanatorium in order to convalesce and to accustom myself once more to the old conditions of life, especially to the sunlight. It was years before I felt any confidence in my surroundings again and could pursue my profession as usual.

The participants in the expedition, after sending a telegram, TERRITORY OF DREAM STATE COMPLETELY OCCUPIED, issued no further statements – as was proper for Europeans who had been made to appear ridiculous.

The phenomenon of Patera remains unexplained. Perhaps the blue-eyed ones were the true masters and, through magical powers, galvanized a lifeless Patera puppet and created and destroyed the Dream Kingdom to suit their pleasure.

The American is still alive and known to all the world.

Epilogue

Man is but a self-confident nothing.
– JULIUS BAHNSEN

In the sanatorium I was compelled again and again to reflect upon the magic of the mighty drama through which I had lived. My capacity for dreaming was obviously hypertrophied, and the dreams threatened to overwhelm my mind.

I lost my identity in them. They often reverted to historical periods. Almost every night brought me events far off in time, and I am firmly convinced that these dream images were very closely connected with experiences of my forebears, whose psychic convulsions left organic traces that were perhaps transmitted by heredity. Deeper dream layers opened, and I lost myself in animal existences – yes, in a less than semi-conscious way, in the primal elements. These dreams were abysses in which I saw myself being helplessly engulfed. They ceased when the weather improved and we had fine clear nights.

The days now passed monotonously. I was a prey to in-activity and boredom. I wished gradually to restore my strength and to get back to work again. However, I realized that I was no longer good for anything. By contrast with the Dream State, reality seemed to be a repulsive caricature. The only thing that rekindled my interest was the thought of expiring, of death. I embraced it with all the ardour of which I was capable.

I loved death ecstatically; I was filled with transports as

though I had been a woman. In the moonlit nights that followed I gave myself to him completely, I gazed upon him, touched him, and enjoyed supernatural blisses. I was the intimate of this prodigious Master, this glorious Prince of the Universe, whose beauty is indescribable for all who have felt him. He was my last, my greatest, happiness. In every fallen leaf, in the damp sod, in the soil itself, I recognized him. To surrender to his catlike wooing, to feel his ravages as amorous embraces – this made me happy. My predilection to this day for half-wilted flowers is significant.

I thought of my own death as the greatest celestial joy, the beginning of a perpetual wedding night.

How all struggle against him – and how kindly disposed he is! In every face I sought eagerly for his signs; in the wrinkles and furrows of old age I recognized his kisses. He seemed always new to me; how exquisite were his colours! His glances were so glistening and so seductive that the strongest were forced to submit to him, then he threw off his disguise and the dying man saw him uncloaked, surrounded by a blaze of diamonds, mirrored in their thousand glittering facets.

Afterwards, when I ventured back into life again, I discovered that my god possessed only a partial dominion. In the greatest matters and the least he shared sovereignty with an

adversary, who wanted life. The forces of attraction and repulsion, the poles of the earth with their currents, the alternation of the seasons, day and night, black and white – these are battles.

True hell consists in the fact that this contradictory double game has its continuation within us. Love itself has a central point, *'inter faeces et urinam'*. Sublime occasions can fall victim to ridicule, contempt, irony.

The demiurge is a hybrid.

ALFRED KUBIN'S
AUTOBIOGRAPHY

Alfred Kubin's Autobiography

NOTE: Alfred Kubin wrote an autobiography to accompany the second edition of *The Other Side* in 1917, and as the book was re-issued from time to time, he added to it, carrying the story of his life almost to its end. The present version of it, which not only has great intrinsic interest but also gives rare insights into his writing and his art, includes a supplementary section never before printed and constitutes the first publication of his complete autobiography.

I

I was born on April 10, 1877, in Leitmeritz, a small city in northern Bohemia. I have no recollection whatever of the first two years of my childhood. That I was an infant given to bawling my parents assured me often enough later on. However, from the early part of my third year I retain memories of toys, green arbours flooded with sunlight, and of my mother's pale, narrow face. My father, a former officer who had become a government surveyor after the campaign of '66, first came to my attention in Salzburg; he had been compelled to abandon his small family for two years in order to carry out duties in distant Dalmatia. My mother and I had just settled ourselves comfortably in our new home when one fine day this, to me unwelcome, character broke in upon us. The gift of a red Dalmatian cap led to a reconciliation, my jealousy abated, and we achieved an uneasy truce. Beginning with the Salzburg period, my memories increase in number and become more orderly

A self-portrait of the artist, a lithograph privately printed by him for friends. In this instance he added pen and ink drawings (at bottom) that showed his preoccupation with death.

and complete. I was a most unruly child, and my habit of running away to the homes of acquaintances in the neighbourhood, and sometimes to those of strangers, caused my mother much pain – and, as I recall, it resulted in pain to me, too. At the beginning of my fifth year my father was transferred to Zell am See, and this tiny, high mountain village became the real scene of my childhood.

School effectively spoiled this period. What I hated most, continue to hate, and will always hate, is external constraint. I wanted to lead an unplanned, untroubled life, and in trying to do so continually encountered the opposition of grown-ups and of my older companions as well. And so it was only natural that, in my weakness, I should resort to cunning and trickery in order to be able to follow my inclinations undisturbed.

It was at such times, alone and in complete secrecy, that I gave free rein to my suppressed sadistic instincts. Lying on the ground in a hidden corner of the garden, I would stage ingenious scenes of torture with any wretched creatures unlucky enough to come into my power, and I must confess that, horrible though I find this today and often though I have repented it later on, nevertheless at the time it gave me a feeling of acute pleasure. After a short while I lost my joy in this horrid pastime. Only while I was at play, alone or with strangers, did I feel completely happy, self-confident, and free. And what splendid opportunities there were for that! As though in a long, long dream I think back today to all those barns, stalls, workshops, and mills, to the sandy shore of the lake, and the forest, which seemed to me a single, inviting moss-upholstered dwelling. We constructed huts in the high mountain meadows or set off in hot pursuit of robber chiefs. Alas, the joyous hours of play always sped swiftly, whereas the five daily hours in the classroom seemed to defy all concepts of measurable time. I must in fairness admit that the teacher and the catechist too, as soon as they revealed a human side, instantly won my confidence. And when I recall today the emotion that filled me during Holy Week at the reverend gentleman's descriptions of the suffering and death of Jesus Christ, I am still overwhelmingly moved.

And above all the church, the ancient church of Zell! What

countless times has this shadow-filled edifice heard my sighs, my good resolutions, and my yearnings, sometimes with silent rejection and then again, as I imagined, consentingly; and often it has seen my youthful heart uplifted in mystic exaltation and true contemplation.

It is true that this gloomy Gothic house of God with its solemn pomp was an object of awe, but in that small, vividly Catholic village it was possible for schoolboys like us to be on truly intimate and comfortable terms with it. Some of my friends were acolytes; I helped pull the rope of the big bell, pumped the organ, exerted myself as a chorister, and very often was thoroughly bored with the endless services. Nevertheless the years of my boyhood were so thoroughly permeated with the pervasive scent of religious mystery that I only need enter a handsome church and smell the incense for those youthful emotions to leap into life again. Church and school laid inexorable restraints upon the infant brute. I had no fear of my mother's punishments. She was already consumptive and very nervous; much of her time was devoted to music, no doubt in memory of earlier triumphs as a pianist. My father, who was very often absent at the times of my misdeeds, restrained his heavy hand during this period in the interests of peace and quiet in the household.

In the meantime I had acquired two sisters, who were a source of great irritation to me since they were constantly being held up as models of behaviour.

And so the lovely hours of my first days in Zell became rarer and rarer; I suffered almost constantly from bad conscience, if only from trivialities such as clothes torn or soiled in the heat of play, or some ill-starred expedition into the neighbours' orchards. My greatest joy at this time came from collections of fairy tales; I was also much interested in natural history and devoted my spare time to fishing and catching birds.

Then came a period when I covered countless sheets of paper with pencil sketches and paintings. From the beginning I had a natural tendency towards exaggeration and fantasy; a cow with four horns always seemed to me more interesting than those with two, which could be seen in those days at every street corner in Zell am See. My childish drawings corresponded accurately with this inclination. They teemed with magicians, comic and terrifying cattle, landscapes consisting entirely of fire – in short, the seed of the whole later Kubin was contained in them.

I was ten years old when death freed my mother from illness. She was the first person I had seen die. I was present when she received extreme unction; afterwards she said farewell to my father and me. Her death throes made a permanent impression on me, but much stronger were the terror and confusion inspired in me by my father's complete despair; he lifted his wife's long, emaciated body from the bed and ran weeping with it through the whole house as though crying out for help. At that time he was still an image of masculine strength and beauty, and although we were often in straitened circumstances, almost poor, I considered him through all the years of my childhood a rich man and most certainly the cleverest man in the whole world. Since he was usually reserved in manner and spoke in a low voice, his completely helpless sorrow was so uncharacteristic that it frightened me. I myself had never thought of mamma's death, rather I had believed that she would, of course, go on being ill, but that she would always be with us. Her loss did not penetrate to my consciousness, and I could not understand why I was so much pitied by so many people.

At the end of a year of mourning, my father married again, choosing as his bride my mother's sister. In this autobiographical sketch, I can safely pass over the following period up to my admission to the *Gymnasium* in Salzburg. There is only one essential point I must touch on here. I was just eleven and a half years old when I became involved in sexual play with an older woman, something that excited me tremendously and cast its shadows as far as my early manhood. One fine September day I found myself settled in Salzburg for the purpose of attending the Latin school there. In my first year, thanks to my excellent memory, everything went splendidly, but in my second year I failed completely. Mathematics and Latin were my particular bugbears – I tried to substitute novels about Indians and desert islands for these hated subjects. In religion, history, and the natural sciences, on the other hand, I always made satisfactory progress.

Salzburg is a wonderful city, and its buildings, evidences of its mighty past, are a constant element in my dreams. When my stepmother died in childbed at the end of a single year of marriage, and I soon thereafter returned home miserably as a failed scholar who had not yet completed primary school, I experienced for the first time a period of real hell. My father, himself deeply unhappy and confused, had lost all confidence in me. I was no longer permitted to come into his presence and had to live completely alone. I could no longer accompany him on his bird-catching expeditions or help him with his flower garden, to which he was much devoted; I was no longer permitted to come and listen when he told my sisters stories in his marvellously realistic way; woe to me if he ever caught me laughing happily! On these occasions I was severely caned and cuffed on the ear. To add to my woes, my younger sister's nurse, a rough peasant girl, had charge of the household and neglected it. She was a spiteful person who inflated my small misdeeds into crimes and completely hoodwinked my father. He himself was lonely, living only for his sorrow, and he punished me without question and without mercy, so that my life now became unbearable. At this time, when I had no human being to turn to, when Christ and all the saints turned a deaf ear, I became completely withdrawn; I took my beatings with bowed head, and in my heart I felt only hate, hate, hate towards my father and all men. Oh, if only I could have murdered them!

Every day I got up very early and took a long walk in the mountains in the grey dawn, so that children and grown-ups might not witness the shameful sight of a student expelled from Latin school.

This time of isolation, however, proved remarkably stimulating to my fantasy. From the start I had found keen pleasure in dwelling in imagination on catastrophe and the upsurge of primeval forces; it was like an intoxication, accompanied by a prickly feeling along my spine. A thunder storm, a conflagration, a flood caused by a mountain stream – to observe these was one of my greatest joys; I was always an interested onlooker at fights, arrests, and cattle fairs. However I took at least an equally lively interest in the play of controlled force and the evidences of power; it is easy to imagine how I was electrified by the music of the troops that occasionally marched through Zell; whatever I heard about military life struck a responsive chord in my breast. We saw little enough in our small corner of the world – a runaway Arabian steed once, and occasionally in summer time a general (in uniform!) was entertained as a guest. The Emperor Napoleon was a demigod in my eyes, and I only regretted that he had not been an Austrian. How I would have loved to talk to my father about him, but that was not possible, for we were enemies, and I was the blot on the family escutcheon.

There were all sorts of other things that aroused my burning curiosity; for example – corpses. The fisherman Hölzl, my benefactor, who was the gravedigger and a jack of all trades, quite often dragged decomposed bodies out of the lake, for there were many careless persons who drowned there. This was the origin of my admitted interest in grisly scenes. In my eyes, death was incomprehensible and astounding. How did it happen? Familiar men, women, children ceased to be seen; they were said to be ill; after a longer or shorter period, one could go to view them in their homes, where they lay stretched out stiff, stark, and yellow – dead. I also observed the operations of the butchers and tanners, but now with a clear, cold curiosity and no longer with the demonic feelings of pleasure of my earlier years.

In the hope that I could learn something useful, my father sent me to the trade school in Salzburg. He wanted to see what could be made of me – a stucco-worker or something of that sort, perhaps. So now I was in Salzburg again for two years, and I attended trade school regularly, mindful of my father's admonitions and his threat that I would not be allowed back into his house but would be sent to a reform school if I failed to make progress. Moreover, I did very well, even managing to make friends with mathematics, in which I received honour grades; my worst subject was freehand drawing.

In the meantime my father had married for a third time, a young lady from Klagenfurt, and through this circumstance I had the chance of becoming an apprentice to a landscape photographer, who was now my 'uncle.' So I said farewell to my schoolbooks, whose margins were decorated with drawings of campaigns, hunts, tortures, and the like, and entered my uncle's large business in Klagenfurt. Here too I kept my innermost hopes and thoughts strictly to myself, having had my wits well sharpened by the recent years of harsh treatment. And I worked hard, especially during the first years, to do everything according to my uncle's wishes and thus some time to become a competent photographer.

I regarded my uncle in a certain sense as a substitute father, yet because of his chilly manner I always felt some dread of him; sometimes, to be sure, he could be enchanting, so that more than once I wondered whether I might not fall on his neck and tell him everything, everything that oppressed or delighted me. However, I continually postponed this action, for I felt no real confidence in him; my uncle remained inwardly alien to me. Then, too, he was usually away on trips and would send us great numbers of his photographic plates to be developed and printed. And I must say that these four years, which I spent amid many thousands of pictures, greatly enhanced my appreciation of landscapes. The sea, Italy, the Orient – things that I had never actually seen – left an accurate and enduring impression on my mind, an imperishable, ideal standard. In other respects, however, I was in bad shape.

It is obvious that in any large-size business division of labour increases efficiency of production. This principle, which was introduced into my uncle's operation, had the disadvantage for me that I was assigned only the completely non-essential chores and therefore, after four years of work, had not even begun to learn how to produce a photograph, although this is no art but simply a mechanical process whose principles can be mastered in two weeks by anyone of average intelligence. However, during my first few years I had exhaustive training in sweeping rooms, making fires, washing, and the like. Later, to be sure, I was brought into the laboratory for a few minor chores. But I learned practically nothing. It was only many years later when I had made the acquaintance of the managers of certain world-famous companies specializing in reproductions that I acquired, incidentally and almost in a spirit of play, all the essentials of this fine technique. On the other hand, in Klagenfurt, my knowledge of the nature of human experience made rapid progress. As a result of my odd situation as nephew and apprentice at once, there arose a continuing strain which, combined with the idiocy of my menial labour, effectively put an end to any desire to become a professional photographer.

During this period I was overcome with a feverish desire to read, and would spend whole nights immersed in some exciting novel. Finally my complete indifference towards everything connected with the business could be clearly read in my face, and my uncle's interest in me declined visibly and irrevocably. Nevertheless I shall remain grateful to him for what little understanding he imparted to me during my scullery-maid's existence.

At the end of my third year as apprentice I was given a monthly salary; I was now a junior assistant, seventeen years old, and at least did not have to spend every evening at the family table. It was enough of a good thing to be on a treadmill from seven in the morning to eight at night, not to mention being constantly harried into the bargain.

There followed a year of licence. It began with high-flown, idealized infatuations, which regularly remained unreciprocated and so dwindled away in sexual dreams. Up to then I had had an outspoken contempt for the female sex, excepting only well-preserved, mature women of thirty to forty years of age. Now I began to take an interest in all young females as well.

In addition to these emotional outbursts, I enjoyed my freedom to the fullest. I bought a bicycle, kept snakes and all sorts of reptiles in cages, and made a habit of frequenting inns and joining in general revelry. Excessive drinking was never my habit, a half-litre of beer or wine being the limit.

During this last year in Klagenfurt, my indulgences were easily concealed. Since my uncle was usually absent, full beer-pots were often circulating in the workrooms before noon; drinking songs, choruses, and solos rang out; it was a merry sink of inquity by day – the nights were full of dark secrets. From time to time the 'master' arrived and quickly restored discipline. In the long run, however, my health was undermined by the many nights of dissipation; I grew pale, bad-tempered, and felt quite miserable. I was afflicted with a constant hangover, and this very appreciably reduced my joy in this form of indulgence.

Now I turned to books once more and by accident came upon Schopenhauer's *Parerga*. This work gripped me to an incredible degree; in fascination I recognized a completely original way of thought; I had had no inkling that anything of the sort existed. I brooded over it, tested the conclusions again and again, and ended by becoming completely confused.

At this time, a hypnotist was holding much-talked-of seances in a large public hall. I considered the whole thing a gross fraud; nevertheless I went there one evening in the company of some reserve officers who liked me because of my trenchant wit. In great astonishment I saw with my own eyes how sane, grown-up people crowed and grunted like animals at his command. Then I enthusiastically volunteered as a subject; in a few minutes the man, a former locksmith with a rough, common-looking face, had me completely in his power. On his suggestion I quite literally gave finished dramatic performances – he had never before had such a success.

In the next few days my friends and I carried on a series of these experiments, which interested me greatly, but which resulted in giving the finishing blow to my nerves. In short, I became more and more confused and was absolutely no use at my daily work. I was nervous and extremely irritable; I had nasty rows with the other employees, for a casual, stupid joke would put me in a towering rage; I felt a constant excited quivering inside me, as though all restraints had fallen away. This could not be allowed to go on! A sombre distaste for life overcame me, and after a violent scene with one of my colleagues I reached the desperate resolve of putting an end to an existence that seemed to be useless and wasted. With this in mind, I bought a cheap old revolver and set out for the distant scene of my childhood with the intention of shooting myself on my mother's grave. Today I have to smile sadly when I think back on that romantic crisis of my youth. The first thing that happened, after a few hours on the train, was that the engine was halted by a flood, and so it was only after two days of detours that I came late at night to Zell am See, much sobered but all the more determined in purpose. Arriving at my mother's grave, I prayed to dear God, just to be on the safe side, and in the same spirit besought my mother's soul to give me firmness of resolve and to shield me from cowardice. Then I waited for the clock to strike again in the hope that help would arrive from some quarter; but no one came, and the thought of going straight over to my father's house, only to be sent back to Klagenfurt and having to beg everyone's forgiveness, was too much for me. I rejected it as too humiliating, as simply impossible. Placing the muzzle of the revolver against my right temple, where, after consulting a drawing in an anatomy book, I had made a scratch with a needle so that I would not fail to hit the brain, I pulled the trigger. But the ancient rusty weapon missed fire, and I lacked the moral strength to try again. I became wretchedly sick. After I had lain in bed in an inn for a few hours, I went to my parents' house, where my father – without further reproaches, by the way – sent me back to Klagenfurt forthwith.

In the meantime my uncle had returned from one of his journeys and had been told of my flight; turning a deaf ear to my pleas and promises, he relentlessly turned me out. Now I was quite alone, I was nothing, and I possessed nothing. That I had learned the trade of photography I read for the first time in the letter of reference I was given.

The worst of it was that I had now lost another important opportunity. As can be seen from the foregoing, I had not yet earned my right to my one-year voluntary military service; it was my father's plan, since he himself had been an officer, to have me take a one-year course with an elderly major whom he knew. For the time being, relatives in Styria took me in. At that point, however, I decided to give up the one year's service and to enlist in the army as a volunteer. I sent in my application and waited. Finally it was acted on, and I was ordered to report to the enlistment board in Graz. But the army would have none of me; the army doctor said I had better wait a few years.

It was a crucial moment for me when I stepped before the presiding staff officer, stark naked and holding myself as straight as possible, and urgently begged him to accept me then. I told him that later on I planned to become a military cartographer and that I had the most ardent enthusiasm for all aspects of military life.

My request was granted, and the very next evening I was given my orders and took the train for Laibach, the capital of Carniola, to join my regiment. There I served for exactly eighteen days and actually felt much better than in the preceding eighteen years. For here subordination and constraint were the order of the day, and I never had the feeling of being the only one to be oppressed. Moreover, it was a wholly new and interesting life that I saw and I was often swept by a feeling of happiness when I reflected that I, though only a common soldier, was privileged nevertheless to belong to so mighty an establishment as the Austrian Army. Sometimes it seemed as though I literally felt the inseparable bond of complete submission to duty and honour that extended from the Emperor through all grades down to me, the least of all. With cheerful determination I carried out even the meanest chores, such as scrubbing floors, and my open, friendly behaviour as well as my intelligence, which showed in my brief meetings with my superiors, brought me the good opinion of all during this brief period. Alas, with the best will in the world I could not stand severe exertion or heavy labour; I often had to be helped, and I tired easily.

Fate had decided that I was not to remain a soldier. The external cause of the new turn in my fortunes was the sudden death of our divisional commandant. Amid the general confusion of getting dress uniforms ready for the funeral, my extreme nervousness attracted attention; all I know is that I felt the greatest anxiety that everything should go right and that my company should cut a good figure. When the time came for the burial, my captain ordered me to remain in barracks. I watched through the window as the regiment marched off, and the funeral music seemed to pour through me like a warm, agreeable stream. I threw myself on my new straw mattress and lost consciousness.

A delirium, which no doubt had lain dormant for some time, now took hold of me; only faint and shadowy memories remain of its crisis, which was accompanied by frequent convulsions. The notion that I was a Bourbon prince living on the island of Borneo superimposed itself on the actual circumstances of my life. The nervous predisposition to this illness had no doubt been inherited from my mother, who had often suffered similar convulsions. I was taken to the garrison hospital in Graz and remained there for three months in this abnormal state. I shall always remember the commandant of that great hospital for his truly fatherly and benevolent attitude towards me during this grave illness. After I was once more in possession of my faculties, I remained for another full month in the hospital to recuperate and to be under observation. In the process, of course, I did some observing of my own, very acutely, as a matter of fact, watching all the miserable sick and dying and the suicides that were brought in – in short, the whole operation – and I did my best to make myself useful, writing out charts, taking temperatures, and doing similar chores.

When my father finally came to get me, I saw from the great joy he displayed that he must after all really love me. Outbreaks of emotion have always been very painful to me – I believe they should be repressed. But my father must actually have suffered frightfully from my illness; perhaps because he saw in it Heaven's punishment for his harshness towards his only son.

I was now made comfortable in my parents' house and treated with every consideration, although the whole family suffered a great deal from my extreme excitability, which at first regularly resulted in convulsions. I once more ate well, took long walks, and as a pastime copied pictures from the *Gartenlaube* (a popular family magazine).

As for my military career, that was, of course, over and done with.

2

A friend of the family, an elderly lawyer who had seen my drawings, advised my father to send me to the artists' Academy in Munich. Since at that time I had inherited from my grandparents a few thousand gulden which could be used for my education, my father put the proposal up to me and I greeted it with enthusiasm. I knew that I had a certain talent for drawing, but it had never entered my mind that this gift might be the foundation of my future profession. And so I went off blithely in the spring of 1898 to Munich, where I rented a small room and entered the private school of the late Schmidt-Reutte. There I busily made drawings of nudes and heads, and Schmidt remained my only teacher, for when two years later I enrolled in the Gysis drawing class it was only to please my father, who wanted me to have some connection with a government institution. I went there very seldom and did not exert myself at the Academy.

Before going to Munich I had never consciously observed a true work of art. Sacred pictures bored me, and I could not imagine that anyone could find pleasure in painting them. I conceived of artists as people living romantic lives very much like those of circus folk. In my home, where the traditions of an old military and official family prevailed, art was almost never mentioned. Of course, I had often seen drawings of pretty girls in the *Gartenlaube*, as well as monastery scenes and scenes of peasant life; by contrast I found the battle pictures in that magazine far more interesting.

On my second day in Munich I entered a great gallery for the first time in my life, the Alte Pinakothek; it was a turning point in my life. I felt as though dissolved in delight and amazement, and ventured only on tiptoe from hall to hall. I was completely overcome by such an immense accomplishment and such a radiant outburst of the human spirit; without eating or growing tired, I stayed from nine in the morning until closing time at six in those rooms that seemed to me heaven itself. No one work of art stood out for me, giving me a dominant impression; on the contrary, it seemed to me as though those hundreds of pictures had been painted by a single hand. Finally I had to leave, but I could not sleep at all that night. Never since has a gallery had such an overwhelming effect on me.

My first years in Munich will always remain among my fondest memories. The contrast with my wretched past was very sharp; most of all, the removal of all outward coercion did me good; I was free, and no one could order me around. The torments of my earlier life as well as the feeling of my own absolute uselessness and unworthiness, which had been instilled and constantly confirmed in me, had distressed me very greatly. My new existence was full of cheer, and I was aware from the start of a happy desire to work. I formed a close acquaintance with two fellow students who lived in a studio in the back of the house where I lived; there we held our interminable artists' arguments (the works of Stuck played a leading part in them), there we brought our food and managed to do the cooking for one another. We played music, drew caricatures, read, and made love – in short, we led a free existence modelled on Murger's *Vie de Bohème*.

There is not much to report of my studies during these first few years. I worked conscientiously, like all the others, in accordance with the rigid system of our exemplary teacher, which consisted principally in the recognition of proper measure and proportion derived from sculptural anatomy; all trickery with tones, any experimenting with shadow effects or highlighting was strictly forbidden. No pulse-quickening model ever appeared, and when now and then a female nude was inserted in the series of athletes, she was instructive, to be sure, but from any other point of view a total loss. The studies we produced were therefore pretty much alike, although of course, as in every other school, we had one or two 'geniuses'.

There is more to be said of an artists' club that had its stronghold in the Café Elite in Schellingstrasse, and which none of its former members is likely ever to forget. It was called Die Sturmfackel, an independent society that, grotesquely enough, maintained that its chief purpose was the suppression of individualism.

Of the club's members the following made names for themselves: Ernst Stern, Weissgerber, Salzman, Levi, Finetti, Korzendörfer, Cardinaux, and several others. In its heyday, however, around the year 1901–1902, no fewer than thirty choice spirits bowed to the strange ceremonial statutes of the club. Many of them alas, are now dead, among them the much admired E. Mantels, the future Arcus Troll of the cabaret Die

Elf Scharfrichter. If we were not brought together by any one artistic tendency, as is the custom in Paris – for secretly each of us was an individualist – at least we all profited from the boisterous, witty, and intellectual atmosphere that prevailed. Each felt sincere interest in everyone else and was concerned for his welfare, a fact that was of particular value to me, for I was much in need of confidants.

This prolonged happy time was ample compensation for everything that had happened, and it gave me courage and strength for the future. Despite all sorts of meetings and festivities, we managed to accomplish a lot of work, and each had as much time to himself as he wanted; for me this was a real boon.

When I entered the Gysis class at the Academy at the end of two years, I found my artistic destiny. This, however, did not come about in the Academy, but in a quite different fashion.

I had never forgotten the enormous impression my first visit to the Pinakothek had made on me, but from my unbounded admiration for the old masters there had sprung a deep feeling of discouragement. Photographs of the works of Holbein, Velasquez, and others hung in the school, and I had them daily before my eyes. But it seemed to me as though my works had not the slightest connection with the purposes of these masters. My portraits and nude studies had nothing whatever to do with the demonic surge and power that were what fascinated me in painting. To be sure, the canvases were not bad, but even if they had been a thousand times better, they would still have been something completely different. Modern paintings meant almost nothing to me in comparison with ancient ones; they simply aroused my respect for the diligence and skill they displayed. I was very depressed, and in order to stifle this mood I gave myself up to all kinds of adventures and diversions. This only made matters worse, and my way of life became utterly repulsive to me, until finally I sought refuge in my old love, philosophy.

I returned to Schopenhauer and in a few days devoured his principal works with intense ardour. In my desperate mood I found his pessimistic *Weltanschauung* the only correct one, and I revelled in his ideas – with the consequence that my universal discontent only grew greater. In a mad and moody temper I wrote down, mostly during my walks in the Englische Garten, all sorts of philosophical notions, and finally I worked out a weird cosmogony. I shall set down here the strange central idea it contained.

My conception was that an eternal, extratemporal principle – I called it the Father – for some unfathomable reason created Self-consciousness – the Son – together with the world, which was inseparable from him. In this scheme I myself was, of course, the Son, who deceives himself, torments and persecutes himself as long as this is well pleasing to his true and gigantic Father, who spontaneously creates him as a sort of mirror image. Such a Son can therefore disappear at any instant along with his world and be assimilated into the superexistence of the Father. There is always only *one* Son, and from his conscious point of view one might say, comparatively and allegorically, that this whole deceptive and tormenting process takes place in order that the Father may for the first time observe and measure his own omnipotent clarity and eternity by contrast with this confusion. During the hours of the night, I filled dozens of notebooks with philosophic and poetic elaborations of the theme of 'The Son as World Wanderer'. These I kept secret from the intrusive curiosity of my friends and only showed them and read from them to a single person. I still have most of them, but they were written in such a feverish scribble that they are no longer decipherable. This febrile and tumultuous period came to an end with a severe inflammation of the throat that kept me in my room for a number of days. During that time I drew a great deal and managed to get down on paper spectral inspirations and caricatures that corresponded exactly with my wretched state.

At this time I had a special friend, a very intelligent musician, who was particularly valuable to me as an antidote to Die Sturmfackel. Visiting me while I was ill, he saw my new drawings. He said they reminded him in many respects of Klinger's engravings, which he strongly recommended to me as examples. And so as soon as I was well enough I sought out his collection of copper plates and saw the series called *Fund eines Handschuhs*. I looked, and quivered with delight. Here a whole new art was thrown open to me, which offered free play for the imaginative expression of every conceivable world of feeling. Before putting the engravings away I swore that I would dedicate my life to the creation of similar works.

I wandered about the city with an overflowing heart, and in the evening went to a variety show. I was seeking impersonal yet noisy surroundings that would lessen the steadily increasing pressure within me. There a psychological event took place that proved to be a turning point for me. Even today I do not completely understand it, although I have thought about it a great deal. When the little orchestra struck up the prelude, suddenly all my surroundings seemed to grow clearer and sharper, as though seen in a different light. All at once, in the faces of those sitting around me, I saw something strangely mixed, part animal, part human; all noises were oddly alien, separated from their sources; they sounded to me like a derisive general conversation carried on in threatening whispers, which I could not understand but which nevertheless seemed clearly to have some quite ghostly inner meaning. I grew moody, although at the same time I was filled with an unfamiliar sensation of well-being, and I thought again of Klinger's engravings and reflected upon the course of my future work.

And now I was suddenly inundated with visions of pictures in black and white – it is impossible to describe what a thousandfold treasure my imagination poured out before me. Quickly I left the theatre, for the music and the mass of lights now disturbed me, and I wandered aimlessly in the dark streets, overcome and literally ravished by a dark power that conjured up before my mind strange creatures, houses, landscapes, grotesque and frightful situations. I felt indescribably at ease and I exulted in my accursed world, and when I had grown tired from walking I went into a small tearoom. Here too everything was out of the ordinary. As soon as I entered it seemed to me as though the waitresses were wax dolls actuated by God knows what mechanism, and as though the scattered guests – who appeared to me as unreal as shadows – had been surprised at some satanic rite. The whole setting, including the phonograph and the buffet, was suspect; it seemed to me like a trap whose only purpose was to hide the real mystery – probably a dimly lit, stall-like, blood-drenched inferno.

With a few bold strokes I put down in my notebook all that I could retain of these impressions, which changed with bewildering speed, while I held myself in a state of complete passivity. On the way home the inner tumult continued, Augustenstrasse seemed to hunch itself together, and a mountain range reared up in a monstrous ring around our city.

Once home, I sank into bed like a dead man and slept soundly and dreamlessly until towards evening of the next day. In the time that followed I stayed very much by myself. I finished whole series of India-ink drawings; I made myself acquainted with the collected art works of Klinger, Goya, de Groux, Rops, Munch, Ensor, Redon, and similar artists, who in turn became my favourites and who exercised an occasional though unconscious influence on me. But I clearly realized that my own works had a marked personal style.

Miraculous intoxications of the sort I have just described overcame me from time to time after that, but never with the same sudden power. My principal worry during this early period was due to the fact that my drawings were so unequal in technical accomplishment. Often only two or even one turned out as I wished. But to select individual ones and do them over again and again, for this I lacked the requisite calm; I was helplessly hurried along by a jostling crowd of new inspirations; to withstand them would hardly have been possible. On one occasion I became so involved in this storm and stress, this up and down of hope and despair, so shaken, that I fell into a state of confusion similar to the one I had experienced in the army, and this was followed by the same convulsions; my friends hurriedly placed me in a carriage and delivered me at Professor Gudden's ward in the hospital. The professor kindly released me the next day once more hale and hearty.

By this time I was not attending the Academy at all and seldom went to Die Sturmfackel. The club was disbanded not long after, having shone in its full glory in a final orgiastic 'Roman festival'.

During the periods when I could not work because my hand

trembled from over-exertion – in those days my mind was always alert – I acquainted myself with the principal works in all modern and classic literatures insofar as they were available in translation. I also read historical works, travel books, medical treatises, and much else largely at random.

Little by little I had got together more than a hundred of my drawings, everything was going splendidly – except that my money was running out. Then I received an invitation from Paul Cassirer to give an exhibition in his Berlin gallery. This made my heart leap up. I surrendered to the happy expectation that an exhibition in a well-established gallery would make me famous and be the beginning of a splendid future free from material anxieties. Accordingly I spent almost the last of my money on frames, mats, and the like, and sent the package off to Berlin with a happy heart. I myself soon followed and was very pleased and proud to see my things, rather strange and solemn-looking, hanging on the fabric-covered walls. Alas, the pecuniary success of the exhibition was hardly worth mentioning; however I received a great number of favourable notices, which hailed me as a new artist. Some, to be sure, expressed dismay at these 'chambers of horrors'. This encouragement from the press cheered me a great deal, but the fact that my money was so nearly exhausted was depressing. What should I do, now that my small inheritance was used up? Penury, alas all too familiar, threatened to engulf me once more. But then a friend bought twelve drawings, and my little ship was afloat again. Soon, quite unexpectedly, things were to go even better.

In the meantime in Munich I had come to know the poet Maximilian Dauthendey, who was most enthusiastic about my art and introduced me to his friends. The latter then talked about me to their acquaintances and made them aware of my work, thereby doing me a great service. Then one day I received a visit from Herr von Weber, a lover of original art, who was so pleased with my things that he immediately took forty-eight drawings away with him. From then on things improved rapidly. A crowd of people came to my little room in Theresienstrasse, all with a lively interest in my productions, and many of them made purchases, so that in a short time I was in possession of six thousand marks. In addition, Hans von Weber, who had now become my good friend, arranged for a portfolio of fifteen reproductions of my drawings to be printed, and this brought me to the attention of wider circles and received excellent reviews. This was a delight!

From this time on I went out a good deal in society and had invitations for almost every evening. The happy change in my situation had a very favourable effect on my creative powers, and a great mass of drawings emerged, of steadily increasing artistic quality. In October, 1903, I went to Berlin for a second time and spent several weeks in Friedenau with Hans von Müller, the well-known expert on E. T. A. Hoffmann. One evening towards eleven o'clock when Müller had gone out, I was alone in my room reading one of Kant's works and striving mentally to make my way through his difficult ideas. With me, all conceptions are accompanied by a faint aura of sensualism which alone makes it possible for me to grasp the ideas. This tendency, almost always on the alert, used to pounce upon abstract concepts (as I had noted again and again) whenever I read works of philosophy. On this occasion, for what reason I know not, I must have reacted differently, for my consciousness quite suddenly attained such a degree of inner illumination that I felt myself, perhaps only for the space of a second or two, in a state of indescribable quietude, like a being for whom physical objects, the room and all my familiar past experiences, existed only as a delusion. This strange experience, which occurs suddenly and departs without leaving a trace, is as completely convincing in itself as it is incommunicable to others. I mention it here only because from then on it became a recurrent phenomenon with me, in varying degrees of vividness, and proved to be a principal fountainhead of my existence.

I had attained a very cordial relationship with my father, who was proud of me now that I was successful. Perhaps I could have earned more money if at that time I had followed my friends' advice and devoted myself to etching, but since I always suffered from a plethora of inspirations that demanded to be given form, I stuck to original drawing and declined the offer of certain gentlemen to present me with a press.

During this time I met in a 'family pension' a young lady from my own section of the country and soon thereafter became engaged to her. Now my earthly good fortune had reached its zenith. Everything that I had heretofore experienced under the name 'love' paled by comparison with the true, deep passion that now laid hold of me. To be sure, from time to time I was assailed by doubts as to whether it was prudent to seal this love pact by marriage. I was afraid of losing my freedom and putting myself in a straitjacket. But my strong yearnings prevailed. I went to see the relatives of my secret bride and begged them to acknowledge me as her bridegroom. And so at the age of twenty-five I was occupied with serious thoughts of becoming the head of a household. But everything turned out contrary to my expectations. My bride fell ill during one of her visits with me in Munich and died ten days later in the hospital. As I stood beside her body, I was overwhelmed by the realization that for me the highest form of happiness was forever a thing of the past. I wanted to cry aloud in dreadful despair, and yet not a sound could I utter to relieve my sorrow. Henceforth existence seemed to me horribly barren and futile. I lost all courage to live, and I squandered my savings senselessly because they seemed to me no longer to have any purpose. During this time I was constantly tortured by memories of the beautiful young creature who had been taken from me as though by black magic. Extravagances and dissipations followed in mad succession; I withdrew from all my acquaintances and allowed my affairs to fall into confusion. When my unhappy state had reached its climax and my mind threatened to lose its equilibrium as a result of these months of dissipation, I decided one Sunday to visit a small circle of my acquaintances again. There by accident I met my future wife. She showed an understanding of my state and this brought us closer together. She inspired me with confidence and love; I visited her frequently and after a short time we decided to marry; through this union I came into easy circumstances. That was in March, 1904.

The first thing I did was to try to take a more rational view of my past fate, to put out of my mind as unalterable the overwhelming tragedy that still tormented me, and to adjust myself as comfortably as possible to my new household. To be sure, I was no longer capable of such flights of soul as formerly, a deep scar had been left, and I had to make my peace with it. But my marriage brought me so much new happiness that I soon felt once more the impulse to work.

The result was a series of harmoniously composed pictures, which I painted in delicately modulated colours in order to give them greater variety and richness. Formerly I had limited myself to grey and closely related shades of blue, brown, and green; now I added to my palette yellow, true green, orange, and various tones of red. This went on for quite a while, half a year I imagine, but I must add that the inspiring visions that had used to rise as though clairvoyantly from my unconscious became rarer and paler and finally ceased. This, added to the fact that my wife fell ill and had to go to a health resort, leaving me alone to keep house, put me in a state of inner dissatisfaction.

In order to free myself from this melancholia and provide myself with new material, I went to Vienna. The beautiful city was still new to me, and it was here in the Court Museum that I saw the collection of pictures by Brueghel. I had, to be sure, heard a great deal about this master, but I have to admit that I was not prepared for such splendours, so perverse and familiar, so appealing to an artist's perceptions. This day belongs to the most rewarding of my life, and if I have already told how my first visit to the Pinakothek filled me with astonishment and ecstasy that first lifted me to the heavens, only to plunge me later into a consciousness of my own insignificance in comparison with those eternal works; if later on I said that my introduction to the early work of Klinger proved decisive for my career by converting me to drawing, this experience was something totally different. It was something completely *sui generis*, familiar, mad, and holy, something profoundly exciting that was nevertheless infinitely well known to me and that brought every string of my inner being into vibration in a way that the sight of no other work of art has ever done before or since. It was not only the content of his pictures that appealed so strongly to me but above all the elemental visionary quality of his art, which arose from the unconscious, and the simple, almost commonplace artistic means by which he exercised such marvellous control over the flood of images.

I immediately purchased whatever reproductions were available of Brueghel's paintings, drawings, and etchings. My admiration for them was so unbounded that my own efforts seemed to me superfluous since what I was striving for had been exceeded so splendidly centuries earlier. I concluded my series of well over a thousand pictures with a big canvas, a hundred centimetres by fifty, entitled 'The Englishman's Island', which I composed in a great variety of colours.

Since my old works now struck me as tasteless and since I felt a certain repugnance for them, I had to look about for some new field of activity.

In Vienna, Kolo Moser had shown me a technique that consisted of mixing water colours with paste and made it possible to achieve very striking colour effects. I devoted myself wholeheartedly to this new procedure and succeeded in producing a whole series of pictures that shimmered and glowed. Magic forests, flowers, fishes, and birds that looked as though dipped in a rainbow, such things could be most effectively represented. In the fall of that year, my wife and I made an extended journey to the south of France and to Italy, which left with me a memory of bright colours gleaming in the strong sun and which contributed to my development as a colourist. Returning home, I painted a great number of pictures of primeval and tropical forests, which for the most part were inhabited by prehistoric or still extant fauna. More thoughtful considerations followed the first period of intoxication, and I recognized that my technique made me too dependent on accident; so I decided to give up the subtle effects of the paste and returned to pure tempera. Although I had now become an accomplished artist and fulminated with rage against anything except the purely artistic content of pictures, I nevertheless felt from time to time a profound conflict, a sensation of being torn apart. My pictures were after all not above reproach from a colourist's point of view; on the contrary, a pronounced feeling for tone was once more asserting itself. Now I began once more in complete secrecy to draw grotesques, for relaxation and because they absolutely insisted on being set down. My patrons' inclination to buy fell off rapidly – new troubles! In order to put an end to these things, I went with my wife to Paris in the winter of 1905 to see the real masters of colour. There it was the artists of the earlier generation, the Barbizon school, who excited me: Corot, Diaz, Daubigny, Rousseau, with their subtle, airy style; above all else, however, I remember that Constable's speckled manner enchanted me. During our visit, I could not refrain from paying a call on the aged Odilon Redon, who was an object of veneration to the draughtsman Kubin. I succeeded, too, in acquiring some rare and beautiful works by the master.

The Impressionists, of course, made a strong impression on me, the strongest of all French art; for my own private purposes, however, they had no great significance; in my eyes they were not dreamlike enough, and yet the facility with which they expressed themselves delighted me.

When I had returned to Munich and set about painting again, I attacked everything in a much bolder and more ambitious way than before; I no longer had any dread of brushes and colours. The themes remained the same. So it went for quite a while, and I believe my pictures painted in those days are perfectly presentable, especially since I had now completely overcome my earlier inadequacies in composition, as was generally recognized. Almost every day people came to see my work, but many of them preferred my older things. However, I was reluctant to talk about my drawings and it pained me to bring them out. I much preferred it when people looked at the temperas. And so two separate groups were formed; their difference of opinion would certainly have made no impression on me had I not myself been secretly torn and plagued by doubts.

It was now perfectly true that my paintings, with their plastic effectiveness and faithful representations of physical objects, were, in fact, from a formal and artistic point of view, far better than my drawings, and yet the latter often possessed even in quite distorted and tormented instances, a charm that the work of my later period did not in any way equal. I was much confused in mind, and when my attention was called by my father to an opportunity to acquire a small country property near the River Inn, I was at once attracted by the idea. It appealed to me all the more since, under the burden of my artistic dilemma, the city had become unbearable. Since that time we have lived in Zwickledt near Wernstein.

At first I continued to paint more determinedly and stubbornly than ever, but my inner conflict and scruples became worse and worse. Nevertheless, I would rather have given up than produce anything weak, and so I set about finding new material to make my painting meaningful. The first thing I hit upon was underwater landscapes, as a result of my vivid memories of certain great aquariums, which had enchanted me with the intoxication of their colours and forms. But even that did not suffice; driven by the conflict of my emotions, I wanted to rise above myself, above nature, above everything, and when I had a chance to study through the microscope the fairy-like images of the most delicate animal and plant substances, relief came as though of itself. I had been working under enormous pressure, which now happily relaxed, but what I created is difficult to describe. I now consistently rejected every memory of the given organization of nature, and I created compositions out of veils or bundles of beams, out of fragments of crystals or parts of seashells, from layers of flesh and skin, from the pattern of leaves and a thousand other things, and these compositions, bathed in a warm or cold light, would astound me as I worked on them over and over again, and satisfied me deeply; yes, they made me happy in a way that the act of creation has seldom done before or since. Is it surprising that at this time I was filled with enthusiasm for the most radical, the most far-out of our modern poets, Paul Scheerbart, and that we exchanged baroque and completely nonphilistine letters? I painted about twenty such pictures, and the few friends who saw them were much amazed but could not come to any clear judgement about these monstrosities. In short, they would wait and see! And I was one hope the poorer. For, once the first intoxication was gone, I had to admit to myself that this procedure could not form the basis for any sustained future work.

Our country place is completely isolated. My father lived in a small town near by, and I visited him frequently; with increasing age he had become very gentle and friendly. I, too, in the meanwhile had acquired enough knowledge of the human soul and had made enough instructive comparisons to be able to understand my father better, and I honoured him and loved him greatly. Today I consider it my good fortune that I was able to make the last years of his life happier.

In my work I had reached another turning point. I was surfeited with experiments in form and colour, and I switched to the opposite extreme: I restricted myself to the flat, harmonious forms of composition employed by the young French and German artists who had found their inspiration in Gauguin. I renounced all originality and indeed guarded myself strenuously against it. All that I aspired to do was to serve art simply and humbly.

During a visit to Munich I met as though by predestination the Benedictine father Willibrod Verkade, who had been a personal friend of Gauguin's and of the members of his circle. This modern painter in priestly garb took a warm and kindly interest in my work and for my edification sent me in Zwickledt a box filled with studies by Denis, Bonnard, Serusier, Filiger, and others of their group. It was thus that I came under this really alien influence, to which I submitted willing enough, essentially out of simple pleasure in opposites.

One day it occurred to me that in doing this I had been subjecting myself to constraint, and in an instant I threw aside the whole carefully elaborated structure and fell into a state of moral confusion, which unfortunately had a physical result, for I fell ill with a prolonged intestinal disturbance. To rid myself of these worries and to escape hypochondria, I took a trip in the fall of 1907 as far as Bosnia and Dalmatia.

On my return, I recognized with horror that my father, who had been in poor health for some time, was rapidly and inexorably nearing the end. He died on November 2, 1907. The effect of this loss is something I have not yet been able to surmount; I have to suppress forcibly every memory of it. The true, inner nothingness of our existence was so deeply engraved upon my mind by this misfortune that probably no change of fate or later reflections will serve to alter it.

It was not so much my father's death that stirred me to the

depths as the intellectual realization that a whole chapter of my intensive emotional life had suddenly been turned into nothing. Since then, I experience a similar though weaker shudder whenever I hear of the death of a dear friend, for I feel on those occasions with greater or less intensity the whole meaningless contradiction of the world, which only becomes grandly and profoundly significant through true mystico-artistic contemplation. The transitoriness of earthly things is a sublime horror; to reflect on this and to see the good in it demands true heroism. My physical circumstances at that time were rendered more difficult because my wife suffered a new and serious illness that compelled her to go away to recuperate. Thus I remained quite alone in Zwickledt, and my melancholy insights extinguished all desire to work. In those difficult days most of my desire for life turned to ashes, and in place of wild alternations of mood I now experienced a more relaxed state; since that time it has no longer been possible for me to feel fear, desire, or hope with the old fiery intensity. I have been impoverished by this loss.

In the next three months I did less work, but to make up for that I read the works of various of the old mystics, both occidental and oriental, who had always attracted me; I devoted myself to observing my various animals, among them a mischievous monkey, a tame deer, cats, fish, and collections of beetles, and I wandered for hours at a time in the woods and fields; it was only by degrees that I found myself reaching for a pencil, whereupon I filled a dozen notebooks with my sudden ideas; each sketch consisted of only a few lines, it was more in play than in earnest, for I lacked both desire and strength to do serious work.

The spring and summer were devoted to these activities, and I should have been in despair had it not been that my sketches revealed something unmistakably new. I saw with delight that I now drew with incomparably greater sureness than in my earlier periods. This greater certainty of hand, which seemed to have come of itself, was in reality the result of the two years I had devoted to painting. It was now possible for me to hit upon the essential point that has to be grasped in order to express an idea in line; this I could now find much more surely and consciously than at the time of my old and strangely monomaniac working methods. But, as I have said, though the seed was there, the desire was lacking, and in order to get myself out of this bad mood and perhaps to achieve the impetus I needed, I travelled that fall with my friend Fritz von Herzmanowsky to northern Italy and to Venice. I surrendered quite indiscriminately to the impressions of the journey, and already on my way home, at Lake Garda, I felt a tremulous deisre to occupy myself again with drawing – to what end I did not know myself, nor did I wish to speculate about it. But I was clearly aware that I was looking at my whole world with new eyes and that an inner splendour had dawned within me. I returned home full of impatience and eagerness. But then when I tried to start a drawing I simply could not do it. I was not capable of putting down coherent, intelligible lines, it was as though I were a four-year-old child trying for the first time to counterfeit nature. This new phenomenon filled me with alarm, for, I repeat, I was inwardly bursting with the need to work. In order to do something, no matter what, to unburden myself, I now began to compose and write down an adventure story. The ideas came flooding into my mind in super-abundance; they forced me to work day and night, so that in twelve weeks' time my fantastic novel *Die andere Seite* (The Other Side) was finished. During the next four weeks I provided it with illustrations. Afterwards, to be sure, I was exhausted and irritable, and I entertained serious misgivings about my daring enterprise. I possessed no reliable judgement in literary matters, I had never before written anything for publication – indeed writing itself is an uncongenial activity; never in my life have I made a poem. I was afraid I would endanger my artistic reputation by publishing *Die andere Seite* especially since some people already believed that they detected literary elements in my drawings.

I read the manuscript first to my brother-in-law, Oscar A. H. Schmitz, in whose judgement of these matters I have great confidence. He found my work exceptionally pleasing and reassured me to a certain degree in regard to its quality. And so that summer the book was published by Georg Müller. It brought me wide acclaim. *Die andere Seite* stands at a turning point in my spiritual development, a fact that is indicated in it openly and covertly in many places. During its composition I achieved the mature realization that it is not only in the bizarre, exalted, or comic moments of our existence that the highest values lie, but that the painful, the indifferent, and the incidental-commonplace contain these same mysteries. This is the principal meaning of the book. About the other references in it – and there are many of them – I prefer to say nothing because my intention is simply to present the course of my development in rough outline. Let the reader himself seek them out. The fact that I wrote instead of drawing lay in the nature of the problem; this happened to be the right means to discharge my thronging ideas more rapidly than would otherwise have been possible.

Shortly after this clarifying interlude I experienced a great feeling of relief and a renewed desire to work. I now clearly recognized my artistic abilities and their limitations. I know that I possess no marked formal talent and that a certain roughness will always characterize my work; besides being an artist, I am a ponderer, a seer. The new problems that fascinated me, when seen in the right light, turned out to be the same old ones but filtered through a purely artistic medium. A further change in my subject matter is worth noting: the representation of fantastic combinations – for example, pigs with halos, houses with huge ears, volcanoes erupting fountains of blood, and so forth – no longer exercised the old attraction for me. Perhaps this form of fantasy is a tumultuous, youthful stage in the development of many people's imaginations.

Now it was no longer the purely personal needs of the heart that cried aloud in me and found strange, distorted expression in my vision. Now I found a greater fascination in the universal life that mysteriously intermingles in men, animals, and plants, in every stone, in every created or uncreated thing. Once more I depicted massed men and animals, magnificence and decay, luxurious sin and repulsive putrefaction, reverence for the sublime and desperate torment, in short, everything that had occupied my heart from the beginning; but in artistic expression the new pictures were substantially better.

I gave up all shading and colouring and devoted myself exclusively to pen and ink. The simplest means, lines, specks, and dots should suffice to bear the whole imaginary structure of the drawing. After straying far and wide, I believe I have finally found my own territory and I hope I can go on perfecting my art and thus hold a mirror up to this distorted world. My wealth of ideas and my whole working method, which makes it possible to produce in essence any effect and which also makes possible reasonably easy reproduction, mark me as an illustrator. My publisher, Georg Müller, recognized this, too; on commission from him I have thus far illustrated a six-volume edition of Poe, the story *Aurélia* by the French romantic Gérard de Nerval, and Hauff's *Fairy Tales*, the novella *Samalio und Pardulus* by Bierbaum, and E. T. A. Hoffmann's *Nachtstücke* in addition to *Haschisch* by Oscar A. H. Schmitz, and *Lesabendio* by Paul Scheerbart. At the same time there has appeared a monograph by H. Esswein adorned with many pictures from all periods of my work.

We have now arrived at the present. Glancing back at the course of my life, I believe I have depicted the trends and the most important turning points in my development without leaving any large gaps. My work shows increasing technical refinement, which, however, does not reflect upon the originality of the earlier pictures, a quality that evoked immediate response from even the simplest souls. It has not been my intention here to identify the hidden influences. For a long time and more particularly during the last few years, I have studied a very extensive collection of graphic material, embracing all cultures, and this intense labour may well explain many subtle variations in my pictures. My collection *Sansara*, designed for art lovers, came into being this last year. In the circuitous course of this autobiography, or rather in the very substance of it, I think I have given to the best of my ability an answer to the question that is often put to me: How did I come to create such things? I hope most of all that I have adequately demonstrated that it was one and the same power that led me to dreams and silly pranks in childhood, later to sickness, and finally to art. To give a clearer definition of this authentic and ultimate mainspring of my creativity lies beyond my power. If formerly I looked to the philosophers for enlightenment without ever quite achieving it, I nevertheless continue to read them today with equal pleasure, for my fantasy plunges me into a tormenting chaos, and I can regain some measure of calm from their icy thoughts – a seeming paradox that will have to be accepted as fact. I read philosophy with passionate curiosity, the way one reads novels, eager each time to find out 'how will it turn out'. Nevertheless for years my essential attitude has been one of profound resignation.

One thing is certain, fantasy has put its hallmark on my existence, it is fantasy that makes me happy and makes me sad. I recognize it constantly inside and outside me. Now that I have seen and suffered a great deal and no longer cling to life as tenaciously as once I did, now that many varieties of bodily weakness and sensitivity to pain repeatedly darken my mood, I accept the idea of death without much concern, nor does it very much matter to me whether, according to those who profess to know something about the matter, death will lead to nothingness, to omniscience, or to some new individual existence.

3

1917

On this sceptical note I ended the autobiographical sketch with which I prefaced my *Sansara* portfolio. Now, eight years later, *Die andere Seite* is being reprinted, and I welcome this opportunity to extend in the same concise manner the account of my development from my old viewpoints and to continue my narrative as a clarification and rounding out of a number of matters.

I now have my artistic style firmly in hand and, although it has no doubt been stimulated by impressions from outside, it has not again been remoulded. To make use of the same hard-won methods to achieve constantly simpler and deeper forms of expression is still my goal today.

After the great *Sansara* cycle, I hit upon the idea of capturing dreams in picture form as they are still reflected in one's memory immediately after awakening. For years, night dreams as well as the so-called daydreams or waking dreams were a rich mine in my opinion, one whose artistic treasures awaited the right miner. I determined to be that man. Without conscious intent I had already in my earlier periods derived excellent ideas from my dreams, a fact that many people had recognized, for example Ferdinand Avenarius, who had referred to me as early as 1903 in his *Kunstwart* as a 'dream artist'. Now, however, I made a really methodical study of dreams. I read old as well as quite recent theories about them. Inasmuch as I was in search of pictures, direct observations of my dreams turned out to be what was most fruitful. The scraps of memory – that is all they are – that stay with us after a dream seem illogical only to superficial observers, on whom the splendid power and beauty of this kingdom are lost. In a great 'dream series' on which I worked for several years, I began at first to include drawings straight from dream fragments; then, however, after I had gained an understanding of certain dream laws of equivalence and combination, I exercised selection more and more and achieved rich compositions made up of various individual dream-motifs. Finally I became completely at home in this ghostly dream world, which for many people does not exist at all, and I succeeded in producing compositions in tune with it while in a psychic state like that of 'daydreaming'. Perhaps later on, my great dream series, of which only a few pictures have been made public, will be published, and I may then set down some of my thoughts about dream life by way of introduction, for I believe there is much that is marvellous and hopeful to be encountered there. For the moment I must content myself with this mention of a realm that I consider still rich in promise.

While engaged in this major effort I did not neglect the business of illustration. For my principal publisher, Georg Müller, I adorned various interesting volumes with drawings. Because of the present unfavourable circumstances some of them will not appear until later. Among these works I mention in particular *Les Diaboliques* by Barbey d'Aurévilly, for which I supplied full-page illustrations and vignettes, and a passionately written and exciting tale from the Catalan, *Josaphat*, which inspired me to make numerous pictures. The handsome collection of

Poe's work was completed by two additional volumes, and a second volume by Hauff was brought out, *Phantasien im Bremer Ratskeller*. The most copiously illustrated work of this kind was *The Double* by Dostoievsky, which R. Piper published in very handsome format and for which I provided sixty drawings. For J. B. Neumann, who had established a 'Graphic Cabinet' in Berlin, I made a small series of lithographs, *Die sieben Todsünden*. At that time Franz Marc, the co-founder with Kandinsky of Der blaue Reiter, a small group to which I too belonged, made the tempting suggestion of a representative modern edition of the Bible. Each artist was to choose his own book. I did so at once, selecting the prophet Daniel. I went to see Marc myself out in Sindelsdorf, and spent two sunny days of companionship with him. These seemed in general good and propitious times for all modern art. Sometimes one would almost feel frightened that such an impetus and such daring recklessness had seized not only many young people but a large number of their elders as well. To me, however, it was a delight to observe this creative destruction and rebuilding and, in the course of my repeated visits to Munich, to experience it and to discover each time new pinnacles. Support came from all sides for this new movement in art, whose individual exponents called themselves cubists, expressionists, synthesists, constructionists, neo-classicists; others were childishly naïve, half or entirely barbaric, primitive, or particuarly self-centred, or simply affected. Well-informed art experts brought into juxtaposition the artistic activities of thousands of years with those of the most recent date, unearthing contradictions where I could see none. Of all the comment that came to my attention the warm and understanding articles of Wilhelm Hausenstein pleased me most. Although I had foreseen this development, which ran parallel with other phenomena of our times, I was nevertheless astounded at the speed with which it proceeded. It was like a brotherhood of all young European artists, for nationality no longer played any role. The commercial art world, which at first had been suspicious and inattentive, opened up more and more to the new works, since collectors and the directors of art galleries began to show interest. Dealers in modern art were now turning up in important places – in

Munich no one so impetuous and idealistic as dear old Max Dietzel.

All that I can say in general about the new art is that it had an extraordinary indirect effect on me. However, the more abstract, abbreviated, and crude the forms became, the quicker I became tired of them. In my own work I could not prevail upon myself to hazard on new experiments what I had already attained by abandoning the intimate, organically related subtleties that I had spent so much effort in learning to portray. My enthusiasm for art operates on all levels and, naturally enough, puts a higher value on a powerfully creative spirit than on an instant's transitory charm or something crudely representational. I love the ancient, the middle, and the latest masters, and even what is only half successful or spoilt arouses my sympathy if I perceive in it the evidence of honest effort.

For instance, if I see years of remarkable persistence at work, as in the case of Paul Klee or Franz Marc, Feininger, or Picasso, I take pains to understand and to feel my way into it and not to stand aside deprecatingly or sneeringly. The prerequisite for true seeing and understanding is always a willingness to re-evaluate.

Through trades, gifts, and purchases, I got together a varied collection of graphic art, both old and new, in the form of originals and prints. This, combined with my library, has helped me through many critical periods and almost daily brings me new joys.

Evidence of various kinds shows me that my pictures and books are gradually reaching wider circles. In the course of its various transformations my art has lost friends and won them back again years later. Others have remained alienated. Still others have followed my work with uninterrupted enthusiasm; such a one is Felix Grafe, who has a collection of my principal pictures from every stage of my development.

By this time, journeys no longer played any important role in my life; nevertheless I remember with pleasure an especially beautiful trip down the Danube with Karl Wolfskehl in 1909, which was followed by a Balkan excursion. Moreover, on several occasions I was the guest of Alexander von Bernus in the extremely congenial Stift Neuburg near Heidelberg. In 1912

I saw old Prague again. I went there in order to visit the highly gifted but gravely ill painter Eugene von Kahler, who died shortly thereafter. The state in which I found him remains one of the saddest memories of my life.

In Prague, too, there was a circle of moderns, especially modern poets. The new spirit compelled everyone to whom art was of any consequence to take a position. However, I had now become completely a countryman and I found that the unaccustomed life in a city depressed me. There was no real comfort for me except at home in the quietness, which from time to time was most agreeably interrupted by the visits of friends from the city. It was through them that I kept abreast of the times, and this much was clear to me: 'the new spirit', vague though the phrase was, nevertheless had a clearly discernible countenance, there was something magnificently germinal in the air.

In January, 1914, I decided upon another trip to Paris, to have a look again at the works of the representatives of modern art at its source. In Munich I secured letters of introduction; at Strasbourg we made an excursion – I was travelling with my wife – to Kolmar in order to see the Isenheimer Altar. On the very first day in Paris I noticed, alas, that my nerves could no longer endure the furious alternation of sense impressions; I became anxious, moody, excited, and my whole stay would very likely have been ruined had it not been that Ernst Sonderegger, to whom I had an introduction, appeared at exactly the right instant like a rescuing angel. He took conscientious charge of us and contributed greatly to the swift restoration of my equilibrium. Despite the fact that this time under the guidance of my new friend I could do much more sightseeing and explored many hitherto unknown aspects of the day and night life of that unique city, my impressions were far from being as startling and crucial as those of my first visit. I was struck by the large number of cars on the streets, which were taking the place of the old nags; there were more moving-picture theatres, everything was more frantic, the food in the restaurants was expensive and even more adulterated – in a word everything had been further Americanized.

There was not a great deal to satisfy my graphic interests;

today the French have no illustrator of the stature of Max Slevogt. The art that proclaimed itself as most modern did not appeal to me as strongly as I had expected. I saw works by Picasso adroitly glued together from strips of newspaper, pieces of wood, and sheets of music, works that demolished all established frameworks and filled me with astonishment.

To see these new tendencies in art today it is no longer at all necessary to go to Paris. These interesting objects, which so often bear a common benchmark, are to be found at least equally well represented in other big cities.

As I sat in the train, almost asleep and very much affected, I was still immersed in the deluge of extravagant toilettes, strange faces, tango melodies, old painting, and cubism.

Then, in August, 1914, the horror came. What artist, indeed what man of any sort, would have dared to prophesy that there could still occur such a flood of hatred, rage, and obstinacy as now broke over us? It oppressed me in my lonely retreat like the scent of carrion, and a dreadful persistent sadness and depression held me captive for the first four or five months of the war. I was, to be sure, impressed and shaken by the gigantic organization of the war machine, the frightful acts of destruction, and the heroic spirit of individuals; but I was completely untouched by the primitive enthusiasm that so many felt; I stood to one side. Three times I endured the torment of military examination and on each successive occasion I was found in weaker physical condition, until on the fourth screening of those in their forties I was officially excused from further appearances. Everyone was deceived about the duration of the war; brutality and every sort of horror penetrated constantly deeper into every corner of private life. Food gradually grew worse, all sorts of abuses increased; I discovered that hardship forced into the open all the meanness of human nature; although in the case of many people it revealed fine characteristics as well.

Certain of my acquaintances thought that these circumstances would be sure to act as a stimulus on me. However, I was so weary. The many deprivations, the devaluation of money, all this caused me continual anxiety. Frequent deaths, among them those of my worthy and beloved friends, further

275

impaired the state of my health. My head and limbs felt as heavy as though my veins had been stuffed with sand, and I lay for hours at a time on my couch as if numbed, even during the day. A. von Heymel, Scheerbart, Max Tietzel, Weissgerber and many of my younger acquaintances, all these deaths came as a result of this inconceivable madness or were hastened by it.

From time to time I would give myself an energetic shaking, and then I could find something splendid in the silent, literally depopulated landscape in which I lived. But soon I would encounter once more the embittered or anguished faces. The phrase 'heavy losses' was something I could no longer bear to hear. In such a state, I should have gone to pieces despite the prescribed nursing care, if I had not found an elixir of life in the creative impulse that filled me. At just this time, it is true, work was made more difficult because I had used up my excellent old hand-made paper. For fourteen years I had made use almost exclusively of the blank reverse sides of old registry office charts for my drawings, and I found it difficult to accustom myself to any other material. Fortunately, after a short search, I discovered a satisfactory new kind of paper. I summoned up my strength and in the years of 1915 to 1916 I completed my *Totentanz*, based on inspirations that had been in my mind for a long time and that had grown constantly simpler. I chose twenty-four pictures from the whole series, and these will be published in Berlin by Bruno Cassirer.

Along with this creative activity I did what I could to improve my powers of understanding. I was still under the spell of that silent, awe-inspiring experience that evening in Friedenau, an experience connected with the name of Kant and one that I have already mentioned in these notes. I now declare, though with a certain constraint and secrecy, that it was the noble discoveries of Kant that gave me the strongest conception of the value of philosophy. The proper tribute to this, the most rational mind our world has ever seen, is not noisy praise but deep silence and profound awe.

His followers – for me they were in succession Schopenhauer, Mainländer, Bahnsen – managed their great inheritances each according to the degree of his talent, and during my younger years my own thinking remained for the most part under the influence of their teaching, until by degrees I discarded all completely negative views of life and about 1909 fell into the stubborn scepticism expressed at the end of the second part of this autobiography.

Joy in creation proved so turbulent a vital force that again and again I was compelled to direct my thoughts to that enigmatic fountainhead, and my icily sceptical attitude proved in the long run untenable.

Next to Kant, I know of no work of such immense value and such ambiguity as that of Friedrich Nietzsche. From the start it attracted me like a subterranean magnet, but whenever I attempted to come to a clear-cut understanding of it, I was again and again repelled by the obvious, indeed dreadful, errors of thought. The personal magic of that sphinx-like yea-sayer seems to me clearest in *Ecce Homo*, his late work, which through a happy accident became known to me long before its publication. It was considerably later, however, that Nietzsche's ideas first bore fruit for me. He is, in truth, our Christ!

On a day when my inner exaltation had raised me to a dizzying height, armed with the clear-headedness acquired from Kant, I dared to gulp down the hot, intoxicating brew of *Zarathustra*, and from it I gained what I had wanted, a point of view that would hold good for every conceivable life experience. An infinite mystery seemed to have been revealed to me, which shed splendour on everything and, for me too, imbued the beauties of earth with a special shimmer of eternity. At the same time it was the most obvious thing possible.

If I had now found the right solutions, that does not mean that they immediately penetrated into my blood so that a complete harmony was achieved. And so my eager attention was directed towards all the intellectual movements and their effects, movements which, running parallel to the new directions in art, seemed to me so indicative of our yearning. Derleth's *Proklamationen*, Weininger's *Letzte Dinze*, Al Raschid's *Hohes Ziel*, Volker's *Siderische Geburt*, Dom's *Odyssee der Seele*, Knoop's *A und O* – I single these out from a great number – are in my opinion just as significant individual witnesses to our times as the new editions of old cosmogonies and the renewed interest in occult works.

Of all the things I read at this time, by far the strongest impression was made on me by the short pieces and philosophical drolleries I came across by Dr S. Friedländer-Mynona, written with unique pregnancy, often derisively ironic, and then again completely absorbing for anyone who deeply understands the values that are at stake today. On my first acquaintance with these essays I detected the lion's roar, and overcoming my hesitation I wrote to this new philosopher and was most happily surprised when I learned that he had long known about my efforts, was acquainted with *Die andere Seite* and indeed admired it. I had been helped to overcome my awkwardness in abstract thought. And so I was overjoyed when an echo, were it only a single one, came from a register that seemed comparable with my own.

Despite all insight, it was still not possible for me to govern my daily life as I should have liked. The morning radiance of interrelationships finally recognized was alas not immediately available for practical application. In the muddy dregs, in so-called human nature – and one can never be careful enough to distinguish between that and the living 'I' – there continued to lurk, usually unnoticed, the negative forces that had been conjured up at the same time as my new clarity.

An old, seemingly demonic love of confusion, which compelled me to go searching secretly in all directions and which was undermining my new-found, positive principles, gave a moody, restless cast to my days. Outer distractions, a trip or a visit to friends, were no longer feasible because the policemen, costumed now as gods of war, imposed restrictions on any such attempt. And so once more I spent many daylight hours lying on the divan in a state of nervous exhaustion, distressed most of all by a troublesome weakness of the eyes, which later compelled me for a time to abandon my exacting black-and-white drawing that I had practised for so many years and turn for a while to painting.

But the secret and suppressed frenzy had to find vent in some fashion, and two unhappy accidents paved the way for the extraordinary crisis that I shall now describe. A single postcard brought me the dreadful news of a double tragedy, the death in battle of my dear colleague Franz Marc and the suicide by poison of a lady in Paris whom I knew well.

Just at that time I was reading a very persuasively written work by Georg Grimm about the teachings of Buddha. The emotional shock bore me along like a growing avalanche and cast me on what was closest at hand, Buddhism. In the course of a few hours this ancient doctrine sprang to life for me in such an incredibly plastic and convincing fashion that everything else really seemed to become 'the veil of Maya'; my thinking and creating turned into an illusion of knowledge, my life an illusion of existence.

I withdrew from my surroundings, even from my wife, I broke off all correspondence with family and friends, and made certain final arrangements about my possessions, which, like my art, had become completely indifferent and alien to me. My wife begged me at least to sleep in the house, and so I fitted up a little room as a cell, leaving nothing in it but a straw mattress and a washbowl cabinet.

For the most part I experienced a peculiar, sweet lightness; I arose very early, brushed my clothes, and tidied the cell, which no one else was allowed to enter.

I ate less than usual, when possible no meat at all, and I wandered about for hours at a time in all weathers. Once, during a rainfall, I removed thousands of earthworms from the road to keep them from being killed; in general, I was very happy, freed from all conflict, and I experienced in a prolonged ecstasy uncanny events such as I had often in earlier times thought up for my pictures, events such as legend ascribes, for example, to St Anthony. There were days when I heard the continuous resounding of multiple footfalls, which approached and then withdrew; a roaring, shrieking, and rumbling, as though from a great crowd of people. If I spoke to anyone, then everything took on a hidden meaning, even the most commonplace and familiar; stones, piles of refuse, the tree trunks, and other things of this kind seemed filled with such tremendous magic force that, although I felt cheerful and well disposed, I hardly dared glance at them because all these objects seemed to me like ghosts and masks that leered at me. The wildest, most intolerable experiences are not suitable for communication, in many cases, indeed, are not describable.

The nights too are hardly to be described. Even in the early days I had put Grimm's book aside and had turned to a collection of Buddha's sermons, which I already owned. In the evening I would read one or two suttas, turn out the light, and, while practising the prescribed breathing exercises, would remain sunk in deepest meditation, usually stretched out on my back, and would lie thus until the grey of dawn. During this whole time I never slept at all, but I was frequently wrapped in a soft, agreeable state of semiconsciousness.

Hidden in the woods and seated on a pile of straw or on my loden cloak, I would inhale in the prescribed fashion until everything within me became strangely quiet; the whispering of the wind and the voice of birds brushed softly against my subconscious as though from an infinite distance; when the last alien sounds died away and the threads of sensation grew even more tenuous, then a grey-white brightness was all that I still perceived before me. If I persisted further, all became night; a few times marvellous, shadowy outlines flashed against the dark background – once, for example, a little fish – and another time everything was covered with unintelligible numerals.

The breathing exercises produced a severe strain, and after a few days I was aware of a constant pressure in the neighbourhood of my heart. This I carried about with me like an incubus. Then a moment came when the recurrent palpitations of the heart grew too violent; fear seized me by the throat – then and there I cast off the whole of Buddhism and returned to my trusted and familiar way of life. This happened on March 12, 1916. The crisis had lasted in all for ten days.

Since that happy hour when I disentangled myself from the clinging vines of that most dangerous magic garden, fifteen months have passed. Like a cold breath, the memory of that insidious attack still often returns to me, and I sniff about suspiciously in all accessible corners of the psychic labyrinth for any possible pitfalls still undetected.

Since that time, not only the most untroubled but also the most blessed months, filled with an unearthly bliss, have been my lot. I carefully cultivate calm in order to achieve more and more control over my creative fantasy.

As I believed I was inextricably caught in the serpentine coils of a cosmic machine, it took many years for it to dawn on me that the whole thing was a game of hide-and-seek of the eternal, infinitely inventive spirit, with the roles assigned by necessity. We, our most individual and enigmatic essence, are playwright, director, and actor of the piece.

In the poor speech of man, who can do more than supply a simile for what is inexpressible?

All that seems certain to me is that nothing more is to be hoped from what is human; the most comprehensive pessimism of a Julius Banzen and others is in this respect quite correct. But it is no longer a question of humanity and the world. That phantom has been exposed! I am determined to act accordingly! Conscientiously, with never wearied patience and with firm resolve, I practise several times a day a loosening of the crust of my humanity; thousands of slag flakes fall away. The stormy tumult of my thoughts is already more obedient to my power. Inner consciousness has become master over the outer senses.

I am filled with the conviction that I am experiencing a fundamentally new beginning. This whole developmental history can be summarized by a few great names, standing like signposts or milestones, past which I hurried until suddenly I stopped, looked about, and rubbed the sleep from my eyes. Out of dull dependence in thought emerged penetration, out of confused fear, a flexible courage. It is indeed the Infinite itself that had forgotten and now refinds itself. Aside from that, nothing exists. The freedom acquired in the struggle for Truth is not a freedom from one's own sentient being. Acting under no outer compulsion, it sanctifies all compulsions by its own free choice.

To reach this point seemed hard; now it sometimes strikes me like Columbus' egg, but it was also Münchhausen's pigtail.

Finally, to return to particulars: I am neither a philosopher nor a writer, but a diligently and passionately committed artist. My best hours are spent with paper, pen, and ink. My deepest joy is in the stubborn practice of my craft. If in seeking my

281

way I have made excursions into abstract thought, I have not thereby given up one iota of my artistry. Riches are no more a disgrace than poverty.

I ask myself: are we then, after all, nothing but this bony framework draped with skeins of flesh? Nothing more than this basket and sack filled with quivering, pumping, sucking organs, like a nestful of naked sea creatures writhing together? Is that all?

A sunbeam is caught in the mirror, as though by accident; disturbed by this flash of light, I glance up and see in the glass my own illuminated face. It is smiling.

4

1926

It is now almost ten years since I wrote the (concluding) words of the foregoing section. They bear witness to the improved equilibrium I had achieved, after countless tensions, in the midst of a horrendous war. My confidence proved justified; never again have I completely lost hold of my inner reins, and up to now I have succeeded in coping in my own fashion with the monstrous things that have befallen us all. We are now in the year 1926. It is my fiftieth.

To give a detailed account of events in the quiet nook where I live lies beyond the scope of a short autobiographical study, designed only to recount my personal development. No doubt we suffered less in the country than the people in the city, but obviously we too had our troubles – and dodges for getting around them as well. It was tragic and grotesque at once. One day when I read in the newspaper that Bulgaria had fallen, I knew that at last the bloody madness was coming to an end.

At that time I was a guest in Micheldorf, which lies in near-by Kremstal, at the estate of my colleague, that very remarkable man Carl Anton Reichel. It was he who, not long thereafter, provided a hospitable refuge for the Crown Prince Rupprecht during his flight from Bavaria after the military collapse. Even in late October, however, when I was with Reichel, we spent most of our time discussing the great political changes that were sure to occur, and together we made all sorts of conjectures. From the vantage point of that dinner table, to be sure, no one foresaw that those changes would be so radical as they actually turned out to be. At all events, I was secretly happy that the tension, which had become intolerable, and the horrible butchery must finally end. Even if I had not known from certain insiders that there could be no question of further military resistance, I should have divined it from a small, half-visionary experience that befell me.

On my way back from Micheldorf I paused for a few hours in Linz and was sitting in one of those agreeable small coffee-houses that still have the atmosphere of old Austria; the taste of the horrible chicory brew that was set in front of me, to-gether with saccharine tablets and a repulsive, watery, bluish milk-substitute, made me want to howl. Through the window I accidently caught sight of a crowd of military prisoners – pre-sumably guilty of insubordination or desertion – who were just then being marched by. Good heavens, what a sight that rabble was! A pack of indigent beggars! And the so-called guards, grey-headed ancient phantoms, were distinguishable from the rest only by their rifles with fixed bayonets – ill-nourished, sallow figures, wearily dragging themselves along in most un-military style. There could be no talk of uniforms, for all uni-formity was lacking, and the only thing they all had in com-mon was the inadequacy of their clothing; almost all of them were shivering pitifully in their thin, greasy rags, whipped by the sharp fall wind. An old woodcut rose like a vision in my memory, 'Napoleon's Retreat from Russia, 1812', and at the same time I had a distinct feeling: this is the end of my old beloved Austria.

A few days later I was told by an official from the district captain's office that the state of war had ceased in our country; however it had been necessary to grant the enemy the right of transit, and so perhaps in the near future we would see enemy troops in our midst. It was in fact possible to observe through a spyglass that earthworks were being thrown up on the far side of the River Inn in Bavaria, presumably for gun emplacements or trenches to repel the advancing Italians. The official also advised me to remove as quickly as possible any valuables that I wanted to keep safe. That was awkward! Where was I to go with my paintings and books? And should I also try to rescue the feather beds, clothes, and silverware? My wife was sick in a sanatorium in far-off Hesse; I had to decide all this hurriedly by myself. There was a rumour that in the near-by village of Schärding worried people were already burying their more valuable possessions. Yes, those were several trying days! People met at the inn, eager for news and full of dread; I myself saw old men weeping for fear, like little children, and I was questioned by the simple folk about my own view of our situation. Men on leave who were present terrified us by asserting that it would go ill for us if Bavaria really decided to defend its borders. The explosion of a single grenade or an aerial bomb could destroy a house, and in a matter of a few hours the buildings of the entire area would be turned into heaps of rubble. Since all this was in the hands of a higher power, the best course seemed to me to be to wait and trust in fate — especially since our old cook swore she would stay with me through thick and thin. As it turned out, none of the things we had feared took place; the phantom disappeared as quickly as it had arisen; Germany too signed an armistice.

Then, when it was all over, one was often astounded by all sorts of postwar scenes. For example, one night I encountered on the country road a ghostly caravan consisting of some ten wagons, pulled by tired, emaciated nags with manes and tails matted with filth. They were accompanied by some officers and soldiers from a German Bohemian regiment. I was asked about the nearest town, and I directed the fantastic troop to our wayside inn; it disappeared into the fog like a phantom left over from the Thirty Years War. Later that evening, I went to the inn myself and chatted with the men, who had brought their wagon train all the way up from Italy. Early next morning, the wagons and horses – not to mention the lice and scabs – the harnesses and blankets, sugar and coffee, were auctioned off. Useful items were acquired at a laughably low price, and this resulted in a lively squabble. Immediately thereafter the warriors disappeared. It was rumoured that they made their way across Bavaria to their homeland, Czechoslovakia, which no longer belonged to us. Two days later, the rural militia arrived and announced that it was forbidden to sell army goods, but they were too late, the peasants would not return a single item.

I am simply telling my story, touching only the surface of events. The world war made a breach in the life of every grown person. Just bring to mind the many surprises, demands, and changes of feeling we were uninterruptedly exposed to, just consider that these most disturbing things were all crowded into two or three weeks, and I wager that no heart and no head could have withstood them; we might well all have gone mad. For me, the most horrifying aspect of war is the lawful unleasing of brutality and cruelty with the consequence of pain and death. The most fantastic, which affected like black magic even the most simple-minded, was the monetary economy.

I have a weakness. Since childhood, figures have been painful to me; every operation involving them, every calculation, chills me to the bone. There is something empty, meaningless, about them – or so it seems to me – and this confirms me in my rebellion. I have no intention of revealing just how meagre my knowledge of this subject had become since I had forgotten the painfully acquired lessons of my schooldays – no, that would be going too far. Every mind has its weak points, and my weakest is mathematics. Since, alas, numbers now play such a vital role in our existence, I have acquired side by side with my innate aversion an anxious and exaggerated respect for the whole system of reckoning. In practical matters the pre-eminent importance of numbers shows itself most imperatively in money matters. In my home we were always in straitened circumstances, and there was a family crisis almost every time my father was called upon for any unusual outlay. Therefore from an early age I was obsessed with the idea of the power of money, and I became a saver whenever that was possible. Money alone certainly does not create happiness, but its lack is disturbing. I believe our whole start in the world would be different if only we had the security of, say, two hundred thousand marks behind us, though this might be no more than a fiction. By about 1915 I had saved up, through care and diligence, the sum of approximately six thousand marks, which was set aside for a rainy day. Mistrustful as I was of savings accounts and banks in general, those institutions where the black magic of numbers held its malignant sway, I considered my capital safe only in my own possession, and for years I had kept it in a cupboard, willingly foregoing interest. All at once, the war, which inflicted so many wounds, gave rise to almost unbelievable possibilities. The value of the Austrian currency sank to half – only temporarily, so it was said. A friend of mine, who was an officer in a Vienna bank, urgently advised me to exchange my German marks for crowns. In this way, without risk to myself, I could practically double my money! If I then subscribed this sum in the recently floated war loan, I would receive five per cent on top of that. An income, willy-nilly, just like a gift. When I saw countless people, rich and poor, intelligent and stupid, subscribing millions, and when I saw the funds of minors being invested in these bonds, my former firmness of mind began to waver and I sought advice from my most reliable acquaintances as to whether I too should venture to invest my savings in this fashion. Everyone said that the war loan was especially designed for people like me. Finally I came to think so too, though a deep, secret premonition had told me at the moment when I first heard of the assassination of the heir to the throne that our so-called peaceful times were over and that there would be a war, which would surely bring an unforeseeable and heavy fate upon all of us. It was said, however, that the war loan would retain its value as long as the earth on which we stood remained earth, that no government would dare devalue bonds to which the whole nation had subscribed. This demolished my last objection, and I handed over my money, though I could not free myself completely from the feeling that I was no longer secure in my possession. A day came when I got it back, to be sure, and at face value – it was at the very worst period of the inflation.

About the inflation itself, there is not much I need say; each of us lived through it. In the beginning, we laughed about prices in Russia; the next thing we knew we ourselves were confronted with figures that are ordinarily used only in astronomy. Oddly enough, artists who knew how to go about it were able to make good money, and many of them believed that the splendid times we had all been waiting for had actually begun. Even the most miserable imitators and incompetents found purchasers for their 'works', though they were by no means always admirers. Since I had a certain reputation, a part of this general blessing came my way. Every day there were letters and often telegrams, sometimes containing the wildest offers. When I sent things out on approval, not only were they usually bought but also more were frequently ordered by return post. My wife and I often looked at each other speechless. Then all sorts of gentlemen began to turn up, gallery directors, art dealers, and publishers, with quite magnificent offers. They did not hesitate to make the trip, which in most cases was a long one. The only absurdity was that the next fellow too was swimming in money! Everyone was a real King Midas on paper!

In addition to certain other inheritances, my wife owned several houses in Frankfurt-am-Main. Since she did not suffer from my total aversion to figures, I learned from her that we were, though not rich to be sure, nevertheless assured of an income that at need would provide us with a modest living. Now suddenly everything was changed. Despite the fact that I had become a Croesus overnight, we could not pay for the necessary repairs, the price of which had risen proportionately. Mending a roof or replacing a drainpipe swallowed up God knows how much. Nor were we able to pay an adequate salary to the superintendent in charge of renting the apartments. In short, the houses had to be sold, and we got from them just enough to purchase, by acting fast, a new stove for our bedroom. But what difference did that make in contrast to the splendid prospects that seemed to be opening up before me! Every sketch, every line, could be sold at once, and we believed that in this new order, the important thing was not one's possessions but only a good steady income, and of this I seemed assured. The story of our bedroom stove reminds one automatically of the fairy tale of Lucky Hans; money lost its value so fast that, with heavy heart, I had to pay the man who installed that stove from my precious, closely guarded dollar hoard, the remainder of which soon after was of no value whatever because like a sudden thunderstorm stabilization broke upon us. People rubbed the sleep out of their eyes and with it the black magic; many, and I among them, planned to start a fresh life on a new basis; only, alas, I soon observed that most of the art dealers and publishers, bearing offers and enticing commissions – I had these lined up for years in the future – were no longer queuing up at my door, so to speak, like the poor women in front of milk stores during the last years of the war. One after another they withdrew, either cancelling their orders or postponing them to a distant future. At exhibitions, it was a rare thing for me to sell a drawing or a water colour. My bundle of war bonds, that sorry remnant of the happy capitalistic time, had shrunk, I learned, to a tiny fraction of its former value. Thus at the age of almost fifty one is left hanging in mid-air, with no prospect of any immediate improvement of circumstances, dependent upon chance sales and chance creative inspiration.

But whoever thinks that this desperate financial situation could upset me permanently is much mistaken. The creative impulse is such an essential part of me and to give in to it makes me so happy that I do not feel any essential difference, now that I am a man defrauded of his savings, from the way I felt before. Indeed, the only real unhappiness is to be unable, for one reason or another, to create – and I have lived through such periods.

The years 1916 to 1926, in fact, were among my most productive ones. Here I shall mention only what has appeared in published form. The works of Poe were completed by two further volumes. Then in rapid succession, *Der Prophet Daniel*, Friedrich Huch's *Neue Träume*, *Kritiker*, Strindberg's *Nach Damascus*, Balzac's *Mystical Stories*, a portfolio *Filigrane*, all of these for Georg Müller in Munich. For the Kurt Wolff-Verlag I made an album, *Wilde Tiere*, as well as drawings for Friedländer–Mynona's metaphysical novella *Der Schöpfer*. For the R. Piper-Verlag I illustrated Jean Paul's *Wunderbare Gesellschaft in der Neujahrsnacht*; moreover this publishing house brought out a portfolio called *Am Rande des Lebens*, with admirable facsimile prints, and my *Bibelblätter*, the latter also in a hand-coloured edition. For other publishing houses I illustrated Voltaire's *Candide* (Insverlag, Frankfurt-am-Main), Arnim's *Major-*

atsherren (Avalunverlag Hellerau), Seidel's *Das älteste Ding der Welt* (Musarionverlag, Munich); also the lavishly illustrated portfolio of lithographs *Traumland* – this meaningless title was, alas, put on the portfolio in place of the original title, *Meine Traumwelt*; then too a book with my own text, *Von verschiedenen Ebenen*, and lithographs for a posthumous fragment of a novella by Heinrich Lautensack, *Unpaar* (these last three published by Fritz Gurlitt, Berlin); a portfolio with *Fifty Drawings* A. Langen, Munich); a portfolio *Masken* (Rembrandt Verlag, Zehlendorf). In addition I made illustrations for Droste-Hülshoff's *Die Judenbuche* (Verlag Fritz Heyder, Zehlendorf), De Coster's *Smetse, der Schmied* (Buchenau and Reichert; the drawings were made into woodcuts by A. Falscheer); G. Hauptmann's *Fasching* (Verlag S. Fischer, Berlin); as well as three fairy tales by Andersen for Bruno Cassirer, Berlin, who also published my *Die Blätter mit dem Tod*. Finally there emerged as though by accident a little book, *Guckkasten* (Johannes-Presse, Vienna), with eight pictures and text by me. These works, as well as the very widely sold *Kubin Brevier* by E. W. Bredt (Verlag Hugo Schmidt, Munich), made me well known in the widest circles.

My *Rauhnacht* came about in a curious fashion. One night in the fall of 1924 I awoke with severe chills and a temperature of almost forty degrees centigrade. As I lay there half delirious with fever, I found myself surrounded by a crowd of strange figures against a familiar and pleasing landscape; in the morning I sketched all this while I still lay in bed weakened by grippe. A picture strip five yards long resulted, and this was published by the Wegweiser Verlag – unhappily chopped up into thirteen single plates. After that I made drawings for the expressionist poet R. R. Schmidt's *Episoden des Untergangs* (Merlinverlag, Heidelberg), and my last large work during the past fall was illustrations for a *Rübezahlbuch* (Verlag Joh. Stauda, Augsburg and Eger), which has not yet appeared.

This somewhat monotonous list, intended for those interested in my work, is by no means boring to me. At each single title I recall the time when the pictures were made and all the pleasant or painful circumstances that surrounded them. Dr Kurt Otte, a young man from Hamburg, has been occupied for some years in tracking down as much of my work as has appeared in the publishing world. He is now about to complete a catalogue that will include it and, in addition, a description of all my individual lithographs.

In the spring of 1921, I had for the first time a retrospective exhibition of twenty years of my work in the Neue Kunst Gallery of Hans Goltz in Munich. The three big salons were filled with especially selected examples of my water colours and drawings, and the occasion brought me very generous acclaim in that beloved city, which I consider my second home. I myself was much surprised to see how naturally my art had grown. I noticed the way in which, from 1916 on, a more deliberate, quiet, and constructive use of line had emerged side by side with my original, strongly impulsive style, which emphasizes light and shade and leans more to the painter's manner. Perhaps this development is the result of my increasingly attentive study of the old paintings in my collection, especially the German masters. These are the two strains that appear from that time on; they alternate visibly in my work and sometimes they coalesce.

The period of life that thus began is unquestionably pleasanter than the confused and stormy days of my youth and the wild years of my early manhood. I recognize this with pleasure, despite the real and imagined disabilities that have come as a result of the years: a certain diminution of sight, greater fatigue during periods of forced concentration, as well as a steadily increasing sensibility to cold. The mountain lies behind me, and my wanderings in the valley in the light of afternoon are much less strenuous and just as fine. But I cannot disguise from myself that during the last few years a dark, premonitory feeling accompanies me always. It is the inescapable consciousness of growing older. I cannot recall when the realization first dawned on me of being perishable through and through. This tragic element is part of life. A day comes when dear friends and beloved companions silently abandon us forever. Of those lost in the last few years I mention only Max Dauthendey, Hans von Weber, René Beeh, Georg Müller; there are, alas, many others, all of whom I cherish in memory and miss, for I expect nothing of the future. The 'wonders of technology', however startling they may be, have always left me cold; I have no taste for skyscraper romanticism. The truth is, I am not in the slightest in love with the conditions of the past, which were often oppressive, but the pictures the past has left to us are all the dearer – a distinction of great importance.

However, as long as one lives, surprises come, filling today, tomorrow, and the next day; let them be savoured freely, but be on your guard. I was almost forty-five years old when I realized I was losing my heart, whose yearnings I thought had been stilled since my marriage, to a young actress. Since my wife, the best friend and beloved that fate could have given me, behaved in this awkward situation with remarkable astuteness and tact, my old affection quickly reasserted itself and I succeeded in extinguishing the flame. One is not a fantasist simply on paper, indeed I will say outright: Fantasy is fate. I have so infinitely much to thank my gifted life's companion for that it seems ridiculous to mention particulars here. She is the good fairy who, in so far as she can, helps me with my work, lovingly concerns herself with my physical state and tormenting sensibilities, and gives our little property a character that makes it possible to feel comfortable there. For us too, to be sure, fate has had its blows. My wife has been ill far more often than is generally the case even with the more delicate sex, and the consequences of these misfortunes have struck me with full force. An especially black day in her life was March 15, 1924. On that date my poor wife, who had barely recovered from a severe illness, met with an accident that resulted in her breaking both bones in her calf before my very eyes. She was attempting to get onto the train at the station in Wenstein, but had to step down again, and it was then that it happened. The greatest happiness I have known next to my art has come from my marriage. The relations between husband and wife contain problems of a deep and secret kind that probably can never be wholly solved. Our forefathers tried for solutions in various ways; among these monogamy seems to me the best. In recent times people have attempted through divorce to dislodge the concept of a lifelong bond with a newly selected partner; this may sometimes turn out well, but it will seldom result in a deepening of personal life.

There were no more long journeys. In 1922 I spent a most agreeable week as a guest of the Gurlitt Publishing Company in their handsome building in Berlin, which is already almost like a museum. A lasting memory remains of the farewell dinner given by our hospitable host. We sat on soft cushions under hanging lamps; Wolfgang Gurlitt was dressed as a rajah in a turban and a colourful silk gown. To the accompaniment of soft music a company of Oriental dancing girls appeared. My friend Grossman got out his sketch book. Exchanging one form of magic for another, I was speeded homewards to my rural isolation in an express train. In the spring of 1923 I passed through Karlsruhe, and there visited the aged Hans Thoma. He was confined to a wheelchair, but for one well into the eighties he was lively and witty; I was much pleased that he knew about me. In the fall of 1924 I travelled with a young poet to Switzerland. There I visited, among others, Dr Ludwig Klages, a friend of the mysterious Alfred Schuler (who died in 1923) as well as the poet Friedrich Huch (who died in 1921), all three of whom I had known from my time in Munich around the beginning of the century. Klages, a fascinating person and a researcher of the first order, is in my opinion the most significant psychologist of our times. He lives in Kilchberg near Zurich in the handsome villa of the great Swiss writer Conrad Ferdinand Meyer. In 1925 I got only as far as Henndorf near Salzburg, where with cordial hospitality Carl Mayr offered me the opportunity for rest and recreation that my tired nerves seemed to require more and more insistently each fall. But here in Zwickledt, too, we entertain many old and new friends.

The most splendid experience of recent years was the Bavarian forest. It was actually an accident that took us to this area, which lies so close to us. There for the first time I could see the true magic of the forest; the woods I had known before counted for nothing by comparison. They had either been partially forested, were cluttered with underbrush, or were tiny by contrast with these enormous forest-covered areas. We visited the painter R. Köppel in Waldhäuser, and our walks through the deep green, from tree to tree, from root to root, gradually aroused in us a strange intoxication that must have had its secret cause in life of these arboreal giants. It is an indescribable primeval world, and the impression it makes on the soul is of an elemental kind. And this forest stretches deep into Bohemia. The axe, alas, yearly fells large segments of this splendour; the mighty colossi crash to the ground, beech trees tall as towers, and ancient rugged pines. A saddening fact – we, however, could still see them.

5

August, 1931

I have the opportunity of extending my autobiographical study a bit further. To be sure, barely five years have passed since I finished the fourth section, and there is nothing for me to report in the nature of special experiences that might have exercised substantial influence on my general development. Instead, these notes, in compressed form, are intended as a sidelight on the circumstances of their now aging author.

As a complete surprise to me, my fiftieth birthday was made the occasion of a remarkable celebration held by certain of my friends in Henndorf near Salzburg, whither we went. Moreover the heavy mailbags, from which poured masses of congratulations from all parts of the world, as well as the numerous published articles, showed me in what esteem I was held and the effect my art had produced. The Drawings Collection in the Alte Pinakothek in Munich gave a very impressive showing of my works on this anniversary. However, it was a trip to Leitmeritz in northern Bohemia, my birthplace, which I had not visited in forty years, that turned out to be a particularly profound emotional experience. I have described it in a small essay that appeared in the *Sudetendeutsches Jahrbuch* 1928. This trip was a birthday present that I bestowed on myself.

Two years later I was elected to the Preussische Akademie der Künste. This official recognition gave me great pleasure, and I considered it an honour since it had been given to me by my own colleagues. It is true that I also saw in it the evidence that my time of life was already well advanced, for it is not long ago that I was spoken of as a revolutionary artist, and now I had become an academician!

For collectors in particular, let me here give a comprehensive review of my productions in these last years. The publishing firm of Johannes Stauda, Eger, and Kassel brought out a portfolio of ten lithographs entitled *Stilzel, der Kobold des Böhmerwaldes*. The Merlinverlag in Baden-Baden published in portfolio form a selection of twenty-five facsimiles from my sketchbooks called *Orbis Pictus*.*

I should also have liked very much to provide illustrations for one of Franz Kafka's novels, which touch me so intimately, but the hour for that seems not yet to have come; just now interest in the tradition of illustrated books is at low ebb. And so I gladly accepted a commission to design the sets for a production of a powerful, elemental peasant drama by Richard Billinger, *Rauhnacht*. It was thus that in the course of the present year a series of colour drawings were created for the Munich Kammerspiele. How far these suggestions will find fulfilment is still in doubt, since the opening is not to take place until fall.

In the intervals between these assignments a respectable number of individual pictures came into being, and in them I recognize that my way of drawing is more and more clearly designed for a broad pictorial effect. In my bold, monumental conceptions I try to emphasize form complexes with my pen but also in part with the aid of the brush. This method is dictated by my increased assurance in handling my imaginary world, an assurance gained through many years of creativity.

Looking abroad, one sees the threatening economic conditions passing by in constantly varied, unsympathetic constellations. One has long since found resignation in the awareness of creating only for oneself and a small circle of truly understanding, friendly spirits. Ever more often one stands, shaken with sorrow, at the bier of some near or distant acquaintance, and this, added to the feeling that in the articulation of one's own body much is changing, brings an inescapable realization of the whole treacherous state of human existence.

But then new lust for life is there, too, to inspire us to seize

* Many works still lie unpublished in my cupboard, and the fact that I have not been able to bring them out as I had expected is in all ways the bitterest misfortune that has befallen me during this time.

the day and advance our work. This no doubt is the final and profoundest meaning of the artist, that in his creative activity he throws a veil over the meaninglessness of life, a thin, concealing veil over the chaotic forces that for us are literally nothing in contrast to that imaginary world that represents truth to us, though it be but an illusion in the flux of time.

6

November, 1946

A surprise : my book *Die andere Seite* is to be re-issued by the Pegasus Verlag in Zurich. To the text I shall add a short continuation and conclusion of my autobiographical study. Fifteen years have passed since I wrote the last section.

There is little that I can say here about the Nazi regime and its war, although that was the most dreadful fate that struck us all. When I think of myself and my colleagues, cultivated men of art, I realize for the first time the full repulsiveness of what came upon us. About the *Kunstkammer* of the Third Reich I prefer to remain silent; there is no use in flogging a dead horse. We are still in the midst of our worldly impoverishment; no one can foresee where this will lead. Oh, those fools, those political revolutionaries, those sinister psychopaths, or whatever you choose to call them, who brought on us war, both inner and outer! The problem now is to find prospects for the future; we have survived that hellish prank, let us forge our way as best we can amid its dreadful aftermath.

The bombardment of Zwickledt on the night of May 1 to 2, 1945, caused three deaths. We spent that night in the cellar, crowded together because of the presence of seven refugees from Upper Silesia and certain of our neighbours who thought that our cellar roof was stronger than others. The barrage was provoked from the German side; I had hidden only my originals, but luck was with us, although the old building was heavily struck by fragments of grenades and to this day has had only makeshift repairs. A mental numbness took possession of me completely during these terrifying hours and helped me through them. Early on the morning of May 3, 1945, our first deliverer appeared, a United States soldier who, to judge by his appearance, was more an intellectual than a labourer. I had already laid out American newspapers as well as a book on modern art containing articles about me and my work. He shook my hand; the worst of the terror lay behind us.

In the meantime our economic situation has, alas, grown worse. Because of the unavoidable neglect of years, I now keep house in a kingdom of rubble, shards, and patches. The destruction of seven years cannot be made good overnight. To speak plainly, a period of bitter impoverishment has ensued. Nevertheless I awake each morning with inner joy that the Nazi horror has disappeared like a mirage! Even if I should have to face physical ruin as a result of its after-effects, my native land surrounds me once more, it will endure! My heart is not grieved, even though a natural force that for several years has made itself unambiguously evident is now no longer to be dismissed: old age is upon me! Luckily the new state in which I find myself has a double countenance. The distress of encroaching weariness reveals itself too as relaxation. The country folk make use of humour and irony in their attempt to bear this sad but all too natural burden, and they come to terms with it, as everyone must. As I grew older my so-called fame redoubled. Ten years ago, on the occasion of my sixtieth birthday, the Albertina in Vienna held a great exhibition that touched me deeply and evoked my gratitude. It contained more than three hundred originals, illustrated books, and portfolios from all periods of my work on loan from public and private collections as well as from me. For two days I left my quiet nook, and in the midst of the speeches of praise and great public success, I could never have dreamed how soon the future would be dealing harshly with us all. What happened was vastly worse than the most confirmed pessimist could have imagined. And yet even that abysmal horror and those dreadful sacrifices have been survived – Austria, our dearly beloved native land, is celebrating its nine hundred and fiftieth anniversary. Therefore, one says with a sigh of relief, in God's name let the evidences of personal decline, weaknesses such as forgetfulness and physical awkwardness, govern my remaining days – to deeper insight this is only a phase, just as youth was. With sobered senses one can literally feel oneself revolve like a moon endowed with self-consciousness. The hidden central sun, the heart of the world, is the cause, too, of this astonishing lighting. Scenes from memory, heavy with dreams and sometimes of great charm, calm our occasional panic at moments of organic crisis. With me, peaceful surroundings are a primary requirement for composure. And so it was a particular torment when the circumstances of war forced on us a refugee family of nine persons, modest and not unsympathetic though they were. For forty years these old walls had been a haven of refuge and an ever renewed refreshment; now one's soul was thrown into a strange state of agitation by the new residents. With a sort of pathological alertness, which, alas, would not rest, I was conscious night and day through the walls of every activity of our guests.

Returning once from a walk in the woods, I found our place transformed into an unusually picturesque scene. There had been a heavy snowfall. A colourful crowd of Croatian men, women, and children were encamped on their open wagons, which had been pushed together to serve as a living and sleeping place. Twenty-six horses had somehow been crowded into our old barn. I sank into silent contemplation of this scene, which seemed to belong to the Thirty Years War. After a couple of weeks the Fata Morgana disappeared just as it had come. Oh, this matter is one on which I cannot compromise: peace remains a prerequisite for my work and I will gladly forego in exchange for it many things that others consider essential to their lives. In recent times, with the decline of those powers that still remain to me, I have been at pains to conserve them for my work. Experience has shown me too often how they can suddenly sink and disappear completely. How abrupt, spiritually like the extinction of a blazing torch, was the end of my dear brother-in-law and friend Oscar A. H. Schmitz! In the fifteen years that have passed, his image has not dimmed in my mind; with increasing age one consorts far more with the dead than in earlier years. So far as the soul is concerned, loneliness is altogether superficial. In 1944 my younger sister, married to an inventor, met a sad end in Vienna. The loss of this unique creature, a being of essential loveliness, is a blow from which I find it hard to recover. In memory Fritzi beckons me gently onwards. A far heavier blow, which struck me and my wife only nine months later, was the incomprehensible decline of her younger sister, a widow who lived in Schärding. On September 4 of last year she succumbed to a kidney disease. This unforgettable lady regularly spent the weekends with us and helped wherever she could. She adorned those occasions with gaiety and wit. What a harmonious triad we formed! 'One of us must go first,' she said about a half year before her death – had some premonition touched her?

If a thinking person places himself mentally at the pivotal mid-point – something that requires, to be sure, a strenuous effort – and, thus free, is as light as he is heavy in every direction, he then obtains an overall view of the whole hurry-scurry of life with its ups and downs, and in this process all that is humanly narrow and distorted sinks into insignificance.

Now, in my seventieth year, a happy turn of events makes possible a new edition of my richly illustrated fantastic novel *Die andere Seite*, which when it appeared thirty-eight years ago was called in one review 'the world view of a visionary'. I do not know about that. The book was written when I was thirty years old out of an inner compulsion and psychological necessity. I am more interested in the illustrations than in the text, which I wrote down in an extraordinary state of mind that was literally comparable to intoxication. I felt as though actually possessed of true clairvoyance. My procedure with the fifty-one drawings was, as usual, a carefully considered one. For this new edition from the Pegasus Verlag in Zurich, I must remake the drawings and pit against the naïve strength of my earlier days the dash and experience of a veteran illustrator. In those youthful times I must actually have been like another person. I was made aware of this fact some years ago when one of my closest friends, Dr h. c. Hans von Müller, the famous authority on E. T. A. Hoffmann, died in Berlin, and my letters to him from 1902 to 1940 were left to me as a bequest. As the events of my reckless youth slowly rose before my mind I found them incredible and was unable to make any judgement about that far-off period. Now I am overcome by a curious – yes, prophetic – feeling that my renewed occupation with *Die andere Seite* is like the closing of a circle. This brings me an almost mystical consolation in our general sorry state, and in place of my former wild conflict something new is emerging, for which I can find no more suitable expression than the words 'troubled peace'.

I have often been asked about the fate of the Kubin archives in Hamburg during the final years of the war. Dr Kurt Otte, its founder and supporter, succeeded in getting the collection through that terrible period with only slight losses. It is true that his family residence on the Fischmarkt was struck by bombs and burned. But at that time the archives were already safely packed away in thirteen chests in the cellar of the Staatsbibliothek in Hamburg. These too were threatened by a conflagration, but with only the slight losses mentioned; just one chest containing press cuttings was damaged, and that not by fire but by water. Afterwards the chests were transferred to a Hamburg municipal air-raid shelter, where they remained with other valuables until the end of the war. Now the archives have been installed in their founder's new home.

In conclusion I shall mention a number of other works of the last fifteen years.

First of all, *Abenteuer einer Zeichenfeder*, a collection of sixty plates with an introduction by Max Unold (R. Piper, Munich, 1942); *Das Meerwunder* by Gerhart Hauptmann, with drawings (S. Fischer, Berlin, 1934); *Die Kartause von Walditz* by J. Durych, with drawings (R. Piper, Munich, 1934); *Vom Schreibtisch eines Zeichners*, text and drawings by A. Kubin (Ulrich Riemerschmidt, Berlin); *Schemen*, sixty heads (Kanterverlag, Königsberg); *Gerade dies* by Peter Scher, with drawings, and *Die neun Planeten*, a small portfolio without text (Staackmann, Leipzig, 1944); *Der Main, eine Legende* by Wolfgang Weyrauch, with twenty-seven drawings (Rowohltverlag, Berlin, 1934); *Schalmoi von Schelmenried* by Hans Schiebelhut (Darmstädterverlag, Darmstadt, 1933); *Märchen aus dem Unbewussten* by Oscar A. H. Schmitz, with twelve drawings (Karl Hanserverlag, Munich, 1932); *Ali, der Schimmelhengst, Schicksale eines Tartarenpferdes*, with twelve original lithographs (Johannes-Presse, Vienna, 1932). This list is not complete, since a number of important works were delayed by the war, among them my major work, *Phantasien im Böhmerwald*, thirty-five plates with text and marginal illustrations; a Münchhausen book; *Prosadichtungen* by Georg Trakl, with twelve plates; a new *Totentanz*; *The Vicar of Wakefield* by Oliver Goldsmith; and others as well. It is to be hoped that a new and more favourable time will put no obstacle in the way of their publication.

Now I conclude these notes. My thoughts continue as always to circle about the uncanny and yet familiar nature of life in this world. It is the dreamlike, transitory essence of all phenomena. To probe it more deeply and to be able to represent it graphically, I would gladly stay here a good while longer, but for years I have been resigned at any hour to hear the call. My single wish would be that I might be spared a prolonged final illness, but after all that is something not within our power to choose.

Each man creates what he must, in his own fashion, to the extent that his gifts permit.

I conclude by saying farewell to the friends of my art.

More About Penguins

Penguinews, which appears every month, contains
details of all the new books issued by Penguins as
they are published. From time to time it is
supplemented by *Penguins in Print*, which is a
complete list of all available books published by
Penguins. (There are well over four thousand of
these.)

A specimen copy of *Penguinews* will be sent to you
free on request, and you can become a subscriber
for the price of the postage. For a year's issues
(including the complete lists) please send 30p if you
live in the United Kingdom, or 60p if you live
elsewhere. Just write to Dept EP, Penguin Books
Ltd, Harmondsworth, Middlesex, enclosing a cheque
or postal order, and your name will be added to
mailing list.

Note: *Penguinews* and *Penguins in Print* are not
available in the U.S.A. or Canada

The Enormous Room

E. E. Cummings

E. E. Cummings was a driver with the American Red Cross during World War I. In 1917, he was detained on suspicion for three months at La Ferté prison; 'entombed within the drooling, greenish walls' of *The Enormous Room*; condemned to abject chores, vile food and the brutality of the guards.

A memorable procession of fellow-prisoners stroll, creep, stagger, shuffle or stride on to the pages of *The Enormous Room*: Count Bragard, the fake R.A.; the detestable Fighting Sheeney; Jean Le Nègre, the pimp who impersonated an officer ...

The Enormous Room, written in 1922, was Cumming's first book and foreshadows the viewpoint and experiments of his poems, authority and 'mostpeople' are castigated; each angry sentence rising hot and strong off the page to fuse in white-hot expression of romantic anarchy.

Not for sale in the U.S.A. or Canada

Franz Kafka

The work of this strange and enigmatic Czech author, who died of consumption in 1924, has earned him a unique reputation in modern European literature and has provoked many endeavours to interpret his view of life.

The Trial

Kafka elucidates some fundamental dilemmas of human life in this account of the perplexing experience of a man arrested on a charge which is never specified. The story reads like the transcript of a protracted, implacable dream in which reality is entangled with imagination.

Metamorphosis and Other Stories

This volume includes Kafka's best short stories. *Metamorphosis* is one of the most terrifying stories ever written. A man wakes up one morning to find himself transformed into a giant insect. His family is at first horrified, then kind, contemptuous and finally negligent.

The Castle

Here the world of Kafka is further illumined; the individual struggles against ubiquitous, elusive and anonymous powers determining and yet simultaneously opposing his every step.

America

America is the lightest and most realistic of Kafka's novels. Yet beneath the surface comedy of young Karl Rossman's discovery of America, the author hints at much more than he seems to be saying.

and

The Diaries of Franz Kafka

Kafka's diaries, edited by Max Brod his lifelong friend, cover the period from 1910 to 1923 and reveal to us the extraordinary inner world in which he lived, his fear, isolation, frustration, feelings of guilt and his sense of being an outcast.